Love Power

A Crescent City
New Orleans Mystery

MARTHA REED

First Buccaneer edition
Published October 2020
Cover art by Karen Phillips – www.phillipscovers.com
Printed in the United States of America.

DEDICATION

To my dad, Samuel Clarke Reed III

and

My dear friend and editor, Ramona DeFelice Long

CHAPTER ONE

"Girl, you're in early again." Calvin Johnson, Jr. swung the channeled vinyl chair sideways using his scuffed heels. "I already told you. They don't pay no extra for overtime."

"Anything up?" Jane scanned the ten grainy security monitors and checked the console clock. Guardian Self Storage, Thursday, December 1, 2016, 9:45 p.m. Home of 480 climate-controlled units, three soundproofed music studios and forty-two seasonally parked RVs on Level Six.

"Cams seven and eight keep cutting out for no damn reason I can see. Must be something electric." Shaking his gray shoulder-length dreadlocks, Cal squinted. "And the exit bubble cam went pure dead again."

"Add it to the maintenance log."

"Already did. And Sonny Rickard stopped by, complaining about the stink on Level Three again. I checked it; man's right. It do smell like something died in the walls." Rising stiffly, Cal slipped into his jacket. "Couldn't ID the unit it come from. You give it a try, young blood, next go round. Your nose is better than mine. Oh, and I almost forgot. You still looking for a new room, new place to stay?" Cal extended a yellow Post It note with a trembling hand. "Spoke to a fella knows of one for rent in The Bywater. Said the landlord's name is Ken Pascoe. Check it out. Might save you a few bucks."

Ken Pascoe? Jane grasped the note. *Why does that name sound familiar?* She tried pushing her brain to trace the connection. The vague hint toyed with her battle-scarred memory, flicked out of reach and was gone. "He keeps a storage locker?"

"This Ken fella? Not that I know of." Cal shrugged. "Every time I seen him he rents one of them music studios. Pays cash, too. Strangest thing. Never seen him carry an instrument. Never heard him play a single note."

"What's he doing renting a music studio?"

"Hee-hee-hee. Ain't my job to ask *why* a man wants to rent one. My job is to make sure he pays for it. Maybe he's hiding out from a girlfriend or his wife?" Checking his wristwatch, Cal fumbled his money clip, which fell to the floor.

Stooping, Jane fingered the cash. "Nice wad, Cal. Where d'you get this? Hit the numbers?"

"Gotta go!" He slipped the money into his pocket. "Can't miss my bus. Marva is waiting up. It's date night. See ya tomorrow."

Tucking the address away, Jane returned to the console. *Straight up ten o'clock. Time for my tour.* Every hour, on the hour, she patrolled the darkened corridors of Guardian's six floors, swiping a security fob at each entry point keypad and double-checking the fire doors to make sure the facility stayed secure. It didn't spook Jane that she worked alone until Christophe arrived at eleven. She preferred the solitude. *And yes, it's mindless exercise. At least I'm getting my steps in.* She poked the fob into her doughy midsection. *I need to back off on the beer. I'm getting soft.*

As she strolled past each padlocked and gated door, the overhead florescent tube lighting buzzed into brilliant life, illuminating the dim corridor ahead before fading into darkness as she passed. Only her steady slapping footsteps disturbed the vibrating white noise OM from the industrial air conditioning. Jane caught the squealing protest of rubber tires against a concrete curb. *That's odd.* Opening Level Three's fire door, she spotted the winking brake lights of a panel van heading down the exit ramp. *Cal didn't say anyone was still in the building.* She shrugged. *A little late for someone to be visiting their unit, but hell that is what they pay for. Secure 24/7 access.*

As soon as the fire door slammed shut, her nostrils started twitching. *Cal's right. It does smell like something died in here.* Sniffing repeatedly, Jane rubbed her nose as she tried to run down which unit housed the coppery stink. *Fucking over-sensitivity. Dr. Wacky said this might happen. I feel like a goddamn bloodhound nowadays.* The best she could do was to winnow it down to three possible units as her eyes watered and itched. *Fuck it.* Clutching the fob in her fingers, Jane pushed on to Level Four. *Let senior management figure it out. It's their pay grade, not mine.*

There it is again. She owned the bitter negativity that stopped her in her tracks. *I hate feeling like this, what's the word? Petty? What does this say about my petty life?* She forced her shoulders down as her ragged fingernails dug halfmoon craters into her palms. *Four years in and it's not getting better, it's getting worse. I still feel hollow and fake, like I'm putting one foot in front of the other like a zombie. What is it going to take to finally get over this shit and to feel normal again?*

Her chin hit her chest. That particular worry was so worn out it repeated itself like a skip on a warped vinyl record. She recalled the parting advice from her PTSD therapist Dr. Walkoviak. *Of course, permanent change is hard. Start by taking baby steps. Take one baby step every day. Eventually they'll add up to real results.* Poking her puffy gut, Jane scoffed. *Baby steps, my ass. Here's my answer: Suck it up, buttercup and hit the stairs. That's something I can do now, something active. Let's make my next baby step fitting back into my jeans!*

Slamming the door's exit bar, she raced up the next three flights of steps, taking them two at a time until her knees buckled and her pounding heartbeat drilled her ears. At Level Six, Jane bent over, sucking in great whoops of air like a drowning sailor. *That's it! I'm going to do this three times every hour instead of once. Baby steps, my ass. I need to get ready.*

CHAPTER TWO

Thumbing the Ducati's kill switch, Jane let the bike roll to a stop beneath the decrepit shed tacked onto her new quarters. 7:18 a.m., and she didn't want the sound of the powerful motorcycle waking the main house. For once, it had skipped the tropical monsoon overnight squall. The rutted driveway was drying out. She noted that the patchy gravel under her tires sounded remarkably like the scratching sound a vinyl record made for a loop or two after the needle dropped before the music began.

Raising both arms, Jane stretched. *Damn. I feel good for a change.* The rising sun's warming blush colored the horizon through the bare treetops, her shift at Guardian was done, and she had a skin full of cheap dollar draft beer. *Life is good.* She was becoming such an after hours' regular at The Double Deuce Lounge that Adele had even started saving her a corner seat at the bar and feeding her a free breakfast before she headed home. Jane contentedly patted her belly. *Never thought I'd be eating white beans and rice for breakfast, but hey, you know what? I'm starting to crave the stuff.*

Looping a finger under the pot metal chain around her neck, she pulled out the new house key she wore like a dog tag. The lock on her apartment door was stiff. She had already learned to lean her right shoulder into the door while lifting the knob slightly as she turned the key. *The things we do that make a place our home.* The deadbolt responded easily once she'd learned the trick of it.

Yesterday morning she had called the number Cal gave her first thing, stopping by after work to see the apartment. It wasn't much, but in NOLA's trendy The Bywater district it was all she could afford. She had feared from the

4

sketchy over the phone description that it might be even worse. On first inspection, half dollar sized plaster flakes had littered the pine floor like fallen dogwood petals, but at least the red brick walls looked dry. Jane was still getting used to the fact that New Orleans was always damp.

Leslie Pascoe, her new landlady, had flicked the light switch next to the door. Leslie was a wiry, petite, middle-aged woman who looked like she knew what working hard really meant. She had deeply dark brown eyes, almost black, and her wavy ebony hair was shot through with plenty of silvery threads which she wore in a braid down her back.

Two table lamps had flickered on, throwing sharp triangular shadows against the ceiling. The condenser on an unseen refrigerator had coughed and started to rattle.

"It's small, but it's solid." Leslie crossed the worn floorboards of the single room. "Used to serve as the kitchen for the Big House." She turned. "No air conditioning back then. Had to keep the heat away from the bedrooms." She laughed easily. "And if the stovepipe caught fire, you didn't burn the whole place up."

Jane surreptitiously dried her palms against her uniform. "Is fire a concern?"

"No, honey." She laughed again. "We got everything rewired properly when we refinanced. In NOLA, you only need to worry about pestilence and the plumbing. It's because all of the water has no place else to go."

"I heard about Hurricane Katrina from a friend of mine who used to live here."

"That bitch Katrina damn near murdered us." Leslie ran her finger over a windowsill before delicately dusting her fingers. "Luckily, Bywater missed most of it. We're three feet above sea level." Moving to the rear wall, she pushed a simple dotted curtain aside. "This here's the galley kitchen. The appliances are oldies but goodies, just like me. Plenty of counter space plus there's extra storage in the pantry. You'll need to visit the coin laundry to do your washing. I wanted to put a washer in but our sewer line won't take it. The bedroom and the bath's upstairs."

"Leslie? Where y'at?"

Jane flinched at the gravelly male voice growling from the garden.

"We're in the kitchen, Ken, honey. Come on through."

A craggy, weather-beaten man blocked the sunlight streaming through the doorway. He was stocky, below average height, about five foot eight, Jane estimated with dark curly hair, thick lips and a pronounced chin. He was wearing an un-tucked Hawaiian shirt loosely over faded jeans. At first glance, she thought he might be packing, but then Jane decided that he was only trying to hide the extra thirty pounds he carried around his waist. Resting his hairy forearms against the brick doorway, he leaned in. "This our new tenant?"

"We're still working that out. Jane, meet my husband, Ken."

Straightening, Ken extended his right hand. It looked as wide as a cranberry bog rake with an oddly flat splayed thumb that almost looked like a fifth finger.

"Jane, was it? Nice to meet you. Ken Pascoe."

An imaginary yellow flare fired off in Jane's mind as soon as he said his name. *There it is again. Why does his name keep pinging me? Was he involved in a criminal investigation I studied?* Yet again, she couldn't immediately pin it down. Her overstrained brain simply refused to process one more thing. She had met so many strangers lately and she had heard so many new names that she had learned to simply file some things away for a private rehash later. She firmly gripped Ken's hand. "Jane Byrne."

He cocked his strange thumb at the courtyard. "That Ducati Monster parked outside yours? You must be some serious kinda bad ass. Had an '82 Harley Sportster, gloss blue, back in the day." He sighed. "Loved that iron-head. Still miss it. How much did that Ducati set you back?"

"Six grand, cash. Bought it used."

Leslie quickly crossed her corded arms. "Don't get any fresh ideas,

Ken. That was way, way back in the day, old man. Those evil days are in the past where they need to stay."

"Leave me be, woman." Ken scowled, scratching his chin. "Jane? You look ex-military to me or like a cop, maybe. What exactly do you do?"

She steeled herself to meet his eyes. "Private security. Work for Guardian. Night shift, ten p.m. to six a.m."

"Guardian Self Storage?" Ken looked surprised. "That outfit on Canal Street?"

"I've checked Jane's references," Leslie inserted quickly. "They couldn't say enough nice things about her."

"Good to know," Jane admitted.

"You carry a gun?"

"At Guardian? No. And I don't have a carry permit for one, either. They issue duty batons and tasers. I won't be bringing those home. We need to check them in and out every shift. Issued security weapons stay on-site in a secured locker."

"And all of that is fine by me," Leslie stated decidedly. "Guns have no place near my home. You hear of too many accidents and tragedies."

Ken cocked his head. "Where you from, originally?"

"Boston." Jane caught herself. "East Coast. Up and down the East Coast mostly."

"Thought so. Leslie? Remember Brian Exton? Played bass for the Tin Foil Puppets? He had that same accent she has. Used those same long 'ah's."

"I do remember Brian. Thought the same thing myself when I first met her."

"What brought you to NOLA?"

"Gravity, mostly." Jane swallowed the bitter lie that stuck in her throat. "Kept heading downhill." She joked uneasily. "Went through a nasty divorce. Starting over now from scratch." She stared out the multi-paned window. "I don't really like talking about it."

"Well then, honey, NOLA is the right place for you." Leslie pulled a key ring from her pocket. "We're home for anyone who can't find a home anyplace else."

"Hold up a second." Raising his hand, Ken studied Jane carefully. "You like throwing wild parties? Having group sex?"

"Stop it, Ken!" Leslie slapped his bicep. "What kind of a question is that? Ignore him, Jane, when he gets like this. I do." Pursing her lips, she thoughtfully removed one key from the ring. "We don't really care what you do as long as you don't do it here. My Aunt Babette lives with us in the Big House on the third floor. She's seventy-four -"

"That woman sees damn near everything from her perch up there -"

Leslie winced. "And we're not looking for any hullabaloo."

"Don't speak for me, woman." Ken roguishly waggled his eyebrows. "I'm still looking for hullabaloo."

"Too bad. You don't get to vote."

"No worries," Jane inserted quickly. "I'm pretty quiet and I work nights, like I said. Sleep during the day. Pretty much keep to myself. Shouldn't be an issue."

"You a vampire?" Ken asked.

"Sometimes it feels like it," Jane admitted.

"One last thing." Leslie tapped her lips. "We want to keep this easy; we won't ask you to sign a lease. Eight hundred a month and we'll do a month-to-month tenancy with 30 days' notice on both sides. That seems fair, doesn't it? And you'll need to pay me the rent in cash. I don't take personal checks or money orders. I like keeping things simple."

Tapping the side of his broad nose, Ken winked. "No need to tell Uncle Sam everything, right? Those bastards in Washington bleed us white enough as it is."

"I can pay cash."

"That's it!" Ken slapped his hands together with a crack like a gunshot.

"Rent it to her, Leslie. Jane's got my vote. It's either her or one of those goddamn hipsters running around gentrifying the neighborhood." Wrinkles channeled his mouth as he scowled. "Can't stand those pretentious little pricks with their goddamned pumpkin spice lattes and fucking avocado toast."

Jane braced herself to stand her ground. "Are the utilities included?"

"Yes." Leslie smiled winsomely as she ticked items off of her fingertips. "That includes water, sewer, garbage and the electric. Electricity can get steep running the AC and the dehumidifier during the season. I've found it's best to just budget it into the rent. And the apartment comes furnished with everything you see except for your own personal linens."

"Trust me, Jane," Ken rumbled. "You won't find anything better in The Bywater at that price."

"I know it." Jane glanced out of the wavy glass panes as a cluster of ravens flapped through the black trees. "And I wanted to stay on this side of the canal. It's closer to work. I just need to watch my budget, you know. Keep it real."

"Tell you what." Leslie rested her hands on her hips. "You help me out a bit in the garden come spring, with the tilling, weeding and such and we'll call it seven-fifty." She cut her eyes at her husband. "It's December first, Ken. I want a tenant. Makes no sense leaving the place standing empty over fifty bucks."

"Hey, you're the boss." He raised his hands in surrender. "She's already got my vote."

"Just so you know, Jane," Leslie wagged her finger, "we're not renovating anything. No fresh paint, no new rugs or curtains. You take the place as it is, lock, stock, and barrel and it's yours."

Jane studied the shoebox space. Four hundred square feet tops, and not a foot more.

"I'll take it." *My new home.*

CHAPTER THREE

Blindly feeling for the light switch, Jane gave it a flick. There was a solid click, but the apartment stayed dark. She arbitrarily flicked the switch again and then again, using more force and getting the same result. *Dammit! No electricity.*

Dipshit! Jane gave herself a mental kick. In her eagerness to move in she had forgotten to ask the Pascoes where the breaker box was or if they even had a separate one for the apartment. *Now I'll need to wake someone up and ask for help.* Leaving the door hanging open she trudged through Leslie's raised garden beds. In the dead of winter, they looked like unmarked graves.

The Big House's screened in back porch was filled with dancing silvery shadows. *I can sleep without the AC on, but there's no way I'll fall asleep without the sound of the ceiling fan drowning out the daytime street noise.* Jane had tried that approach using earplugs twice before. Sensory deprivation had led her straight into a vomiting migraine nightmare.

She heard an aluminum lawn chair's squeaky protest and a soft silhouette rose from behind the rusting screen. Shuffling forward, Ken unlatched the door, holding it open with one huge paw, his gravelly voice deliberately kept low.

"Morning, Jane. Saw you come in. Sun's up. Take a detour this morning?"

Pausing at the base of the steps, she matched his whisper. "Stopped by The Deuce for a beer or two. Helps me sleep."

"Or maybe three?" He chuckled. "Good for you."

"Ken? The electricity's out at my place. Where's the breaker box?"

"I have no idea. Leslie covers that kind of thing." Pushing the screened door fully open, he grasped the railing and stiffly descended the steps. "I'm useless when it comes to housekeeping. Don't even know where to look." Crossing the courtyard, he opened the iron side gate and stepped out into the street. "Leslie has insomnia. When she finally drops off I try to leave her be. We'll go ask Ryan." He studied a clapboard house facing Plessy Street. "I see a light in his kitchen. I know he's up."

"Who's Ryan?" Jane followed Ken along the crumbling sidewalk.

"Ryan Embry, the boy next door. Well, Ryan's a man, now. Family friend. Known him all his life. Works for the electric company. He'll know what to do."

They skirted a boxy Delta Power van parked on a concrete pad, part of a paved driveway leading to a standalone one-car garage. Jane followed Ken up the three short steps onto a wooden front porch protected by a narrow overhang. The Embry's bungalow was roughly one-third of the size of the Big House that loomed across the street, built in the traditional NOLA shotgun style with a single door and three long shuttered windows. The simple unadorned house was painted a pale blue that almost looked gray in the early morning light. Jane felt such a pang of false recognition that she felt sucker punched. *It almost looks like back home.*

Ken gently rapped on the door using his knuckle.

There was a rustle, the deadbolt was thrown, and an older woman peered through the screen. She was wearing a yellow chenille bathrobe with matching terrycloth slippers. Her thin, faded brown hair was tightly rolled in pink foam curlers. Her nose was slightly too big for her face. She had a prominent forehead and piercing blue eyes.

"Morning, Cheryl." Ken whispered. "Sorry to trouble you. We've got a problem at the house. Is Ryan home?"

"He's in the garage checking his gear." Clutching her robe tightly at her neck, she pushed the door open with her free hand. "Come in. I'll fetch him."

"This is Jane, our new tenant."

"How d'you do?" She bobbed. "I apologize for looking like this. I only just got home." Turning, she shuffled down the single hallway. "Have a seat. I'll just be a minute."

The living room was spotlessly clean with a white painted brick fireplace and a gleaming heart pine floor. Pot metal fleur-de-lis crucifixes hung prominently in the center of every wall. The room held a teak mid-century sofa and two matching armchairs sealed in clear plastic slipcovers. Jane was surprised to see that the ceiling rafters had been painted a vibrant turquoise hue.

"Interesting color choice," she noted.

Ken looked up. "Blue ceiling keeps the haunts away."

"Haunts?"

"Ghosts, spooks, evil spirits. Or so I'm told."

"Good to know. Cheryl works nights like I do?"

"She does now." Ken laced his hands together. "Used to work as a call center manager, but they moved the damn thing to China or Mumbai or some fucking place and downsized her out of a job. Too young to retire, so now she cleans office buildings at night when no one's there."

"At least it's quiet."

"That is one way of looking at it," Ken admitted.

"Here he is." Cheryl returned.

A man roughly Jane's own age stood behind Cheryl, wiping his mouth on the back of his hand. He was whipcord slim, about six-two, with neatly parted sandy blonde hair, blue eyes, and hipster mutton chop sideburns and a whiskery soul patch under his lower lip. Jane raised her chin. A friend of hers back home was addicted to watching classic action movies on DVD. *Ryan looks just like Steve McQueen in Bullitt.* He was dressed in a short-sleeved navy Delta Power work shirt with an employee photo ID clipped to his breast pocket. His muscular left bicep sported a tattooed eagle clutching a cluster of arrows and a Confederate flag in its talons above the script *Never Forget*.

"Good to see you man. Zup?" Studying Jane, he blinked. "Who's this, Ken? Bring me a present?"

"Behave." Ken growled. "This is Jane, our new tenant. She's having problems with the electric. Leslie's still asleep. Thought maybe you could come take a look?"

"I'll get my kit." Without a hint of embarrassment, Ryan stooped and gave his mother a quick peck on her cheek. "Have a good day, Chere Mere. See you later."

"Don't be late tonight, son." She gazed at him adoringly. "I'm making jambalaya."

"With double shrimp?"

"Of course with double shrimp." She playfully slapped his cheek. "Just the way you like it."

"Yum!" Ken rubbed his hands together. "My favorite. What time's supper?"

"Go on, you rascal." Cheryl laughed happily. "I know Leslie feeds you fine."

She slowly shut the door as they trooped down the stoop and followed Ryan to the service van. Opening the unlocked rear cargo door, he reached in for a canvas tote bag filled with clanking tools, slinging it easily over his shoulder. Pausing, he reached in again for a chrome halogen flashlight.

"Might need this. As I recall, there weren't a lot of windows in that place."

Ken took the lead as they re-crossed Plessy Street. Jane deliberately slowed her gait so that she didn't mow him down. As she did, Ryan slid in neatly by her side, matching his lanky stride to hers.

"Noticed you moving in the other day," he offered. "Place's been dark for awhile. Been in NOLA long?"

Jane's gut twisted into a knot of uncertainty as she struggled to squash the anxious, uneasy feeling. *Slow your fucking roll, girlfriend. He's just asking you a normal question. Don't get paranoid. This is what new neighbors do.* She swallowed thickly. "About four months. Decided it was time to settle in. I like NOLA. Think I'm gonna stay."

"Hope you do." Smiling, he caught her eye. "Cute accent. Where you from?"

This time she remembered to keep it safely generic. "East Coast." Ryan's eyes were pure cornflower blue. The color was mesmerizing. Jane knew she was staring, but she couldn't tear her gaze away. She felt the heat coming off of his skin in waves. *Jesus. This guy radiates nervous energy.*

The courtyard's broken bricks slowed Ken down. Stepping through Leslie's garden, Ryan took the lead, pushing the apartment's door wide open. "Let's see what's going on here." Snapping the flashlight on, he raised it to his shoulder. "Breaker box is in the pantry. Wired it myself."

"Oh!" Ken scoffed sarcastically. "She hid it in the pantry. That makes perfect sense. I'll try to remember that for next time."

"Let's hope there is no next time. Jane? Slide in here close. You should see this."

Flicking a wire handle, Ryan opened the gray steel box, shining the flashlight's beam up and down a double row of neat black circuit breakers.

"Here's your problem." He thumbed one switch back and forth repeatedly. The ceiling fan began to whirr and the dehumidifier kicked back on. He smiled, obviously delighted. "The problem's not the breakers, it's the wiring. Miz Pascoe didn't want me rewiring the whole place, too expensive, so I had to keep the amps low."

Slipping across the main room on cat feet, he turned off the dehumidifier. "Miz Pascoe should've mentioned you can't run both units at the same time, since they're on the same circuit. Trips the breaker." He lightly rapped the flashlight against his palm. "Do you even own a flashlight? For next time, just in case?"

"Didn't know I needed one," Jane said quickly. "I'll pick one up at the Dollar Store."

"Here." He spun the chrome tube like a gunslinger. "Keep this one."

"You sure?" She turned the halogen flashlight over in her hands uncertainly. It looked expensive.

"Consider it a housewarming present. Welcome to the neighborhood. We've got plenty more back at the warehouse." He slyly winked. "Delta buys 'em by the case."

"Thank you, my boy. We're all set?" Ken yawned, rubbing his hand over his face. "Don't forget. Tomorrow is Leslie's surprise party for her big 5-0. Top secret. Hush-hush. Don't tell a soul. You're both invited. Eight o'clock, sharp."

Ryan thoughtfully scratched his soul patch. "I heard something about that from my mom. Wasn't sure I'd be welcome."

"Why the hell not?" Ken sputtered.

"Will Gigi be there?"

"I hope so! She helped me plan the thing."

"You know we had trouble, Ken, the last time we got together."

"Ryan. Let bygones be bygones." Ken sounded exasperated. "It's supposed to be Leslie's birthday celebration."

"Can I bring a friend? My boy Tyler would crack his nut sack for a chance to meet you."

"Fine." Ken waggled his index finger. "But the spotlight tomorrow night is on Leslie, not me. Your mother is taking her out for an early bird supper at Brennan's. We'll get things set up while they're gone." He turned. "Jane? Be sure to swing by before you leave for work."

"I will." *Shit.* Jane scrambled to come up with an affordable idea for a present. *Wine is twelve bucks that I don't have. Flowers?* She relaxed. *I'll swing by the farmers market and pick up something bright. Sunflowers. Big ass*

15

sunflowers. They'll stay fresh if I keep them in the fridge.

Ken studied her carefully. "You will stop by, Jane? Promise?"

"Yes, I promise."

"Great. See you both then."

Ryan watched Ken leave before he snorted. "New tenant, huh? You sure stepped in that one. You do know who he is, right?"

"Who, who is?" *Crissakes! I sound like an owl.* "Ken? My landlord?"

"He's more than that. Remember The WarBirds band? Kenny Pascoe played monster bass. The finger-popping king? Wrote "Love Power"?"

Jane's brain lit up like a Christmas tree as she finally made the connection. Every heavy metal band on the planet had covered "Love Power" to prove their musical chops. *Rolling Stone* magazine had called the song one of the top five stadium rock anthems of all time. "Love Power" had been adopted by every major league sports team and by the LGBTQ community as their cry of solidarity and defiance.

Turning, she watched Ken climb the porch steps. "He's Kenny Pascoe? I thought he was dead."

"Nope, just got old. There he goes. Last of the dinosaurs, a real T-Rex," Ryan stated. "He's either a rock god, a legend, or a dream. Take your pick."

CHAPTER FOUR

Pumping her arms, Jane double-timed the concrete staircase before sidestepping the corridor to stretch her laterals. Sliding through the office doorway, she scanned the console monitors before reaching for her water bottle, ignoring the siren's call of the emergency family-sized Milky Way Midnight candy bar she had stashed in her backpack. *This is how we do it, girlfriend. Ignore the temptation.* She felt her resolve wavering. *Quick! Focus on something else.*

Ryan said that Ken Pascoe was an original WarBirds band member. Spinning the chair around with her fingertips, Jane sat. Reaching for the wireless mouse, she googled Wikipedia, typed in "WarBirds band," and read:

> The WarBirds were an American four-man garage band from Prairie Village, Kansas. In 1974, while attending Shawnee Mission East High School, electric guitar front man Scottie Brennan founded the band with drummer Alan "Mick" "Madman" Kiesling, Gary "Lemonhead" Meyer on electric keyboard and harmonica and Kenny Pascoe covering electric jazz bass guitar. On their sole 45 single, "Love Power" Marianne Tanner sang female vocal. However, she was not credited on the record.
>
> **Background Information**
>
> In an interview with *Rolling Stone* magazine in 1982, Mick Kiesling stated that he named the band The WarBirds as

a nod to the Romulan military spaceships from the original *Star Trek* television series.

History

The WarBirds enjoyed modest local college campus touring success until they released their rock anthem "Love Power" as a 45 single in April of 1981.

According to Gary Meyer, "That summer, Kenny saw this tubular show called MTV one night on cable. He called me up. He was freaking out, totally amped. I thought he was high. I kept asking him, Dude? What's your damage? He kept shouting that we needed to shoot a 'music video' and get in on this new *MTV* gig or we'd be working in the shoe department at Kmart for the rest of our lives. Hell, I didn't even know what *MTV* or a 'music video' was, but Marianne got all Dexter on us. She borrowed her brother's video camera and his tripod, and we shot our video outside the War Museum in Penn Valley Park. The rest, as they say, is history."

The music video for "Love Power" debuted on *MTV* over Labor Day weekend in September of 1981. According to Gary Meyer, "Marianne kept pushing for it, saying that the timing was critical. She said we needed to get the music video done in time to catch the kids before they went back to school to ride the buzz. I remember telling her to chill-ax. Turns out she was right."

"Love Power" immediately shot to the number one spot on Casey Kasem's *American Top 40* countdown radio program. The song held the *Billboard Hot 100* top-ten singles number one sales spot for a record-breaking (at the time) twenty-three weeks, a record only broken later by Michael Jackson's single "Thriller" in January of 1984.

Discography

"Love Power" was certified platinum by the Recording Industry Association of America (RIAA) for sales over one million physical units. It has since sold over 110 million copies in digital downloads.

After their skyrocketing initial success, The WarBirds signed with the Crystal Prism/Sultana Records label in February of 1982. They entered the Dancing Blue Crow studio to record their debut double album tentatively titled *Blood Sport* with additional songs written by Kenny Pascoe.

Jane looked up. She thought she heard a soft scratching sound. The sound wasn't repeated. She returned to the screen.

In an interview with *Billboard* magazine in 1982, guitarist Scottie Brennan said, "Kenny writes our songs. The guy is genius-o-rama in the mix. Truly. Used to blow me away. He locks himself in a room and comes out with these rad lyrics written longhand on a legal pad. I kid you not. Dude can't sing a note to save his life which is why we never mic him up, but you can't beat Kenny for producing that solid wall of sound. It's kind of psycho. Sometimes, he can't even remember writing the lyrics like he's a space cadet lost in the ozone, a real Major Tom, but nobody does it better. Kenny Pascoe is the real deal."

The street side security door buzzed like a pissed-off yellow jacket. Jane leapt up. *Oops! Eleven-ten.* As usual, Christophe was running late. Pressing the quick keys to delete the web browser's search history she let him in.

CHAPTER FIVE

Stooping slightly, Jane checked her reflection in the bathroom mirror. *I'll stay at Leslie's party for forty-five minutes, an hour tops. Then I'll change into my uniform and head for work.* Unplugging the straightening iron, she smoothed her hair with both palms. The beauty tool was another unplanned for expense at the Dollar Store, but at least the damn thing had worked. Jane pursed her lips. *A touch of gloss and I'll be ready.* She shook out her hands to release the tension. *Why am I so fucking nervous? It's only a birthday party.*

Trotting downstairs, she plopped onto her one upholstered chair, wiping her palms on her jeans before reaching for her phone for a time check. *Fifteen more minutes. Don't want to be the first guest to arrive. I hate standing around not knowing anyone, feeling awkward.* Resting her phone on her thigh, she decided to wait it out. Her busy beehive mind reminded her that she still didn't know what had happened to *Blood Sport*, The WarBirds debut album or why the band had broken up. Kenny Pascoe had been an arena-filling rock superstar. *How did he end up in The Bywater, Louisiana?*

There was a tap on the door. Reaching up, Jane snapped off the lamp. Sliding lower into the cushions, she saw the bulky outline of someone standing on the stoop. *Should I pretend to not be home?* She unclenched her fists. *Don't be stupid! Whoever it is knows I'm here. My lights were on and my bike is parked in the driveway.*

She clicked the table lamp back on. Pushing off the chair, she forced her protesting legs across the floor.

"Hey, Jane. Am I disturbing you?"

Ryan stood under the yellow bug light. He looked extra trim in a tan windbreaker, pressed dress shirt and jeans cinched tight with a brown leather belt. *Nice style.* Jane glanced at his feet. *Alligator boots. He cleans up good.* "No." She mumbled, her tongue feeling uncomfortably thick. "I'm almost ready."

"Didn't see you at the party." He pointed his chin at the Big House. "Thought I'd check." His blue eyes sparkled with humor as he crossed his arms and leaned into the doorway. "How's the electric?"

"No more glitches."

"Good. Thought I saw them flickering, just now."

"That was me. Hit the switch by accident."

"O-kay." Grinning crookedly, he cocked his thumb. "You coming?"

"I'll get Leslie's present." Jane turned for the fridge. "I bought her some flowers. Hope she likes them."

"I'm sure she will. Leslie's easy that way." Ryan stood on the threshold, making no move to enter. "Flowers are a nice touch. Thoughtful." His eyes narrowed. "I like your hair that way. You look cute."

"Thanks." Jane felt a ripple of green unease. *Stop it. He's giving you a compliment.*

"Let me hold that while you lock the door. Safety first."

"Thanks again." Jane fat fingered the key. *What is wrong with me? I'm as nervous as a teenaged girl on her first car date.* Dr. Wacky's wisdom floated to the surface of her mind. *Anxiety is a natural byproduct of change. You're moving outside of your normal comfort zone. Relax. Trust the universe and push through it.*

Check. Firmly locking the door, Jane dropped the key down the front of her blouse, retrieved the sunflower bouquet and skirted the abandoned chicken coop on the edge of Leslie's garden. *Quick! Think of something clever to say. He's making an effort.*

"Have you known the Pascoes long?"

Ryan shared some serious side eye. "Only my whole life. Grew up with Gigi. We used to be best friends."

"Used to be? What happened?"

He shrugged. "You know how it goes. People change." Lankily climbing the porch steps, he politely held the screened door open to let Jane slip past. "Have you met Gigi yet?"

"No, I've only heard of her."

"You're in for a treat. Gee's a force of nature like a hurricane." Ryan ruefully tugged his ear. "Or a tsunami. Either one's a disaster."

Jane heard a peal of laughter and the clink of silverware coming from the kitchen. *Happy party sounds.* An enticing perfume of garlic and butter, onions and a faint hint of celery wafted across the porch. It smelled exactly like her mother's Pepperidge Farm stuffing and her mouth watered. *Tonight might hafta be cheat night.* She'd been ruthlessly trimming her carbs.

Leslie's kitchen was U-shaped and surprising large. It was filled with dozens of cupboards and cabinets and it ran the full length of the Big House. Passing the range, Ryan snatched up a bite-sized crab cake toasting in a cast iron skillet. He tossed it into his mouth.

"Hot! Hot!" His eyes bulged as he waved his hand. "Lava rock!"

"I'll just bet it is." The caterer spanked him with her spatula. "Don't blame me if you scald your fool mouth. Y'all need to wait like them others."

Jane studied the swinging door. *Buck up, girlfriend. It's show time.* Pushing the door open, she entered the hallway that spilled into the formal front room. Roughly a dozen people stood clustered around a sofa and a loveseat. *Twelve strangers. Looks like a jury. And I don't know a single one of them.* A line of sweat rolled down her spine. *When am I going to stop being afraid of strangers standing in groups, judging me?*

"Jane!" Ken boomed. The crowd parted as he crossed the room. "And Ryan. Good work! Glad to see you found our lost lamb. Ryan? Your mother texted me; they're on their way back." Clear liquid slopped on the floor as Ken waved his glass. "Get yourselves a drink! Your boy Tyler has been manning the bar. Makes a mean vodka tonic."

"Yo, 'bro." A sullen twenty-something guy stood behind a card table loaded with half empty bottles and sturdy glassware. His forehead burned with acne and his scrawny neck looked flushed. "Thanks for the intro. Look what he did. Put me to work."

"'The world needs ditch diggers, too'," Ken rudely quoted *Caddy Shack*, squinting as he studied the younger man. "Where have I seen you before? I know I have. Never mind. Can't remember. Doesn't matter." Mindlessly setting the bouquet aside, Ken grasped Jane's elbow. "Come with me. There's someone you need to meet."

"Hey!" Ryan protested. "She's my date!"

Jane wrenched her arm free. "Let go, Ken. And this is not a date."

"Come with me, Jane, please." Ken insisted as he walked toward an elderly woman holding a sweet grass basket tucked in the crook of her arm. "Aunt Babette? Everyone? Meet our new tenant, Jane Byrne."

Aunt Babette was a tiny woman with a face that looked like it had been carved from a polished hickory nut. Her closely cropped hair covered her skull like a silvery helmet. She wore a gauzy linen blouse with a flamboyantly embroidered skirt and matching evening slippers. Huge golden hoops dangled from her earlobes. She reeked of patchouli.

Please, Lord no, not now. Jane started mouth breathing. She was extremely sensitive to any powdery scents that tickled her nose. *Don't let me sneeze.* Strong scents triggered an explosive coughing fit that left her eyes red and her nose streaming. It was not a good look.

Ken swallowed Aunt Babette in a massive bear hug. "Babette is Leslie's aunt, a real part of the family. Rents out our third floor. She's the mad woman living in our attic."

"I'm a cousin, really." Babette struggled free. "We're related through the Dulayne-Broussards." She studied Jane with limpid eyes. "But you know N'awlins. We don't hide crazy. We set it on the front porch and give it a

23

cocktail."

The party crowd laughed appreciatively. A few of the men raised their drinks in a mocking toast.

"It's a genuine pleasure to meet you, Jane. I'm sure we'll be great friends. Please call me Babette, or even Aunt Babette. Everyone does." She extended the basket. It was brimming with handmade paper mache masks. Jane spotted a sly fox, a bucktoothed rabbit and a spectacularly feathered Great Horned Owl.

"Thought we could wear these for Leslie's party," Aunt Babette explained. "To make it more festive like Mardi Gras." She alertly cocked her head. "You're our newest houseguest. You pick first."

"These are gorgeous." Reaching in, Jane selected a pussycat mask covered with shiny black sequins. She trailed the smooth pink silk ribbons over her hand. "Thank you, Aunt Babette. This is really gorgeous."

"I know. Isn't this fun?" Aunt Babette draped a feathered hen mask around her neck before plucking out an angel mask and a grinning red goblin that looked deeply satanic. She passed the basket to her right.

"Go ahead, everyone! Pick out the mask you want." She raised a warning finger. "But do take a minute to think it through. The mask should represent your inner spirit guide or your totem animal. I've made plenty to choose from."

Ryan grabbed a boar mask with plastic tusks and a pronounced snout. He held it up to his face. "Thank you, Miz Broussard. This one looks like me, Jane, don't you think?"

"I think I don't know you well enough yet to make that call."

Aunt Babette stroked the snowy angel mask with her fingertips. It was trimmed with shimmering silver rickrack, opalescent sequins and white chicken feathers. "I made this one 'specially for Leslie, because she's my guardian angel." She offered Ken the satanic one. "This one's for you."

"Sorry, Babette. I'm not wearing that." Ken raised his hands. "I can see the work that went into it, but I can't stand putting anything across my face. Never could."

"Oh, pooh, Ken." She pouted. "You're such a spoil sport!"

"Yes, I am." Ken suddenly set down his glass. "Shhh! Shhhhh, everyone! Places! Places! That's the Uber. They're pulling in."

Chapter Six

A chorus of hushed giggles swept the room as the party guests slipped on their masks followed by the sound of a brass key scratching the lock. Ken excitedly waved everyone to silence. The front door swung open. Leslie stood framed in the arched doorway.

"Ken? Why are all these lights on? Have you seen our electric bill?"

"Surprise!" Ken roared. Still waving his arms, he encouraged the revelers like a front man circus promoter. "Surprise! Surprise!"

Leslie pressed her hands to her heart. "Oh, Ken. You madman! What have you done?"

"I'm throwing you a birthday party!"

"And very best wishes, my dear." Aunt Babette tottered forward. "For many, many happy years to come."

"You didn't need to do this." Leslie accepted the angel mask, swiping away tears. "Dinner out was more than enough." She smiled at the other party guests. "It's been years since we've had a party in this house."

"Long overdue," Ken heartily agreed. Pulling Leslie into his arms, he dipped her back, giving her a melodramatic kiss before setting her back up on her feet. "Happy birthday, sweetheart. I know I don't tell you this often enough, but I wouldn't be standing here today without you."

"Oh my, Ken. That's quite a confession." Pulling her hands free, Leslie pressed them to her face, cooling her blush. "How much have you had to drink?" Peering around the room, she laughed nervously. "Is Gigi here?"

"On her way, but running late, as usual." Picking up his drink, Ken enjoyed a hearty swallow. "Never been on time in her life. Why start now?" He shared his opinion with the crowd. "It's only her mother's fiftieth birthday party -"

There was a ringing metallic sound like a gong from the kitchen as someone dropped a roasting pan. Leslie flinched.

"Who's back there?"

"Sweetheart, relax. I hired Big Mama's catering. You don't need to do a thing -"

"Caterers, Ken? How are we going to pay for them?"

"Would you please stop worrying?" He smiled uncertainly. "I've got it covered."

"How?" The gong sound was repeated. Leslie quickly hung her angel mask on the back of a chair. "You know I don't like anyone in my kitchen. What are they looking for? I'd better go check."

Ken watched Leslie leave and then he shrugged and ruefully laughed. "Oh, what the hell! Best laid plans. Best to just let her go." He drained his glass. "Drink up, everyone! Tyler? We need music. Play us some tunes."

Squinting, Tyler pushed a button on a vintage '80s boom box. The room filled with a surprising musical pick: Benny Goodman's *In The Mood* big band swing. Jane shut her mouth with a click. *Didn't see that one coming. With Ken's WarBirds background, I was expecting Metallica or Judas Priest.*

Snapping his fingers, Ryan started tapping his toes. "*Bonsoir, Chere Mere.* How was supper?"

"Delicious! Why does crayfish etoufee always taste better when you're not the one who cooks it?" Cheryl adjusted her lioness mask with its fuzzy pipe cleaner whiskers. "Chartres House is always reliable and it's Leslie's favorite. I prefer Bon Ton, but it's Saturday and they were closed."

Finishing his beer, Ryan belched. "Jane? Will you be okay for a minute? I need to drain the monster."

"Oh, son. Don't be crude." Cheryl frowned severely beneath her whiskers. "It's nice to see you again, Jane. Don't mind Ryan, he thinks he's being funny. He told me you work nights, too. Is that true?"

"Yes." Jane settled in. "At Guardian Storage. I work security."

"Odd job for a woman, don't you think?"

Don't judge. Jane blinked. *She's entitled to her opinion.* "Fits my background." She shrugged. "Pays the rent."

"You were in the service?"

"Army Reserves." Jane lied. *It's easier than explaining the truth.*

"Is this security job a permanent thing, then?"

"It is as long as they keep paying my salary." She joked.

"Ryan seems quite taken with you." Cheryl sipped her wine. "You're all he's talked about these last two days. I hope you won't break his heart."

"It's a little early for that, don't you think? We only just met."

Cheryl took another sip. "I can't help but worry, the state of the world being what it is these days. Jane? As a mother, I need to ask you something. Are you a true woman?"

"Sorry? I don't know what you mean."

"I mean, are you the kind of woman who sticks by her man? You're not queer, are you?"

Wow. This just got way personal. "No, Cheryl, I'm not gay. And yes, I think I'd stick with the right guy if I found him."

"It's just that Ryan's had such bad luck with his relationships." Cheryl glanced down the hallway worriedly as she smoothed her collar. "Through no fault of his own. Girls these days don't appreciate a steady man, one who's reliable. They're looking for glamor and excitement. Ryan's worked for Delta Power since the day he graduated high school." She tidily tucked a strand of hair behind her ear. "They think very highly of him. He could be quite a catch for the right woman, and he has a very generous heart. Yes," she nodded, "my son is all of these things."

"I'm sure you're right." Jane sipped her club soda. "To be honest, I'm not wild about the whiskers."

"Oh, I know. Aren't they awful? I've been getting after him about shaving that off. I don't know why he insists on hiding his handsome young face behind that scruffy hair, but he says it's the fashion." She pursed her wrinkled lips. "At least that's an easy fix, not like that sinful tattoo." She shuddered. "Our bodies are God's sacred temple; it's blasphemy to deliberately blemish them, but Ryan wouldn't listen to me." Reaching out, she patted Jane's arm. "He was young, and he's changed since then. You'll just need to work on him a little. I know he's ready to settle down. He's turning thirty-three in July."

One year younger than me. I'd be dating a younger man.

"Cheryl?" The kitchen door swung wide. Looking frazzled, Leslie braced it open with her foot. "Could you please give me a hand in here?"

"On my way." She replied, rolling her empty wine stem between her palms. "Nice talking with you, Jane. Please think over what I've said." She stared up, unblinking, from behind her mask. "I won't let anything ever hurt my son. Ryan deserves to be treated better than that."

Turning, she marched to the kitchen.

Okay, then. I've been duly warned. Jane slowly drained her club soda. Crunching an ice cube between her molars, she studied the party guests and shivered, suddenly feeling isolated and alone, surrounded by a roomful of masked strangers. Ryan was MIA and Ken was nowhere to be found. *I don't have it in me to walk up and introduce myself and make witty small talk. Let's go get some air.*

Opening the front door, she stripped off her mask and stepped onto the porch. Her nose immediately caught the pungent scent of mixed cannabis and tobacco smoke. Ken was sitting in the shadows alone in a wicker rocking chair. An orange ember faded and glowed as he inhaled.

"Evening, Jane." His voice squeaked sharply. "Want some of this?"

CHAPTER SEVEN

"I don't smoke," Jane said. "It's one of the few vices I've skipped."

"I'd like to hear your list of vices someday." The ember left a glowing imprint on Jane's retinas as Ken inhaled again. "Don't tell Leslie."

The herby odor was hard to miss. Jane leaned her hip against the railing. "I think she probably already knows."

"Probably." Ken wheezed a laugh. "It's tough getting anything past that woman. I'm amazed this party surprised her. Leslie is … astute."

Ken and Leslie make such an odd couple. He's so laid back and she's wound tighter than a clock. "Where did you two meet?"

"Now, that is a story." Ken flicked the spliff into the shrubbery. Rocking forward, he rested his elbows on his knees. "Leslie saved my life. She really did. I was living in The Dakota, the co-op in New York, 72nd and Central Park West. Same floor as John Lennon. On top of the world." He raised his arms in triumph. "I fucking had it all."

Rocking back, he crossed his legs. "But I was in a bad place, Jane, a very, very bad place. Drugs were involved, major drugs and not just blow. H, 'ludes, X, you name it. Alphabet stew. If it got me high, I ate it, in massive quantities. Used to have shit delivered right to my door. And I was drinking on top of it. Had that shit delivered, too, by the case." His tired sigh carried across the darkness. "Hope you never experience that depth, that depravity. It's the abyss."

Been there. Jane rolled the bland bubbly club soda across her tongue. *Done that.* "What year was this?"

Ken gave it some thought. "1984. Leslie showed up at my door in June

30

of '84. Carlton said there was this girl standing on the sidewalk insisting that she talk to me." Ken coughed a chuckle. "I asked him if she looked pregnant. When he said 'no,' I figured what the hell. It'd been months since anyone had wanted to talk to me. I told him to send her up."

He paused to let an RTA 88 bus rumble by. "I opened the door and there she stood. Leslie Broussard, this tiny little thing with wild and crazy hair. Just turned eighteen, barely even legal. Marched right in like she owned the place. Said she fell in love with me the first time she saw "Love Power" on MTV. Decided then and there that I was her soul mate, that we were meant to be." He chortled another laugh.

"She heard I was in bad shape. Hitchhiked to New York to take me home. Took one look at my place and said I needed to start over, start fresh. Christ! She was a child, still a kid. So fucking innocent. I was charmed." He raised his index finger. "No, that's not it. I was beguiled. There's a difference. Leslie cast her spell on me. And now, here I am. Here we are." He finished his drink. "NOLA was her home, not mine, but Christ! I've been living here for thirty-four years. That's insane."

Jane's curiosity niggled. Digging her fingernails into the railing's rotten wood, she risked a couple of questions. "Ken? What happened to The WarBirds? Why did the band break up?"

"*Et tu,* Jane?" He rattled the ice cubes in his glass. "*Et tu?*"

"We don't have to talk about it if you'd rather not."

"I wondered when you'd finally put two and two together. Did Ryan clue you in?"

"He did."

"That boy." Ken snorted. Raising his eyebrows, he studied the ice cubes in his glass. "Better watch him, Jane. He's using me to get into your pants." The splintery porch boards cracked as he began to rock. "Who's your favorite bassist, Jane? You're too young to remember Cliff Burton or Jaco Pastorius. Can I guess? Was it Geezer Butler or maybe even me?"

"Of all time? I'd have to go with Aimee Mann."

"Don't fuck with me, woman." Ken chuckled. "I'm trying to relax. I meant heavy metal hitters and you know it. Name me a slasher if you can."

"My dad's favorite was Geddy Lee. He played with Rush."

"Christ! I know who Geddy Lee is, damn your eyes! Your 'dad's favorite'? Fuck, Jane. Thanks for making me feel old."

"Ken, all of this happened before I was born -"

"Stop doing that, you heartless bitch!" He wheezed another laugh. "How much do you know?"

"I know you wrote "Love Power". I know The WarBirds were working on a studio album that never got done."

"That's right. *Blood Sport*." Ken rested his empty glass on his thigh. "All of that is very, very true."

"Why did you stop?"

"Death stopped us, Jane. Death stopped us cold."

Ken set his glass down next to his heel. "It's our duty to rattle this human cage while we can. It's an act of defiance, to prove to God we exist." He pointed his index finger again. "The WarBirds were doing just that. Four punk kids from Prairie Village, Kansas, as white bread middle America as you can get. Think Mike Pence." Raising his arms, he roared. "We were shaking the pillars of heaven!"

Wiping his eyes with his odd thumbs, he settled back. "We'd been in the studio for fourteen months, for over a solid year, and it wasn't working. The songs were getting worse, instead of better. They started sounding brittle, over-produced. Frankie Malcolm, our producer, was sweating bullets. Frankie was starting to panic, afraid we were losing our rawness, losing our edge."

Ken paused as another city bus whined by. "Mick heard about this music festival in California that Steve Wozniak was putting together. You remember Wozniak, the Apple guy?" He snapped his thick fingers. "The US Festival in San Bernardino over Labor Day weekend of '83. Sunday was

'Heavy Metal Day.' Mick wanted The WarBirds to play alongside of Ozzy, Quiet Riot, Judas Priest, Motley Crue." He ticked the competing bands off of his fingertips. "Those guys were our heroes, although personally, in my humble opinion, I agree with your dad that Geddy Lee is the closest thing to God that we have on this planet." He dismissively waved his hand. "Anyway, fuck, Frankie didn't want us to go, but we insisted. We went hoping the festival would freshen our sound back up."

The rocking chair slowed to a full stop. "Van Halen was headlining Heavy Metal Day. Can you believe it? Van fucking Halen. Eddie was an okay guy, but that Dave was a showboating ass wipe." He repeatedly drummed his right knee with his fingers. "They got paid a million and a half for a two-hour set. One point five." Ken whispered. "Joe Strummer found out about the money and he went ballistic, because The Clash was only getting half a million. Shit. Half a million dollars for one set. Even that was real money back then. Things were getting ugly, out of hand, and then Bowie flew in on his private 747. The thin white duke shamed 'em all. Told them to stop acting like pussies. Reminded them they were *professional* musicians. Bowie shut everyone down. That's right. He was smack in the middle of promoting *Let's Dance.*"

"Sounds like a dream gig."

"It should've been, Jane. It should've been." Pushing off his toes, Ken slowly started rocking again. "We left New York that Tuesday. Sent the roadies on ahead with the gear. The idea was that we would take four days to drive to California on the tour bus. Take some time to clear our heads, focus on our music and get out of that fucking studio." Ken clutched his throat dramatically with both hands. "The walls were closing in on us, Jane! We felt trapped, like in prison. And we wanted to party a bit, too, I'll admit. First stop was Fulton, Indiana. Scottie had a friend there who owned a farm with a private airstrip." He waggled his eyebrows. "If you know what I mean."

"Scottie's friend grew pot as a cash crop?"

"On the nose." Ken winked. "We got to Fulton and I needed to crash. We'd been going at it pretty hard. Needed a fucking time out. I stayed on the bus to grab some sleep, but the rest of the guys were wired tight and still going strong. Scottie's friend, Rory, had a single engine prop plane. The four of them tried to get me up to go for a joy ride, but I told them to fuck off. I was beat. So Scottie, Mick, Lemonhead and Rory went up in the plane." Ken stared at the ceiling. "I could hear them up there, buzzing the cornfields, coming in plenty low. Then those assholes started buzzing the bus, trying to make it shake. Must've thought it was hilarious. I imagined them up in the plane, yelling: 'Rock and roll, sucker! Rock and roll'!"

Ken's voice faded to a whisper. "I got royally pissed off, because they were fucking with me and keeping me up. I still think about that, that my last thought about those guys was rage. Then there was this BANG and the whole bus rolled over, slow-mo and I heard a BOOM like the ending of the world. I wound up kneeling on the inside of the roof. I crawled to the front of the bus and I kicked out the windshield. All I could see was this wall of flame. The plane had flipped into a bunch of trees. The fire was so hot it melted the windows on that side of the bus."

Holy shit. Jane swallowed. *I remember my dad telling me this.*

"Everyone died in the fire, except me." Ken repeatedly moistened his lips. "Rory's farm was so remote it took the fire trucks forty minutes to find us. There was nothing they could do, really, except put out the trees. That whole forest blackened down to charcoal briquettes. Mick, Scottie, Lemonhead, Rory had to be identified by the fillings in their teeth."

Ken rested his head on the back of the chair. "Never went to the festival. Couldn't make myself go. I was alive, but The WarBirds were dead. So, I turned around and I headed back to The Dakota. Put The Warbirds songs in my axe case and locked my Fender away." He rubbed his huge hands together. "Then I lit a fire and I burned the session tapes."

"What? Why'd you burn the tapes?"

"I was drunk. Seemed fitting, at the time." He shrugged. "Ignored Frankie's calls. Never finished *Blood Sport*. Never wrote another goddamn song. Decided I was done with all of that. Seemed pretty clear to me it was the end of that particular road."

Frowning, he picked at a callous on his palm. "Those WarBirds songs had seriously bad mojo, Jane, an active evil karma. Spent a year trying to drink myself to death until Leslie showed up and carried me to NOLA." He settled back. "She started feeding me health food, making me practice Tai Chi. Yea, how the mighty have fallen." He circled his finger at the derelict porch. "Now you know. That's who I really am. Kenny Pascoe, the man who wrote "Love Power", the world's most notorious one hit wonder."

A vintage convertible Cadillac Eldorado completely ignored the stop sign at the corner of Plessy Street, blasting through the intersection before squealing to a stop in front of the Big House. The driver parked the cranberry red car under a streetlamp before enthusiastically tapping out "shave and a haircut, two bits" on the horn which was immediately followed by a raucous chorus of high-pitched, drunken female laughter.

"Better batten down the hatches, Jane." Ken muttered. "Gigi's brought her friends, Death and Destruction. It's about to get loud around here."

"Come on, girls! It's party time!" Shoving her door open, the driver raised a silvery gift-wrapped bottle that sparkled under the streetlight. "Hiya, Pops! We have arrived!"

"I can see that." Tipping the chair forward, Ken stood. "Gigi, you're late. Your mother's been looking for you."

"Got here as soon as I could." She marched across the rough dirt yard. "Where is the birthday girl?"

"Hiding in the kitchen, as usual."

A tall black woman wearing crotch hugging white shorts and a midriff baring sequined mohair sweater strolled around the Eldorado's trunk. She looked as leanly muscled as a competitive body builder. Her legs were three

35

quarters the length of her entire body.

"Hey there, sex bomb," she called, carefully picking her way over in six-inch silver stilettos. "I can see you standing there. You waitin' on me, Ken? Looking for a date? How you doin', sugar?"

"Hello, Fancy," Ken said. "Glad to see you could make it."

"Oh, honey." Choosing a bare patch of dirt between two tufts of grass, Fancy paused. Digging into her silver evening bag, she pulled out a mother-of-pearl case and lit a cigarette. Jane caught another whiff of sweetly scented smoke. *Correction. It's a cherry blunt.*

"Sugar? I always make it." Gripping the blunt between her eyeteeth, Fancy snapped her fingers. "Making it is what I do best."

Gigi lithely stepped up onto the porch and into the light. Jane felt a spasm of surprise so tight it tingled her toes. *Why am I shocked? This is New Orleans, after all.* Gigi Pascoe was a man.

CHAPTER EIGHT

Jane shut her mouth so fast her molars clicked. Gigi Pascoe was petite like Leslie, but she had Ken's stronger features including his deeply set eyes and full lips. Her pointed elfin chin was all her own. She wore a striped Oxford cloth dress shirt belted tight over fitted trousers and velvet slip-ons without socks. Dark brown curls brushed her collar. She had wide shoulders and slim square hips and an Adam's apple. *If I passed her on the street, I'd call her a man, but when I look closer there is something in her face that's pinging me she's a woman.*

"Come here, you." Ken pulled Gigi into a hug. "Jane, meet my daughter, Gigi. Jane is our new tenant."

"Wattup?" Cocking her hip, Gigi stretched out her hand, meeting Jane eye to eye. "Liking it so far?"

Her voice was mid-range contralto, but Jane gripped a square hand that felt distinctly masculine. The cobalt blue nail polish threw her off balance again. "Suits me down to the ground."

"Fantastic! I know Maman will be over the moon seeing some income again. Delilah? Yo, girlfriend. Meet M&D's new tenant."

Jane blinked as an absolute vision climbed the porch steps. She was still getting used to NOLA's flamboyance. This woman was pushing the limit in a black lace bustier, fishnet stockings and calf-length button up Victorian boots. Her shoulders and bare arms were covered to her wrists with gaily tattooed sleeves featuring twining pink hibiscus flowers, ruby hummingbirds and yellow butterflies. She had a broad moon shaped face with raven-colored hair, heavily mascaraed eyes, scarlet lips, and a silver nose ring that pierced her septum. The right side of her head was shaved bald. Her bare scalp sported a spider web tattoo.

"Good evening, Delilah," Ken offered gallantly. "You look stunning, as always."

"Thanks for the invite, Ken. I brought Leslie a present. Where should I set it?"

Delilah had a childish, baby doll voice. She proffered a gift wrapped in aluminum foil with a black lace ribbon. "It's a selection of her favorite teas hand-picked from my shop."

"That was very thoughtful. I'm sure she'll love it. Put it on the table, right inside."

"Jane?" Gigi said. "Meet Delilah, my roommate."

"Yes." Delilah giggled. "Lucky me."

"Nice to meet you." Still stunned, Jane scrambled for something more to say. "That's some outfit. Are you practicing for Mardi Gras?"

Ken guffawed and Fancy burst into a musical laugh.

"No girlfriend, this is steam punk." Delilah protested. "I always dress this way. I'm a fashionista."

Duh. Jane blushed maroon to the roots of her hair. "Of course it is. Don't mind me. I'm an idiot."

"Cut Jane some slack." Ken chuckled. "She's still learning the ropes. Hey, bay-bee? Fancy?" He called. "You coming in?"

"Just finishing my cigar, sugar. You know Leslie don't like me smoking in her house." Fancy looked up from her phone, her sculpted face lit ghostly pale by the screen. Inhaling one final toke, she dropped the blunt and crushed it out using the toe of her stiletto. "Don't want to waste it. This shit is fucking dope." Sliding the phone into her bag, she strolled over. "I am so loving this new Tinder app. Might have me a date for later this evening."

"Good for you." Ken raised his empty glass. "Let's go get a drink for the now."

"Lead me to the bar, sugar." She grasped Ken's forearm. "You know you got my vote."

"Fancy?" Gee interrupted. "Meet Jane."

"My goodness me, yes, yes." Fancy paused, scanning Jane from head to toe. "You are one big, tall white girl, aren't you?"

"Play nice, Fancy," Gigi stated, pushing the front door open and leading them into the party. Studying the festive guests, she gave her father two thumbs up. "Nice job, Pops! Listen to the gumbo yaya going on in here! Love the masks and the music. Can't beat Gene Krupa. I can see where Jane got her Mardi Gras idea."

"Every day is Mardi Gras with you three around," Ken stated flatly.

"Ha-ha, funny." Gee gave him a playful shove.

"The Decadence parade might be closer to the truth," Fancy drawled, "but I have to say this party is lit."

"There you are, Fancy!" Aunt Babette swooped over with her basket. "I've been waiting for you!" She plucked out a bird mask that erupted into an Aztec spray of blue and green opalescent feathers. "I made this mask for you, special."

"Give me that," Fancy said.

"Good evening, Aunt Babette." Stooping, Gigi gave the elderly woman a kiss on the cheek. "I knew this was all your doing the minute I saw it." Reaching into the basket, she plucked out the grinning satanic mask that Ken had already rejected. "This one's mine. Maman's in the kitchen?"

"She was the last time I saw her, *cher*."

"I'll go see if she needs help." Gigi slid the mask over her face. "Dee? You coming?"

"Babette, honey?" Fancy struggled with the fabulous bird of paradise mask. "I'm having trouble fitting this over my eyelashes."

"Let me help." Babette set the basket down. "Bend lower, Fancy. You know I can't reach you with my short little legs." Stepping back, she clasped both hands over her heart. "Perfect! I knew it would be. Fancy, you look stunning, absolutely stunning."

"Where's a mirror?" Turning from side to side, Fancy studied her reflection from across the room, smoothing her fuzzy sweater over her breasts. "Babette? You are hands down my favorite person in this whole world." She gave the mask a slight tweak. "Always so considerate. Always thinking the best of other people. This world would be a better place if more folks acted like you." She glanced at the Embrys standing nearby. Cheryl was openly gaping in horror. Fancy raised her voice. "Especially those evangelicals. I swear they are the world's worst hypocrites, always talking outta both sides of they mouths. You should see my appointment book on Sundays, right after they done with church. I am booked solid for all of next year. Those evangelical men can't get enough of my chocolate starfish."

One of the male guests blanched. Cupping his wife's elbow, he dropped a quick word in her ear. Setting down their drinks, they moved toward the door.

Fancy primped her hair before spotting Ken at the bar. "Ken, sugar? I'm ready for that drink now." She was so tall that the mask's green feathers brushed the ceiling fan as she crossed the room. "Bartender? Fill me up. I'd like a Vieux Carre."

"I don't ..." Tyler stuttered, "know what that is."

"Boy?" Fancy cocked her hip. "Where you from? The beer pool? Listen up." She rudely waggled her fingers in Tyler's face. "Whiskey, Benedictine, cognac and a tiny drop of sweet Vermouth."

"Give the kid a break, Fancy." Frowning, Ken rattled his ice. "He can't make you that. Besides, we don't have any cognac."

"Ignorance, Ken, honey," she turned, "is no excuse."

Tyler glared. "Who you calling ignorant?"

"Don't mind her, kid. Give her a double Stoli on the rocks. She'll be fine."

"With extra lime. You do have limes somewhere, right?"

"Yes, I've got limes." Tyler splashed a double shot of vodka over a handful of ice cubes. Squishing a quartered lime, he rudely plopped in into the glass. "Here you go."

"Thank you." Fancy delicately accepted the glass, taking a tentative sip. "Delicious! I only hope I don't catch cooties offa this cotton picker."

"Back at you, bitch." Tyler snarled. "Hope I don't catch an STD."

The kitchen door swung open. Leslie backed into the dining room hunched over a heaping cheese plate and cracker tray. Gigi followed carrying a platter of sliced ham speared with glazed cherries and glistening pineapple chunks. Delilah balanced a chocolate layer cake in one hand and a stack of china dessert plates in the other.

Quickly setting down his drink, Ken trotted over. "Sweetheart? What are you doing? You're supposed to be enjoying the party. I paid the caterers good money to do that."

"We've already talked about this, Ken. You can't just drink your dinner." Leslie fluffed her damp bangs with the back of her hand. "Everyone? Supper's on the table. Please, come help yourselves."

CHAPTER NINE

"One minute, Maman." Gigi pulled out an index card. "I wrote you a birthday song."

"Oh, Gigi." Leslie sighed with exasperation. "Make it quick. People need to eat."

"It's short. I promise. Ready, girls? Help me out." Setting the key with a hum, she launched into a rich contralto, supported by her friends who followed her lead, swaying and clapping their hands like an old school gospel choir.

> "Let's take some time
> To recognize what's fine
> In your life and in mine.
> *Happy birthday.*
> You held me up while I walked this path
> Never looking back
> Always holding fast.
> *Happy birthday.*
> You're our rock, our roll
> Always in control.
> This families' heart and soul.
> *Happy birthday.*
> And fifty years ain't … that … old."

Ken roared with laughter over the applause. "That's saying it!"

"Oh, *bebe*. You are so sweet." Leslie brushed away tears. "Thank you."

Ken grabbed her hand. "One more minute - "

"Stop it, Ken." She mulishly pulled free. "You know I don't like being the center of attention. That's your job."

"Too bad. Today it's all about you." He persisted. "Leslie? I have a confession to make. I wanted to take a minute, in front of our family and friends to admit that everything good in my life came about because of you."

"Hey!" Gigi protested. "I resemble that remark."

"Don't interrupt me, Gee. This is tough enough to get through as it is." Ken moistened his lips. "Leslie, we've had some rough patches, some tough times. I'm not an easy man to live with; I never was. That said, sweetheart, you've stuck with me through thick and thin, true blue. Sometimes I think I forget to tell you that. So, well, I got you this as a reminder of what you mean to me." He fumbled with his pocket. "I don't want you to ever think that I'm taking any bit of this grand life with you for granted."

Pulling out a gilded red leather ring box, Ken snapped it open. Leslie gasped as the generous diamond solitaire caught the light and sent brilliant rainbows skating across the ceiling.

"Oh, Ken!" She pressed her hands to her heart. "Is it real?"

"Of course, it's real." He blustered. "I wouldn't buy you a fake diamond."

Her hand trembled as she reached for the ring box. Looking up, she stared into his eyes. "Ken? How on earth did you pay for this?"

"That's none of your never mind. All you need to know is that it's paid for and it's yours." Taking her right hand, he slipped the diamond onto her ring finger. It fit perfectly. "Like Gee said in her song, sweetheart, you are my rock, so I bought you this rock to prove it."

"Oh, snap." Gee groaned. "Dad humor at its absolute *worst*. Didn't know he was gonna go there."

"Ken, you didn't need to do this." Leslie's shoulders softened. "You know you're the only man I've ever loved and I've known that since I was fifteen years old."

"Twenty years ago?" He winked.

Aunt Babette folded her arms. "Saw it with my own eyes. A true *coup de foudre*. She was watching him on TV. From the second he came on she was never the same. Love at first sight."

"That's enough from the both of you." Leslie playfully pushed Ken, but she kept her eyes locked on her new ring. "Everyone, please, eat! I mean it." She blindly waved her free hand at the buffet. "Eat. Eat!"

"That was adorable." Delilah sighed. "Thirty years in and to still be so in love." She caught Jane's eye. "I hope I find that kind of love someday."

"That's nothing special." Ryan's arm brushed Jane's elbow. "Known them all my life. They always talk like that."

"Hey, Ryan. Zup?" Gigi strolled over, elegantly sipping champagne. "How you doin'? Haven't seen you in months."

"Been busy working." He refused to meet Gee's eyes.

"Whoops!" Delilah unexpectedly tottered. Clutching Jane's arm, she threatened to spill out of her bustier. "Jane? I meant to ask: What do you do?"

She had a leggy spider tattooed on her left breast. Jane blinked. *Is that a black widow?* "Private security. You?"

"Me?" She giggled. "I own a shop in Jackson Square. Been there forever. Le Maison Grise. Sell essential oils, healing crystals, jewelry made by local artists, you know. I try to support our community as best I can. Oh! And I do Tarot card readings."

"Dee gives great advice." Gee knowingly smiled as she studied Jane over the rim of her crystal flute. "Dee? Not for nothing, girlfriend, but I think Jane needs some space."

"Oh! Sorry!" She released Jane's arm, smiling winsomely. "Jane, you should stop by sometime for a reading. First one's on me."

Voo-doo, hoo-doo. No, thank you. New Orleans' gris-gris was one of

44

the three things Jane had sworn to steer clear of in her newly adopted city. Vampirism and law enforcement were the other two. She flinched as Delilah suddenly grabbed her left hand. She shivered as Dee ran her pointed scarlet fingernail across her palm.

"You have fascinating lifelines." Dee squinted. Cocking her head, she looked up. "What's this dark secret you're hiding from the world?"

Jane snatched her hand back. "There's no dark secret. I'm a security guard. That's it."

"Girlfriend, please." Dee scoffed. "You have an 'M' for mystery written in the center of your palm."

"Jane's plenty mysterious," Ryan said. "That's what I like about her." He stretched out his hand. "What's mine say?"

"I wouldn't know." Rolling her eyes, Delilah gave him her standing bitch face. "You'd need to make an appointment." She smoothed her bustier. "It's forty bucks."

Jane's trained senses flipped to high alert as Ryan's jaw clenched. *Quick! Change the subject.* She rolled up on her toes. *He's about to blow.* "Where did you and Gigi meet?"

"Where else?" Gigi laughed, raising her champagne flute in a toast. "Femme Du."

"That's our nickname for it." Delilah dimpled. "Club Femme du Monde."

Jane frowned. "Where's that? On Bourbon Street?"

"Oh hell no." Gee stated flatly. "The Quarter is only for drunks and tourists. Femme du is on Frenchmen near Washington Square. That's where the real people go."

"Now that's a place you should visit, Jane," Dee agreed. "In NOLA, queer life is where it's at. Let me know when you want to go. I'll introduce you to the crew -"

BANG. Jane flinched so fiercely she cricked her neck. Cheryl Embry was stooping next to the couch, working to right a mahogany candle stand lying sideways on the floor. There was a nervous ripple of laughter from the party guests and more than one raised eyebrow. *Okay.* Jane thumbed the suddenly sore muscle behind her ear. *I'm not the only one feeling jumpy.*

"Ryan?" Pushing past an armchair, Cheryl hurried over. "Where've you been hiding, son?" Fingering her crucifix necklace, she lowered her voice. "You need to remember who these people are."

"Sorry?" Delilah blinked her kohl-rimmed eyes. "What do you mean by, 'these people'?"

"You know perfectly well what I meant." Wincing, Cheryl crooked her fingers into quotes. "People who practice 'alternative lifestyles'."

"Hold it right there, sugar." Fancy cut through the crowd, stripping off her mask. "I believe you're talking about me, and I prefer that you say it to my face. Personally, honey, I love my alternative lifestyle." She snapped her fingers. "I am free to be."

"Don't get your knickers in a twist, Fancy." Gee stated uncertainly. "It's a birthday party not a debate."

"Relax, *chere mere.*" Ryan thoughtfully rolled his beer bottle between both hands. "We were just talking -"

"That lifestyle goes against our faith, Ryan. It's moral degeneracy and perversion." Cheryl nervously plucked his sleeve. "I've been told that one's a prostitute."

"It's called sex work." Fancy glared. "And people got to live."

"Sodomy is a sin." Cheryl clutched her necklace. "And prostitution is against the law."

"Honey!" Fancy crudely slapped her ass. "You can outlaw sex all you want, but it won't make it any less popular!"

"Thankfully," Cheryl blushed a deep cherry red, "we have a new president who will reset this country's moral compass. It's almost too late. End signs have been seen, almost daily."

"Moral compass? Who you talking about?" Fancy's eyes bulged. "Donald Trump?"

"I have every confidence in President Trump." Cheryl stoutly raised her chin. "He's going to make America great again before our nation degenerates any further and turns brown."

Delilah choked.

"Jesus was brown, you do know that, right?" Fancy snapped. "Where the hell did he go in all of this?"

"Don't you dare bring our blessed Savior into this sinful conversation!"

"I can remember," Delilah interrupted, "waking up on November tenth and feeling like I woke up in an alternate universe, bizarro-world. Went to bed thinking we had voted in Hillary Clinton and woke up to find out we got Donald Trump." She dropped her hands to her hips. "Seriously? Donald Trump? I can tell you it's been a waking nightmare for the LGBTQ community and it's only gonna get worse."

"Things have gotten crazier since November," Gee agreed. "Seems like we're going backwards." Setting her champagne flute down, she gestured like an airport marshal directing planes. "I thought we were all pushing one way, you know, forward, and now everyday it seems like we're moving in the opposite direction, like somehow we've ended up over here." Her forehead puckered. "I'm not sure how it happened."

"It's gonna get ugly." Fancy warned. "Some girls I know have even started to carry."

Delilah frowned uncertainly. "Carry what?"

"Baby nines, mostly." Smoothing her blonde hair, Fancy gently explained. "It's a gun, sugar. Nobody feels safe no more. We're not even sure the cops are still on our side," she rolled her eyes at Cheryl, "ever since the crazies been given permission to act."

"Crazy?" Tyler's barking laughter captured the crowd's attention.

Pressing both fists onto the table, he leaned forward, staring at Fancy, his eyes glazed. "Who you calling crazy, you ugly fucking bitch? You're the one walking around with your dick taped to your leg. How's that for crazy?"

"Ryan?" Ken quickly downed his drink. "Better take your friend home. He's drunk."

"And who you calling drunk, you washed up old fart?" Hefting a tequila bottle in one hand, Tyler sighted down his index finger. "Rock star, my ass." He spat. Taking a belligerent swig, he flipped Ken the bird. "You're not a has-been. You're a fucking never was."

"Shut the fuck up, you goddamned peckerwood!" Gigi crossed the room in three giant strides. "Don't you dare call my father that!"

She launched over the makeshift bar. Tyler raised both arms defensively to fend her off, and the card table collapsed into a skittering wave of shattered bottles and crystal stemware that sped across the polished floor like a glass tsunami. Shrieking in panic, Leslie's party guests stampeded for the door.

CHAPTER TEN

"And that is why," Leslie calmly sipped her peppermint tea, "we never have big parties, in the Big House, anymore."

"How's Ken feeling this morning?" Stretching her right hamstring, Jane pressed the tread of her cheap sneaker against the splintery porch step. Her heart was hammering and sweat was rolling in sticky beads down her spine, but she had completed a full lap for the first time without stopping, not once. *Acknowledge the small wins,* her therapist had advised. *That has to count for something, right?* "How's his wrist?"

"It's not broken, only sprained. I wrapped it in an Ace bandage. He'll survive. Ken can act like such a diva sometimes." Reaching for the electric kettle, she refreshed her fine china cup. "Serves him right," she added brutally. "He should know better. Ken's too old for a bar fight brawl."

She raised the kettle. "Jane? Would you like a cup? Some of these teas are herbal." Pulling Delilah's gift box across the wicker table's glass top, she rifled through the slim paper packets. Choosing one envelope, she gave it a sniff. "This one's valerian. It'll help you sleep."

Why not? Jane reached for the porch door. *I need to grab a shower anyway. Might as well sit down for a few and cool off first.* The shower suggestion pinged a reminder. "Hey, Leslie? Nothing urgent, but the shower needs to be snaked. That drain is super slow. I'm in water up to my ankles."

"I'll add it to the list," she replied promptly. Her new diamond ring sparkled in the sun and twisting her hand, she admired it. "That Ken is such a rascal. I still can't believe he bought me this." She snorted. "Still won't tell me where he got the money for it."

"It's a beauty." Jane lifted the soggy teabag from her cup. "Where is Ken? He's usually puttering around by the time I get back. He sleeping in?"

"No, he snuck out of the house at dawn. Being all mysterious again. Won't tell me what he's up to or where he's going." Leslie adjusted the wooly cobalt blue shawl draped around her shoulders. The December air was chilly. She sipped her tea, smiling serenely. "It's his new big secret."

"Aren't you worried about that?"

"No. Maybe I'm blind and foolish, but I don't need to know every single thing Ken does. Jane? Have you ever been in love?"

"Not like what I saw between the two of you last night." Pressing the spent teabag against a spoon, Jane set it aside. "But I have hope." She lied.

"I hope so for you, too." Leslie rested her head on a cushion. "Love is the strangest thing, because the idea of it changes as you get older." Setting her cup down, she linked her fingers, and stared at her hands. "When you're young, you're looking for that one special person; at least I know that's what I did. But as I get older, as Ken so kindly reminded me last night, the more I think it grows out of caring for all of the people you live with or that you meet, day to day. It turns into being part of a bigger community, part of a bigger family, and that's where our comfort is. Even the people you work with figure into it somehow."

Jane considered her world at Guardian Storage, of Calvin, and of all the new people she had met: Leslie and Ken, Ryan Embry, Gigi, Fancy and Delilah, even Aunt Babette. *These people are making NOLA my new home. I'm starting to care for them. I'm building my new family.* Flaming anxiety torched her esophagus. Doubling its grip, the PTSD trigger pinched off her air pipe. *Relax.* Jane forced her shoulders down. *Crissakes! Relax!* Rapidly flexing her fingers, she released the tension, acknowledging the fear. *It's* normal *to care for people. It's* human. *It's not a bad thing to feel emotion. I acknowledge that it's uncomfortable.* She admitted the full truth. *It fucking hurts.*

Leslie looked up. "That's why I think it's important that all of us spend time talking to each other, face-to-face like we're doing now." She dimpled. "It's the only way to really get to know someone. I enjoy having my tea outside, most mornings. Feel free to stop by after your run anytime if you like. You're more than welcome."

"Thank you. I will." Jane said, and she meant it. Her heartbeat had simmered down and her breathing had returned to nearly normal. She picked up her teacup. Warming her fingers on it, she sipped the bitter brew that curled her tongue before reaching for the clover honey. "Leslie? Why didn't you tell me that Gigi was a man?"

"Because she's not." Leslie adjusted the striped cushion under her elbow. "My daughter is a transgender person. Gigi is female in a male gendered body."

Is this really any of my business? Why should I care? Jane studied the sunrise warming the treetops as her ingrained investigative training niggled her unmercifully like a persistent redbug itch. *Because this is who I am; This is what I do best.* "Forgive the twenty questions. This is new to me. I've never run up against it before."

"It's natural to be curious, Jane, and it's nothing to be ashamed of. Gigi's gender is a fact that we live with, in this family, every day. Although," Leslie quirked a gentle smile, "as you saw, it does tend to cause a ruckus."

"When did you know?"

"Know that Gigi was transgender?" Leslie pursed her lips. "I suppose I knew it when she was six, maybe seven? She was still very, very young." She toyed with her ring. "I remember thinking there was something odd about the way Gigi smiled in her grade school pictures. It looked … unnatural. I know now, of course, that she was hiding from us, even then, poor little thing, as best she could. God bless her, she thought there was something wrong." She sipped her tea. "I thought Gigi was going to grow up to be an actor because she was always playacting. Now I know she was acting at being male."

Jane was struck by a sudden thought: *'Gigi' is an AKA.* "What was her real name, I mean her birth name before it was Gigi?"

"Paul. Paul Pascoe. We named her for Ken's father." Leslie wound a stray strand of hair around her fingers before tucking it behind her ear. "Everything came out in spades when Gigi hit puberty. That was a rough few years, I can promise you that. Gigi hated growing muscles and hair and turning more obviously male. She hated it! We had an active teenage rebellion on our hands until we visited Dr. Benedict, our holistic therapist, and got things squared away."

Jane settled her hands in her lap. *Everyone has a story to tell. The trick with getting witness testimony is letting the witness speak.*

Leslie smoothed the fuzzy afghan around her neck. "I thought that was going to be the hardest part about her gender change besides the pronouns," she joked, "but I was wrong, because even though I accepted Gigi as my daughter," her voice softened as she grew still, "I still wondered what happened to my sweet little boy? Where did *Paul* go?" Her hand trembled as she reached for the kettle. "I had to remember that Gigi is still the same person we have always loved and it did get easier with time. Ryan, of course, was devastated."

Ryan Embry? "Why was Ryan upset?"

"Because up 'til then they'd been best pals. Ryan and Paul were practically twins, growing up." The water sloshed as she checked the kettle. "I knew something had changed when Ryan stopped coming by. That boy practically lived here when Cheryl was working or busy with her church. When Gigi turned thirteen, though, I think that's when Ryan finally figured it out."

Refilling the teapot, she replaced the lid. "Of course, you worry about it, as a parent, the same way you worry about any child." She shuddered. "Some of the way Gigi lives now is called 'high-risk.' I hate that phrase, hate it, but I can't help it, it's stuck in my head." She straightened. "I need to be brave because I want Gigi to be happy. I don't want her going through life pretending to be something she's not. That's no way to live. There's no happiness there." The wooly wrap slipped as her shoulders slumped. "But there's only so much I can do to protect her. I would never tell Gigi this, but I still struggle with it every day, the minute I open my eyes and my feet hit the floor."

"Struggle with her gender?" Jane asked, suddenly feeling foggy. The Valerian was kicking in.

"No." Leslie studied the line of dark trees. "I struggle with my fear."

"Fear's a raw bitch," Jane agreed. *And don't I know it.* The electric kettle steamed gently. Leaning forward, she chose a fresh teabag. *Sleepytime. That'll do it.* "I've studied DNA and genetics some, as a hobby on my own. This kinda fits in there, somewhere."

"It can." Leslie readjusted her shawl. "I've read everything I can get my hands on, on the subject. There's not a lot of information out there."

Jane's curiosity prickled. "Does this transgender thing run in Ken's family, or in yours?"

"Not that I know of." She smoothly linked her fingers. "Ken's never mentioned it and if it ran in my family it wouldn't matter, since Gigi's adopted."

Jane set her teacup down with a click. "I'm sorry? What?"

"Yes." Leslie turned. "Gigi is Ken's natural child, not mine. Her mother abandoned her when she was a tiny infant and we took her in."

I did think Gigi looked more like Ken than like Leslie. Jane blinked. "That was very generous to open your heart to her."

"Any child of Ken's is a child of mine." Crow's feet lined Leslie's eyes as she smiled. "Gigi may not be my blood, but she is my daughter. She always will be. That's how love works."

"Who was Gigi's biological mother?"

Leslie shifted uncomfortably. "Some WarBirds groupie named Marianne. Turned up here one night with Gigi in her arms, the cutest little peanut you ever saw." She slowly stroked her throat. "We still don't know when Gigi's real birthday is. I had to invent one for her birth certificate." She stared blindly at the floor. "I had to lie to the judge. I'm not proud of that. I had to swear that I was Gigi's birth mother and that she was born at home without a doctor." She suddenly looked haggard. "I couldn't let them take her. Luckily, it happens more often than you think, children born at home. Nobody raised a fuss."

Jane shook off the foggy feeling. *Marianne Tanner was mentioned as the backup singer on "Love Power".* "What happened to her? To Marianne? Why did she leave Gigi here?"

"I have no idea and honestly, I don't care." Leslie dusted her hands. "She took off in the middle of the night and left that sweet little baby sleeping in my laundry basket next to my washing machine. I found Gigi there first thing, wailing away. Poor little peanut got hungry."

The floorboards creaked.

"Who there?" Leslie leaned forward. When no one answered, she settled back.

"I don't think Ken was ever serious about Marianne. Didn't even want to talk to her when she showed up. He told me to send her away, baby and all. She insisted on talking to him. Stood right out in our driveway, screaming Ken's name at the house at the top of her lungs over and over, and that woman was loud. I could hear her shrieking from inside the kitchen," Leslie flushed, "so did the neighbors. She kept screaming that Ken owed her the royalties from "Love Power", that the money was hers, that she needed it to support their child. It was a terrible scene, horrible." She swallowed hard, staring at the floor. "And when she left, she stole Ken's guitar, his Fender bass. All of his WarBirds songs were in that case."

And Ken burned the studio session tapes. "So, his other WarBirds songs are really gone?"

"Gone, all gone. And Ken absolutely refuses to write anything new or to even try." She croaked. "I try bringing the idea up; we could sure use the money, but it only raises a fuss." She shrugged. "We're limping along." She chewed her lip. "I still think Ken listens for those missing songs. Every once in a while, I'll catch him listening to a riff or to a certain bass line, and he gets the strangest look on his face, like he's still hoping they'll turn up again, that they're still out there, somewhere in the universe. Who knows? Maybe they will turn up one day. Stranger things have happened. You hear about people finding lost things all the time."

The kitchen door creaked open.

"I thought I heard voices. Good morning."

"Babette?" Leslie leaned forward. "You there? Come join us, dear. We're having tea."

CHAPTER ELEVEN

Jane straightened as Aunt Babette shut the kitchen door. *I feel like such a slacker.* The elderly woman was carefully made up and dressed for the day in a black linen skirt with a ruffled white blouse and sensible low-heeled pumps. Her gray hair was neatly combed into tight curls that lay flat against her scalp. She wore a necklace of colorful carved wooden birds with matching bird earrings and a jangly collection of silvery bangles on her knobby left wrist.

"You sure I'm not interrupting?"

"Don't be silly. This is your home, too." Leslie pushed a decrepit wicker chair closer using her toes. "Take a seat. How about a nice cuppa tea before you leave? What time is your bus?"

"Quarter past. I'd love a cup, but isn't that the gift Delilah gave you?" Her shoulders dropped as she folded her hands. "I don't want to take your nice present."

"Babette, please! Look what that crazy girl did." Turning the gift box sideways, Leslie displayed the selection as she reached for a fresh cup. "She is too generous by half! Gave me fifty different kinds, one for each year of my life. Which one would you like? Orange Pekoe? Lemon Splash? Lady Gray?"

"Orange Pekoe would be lovely." Babette sat. "*Merci.*"

She's got to be close to seventy. I thought she was retired. "Where do you work?" Jane asked.

"Le Maison Grise. Delilah's shop." Repeatedly dipping her teabag, she neatly set it aside. "This time of year between Christmas and Mardi Gras she

56

gets *fou occupe*." Her dark eyes twinkled. "She gives me twenty hours a week. It helps us both out."

"Retail sales is tough," Jane commiserated. "Personally, I am through dealing with the public. Never again."

"*Alors pas*, no, dear." Babette shrank back, horrified. "I don't work the counter! I'm mediumistic. I do readings. Worried souls come to me seeking spiritual advice. I have the gift." Pursing her wrinkled lips, she cooled her tea. "Did I hear you talking about Marianne Tanner?"

"Jane was curious," Leslie said.

Babette frowned. "I hardly remember her. I only saw her that one time, the night she left the baby behind."

"Are you sure that Gigi is really Ken's child?" Jane blurted.

"Jane!" Babette laughed nervously, fingering her bird beads. "So many questions! You should've been a detective like on TV."

"Yes, we are sure of that." Leslie sipped her tea. "Gigi bought us one of those ancestry kits last Christmas. She wanted to know." Her cup rang as she tapped it with her spoon. "Ken and Gigi are originally from Italy, Germany, and Wales." She raised both eyebrows. "Gigi got a surprise; she showed Central European which was identified as Jewish." Setting her cup down, Leslie placed both hands over her heart. "Babette and I are northern Spain, La Belle France, and sub-Saharan Africa, which is proper for Creole and exactly as it should be."

"An all-American family," Babette agreed.

A songbird's bright trill caught Jane's ear. *It's still strange to hear birds singing in December.* She studied the threadbare porch, the unmortised bricks and the scruffy courtyard. "It's a shame Ken's songs are gone. They'd be worth some serious money. At least he's still getting royalties from "Love Power", right?"

"No, he is not!" Leslie snapped. "Ken sold those royalties before he left New York. He's never made one dime offa that song! To this day that money still goes to those crooks, those New York record company thieves!"

No royalties? That's got to sting. Explains why this property looks so run down. "Love Power" is a hall of fame classic. I hear it played everywhere I go.

"I know I shouldn't let it upset me." Leslie smoothed her hair. "It happened so long ago, it shouldn't even matter." Circling her finger, she indicated the Big House. "I keep warning Ken we're only one disaster away from having to sell this place. If anything big happened, I don't know what we'd do. We spent our savings repairing Katrina. There's no way we could pay for a new sewer line or fix the roof again. When we die, all Gigi will inherit is old Tupperware and debt."

"This property has to be worth something." Jane stood. She had cooled off and her nap time clock was ticking. "The Bywater is booming. I see flippers working on a different house every day. This house has a big corner lot. You'd get a good price for it, as it is."

"That's what Ken says." Leslie blotted her eyes with a ragged corner of the afghan. "I suppose we could move into an apartment, if we needed to. It's not such a sacrifice to make."

"Leslie! Please don't talk like this!" Babette clapped both hands over her ears. "You know how it upsets me! We belong here! This is our home. Where else would we go?"

"Of course, Babette, of course. I'm sorry, you're right." Leaning forward, Leslie patted Babette's bony knee. "Ignore what I said. I'm being foolish. Of course we're not going to sell the Big House. For some reason I woke up feeling blue this morning -"

She turned as Gigi pulled The Boat into the driveway. Slamming the Cadillac into park, Gee left the driver's side door open, sprinting across the side yard.

"Heel, Piddles!" She shouted. "I said heel, goddammit!"

A black standard poodle wearing a rhinestone collar hopped off the passenger seat and loped toward the porch. He had a ridiculously long purple tongue and a scarlet pedicure.

"Maman?" Gigi shouted, taking the porch steps two at a time. Snatching the screened door open, she waved her phone. "Maman? Why didn't you answer me?"

"I'm sorry, dear." Leslie rose, looking confused. "I didn't hear it ring. What's wrong?"

"Fancy never made it home last night." Noticing that Leslie had company, Gigi nodded a greeting. "*Bonjour, ma tante.* Something's happened. We need to call the police."

"Let's think about this for a minute, honey. Maybe Fancy met a new friend?"

"No." The china tea set rang as Gigi dropped her phone on the table. Shaking out both hands, she cocked her right thumb at the dog. "She would've texted me and had me check on Piddles." She nervously tucked her hair behind her ears. "Fancy hasn't been home. I'm telling you, Maman, something is wrong, bad wrong."

"You should file a missing person's report," Jane said, "in person. They can add her to the NCIC Missing Persons file. It has national reach."

Aunt Babette frowned. "I thought you needed to wait forty-eight hours?"

"That's a myth," Jane stated. "The force is much more responsive these days. Sooner is always better."

"It's kinda weird, Jane." Gigi's brow furrowed. "That you even know that."

"I've seen it on TV."

"I watched you move in, Jane." Aunt Babette slowly lowered her teacup. "You don't own a TV."

CHAPTER TWELVE

"Thanks for coming with me. Something's not right."

"Not a problem." Jane restlessly drummed her fingers on the Cadillac's passenger door. The rising sun had warmed Lake Pontchartrain, stirring up a whispery breeze that set her teeth on edge. Gigi Pascoe had hesitated over filing a missing person's report on Fancy Abellard, so she had volunteered to go to the police station to offer support. Reaching up, Jane massaged the back of her neck, rolling the tense muscles under her fingertips. *Why do I feel nervous? I haven't done anything wrong. This isn't even about me.*

She had skipped taking a shower, but she had scrubbed her face, slicked back her hair, and changed into what felt more like her native uniform: a V-necked T-shirt, jeans and her favorite scuffed patrol boots. Her lined windbreaker, wallet, and iPhone were tucked into the backpack on the floorboards next to her feet. Four years of road living had thinned down her vital necessities list.

Spinning the wheel with one hand, Gigi maneuvered The Boat around the construction dumpsters permanently parked the length of Poland Avenue before turning left on North Claiborne. The Lower Ninth Ward still looked like a bombed-out war zone. When Hurricane Katrina breached the MRGO and Industrial Canal levees in 2005, storm surges from Lake Pontchartrain had swept the Lower Ninth Ward off the map. Upriver The Bywater had mostly been spared, but as they headed for the Fifth District NOPD station they passed whole city blocks of barren devastation. One blighted little house painted a fading shell pink stood alone in a wilderness of bulldozed earth and shattered trees. Crumbling plywood sheets splayed with black mold boarded its windows. *We Will Be Back* was spray painted across its door.

"Looks like they didn't make it back." Jane pointed. "Where did all of these people go?"

"Houston, mostly." Gigi puffed on her cigar. "Half a million. It's the diaspora that everyone ignores." She frowned at the vacant lots and the shuttered small businesses. "Most of this ward was owned by black folks. These homes were the only equity they had."

Diaspora? Jane blinked in surprise. *That's a five-dollar word, but it fits.* She studied the acres of blasted desolation. *How do you bounce back from taking a hit so hard that it doesn't just disrupt your life, it ends it, snap, just like that like these people did? Something so overwhelmingly immense that you lose everything you knew and you simply give up and move on, leaving everything you knew before behind?* Insight connected the dots. *Like I did. Like Ken did when The WarBirds died. Who are you after you take a catastrophic hit like that? Are you even the same person anymore? What do you do when the whole question of you are becomes who you were? Who is Ken now?* She swallowed. *Who am I?*

Pulling The Boat into a shaded spot in the gated NOPD lot, Gigi reached over, clicked off the ignition and stubbed out her cigar.

"Sit, Piddles," she snapped. Stepping from The Boat, she smoothed the pale yellow polo shirt that complimented her tan. "Stay put. We'll be right back."

The poodle in the back seat cocked his ears at her command.

"You ready to do this thing, Jane?"

Butterflies battered Jane's stomach. "Let's do it," she agreed.

Her boots firmly slapped the asphalt as they headed for the spanking new police station looming over the shattered neighborhood. The two-story cream-colored building possessed an entire city block with its end corner unit separately painted brick red. A double row of windows had permanently installed metal awnings that on a good day might look like eyebrows raised in

61

surprise, but on a bad day look like drawbridges poised to drop on your head. PTSD sent a tremor through Jane's fingertips. *Evidently, today I vote for the drawbridge idea.*

Gigi turned. "You okay? You look pale."

Gripping the handle, Jane opened the door and pushed through the epicenter of her fear.

"I'm fine." She crossed the threshold. "I'm not partial to law enforcement."

"You and me both, sister." Taking the lead, Gigi grimly marched across the open vestibule, muttering over her shoulder. "At least you're honest about it."

Four years since I've stepped inside a police station. Jane swallowed thickly, crooking her neck from side to side to ease the tension. *It never changes though, does it? They all have the same look, the same smell. Like male locker room and that nasty ass pink industrial cleaner.*

Spotting a black-framed photo displayed on an easel, Jane eased closer. **Officer Roberto Garza. We Remember.** A milk glass vase held a handful of red carnations. Reaching out, she fingered a leaf. *Real flowers and they're fresh.* She smiled. *Law enforcement stays the same, no matter where I go. It's about duty and honor and that crazy deep fucking brotherhood that burrows into your bone marrow.* She straightened. *The thin blue line stands strong.*

She heard a roar of laughter and looked up. Four fit men with regulation haircuts stood in a circle down the hallway. Two of them, the younger two, wore the NOPD patrolman's uniform: powder blue shirt, black tie, black slacks. The other two looked like detectives with brass star and crescent badges clipped to their leather belts. The uniformed Latino guy stepped back. Raising his hands in surrender, he delivered the punch line and they all roared again. Jane tasted an aspirin-like pang of homesickness so bitter it curled her tongue. *This used to be my world.* She stared at the grouted tiled floor. *But I don't belong here anymore.*

"Jane?"

Gigi was talking to a woman officer seated behind a plexiglass desk that looked like it belonged in a modern hotel lobby. Even the public reception room walls were painted a creamy and inviting yellow.

"You still with me?"

"I'm here." Jane's palms slicked with a sudden nasty sweat as silvery stars flared around the edges of her vision. Willing her protesting legs forward, she moved deeper into the station, each forced step taking her further away from the safety of the exit sign and her freedom.

"Yes, sir. Let me get you some help." The desk sergeant wore her hair in stubby plaits. She had one gold front tooth. She pressed an intercom button. "Detective Bordelon heads up our Missing and Exploited Persons Unit. I believe he's here."

She called Gigi 'sir.' The gender game rattled Jane's distracted brain like dice in a cup. *Just when I'm getting the hang of it this new world gives me another toss.*

"You were right." Gigi flattened both hands on the Formica counter. "They do like getting these reports right away. It's a good thing we came in when we did."

Jane caught the unmistakable slap of shoe leather on tile and she turned. One of the two detectives she had noticed earlier was approaching. 'Detective Bordelon' was a squat, balding, bullet-headed man with black-framed glasses and a non-existent neck. He was wearing a crisp dress shirt that nicely matched his good tan suit with a patterned blue silk tie. He gripped a slim laptop in his right hand. A gold Katrina survivor badge was pinned on his lapel over his heart. His eyes shone bright with curiosity behind his glasses and he had an active and obvious intelligence.

"I'm Detective Felix Bordelon. You needed to see me?"

"Gigi Pascoe." Gigi extended her hand. "One of our friends is missing. We wanted to file a report." Looking at Jane, she nodded. "We're worried about her. This is another friend, Jane Byrne."

Detective Bordelon settled into a wide stance. "Is this missing friend an adult?"

"Yes. Fancy's around my age, thirty, thirty-one?"

He cocked an eye. "It's not a crime for an adult to go missing. Sometimes people don't want to be found. They're hiding from creditors or from an abusive relationship. How long has your friend been missing?"

Gee checked her phone. "About ten hours. But I'm telling you something is bad wrong. If Fancy was okay, she'd be texting me, and she didn't ask me to take care of her dog. She'd never leave Piddles locked in his crate all day, never. She would never do that. She loves that dog."

"I'll buy that." Detective Bordelon worked his lips before turning on his heel. "Follow me."

He stepped into a conference room and pointed at two chairs before shutting the door. "Take a seat. We'll get started." He sat and opened his laptop. "I'll need some preliminary information for the NCIC database."

Fluttering panic tightened Jane's chest. *NCIC?* She swallowed past the hard lump in her throat. NCIC was the National Crime Information Center. *I'm only one step away from pinging the fucking FBI.* Balling her fists in her lap, Jane fought the compelling desire to reach up and swipe her mouth, a giveaway nervous tell.

"Missing person's name?" Detective Bordelon looked up expectantly.

"Abellard, Fancy Abellard." Gigi smoothed her khakis over her knees. "Her Christian name is Lester Wayne."

"So 'Fancy' is an AKA?"

"Not anymore. She had it legally changed when she came out."

Bordelon started typing. "Address?"

"5602 South Dauphine, Faubourg Marigny, between Piety Street and Desire."

"A foot in both camps." Bordelon smiled to himself. "SSN?"

"I have no idea," Gigi looked confused, "if she even has one."

The detective squinted. "How good of a friend is she?"

"She's one of my besties." Gee sputtered. "I just don't know that information."

"Have you tried contacting Ms. Abellard's workplace?"

"Sir? They're not going to answer their phones." Smoothing her shirt, Gigi explained. "They only just went to bed. Fancy works at Club Oz on Bourbon Street." She combed her fingers through her curls. "Listen, detective. If anything bad has happened, it could happen to any one of us. We run in the same circles, hang at the same clubs. Things have been getting crazy lately. I'm thinking it might be bigger than just this one thing."

"Let's work with what we know." His hands hovered over the keyboard. "Distinguishing features? Height? Weight? Race?"

"Fancy's about six two, black," Jane offered. "Approximately two hundred and twenty pounds."

"She is not two hundred and twenty pounds!" Gee gasped. "She's an easy buck seventy-five. I am so going to tell her you said that!"

"Hair color is blonde, but that could be dye, an extension or a wig."

Bordelon settled his chin to his chest. "Last seen wearing?"

Here we go. "White shorts with a silver mohair sweater and pink stilettos."

"Tough to miss." He kept typing smoothly. Jane was impressed. "Any tattoos or distinguishing scars?"

"No scars or tattoos that I know of." Gigi tapped her chin. "But Fancy's really good with makeup."

"She's got the longest legs I've ever seen on a human being," Jane added.

"Noted. History of substance abuse?"

Gigi squirmed. "I'm not going to answer that. Like what, specifically? Fancy likes to party; we all do. Honestly, detective." She waved a hand to indicate the general area. "It's NOLA. Who doesn't?"

"Fair enough. Any mental health issues we should know about?"

"Not really," Gigi stated slowly. "Unless you consider working as a drag queen to be a mental health issue."

"Personally, I don't." Bordelon's eyes warmed with humor. "Is Ms. Abellard subject to debt? A recent victim of a crime or a workplace incident?"

A recent incident? Jane considered the fracas at Leslie's party. "There was a fist fight at a family party that got heated."

"A fist fight?" He perked up. "When was this party?"

"Last night." Gigi picked up her phone. "Ten hours ago."

"Did Ms. Abellard participate in this fight?"

"Yes, but so did almost everyone else," Jane stated. "I don't think you could single Fancy out for anything special."

"I'll make a note of it." Bordelon studied his laptop over his glasses. "Anything else you can recall? No detail is too trivial."

"No." Gigi tapped her lips. "I think that pretty much covers it."

"Alright, then. This looks solid so far. I'll need your contact information next, Ms. Pascoe as the reporting person."

"Not a problem." Gee eagerly pulled her chair forward. "Gigi Pascoe, 504-581-6476. Address, 3726 Chartres Street, Apt. 2B, Bywater. My email is GoYouBadGirl69@gmail.com. Text works best."

"Thank you." He started typing again. "And I'll need to see your ID as the reporting person."

"Got it right here." Reaching into her back pocket, Gigi pulled out her wallet. Flipping it open, she handed over her Louisiana driver's license.

Detective Bordelon propped the plastic card next to his keyboard and adjusted his glasses, entering the data into the NCIC system before he paused. "This license doesn't match the address you just told me."

"Correct. That's my parent's address on St. Claude Avenue." Gigi flicked her fingers dismissively. "I've moved to my own place. I was going to update it when it came time to renew."

Bordelon frowned severely. "It's best to keep your documents current."

"I'm quite sure you're right," Gigi easily agreed.

What will I do? Jane felt a frosty warning shiver brush her skin. *If Bordelon asks to see my license? Will he try to stop me if I bolt for the door?*

"Detective Bordelon?" Gigi asked. "How many missing persons do you see in a day?"

"More than you'd think." He handed the license back. "About a dozen. Half are adults like your friend. The others are late teens, runaways. To ease your mind, about half are found, just fine, in about three days." He folded his hands across his stomach. "We've established a solid search process. I'll start by checking the hospitals and the jails. I'll check the transport hubs next."

He paused. "There's one more thing. We need to respect Ms. Abellard's right to privacy. If she's fine, we'll need to get her permission to contact you as the reporting person to let you know that. As the reporting person, you have the right to be concerned, but her right to privacy supersedes your right to know where she is."

"Just ask her to text me. That's all I want, to know that she's safe."

"How many of these cases turn into homicide investigations?" Jane asked.

"Really, Jane?" Turning, Gigi stared. "You had to go there?"

"In a year?" Detective Bordelon shut his laptop. "About a dozen, in which case I'd partner with our homicide unit, but my goal," he repeatedly tapped his chest, "is to reunite people, the missing and the reporting person who is concerned about them. I like that part of my job. It's a good feeling when that happens."

Gigi leaned in. "Is there anything more we can do now? For Fancy?"

Bordelon considered her question. "You could post flyers in areas she's known to frequent. Some families do that to make people aware, to get the community looking. Or, if you're IT savvy, you could create a social media dragnet using a Facebook case page. That's proven effective. You could also hire a private investigator to assist with the search effort." Pushing away from the table, he stood, smoothing his tie. "In any case, you'll be getting daily updates from me. I can promise you that."

"Thank you, detective." Gigi stood, firmly shaking his hand. "I'm feeling much better about this now."

"That's what I'm here for." Bordelon smiled warmly. "I'll be in touch."

Get me outta here. Jane almost tapped Gigi's heels as she followed her outside. Pausing on the top concrete step, she sucked in a breath so deep her lungs ached. *Hold it; hold it for three seconds, then release.* She practiced her instant calming technique. NOLA's climate was infamous for its overripe, sub-tropical tang and she inhaled deeply again. *If this is what liberty tastes like, it is sweet.*

Reaching into her breast pocket, Gigi unwrapped another cigar. "That wasn't so bad."

The rising sun warmed Jane's uplifted face like a mother's blessing. "What were you expecting?"

"Honestly?" Cupping her hands around her lighter, Gee hissed a smoke plume through her teeth. "Hostility. I've heard reports. LGBTQ isn't accepted as it was six months ago before Trump got elected." She gazed across the parking lot with unfocused eyes. "I'm worried about the direction we're heading in the good Ole US of A." She smiled sardonically. "Our circle tends to live beyond the pale."

"I don't know what that means."

"Beyond the pale?" Gee dug for her keys. "It means that we live outside the normal reach of the law and that the law has not always been on our side." Juggling her glittering skull key ring in one hand, Gee stared unblinking with her strange, elfin eyes. "And don't mind me saying so, Jane, but from what I've noticed lately, I think that maybe you do, too."

CHAPTER THIRTEEN

Piddles waggled his ridiculous pom-pom tail as Gigi slid behind the wheel.

"Jane? You hungry? I'm starving. Want breakfast?"

Jane's stomach rumbled at the suggestion of hot food. *Anything beats that dry protein bar I stashed in my backpack.* She checked her iPhone. Cruising past 9:30 a.m. "The Deuce will be open. They serve white beans and rice."

"Girl? Where you from?" Gee sputtered. Sticking her cigar in the ashtray, she shifted the Cadillac into gear. "I said *breakfast.* Meaning beignets and café au lait." Squinting, she pointed her finger down the road. "I know a good place, nearby. Café Irene. It's on the way. I want to stop by Fancy's. Maybe she's home, just not answering her phone."

"You said she lived in Marigny?" Jane yawned.

"She has for as long as I've known her." Glancing both ways, Gee pulled onto North Claiborne. "Got herself a sweet little crib some sugar daddy paid for." Gripping the wheel with both hands, she changed lanes. "Fancy's smarter than she looks. She only plays bubble-headed for TV."

Jane's inquisitive nature urged her to investigate, but the sun was up and her naptime clock was ticking. "I will need to get some sleep before my shift."

"When exactly is that?"

"Ten p.m. to six a.m."

"Shut your eyes now." Gee suggested reasonably, reaching for the cigar again. "Catch a nap. I'll give you a nudge when we get there."

"No, I'm good." Jane looked away, lying through her teeth as her gut flared with anxiety. *Goddamn trust issue. Can't sleep unless I'm behind a bolted door, which needs to be checked not twice but three times to make sure it's secure before I can finally let go.* Reaching up, she knuckled her temples hard, grinning ruefully. *Be honest, girlfriend. Half the time that doesn't work either, because I don't trust anyone, not even the lock.* Chilly fingers of doubt and self-pity sidled in, deflating her battered confidence. Her shoulders slumped, and she dropped her hands into her lap. *It sucks that I'm not getting better. I'm doing everything they told me to do.* She tightened her hands into fists. *Enough of this whiny ass shit! On your feet, soldier! When did I let it get this bad? How do I fucking turn it off?*

Taking her eyes off the road, Gigi checked her phone. "It's quarter to ten. If I get you home by noon, does that give you enough time for sleep?"

"Yeah, sure." Jane settled back sourly.

"Good. Then we do have time for a treat."

She swung The Boat left onto Louisa Street and slowed, hunting for a parking space. Café Irene was on the corner, a ramshackle single-story clapboard building painted lime green with a florescent fuchsia door. *Typical NOLA.* Jane folded her arms. *Hide the best eateries from the tourists. The only way you'd know this cafe was here was if you spotted the bicycles parked out front or if you were local.*

A Crescent City Seafood delivery van pulled away from the curb. Clicking the turn signal on, Gee grabbed the spot.

"Parking karma. We're in luck." Checking her mirrors, she backed in, resting her arm on the seat while looking over her shoulder. "It's a sign. We're doing God's work."

Jane unlatched her seatbelt. "God is in the doughnut business?"

Gee bounced The Boat off the curb. "A beignet is not a doughnut, you savage!"

"Relax. I'm fucking with you." Stepping out, Jane shut the heavy door.

"Out of curiosity, what kind of gas mileage does this thing get?"

"And will you please show some respect? The Boat is not a thing. She's a ton and half of fine American-made steel." Gee smoothed the wrinkles from her shirt. "About eight miles to the gallon. Stay put, Mr. P. We'll bring you something back."

A tinny bell rang as they entered. Café Irene was narrow with an open kitchen in the back beneath a chalkboard offering daily menu options. The ceiling and the rafters were painted vibrant cobalt blue. Wooden booths lined both walls and a sprinkling of two-person tables cramped the single center aisle. Every booth and table was occupied. Bright cartoonish canvas paintings covered the walls. A few were wet looking NOLA Bourbon streetscapes, but most depicted voodoo devils and skeletons drinking steaming cups of coffee or raising brimming red cocktails in a grinning, toothy toast.

"Hey, girl, hey." A woman called from the kitchen. "How you doin' this fine new day? What can I get you? The usual?"

"Yes, please, for me. Jane? How 'bout you?"

"Ditto."

"Double it up for us, Celestine, if you please."

"You got it." Flicking her wrist, she popped a waxed paper bag open and reached for some tongs.

Gigi drummed the countertop. "Have you seen Fancy around?"

"Haven't seen Miss Fancy in the past couple of days." Creasing and folding the bag, she carried it to the register and then turned and filled two takeout cups. "Thought she might be slimming. You know she's always trying some damn new fool diet thing."

"If you do see her," Gee reached for her wallet, "will you ask her to text me?"

Celestine cut her eyes. "You two been fighting?"

"Nothing like that. I just haven't heard from her today and I've got her dog in my car."

71

"Alright." Celestine agreed, slowly pressed the coffee lids down firmly with her thumbs. "That's easy enough to do, but it's still early, knowing her schedule. I'll tell her what you said, if I do see her. You all set?"

"Yes, ma'am." Gee handed over her VISA card. "Jane? First time's on me. Next one's yours." Picking up a cup, she risked a hurried sip. "Ahhhh. Delicious. Celestine? You are the voodoo queen of NOLA caffeine."

"I'll need to remember that." She giggled. "Sounds like maybe that's my new jingle." She returned the credit card. "Coffee mojo, girlfriend. Blessings on you both. Y'all have a great day."

"Let's eat these on the way." Grasping the waxed bag, Gee turned. "I know we're watching the clock, but we seriously need to wean you offa that Yankee thing about always being in a hurry." She slipped through the door Jane held open. "Thank you. You're halfway there, but there's definitely room for improvement."

Piddles yipped when he saw them coming. He started dancing back and forth across the back seat.

"You know I brought you some of this, Mr. P.," Gee crooned. "Did you think I'd forget?" Setting her cup on the dashboard, she slid behind the wheel, gripping the folded edge of the waxed bag and giving it a vigorous shake. "Stirring up all that good powdered sugar." She winked. Opening the bag on her lap, she selected one beignet, tossing it between her palms. "Smoking hot, too! You cannot have a bad day when it starts with Café Irene."

Jane's mouth watered as she scented the sugar and hot grease. Securing her coffee cup in the console holder, she reached eagerly into the bag. Hot oil scorched her fingertips as they slid across the powdery melted glaze. Pinching one beignet between her fingers, she raised it to her lips and snapped off a toasty bite.

"Oh my God, I'm drooling. I haven't eaten carbs in three days." Jane licked the sweet stickiness off of her fingers. "You want any more?"

"Nope, they're all yours. One's my limit." Gee relit her cigar.

"Keeping this slim takes work."

The second beignet had slightly cooled. With a chomp, Jane bit it in half. It was even tastier than the first. The beignet had the perfect chewy texture and a golden sweetness that gilded her tongue like honey. It was orgasmic. She closed her eyes. "This shit is crack. We should never have got these." Stuffing the beignet into her mouth, she playfully extended both arms across the dash. "These are so good, I've gone blind."

"Look at you." Gee chortled. "Glad to see you finally enjoying something. You are wound way too tight." Hooking her fingers into horns, she set her right hand on top of her head like a tiara. "Stick with me, Jane. I'm the good kind of devil. I only have fun."

The fine powdered sugar tickled Jane's nose and she sneezed.

"God bless you." Gee snorted, before pointing at the pebbled dashboard. "Better wipe that down. If the cops stop us, they'll arrest you for doing blow."

Jane swiped the dashboard with her greasy hand. "Shit! I'm only making it worse. Did you grab any napkins?"

"Napkins? You mean serviettes? Oh-mi-god, look what you've done to my car! Get out!" Gee ordered. "Get out of my car this instant!"

"What?" Jane cowered, blinking and confused. "Huh?"

"Get out! People like you are why we can't have nice things."

"I'm sorry!" Jane scrambled to unlock the door, smearing the door with even more greasy fingerprints. "I'll pay to have it detailed. Send me the bill."

"Girlfriend, relax!" Gee howled with laughter. "Back at you, babe. I'm just fucking with you now." Reaching over her shoulder, she fed Piddles her final bite. "Jane, we need to seriously work on your sense of humor. You can't hurt The Boat. She's seen it all. That's why I bought her." Swiping her greasy fingers on her knees, she restarted the car. Taking another slurp of her coffee, she eased away from the curb before banking left for South Dauphine Street.

Ryan Embry called Gee a force of nature. He was right. Leaning forward, Jane set the beignet bag on the floorboards next to her boot. *She sure knows how to live and she just puts it out there. She's fearless.* Doubt darkened Jane's admiration. *Or is she reckless? I do feel a connection, but can we be friends?* Reticence raised a caution flag. *We only just met.*

Come on. No games now. Her chronic fear rippled uncertainly. *What's the real issue?* Settling in, Jane dove deeper. *This is really about* trust. *When did I stop trusting my judgment about people? Sure, it's easier to not trust anyone, but when did I include not trusting myself?*

The Marigny neighborhood was beginning to stir. The gutters and sidewalks were littered with empty pint glass bottles and flattened red Solo cups from the previous night's revelry. The corner bars were shuttered and hushed, still grated, but the old black men were already parked on their benches and their broken stoops sipping their daily malt liquor 40s. The quick stop grocery stores were open, bustling with the new day's cigarette and lotto needs. Gigi blatantly ignored the orange construction fencing and the plastic traffic cones and the concrete barricades running along St. Claude Avenue like they weren't even there. She roared around a trolley stopping to pick up downtown commuters and deftly wove The Boat through clusters of hipsters pedaling their bikes toward Crescent Park and Washington Square. Jane clutched the padded armrest as they blew through an intersection on a yellow changing to a fully red traffic light. She closed her leaden eyes. *That's it, universe. I surrender.* The channeled leather seat cupped her in upholstered comfort and she dropped her chin. *I will trust you enough - again - to do whatever it is that you want me to do.* She scented sweet country ham spiced with cinnamon, mustard, and clove and the smooth, chocolaty aroma of freshly brewed chicory coffee. In spite of the beignets she had eaten, her stomach rumbled and Jane opened her eyes.

"Enjoy your nap?" Gigi grinned. "Fancy lives about three blocks down. I'm going to kill her if we get there and find out she's been ignoring my texts."

CHAPTER FOURTEEN

Jane straightened. The shot of caffeine buzzed through her veins like a live electrical wire and her brain fog had lifted. She felt invigorated and refreshed.

"Gee? I'm just going to put this out there." She shifted in the seat. "Leslie said you're transgender. Is that right?"

"You're close." Spinning the wheel, Gee avoided a cluster of pedestrians huddled protectively in a marked crosswalk. "I'm a transgender person. It's an adjective, not a noun." She grinned crookedly. "I'm a straight woman in a male gendered body." She squinted. "You look confused."

"I am, a little." Jane admitted.

"You never met a gay person up north before?"

"Not this gay."

Gee howled. "What does *that* mean?"

"I'm not sure." Jane blushed.

"How do I explain this?" Gee looked to the sky. "Gender identity is different than sexual orientation. I like men same as you. Actually, I don't know that. You're straight, right?"

Jane folded her arms over her chest. "Yes, I'm straight."

"Thought so. You look it."

"Excuse me? That sounds like a judgment."

"Hell yes, it's a judgment," Gee snapped. "Welcome to my fucking world. I deal with judgments about the way I look every goddamned day."

I'll just bet you do. Jane chewed her lip. "And Fancy's a drag queen?"

"No." Gigi drummed her thumbs against the wheel. "Fancy's a gay man who's a drag queen if we're still talking about gender identity and not a lifestyle choice." Blocked by the car ahead, she braked for a solid red light. "Fancy's a man who likes fucking other men."

"But we call Fancy 'she.'"

"We do. Because," she drawled, "that's the pronoun she prefers." The traffic light flicked to green. "Whether we admit it or not," she laid on the horn, "NOLA is the south. Sometimes it's about courtesy and good manners."

"I'm getting the hang of this." Jane's head snapped back as Gee floored the gas pedal. "And Delilah? What is she?"

"Besides being my roommate and my very BFF? Dee's bi. She likes fucking men and women." She snorted. "Better watch out, Jane, if you ever see a red dot moving around on your body. Dee likes you. I can tell."

"Thanks." Jane tore the cuticle on her thumb. "I don't play for that team."

"Snap!" Gee laughed musically. Reaching into the console, she shook a slim brown cigar from a pack and pressed the dashboard lighter. "You should see your face right now." She ducked her chin. "You sure?"

"Yes, I'm sure."

"Hell, girlfriend." The lighter popped. Gee spoke through the smoke snaking around her eyes. "This is NOLA. You can always change your mind. Most of us reinvent ourselves every day. Whatever it takes to make it work and get by, you know?"

"Tell me about it." Jane studied Gee's plucked eyebrows and strangely hairless arm. "What do you do for a living? For money? Are you a beautician?"

"Oh, hell no!" She repeatedly puffed the cigar. "I'm a go-go boy."

"A what?" Jane sputtered.

Gee exhaled a steady smoke stream. "A go-go boy, a dancer. I don't strip, if that's what you're thinking. I start off pretty much naked. Got my gold lame trunks and my pole," she fluttered her eyelashes, "and that's pretty much it."

"I've wondered why your skin was so smooth."

"Get everything waxed, girlfriend. Smooth as a Barbie doll. Customers hate seeing hair. Hate it! One girl I know got fired for letting her tampon string show." She inhaled again. "Can't be human. Not allowed. Got to be a thing." She stubbed out the cigar. "Work at Club Oz on Bourbon Street. Hate the drunks, but the tips are solid. My boss loves my androgyny. Asks me to play it up. I'm featured on the club's web site," Gee announced proudly. "Cater to the tourists. Mid-Westerners eat my act up. They love feeling naughty."

She straightened her arms against the steering wheel. "But I need to change my game. I'm getting to old for it. I'm dancing now against boys half my age. What I really want to do is own my own club. A dance club, a real old school disco, know what I mean? Someplace young, and fun, down on Frenchmen Street, a real dance party place where me, Dee and Fancy can sing. Shit! We'd belt it out like a Donna Summers version of the Supremes." She guffawed. "Can you imagine how much fun that would be?" She rubbed her right thumb and fingers together. "But that shit takes money and backers, and we don't have that, yet. *Yet.*" She emphasized. "We tried busking on the street, but the drunks got plain ass nasty. Fancy's tough enough and don't fuck with me, but they made Dee cry." She worked her lips over her teeth. "Can't have that. Dee deserves better. She sings like an angel. She deserves some goddamn respect."

Jane's curiosity about Gee's lifestyle prickled and itched. She framed her next question carefully. "Have you ever considered the surgery? The sex change surgery?"

"Gender reassignment?" Gee fingered her throat. "I'd love to get my Adam's apple shaved and buy a decent pair of tits. You have a nice rack, by the way. Lucky girl. Mother Nature blessed you."

Jane shifted uncomfortably. "Thanks, I guess."

"Some of my friends have transitioned." Gee reached for the cigar. "But I have a problem with it." She glanced over with haunted eyes. "I'm

77

terrified of hospitals. Had a dream once, when I was a kid, a fucking vivid nightmare." She shuddered. "Saw myself lying dead on a table under a red sheet sopping with blood." She blinked repeatedly. "There were bloody footprints everywhere, hundreds of them, thousands, and bloody handprints on the walls." She moistened her lips. "Put the fear of it in me." White-eyed, she raggedly puffed the cigar. "Can't get past it. When I think about transitioning, I flinch."

"I get that, I do," Jane said slowly. "But I think eventually I'd have to get the surgery, if that's who I really was. I don't know how long I could keep up the fake. I'm not that good of an actor."

"Everybody's working through something though, right? Evidently, I'm not there yet."

Stubbing the cigar, Gee pulled up in front of a shotgun house painted minty green. The wide sheltering porch roof was supported by mango orange corbels that matched the shutters on the two tall windows on either side of the single lemon yellow front door. A black wrought-iron railing framed the porch, flowing gracefully down the porch steps to become a fence that protected the two palmettos growing in the miniscule front yard.

"Nice digs," Jane noted. "This is Fancy's place?"

"She did good with this one." Slipping the keys into her pocket, Gee stepped into the street and started up the sidewalk. "Scored big. Got this place ten, eleven years ago, right after Katrina flattened the Ninth Ward. Folks then weren't sure about staying in Marigny, but Fancy sure was. Said Marigny was her home and she was staying put. Took a big chance, but it paid off." She thumbed the iron latch. The gate squealed as she pushed it open.

Piddles cocked his ears alertly at the sound. Leaping from the back seat, he snaked around Gigi's legs and raced for a palmetto. Raising a hind leg, he released a steaming torrent of neon yellow pee.

"Is Fancy alright?"

An elderly woman rested her twig broom against the railing of the rundown house next door. Grasping the railing, she shuffled over. She was about five feet tall, rail thin with arms of corded muscle. All of her lower teeth were missing and her gum line was a mass of pink tissue. Her head looked like it had been carved from a block of coal.

"I see you got her dog. I was worried. Is Fancy okay?"

"We're worried too, Miz T." Gigi strolled across the sidewalk to meet her halfway. "We're trying to figure out where she is. Haven't seen Fancy since last night. This is another friend of hers, Jane."

"How'd you do?" She bobbed. "I can tell you that Miss Fancy didn't come home last night or I would've heard her. That one truly belongs to the *Ghede nanchon*, for sure. She do like to make herself some noise." She slowly blinked like a tortoise. "Maybe you should call the po-lice?"

"We just came from there," Jane said. "They've initiated a search."

"Good. Good." Miz T rolled her lips. "They're good enough fellas." Smoothing her purple blouse, her fingers checked her black pearl buttons. "Do you have a key?"

"I have a spare." Gee reached into her pocket. "Used it this morning to let Piddles out."

"Then unlock this door." She started up the steps. "And let's have a look."

CHAPTER FIFTEEN

That's not safe. Jane's instinct tripped to high alert as Gigi unlocked the door and politely held it open to allow the older woman to enter. *I should go first.* In the split second of hesitation, Miz T slipped in.

Jane rapidly followed. Fancy's house had a simple floor plan with one long narrow hallway and all of the rooms strung off to the right. The kitchen and the bedrooms were tucked into the rear. The tall living room windows were shuttered and the atmosphere felt airless and stale.

"Fancy?" Gee flicked a wall switch. The ceiling fan slowly began to stir. "Hello the house?"

The whirring paddle fan made the only sound.

"Fancy? Answer me, girl. You here?"

There was a high-pitched nervous whine. Gee spun around. Piddles still sat on the front porch, white-eyed and trembling.

"Dammit, Piddles. Heel." She snapped her fingers. "I don't have time to fool with you now."

Bunching up, the poodle leapt over the threshold, his painted toenails scrabbled for purchase against the polished floor. He raced around the couch and skidding around the turn, heading straight for the kitchen like a wooly black blur.

"You two to check them bedrooms," Miz T directed. "I'll check the kitchen and the side porch."

"Stay behind me, Gee." The hallway was so narrow Jane could have stretched out her arms and brushed both walls with her fingertips. *Gee was here this morning,* she swallowed, *but that was hours ago. Things might have changed.* Her right hand itched to hold a weapon. *Lame ass as shit, but even a taser or a duty baton would be something.* "Stay ready to move."

The first bedroom door hung slightly ajar. Pushing it open with one hand, Jane tucked her shoulder defensively against the interior wall.

Gigi peered around her. "See anything?"

"Clear." The room was set up as a dressing room with a mirrored bureau and a rolling rack of gowns hanging neatly in clear plastic dry cleaner bags. Matching shoes were stacked beneath each dress in boxes overflowing with tissue paper.

"Where can she be?" Gee recklessly continued down the hall. Marching toward the second bedroom, she pushed the door open and stepped inside.

This bedroom was simply a showplace, a piece of theater, a show-stopping set. A queen-sized mattress owned the space with its leopard print duvet and matching black and gold ruched silk toss pillows. The walls were painted pale lavender and a square white shag rug covered the floor. Instead of a ceiling fan, this room held a crystal chandelier. The duvet was neatly made up, and the room was empty.

"I don't get it." Gee walked around the foot of the bed. After checking the bathroom, she turned back, placing her hands on her hips as her face tightened like a fist. "This is so not like her. Sure, she may stay out all night, but Fancy always comes home to sleep in her own bed. Miz T?" She called, trotting back to the living room. "Find anything?"

"She's not in this kitchen." The elderly woman's voice quavered. "I'm gonna feed this poor dog while I'm in here. There's a good bag of chow in this pantry."

Gee looked perplexed. "I don't know what to do next."

"Too bad we're not the police." Jane studied the landline phone. "We could check Fancy's phone records and credit card usage. That's where I'd start."

"Won't the police already be doing that?"

"They should be." Jane turned to open a window. The stuffy air was parching her sinuses. She felt light-headed and dizzy. Reaching up, she unlatched a shutter and raised the double hung panes. Cooler fresh air immediately spilled into the room, refreshing her face. "They'd need to ask a judge for permission to release the records and subpoena the phone company, but it's not that big of a deal."

"Any way we could do that on the sly?" Gee asked.

"Only if you know someone who works at the phone company." Jane unlatched a second shutter. A triangle of bright sunlight fell on the Toulouse-Lautrec cat print hanging over the mantle. She shrugged. "And it would be illegal."

"Rules were made to be broken," Gee stated firmly. "It's easier to ask for forgiveness than to ask for permission." She squinted narrowly. "You seem to know an awful lot about breaking the law."

"I used to be a cop." Jane stopped. *Wait. Did I just say that out loud?*

"What? Huh? Hold up." Gee gaped. "When were you a cop?"

"Four years ago." Jane swallowed drily. "A different place, in another world." *Out of everything I went through, why do I keep pinging off that rattle my locker made that final day when I slammed it shut for the last time?*

"Where were you a cop?" Gee persisted.

"Back east, in Massachusetts, on Nantucket. It's an island, thirty miles off the coast."

"I had no idea. Why didn't you say so? Why did you stop?"

Jane studied the sunlight dappling the floor. *Don't make this any harder than it has to be.* "I resigned. I was forced to resign," she admitted. "I responded to a kidnapping/assault call. A hostage situation got ugly." Taking a ragged breath, Jane faced the searing truth. "I shot a scumbag, shot him dead. Removed the threat." She lifted her chin. "I'm not sorry I did it, not one bit. He was torturing a friend of mine." She pressed her fingertips to her eyelids. *I can still see Sarah zip-tied to that bed, screaming, with that fucker Mason holding that knife to her throat.* Jane dropped her hands. "The Grand Jury dismissed the charges. 'Excessive use of force,' but his father sued me in civil court. Took me two and half years to get through that legal shit. Lost everything I had paying for the lawyers." She shrugged resignedly. "Could've been worse. I was facing prison time with the federal charges until they got dropped."

"Jane, I'm so sorry. I had no idea -"

"Don't be." She straightened. "I knew what I was doing. Needed to get done. It was the right decision to make. That scumbag deserved everything he got."

"That's incredible, Jane." Gee paused. "Do you miss it? Your old life?"

"I miss the people," she admitted. "I do miss them. I miss my family and my old crew." She sighed, staring at the sunbeams streaming through the windows. "But you have to let that shit go. Doesn't do any good trying to get after it once it's gone. After that, it's dust and ashes. Some part of me died after that trial. That's not my life, anymore. That's not who I am, anymore." She tapped her heart. "I can't go back. When I think about it now, I feel hollow. There's nothing there left for me to go back to."

"I could never leave NOLA." Gee whispered, horrified. "I'd dry up and blow away if I ever tried living someplace else. I wouldn't know who I was any more."

"Sometimes," Jane said, bitterly, "you don't get a choice."

"Girls?" Miz T reentered the room with a satisfied looking Piddles tagging happily on her heels. Jolting to a stop, she spread both hands like starfish. "Who opened them shutters?"

Jane flinched. "I did. Why?"

"You stupid, ignorant girl!" She spat. "You let Fancy's spirit out! Now she's truly gone!"

Gigi blanched.

"What the hell are you talking about?" Jane sputtered. "Did you find Fancy in the kitchen?"

"I told you there was no one in that kitchen," Miz T argued, "but as long as them shutters stayed shut Fancy's spirit kept inside the house." Tottering over, she stretched out her right hand. "Quick! Give me twenty dollars. It might not be too late."

"Twenty bucks?" Jane retreated a step. "What for?"

"To quickly go buy rum for Baron Samedi. If I pour it out for him he might not take Fancy or if he has, he might bring her back."

Voodoo. Superstitious dread ruffled the hairs on Jane's neck. "You're talking voodoo. And I'm not giving you twenty bucks."

"Miz T., wait." Quickly pulling out her wallet, Gee rifled through her cash. "Please take this and go buy rum, some good rum, and maybe a fine cigar and ask Baron Samedi for his help finding Fancy. We're going to need it."

Miz T held the sawbuck up to her milky eyes. Puffing on it twice, she folded it carefully before tucking it into her black bra. "You maybe he'll listen to." Pointing her bony finger, she shuffled for the door. "Her? I'm not so sure. Tonight, I'll offer Legba a special prayer and light a candle for Saint Expidite, regardless."

Gee waited for the door to close before she spun around.

"Jane? You cannot talk to her like that! Miz T is one of the most powerful voodoo priestesses we have. She has special powers! You cannot piss her off."

"I don't believe in any of that voodoo crap." Jane mulishly folded her arms.

"Doesn't matter what you believe," Gee sputtered, "but if you're going to live in NOLA you'd better understand it because we do."

"Really, Gee? Voodoo queens? Hoodoo dolls? Stick a pin in me, I'm done," Jane scoffed. "Besides, how was I supposed to know who she was?"

"Didn't you see what she was wearing?"

"That purple blouse?" Jane shuffled uncomfortably. "Sure, I saw it. Hard to miss. It was so butt-ugly."

"With a black skirt," Gee explained patiently. "Those are Baron Samedi's colors. It was all there right in front of you. You were just too ignorant to see it."

"Listen." Jane bridled, raising her hand. "Voodoo is a long con job. We don't even know if anything has happened to Fancy. We don't have any hard data or facts. That woman is a grifter, playing off your fear."

"Lower your voice." Gee bounced both hands like she was dribbling a basketball. "She might be listening." Slowing cracking the front door, she checked the street before waving Piddles through. "I'll go talk to Aunt Babette. She may be able to help us."

Halfway down the sidewalk, Miz T stopped dead. Her pleated black skirt puffed up like a pumpkin as she spun around.

"You'll be calling on Babette Broussard, next? After me?" She shouted. Hawking loudly, she spat into the gutter. "That busybody? That witch? She can't help you," she stated, scornfully. "That woman works red magic." She dug into her pocket. "You'll need a powerful *gris-gris* to protect you from her, now."

"Step on it, Gee." Jane quickly opened The Boat's passenger side door. Waving Piddles into the back seat, she slid in, pointing at the ignition. "Fire this thing up before she hits you for another twenty."

"Didn't you hear what I just said?" Gee hissed. "Don't antagonize her! You are messing with something you don't understand."

Checking both mirrors for traffic, Gee cranked the wheel hard and peeled away from the curb. "I'm going to drop you back at the house and go make up those flyers like that detective said. Sounded like a good idea. Something I can do." Frowning, she slowed The Boat for a busy intersection. "I'm a little worried about Piddles. Can't lock him in a crate all day; that's not fair." She turned left. "Maybe Maman can watch him. Dee would pitch a hissy fit if I brought him home. She's allergic to pet dander."

"I'll take him," Jane blurted. "Piddles can stay with me."

"Really?" Gee looked startled. "It would only be until Fancy gets back."

Take it back! Jane winced as the imaginary shrieking klaxons blared in her ears. *Rescind the offer! Live free and ride light, right? I've avoided every other personal responsibility for years, so now I'm going to foster a dog?* Jane tentatively poked at the crusted scab that stitched her bitter heart together. She was surprised to find it resilient; the thick scar held firm. *Yes. My answer this time really is 'yes.'* Her heart softened and her resistance melted like hot candle wax before it erupted into a geyser of blindingly fresh possibility that felt so overpoweringly magnificent it left her breathless. *Yes. I'm going to take Piddles home with me and I'm going to trust my judgment that this is the right decision to make, the right action to take, the right fucking thing to do.* She fell back against the cushioned seat, astonished by the sudden and unremembered feeling of benevolent universal promise and of hope with an upwelling gratitude so bone-shakingly deep she felt reborn and exposed to the world. *Yes. I'm going to trust that everything will work out fine because I care about these people and I can help.*

CHAPTER SIXTEEN

Jane adjusted the black elastic brace supporting the damaged ligaments and the lumpy scar tissue in her left knee. It had taken tough love discipline, a boatload of avoidance, and outright self-shaming standing naked in front of the dim bathroom mirror, but she had decided to run for an hour each morning straight after work instead of heading to The Deuce to drink her breakfast beer. Her heels were chapped and sore and her breathing was ragged, but her core already felt stronger. *Baby steps. This will get easier the more I do it.* Locking the door, she dropped the key down the front of her T-shirt, zipped her windbreaker up to her chin, settled her ball cap and studied the pink clouds and the baby blue dawn sky. *Repeat an action for ten days and it becomes a new habit.* She snorted. *I could use a few new good habits in my life.*

"Ready, Biggy P?"

Piddles yipped. He was evidently delighted to go for a run although the city sidewalks had already ruined his fancy pedicure. Jane had coughed up sixteen bucks to buy him a running harness with a retractable leash from the Dollar Store. It was well-made gear and she didn't begrudge the expense. *It's nice having a running buddy. Spending part of my salary on a dog isn't necessarily a bad thing, right? That is what the money is for, to help me enjoy my life.* Her hidden cash stash wasn't doing her any good rolled up in her hollowed-out copy of *The Murderer's Vademecum* sitting on the bookshelf. *I have $3,600 saved up. How much more do I need?*

They started for the park. Yesterday, after Gigi had dropped them off, Piddles had been so terrified at being left behind that the poor dog had frozen stock-still in the middle of the courtyard, trembling until his pointy little teeth had chattered. Jane had instantly connected to the fearful uncertainty she saw in his intelligent brown eyes. Leslie had raised no objection to keeping Piddles temporarily; she had simply stated that it was Jane's apartment and she could do as she pleased as long as she was prepared to pay for any damages. Jane had enticed Piddles inside using a wiggling slice of processed American cheese, knowing that she needed to do whatever it took to erase that kind of pain from his eyes. No one, not even a dog, ever deserved to feel that way.

She had fashioned a dog bed out of an armful of random musty pillows and a faded duvet she found stuffed in the laundry room cupboard and had barricaded Piddles in the kitchen using a wooden chair and a broom until she had the time and the money to buy him a proper crate. As she had climbed upstairs to grab some sleep, Piddles had started to cry. Not howl or whine, just whimper, a low, soft noise that had crushed her heart. Crawling under the covers, Jane had clamped a pillow around both ears, unsuccessfully trying to ignore the cry for fully twenty minutes before finally surrendering, throwing off the covers and bringing Piddles up to her bed. He had hopped up onto the mattress, circled twice, and settled in immediately to slumber next to her feet. *Goddamn fucking dog. Didn't take him long to form a new habit.* Jane chuckled. *Funny thing is, now that Piddles sleeps with me I pass right out. Didn't even dream. Didn't need to drink my breakfast beer or that funky tea, either. So, the question is, who saved who? Did I rescue Piddles or did he save me?*

She scanned the sporadic traffic as they passed the Embry's house on its lot facing Plessy Street, noting that the Delta Power van with bicentennial tag KRM 772 was still parked in the driveway. *Ryan must not have left for work yet. Slow start today. Happy Monday.*

Turning left on Dauphine, she picked up the pace. Her joints felt looser as her muscles warmed up and they cut catty-corner onto Piety running hard for Crescent Park. Jane caught the warning blast of a freight train and sucking wind, they raced for the pedestrian bridge over the riverside railroad tracks and the levee. Even in December, the park's landscape looked lush and green and Jane felt a tingling flicker of nostalgia. *I do miss seeing the changing seasons and the fall colors on the moor near Altar Rock.* Then she recalled hauling the leaden twenty-pound bags of rock salt and battling the icy town sidewalks and frigid parking lots and she shuddered. *No, thank you. I do not miss battling those crippling New England winters.*

Her left knee started pinging 'hello.' Limping, she stiffly started climbing the arching steel bridge she had nicknamed the Rusty Rainbow challenge because of the staircase that led up and over the railroad tracks. The steep climb took resolve and a serious gut check, but the panoramic view of the Mississippi River and the downtown NOLA skyscrapers made the extra uphill effort worthwhile. *Goddamn dog.* Piddles didn't seem to have an issue with the steps. He took them easily, two at a time.

Flicking the sweat from her face, Jane stretched out her hamstrings and took a breather, watching a massive commercial container ship slide by, its roiling wake feathering the greasy brown water into silvery ripples that semaphored the rising sun into her eyes. *Crescent City, indeed. This big ass river is still the heart of this place.* Trotting down the riverside of the arch, they jogged for Piety Wharf. *But its soul is something bigger, something deeper, something darker and maybe something else?*

A hot pink flyer taped to a light pole fluttered erratically with the breeze. Jane stopped in her tracks so suddenly that Piddles yelped when he got snatched back by the unexpectedly shortened leash.

"Sorry, Biggy. Wanted to see this."

Fancy's wide and toothy smile leapt out at her. Gigi had picked an extreme close-up for the *Have You Seen Me?* photo. Studying it closely, Jane could see Fancy's outrageous personality shining devilishly from her eyes. *Yes, that's Fancy alright. So sassy, so full of life.* Flattening the flyer against the light pole with her fingertips, Jane's hand dropped to her side as she made the connection. *I know this person. This isn't someone anonymous, anymore.*

Piddles dodged left as she tripped forward a half step. *I've put down roots. I'm a part of this community.*

"On your right."

Piddles skittered again as a cycling hipster in blue spandex shorts skillfully avoided their standing in the middle of the trail hazard. Turning his helmeted head, he stared over his left shoulder. Jane braced herself for the insult.

"Gonna get hot today," he shouted, "but not as hot as you."

Wow. Jane blinked in surprise. *Positive reinforcement. I'll take it.* Whistling to catch Piddles attention, she started jogging for home. *Maybe the universe is trying to tell me something. Good job? Nice work? Keep at it? Shit. When was the last time that happened?*

The Bywater neighborhood was fully awake now, its denizens up and preparing for work. As they dodged the oddly parked cars and the blue recycling bins that lined the crumbling sidewalk, Jane caught the clink of glassware and the metallic shiver of cutlery from personal kitchens hidden behind long blinds and shutters. Jogging under a spreading lemon tree, she scented rich country sausage with red-eye gravy and cheesy grit casserole and thinking of the Hi-Pro PowerBar waiting for her on the counter she picked up the pace.

At the Piety Street intersection they needed to wait for the light to change because of the increased vehicular traffic heading downtown. Jogging in place, Jane pumped both arms to keep her heart rate in the burn zone. The light turned green.

"Take it home, Biggy P."

She gave the run one final big push, racing for St. Claude Avenue and focusing on the finish, ignoring the pulse thrumming her carotid artery. Skidding to a stop in the driveway, she dropped Biggy's leash and raised both arms in triumph. *Did it! And I didn't need to stop for that painful stitch in my ribs this time, not once! It's a new personal best!*

Piddles barked sharply. Her sneakers spit gravel like lost teeth as Jane spun around. A Delta Power van with Bicentennial tag KRM 772 was backed up to the shed attached to her apartment and her front door stood wide open. *I locked that door before I left. Didn't I?* She clutched the key chain hanging around her neck. *Crap. What's Ryan doing here? I wanted to grab a shower and get some sleep before my shift.* Her jubilant mood soured. *What's wrong with my goddamned apartment now?*

CHAPTER SEVENTEEN

Ken strolled around the back of the van, swinging a claw foot hammer. "Morning, Jane. Ryan's snaking your tub." He loosely waved the tool. "Going to fix this shed next. Got a packet of asphalt shingles. Hated seeing that Ducati getting dripped on. Give us an hour and you'll be all set."

Fuck. Jane fought the flutter of exhausted irritation as her temples throbbed. *Ken still doesn't get that I sleep during the day. He should know better. He used to be a rock star. I know he's worked nights.* She tempered her response. *Behave! He's actually doing you a favor.* She pointed to his Ace bandage. "How's the wrist?"

"Better. Only a sprain." Switching the hammer to his left hand, he lowered his cheap sunglasses and winked. "You should see the other guy."

Unsnapping Biggy's harness, she watched him trot away to sniff the courtyard. "Any word from Fancy?"

"Not a peep." Channels creased Ken's mouth as he grimaced. "I'm doing my best to calm Gigi down. She's been running all over town, posting flyers."

"I've seen them."

"She forgets that Fancy's done this before." Ken tugged his lip. "My bet is that Fancy found herself something extra good." He nodded resolutely. "She'll pop back up by the weekend, with another grand story to tell -"

Ryan Embry stepped out of the darkened doorway wearing jeans and a tight wife-beater tee under a loose flannel shirt. He looked odd out of uniform, but the blue plaid really played up the color of his eyes. *Playing hooky today? Called off sick?* His sleeves were rolled up to his elbows and he had scabby-looking scratches on both wrists.

Flicking water droplets from his fingers, he started coiling a wire drain snake. As he stepped fully into the sunlight, his face looked different somehow, broader, and not so harshly sharp. *He's shaved off his soul patch and trimmed his sideburns.* Jane started. *He's really handsome without that facial scruff.*

Looking up, he caught her staring.

Jane's face blossomed with heat. "How are you feeling today?" She stuttered.

"Embarrassed." He tossed the drain snake into the van. It clunked against a pile of loose tools and wire cable. Reaching up, he straightened his Make America Great Again ball cap. "Sorry about the other night. Hate thinking that's your first impression of me and my friends."

"It was a crazy night for us all," she admitted. "You shaved."

"Yeah, well." He rubbed his neck. "I heard that some folks didn't like it."

He's been talking to his mom about me. I told Cheryl that at Leslie's party.

"I've done what I can, Ken, with that drain." Ryan massaged his bicep. "If that doesn't fix it, you'll need to hire a pro. Digging up a sewer line takes a ditch witch or a backhoe. I don't have access to that kind of equipment."

"Fuck. That sounds expensive." Ken dropped his chin to his chest. "Let's hope we don't need to do that. God knows how old those pipes really are. Probably original to the house." He coughed. "Probably still made of lead."

"Don't tell me that." Jane swallowed. "Those pipes supply my drinking water."

"I'd switch to bottled if I was you," Ryan stated flatly.

"Hell with that." Ken thumped his chest with his fist. "Preservatives are keeping me alive. That, and Leslie's cooking." Stepping back, he settled his stance. "You kids should see what she feeds me. Apricots, walnuts, almond butter." Squeezing both eyes shut, he stuck out his tongue. "Supposed to be anti-inflammatory, and everything's fucking organic. One year, my bad cholesterol was too high. She fed me beans and Brazil nuts. Fuck! I almost exploded. I'm going to live forever with that woman, whether I want to or not."

Ryan laughed. It was an easy, mellow sound. "I love you, dude. You're insane."

Walking under the shed, he reached up and started picking at the damp rafters. Long rotten splinters flaked away in his hands. Shouldering a two-by-four support, he gave it a shove. The whole shed cracked, swaying unsteadily as it shifted.

"You're not gonna like hearing this, either." Ryan dusted his palms. "But this framing is shot. We're gonna need new lumber before we set those shingles. Gonna need new tarpaper, too."

"Fuck. I was hoping we didn't need to spend any money on this." Ken looked up, hopefully. "Couldn't we just jigger something? Lay the new shingles over the old ones and call it a day?"

"I'd rather not do crap work like that." Ryan pursed his lips. "Tell you what. I have a roll of sticky tin in my garage. Won't cost you a dime." He slammed the van's rear double doors shut. "I'll go fetch it."

"I'll go with you," Ken offered. "Give you a hand - "

"No." Ryan snapped. "But thanks. I know exactly where it is. Won't take me a minute."

What's he so suddenly nervous about? Jane frowned. *Listen to him. He's talking staccato.*

"The real problem is," Ryan sucked in a long breath, "is that we still need new lumber. I don't have any extra of that laying around."

Ken obviously searched for an idea. "How about using the chicken coop? Some of that wood might still be good."

"The length looks about right." Strolling over, Ryan studied the abandoned coop before giving Ken some serious side eye. "You sure Leslie won't mind us tearing this down?"

"Oh, hell no. Why not?" Ken clapped his hands. "She hasn't kept chickens for years! It's a great idea."

"You sure she won't mind?" Ryan repeated.

"Of course not. Let's recycle it! She's into that."

Chapter Eighteen

"That Ryan is one good fellow." Ken studied the cloudless sky as the Delta Power van pulled away. "Known him all his life. Not a lot of flash, but pure gold. Loyal as the day is long. Make a great life partner."

Subtle, Ken. Popping the Ducati's kickstand, Jane wheeled the bike out of the shed, parking it on the rough grass in Leslie's garden. "I'll take your word for it."

He idly swung the hammer. "I like this 'take down the coop' idea. It'll tidy up the yard."

"You said Leslie used to keep chickens?"

"She sure did. All part of that organic thing she does. Said the eggs tasted better when they ate the bugs out of her garden." He shuddered and stuck out his tongue. "Yes, I think the chicken experiment is definitely over."

"Why? Too messy?"

"No. She freaked out when the hens kept crowing."

"Roosters. You mean when the roosters kept crowing."

"No, I did not." He slid the hammer on top of the coop. "Down here, hens crow to predict a death in the family and they kept crowing." Raising his hands palm up, he shrugged. "Then some damn critter got into the yard and kept killing 'em. Strangest thing. We'd find the hens outside of the coop, lying around the courtyard, squashed flat, just piles of feathers and guts. Never did figure that one out." He scratched his whiskery chin. "I think the truth of it was there were too many snakes."

"Snakes?" Jane yelped. *That's the bad thing about living in NOLA. Nantucket didn't have any snakes.* "What kind of snakes?"

96

"Great big black fuckers. The eggs drew them in. Leslie won't ever admit it, but that's the real reason we switched to buying store bought, because Babette won't let me kill the snakes." Crooking his fingers into quotation marks, he snorted. "That crazy bitch says snakes are 'messengers from the spirit world.' So now, we buy our eggs from Hailey's Market to avoid setting Babette off and I hafta pay an extra buck and a half for organic to satisfy Leslie. Fuck." He stretched the word. "S'worth the extra dough just to get a little peace outta those women."

"I had tea with them the other day." Jane recalled the conversation although the days had blended together. "Leslie told me Gigi was adopted."

"She said that?" Ken looked surprised. "I suppose it's a good thing Leslie talks about it, right? Not my finest moment, but she sure stepped up to the plate."

"She also said Marianne Tanner was Gigi's birth mother."

"Fuck!" Ken started pacing. "Goddamn women! Why can't you ever leave things alone? Always got to stir shit up." Stopping short, he turned. "Why is that?"

Jane ignored his digression. "What happened to her?"

"To who? Marianne? Fuck if I know." Ken pointed his index finger in her face. "You are asking the wrong person. The last time I saw Marianne Tanner was the night she stuck me with Gigi." White-eyed, he ran his fingers through his hair. "That's not what I meant; that came out wrong. I wouldn't trade Gigi for the world, but Christ! That was thirty years ago."

"Where did she go?"

"I have no fucking idea!" Ken shouted. "I don't remember a goddamned thing about it!" Shaking his head, he stared intently at the ground. "Leslie said we had a fight, but I was still hitting Jim Beam pretty hard." He looked up, suddenly haggard. "She was gone when I woke up. Stole my Fender bass and left the baby. Took off. And that was it."

"You never heard from Marianne again since that night?"

"I just said that, didn't I?" He snarled.

"It just seems strange that now, with social media, she's never reached out to you or to Gigi. It would be easy enough to do."

"I'm not on goddamned social media." Ken splayed his hands. "And if Marianne is as smart as she always said she was, she went back to Kansas City, married some poor schlub from Mission Hills, popped out a couple more kids and spent the rest of her life playing tennis and eating toasted BLTs at the fucking Indian Hills Country Club." He dropped his hands to his hips. "Fuck, Jane. Leave it alone, will you? It's not like we ever had a relationship. She was just a girl I was banging, a girl I was banging with the band."

Jane felt sick. *Is this really how women were treated in the 80's? Like powerless second-class citizens or worse, like cuts of meat?* "Marianne Tanner was a person, Ken, and she had your child. That should mean something."

"I know that. I do know that. I know you're right but you're too young to remember. It was a different world back then. You'll never understand the 80's if you weren't there. We broke the rules. Hell! There weren't any rules. We did whatever the fuck we wanted and they let us do it as long as we brought in the big money." He swiped the corners of his mouth. "Corrupt? Sure, yeah, well hell, maybe. We were all scrambling to make it, and Jesus! We were kids! Kids running loose. Twenty-three, what? Maybe twenty-four years old?" He pinched the bridge of his nose. "But we knew the way the game was played. Oh hell yes, we did. I'm not joking when I said that Leslie saved my life getting me out of The Dakota."

The stupid, mulish look returned to his face. "But Marianne Tanner? She was groupie. Don't scowl at me like that, Jane. Yes, there was such a thing. I can't whitewash The WarBirds history just to make it pretty for you. Yes, this shit really happened. Marianne lived in Prairie Village with an uncle she hated because her mother died and her dad was in Hutchinson for assault. She practically lived on the street, and she hung out in Mick's garage every chance she got. So sure," he shrugged nonchalantly, "she got passed around to whoever wanted her except to Lemonhead because he was queer." Ken laughed oddly. "I think Lemonhead was the only one who really liked her."

Jane's bone-deep need for fair play and justice spouted like a geyser. "Call her a groupie if you want to, Ken, but Marianne Tanner is credited with singing backup vocals on "Love Power" and it's her voice that rocks that song. That has to count for something."

"What?" His jaw dropped open. "Where did you hear that?"

"I read it on Wikipedia." She pointed. "Someone out there is giving Marianne Tanner that kind of credit even if you don't."

"Oh, hell no." Ken stared, unblinking. "Marianne was never part of the band, not like that. Sure, she might have helped out with a vocal track or two, but she didn't have the pipes to be a real singer." He guffawed. "Shit! Are you kidding me? She wanted to be the next Annie Lennox, but she only had one volume, loud." Wiping his eyes with his thumbs, he laughed even harder. "Marianne Tanner a WarBird? She played clarinet with the SME high school band!"

The kitchen door creaked open. Aunt Babette stepped onto the porch, clutching her scarlet Japanese kimono tightly around her leathery neck.

"Ken?" She hissed. "I can hear you hollering from inside the house. What are y'all doing back there?"

Pushing the screened door open, she grasped the railing and side stepped down to the courtyard, being very careful not to drop her ostrich-feathered slippers. Rolling his eyes, Ken reached for the hammer.

"We're fixing to tear down this coop, Babette."

"Y'all need to do that now? That'll make some noise. Wake Leslie up." Hurrying over, she delicately stepped around clumps of dead grass. "Have you asked Leslie about this crazy idea of yours?"

Ken swung the hammer. "I don't need to ask Leslie's permission for every goddamn thing I do."

"You might want to remember this is her property, not yours." She belligerently stared up into his face. "She might have an opinion on it. I know I don't like the idea. She'll want to use this space for growing more vegetables. She has enough beds to manage as it is. I'm not sure it's even safe, growing food where there used to be chickens. The dirt might be contaminated with germs or parasites."

"It's guano, Babette." Ken guffawed. "The best organic fertilizer there is! She'll grow the biggest vegetables in The Bywater next year."

"I know I won't be able to eat them." Babette shuddered. Hearing a warning beep, she turned as Ryan started to back the Delta Electric van down the driveway.

"Took him long enough," Ken grumbled.

The van rolled to a stop near the shed. Ryan slid out of sight before reappearing to unlatch the van's rear cargo doors. Hefting the roll of sticky tin, he paused before setting it back down, his forehead creased with wrinkles. Tapping the van's panels with both fists, he turned quickly and marched over.

"Jane? Before we get started, I wanted to ask you something."

"What about?" A nervous ripple flicked her stomach. She could see the effort the request cost him as he stared at his boots.

Looking up, he met her eyes. "Do you want to grab supper sometime?" He hurried on. "With me? I hafta carry my mom to a couple of meetings this week, but Wednesday's free. It's blues night at The Deuce. We could grab a bite to eat before you report for work."

Folding his hands, Ryan stood quietly, looking hopeful. Ken and Aunt Babette gaped as they waited for her reaction. Jane's face grew too warm.

"Dammit, Jane!" Ken roared. "Say yes! It's "Love Power", baby. "Love Power" in action!"

Quick, say 'no.' Jane's pulse throbbed. *Say 'no' and put a stop to this right now before it gets real, before it gets out of hand. 'No' is the safest answer because then nothing more needs to change.* Digging her nails into her palms, Jane plowed through the decision. *Fuck! Of course! Just when my life's getting comfortable! Do I really want to take the chance and shake things up and toss everything back up in the air again?*

Ryan continued to study her. His crooked, uncertain grin was adorable. *He is a nice thoughtful guy. I know he's generous. He's always helping out Leslie and Ken.* He narrowed his eyes and Jane caught his blink of uncertainty over her hesitation. *Not being alone is one of the things I want to change in my life.* Her ears popped as she swallowed past the lump in her throat. *I'll never know unless I try, right?*

Jane raised her chin. *Time to test out my new theory about a benevolent universe.* "Yes," she agreed. "Let's do that. Sounds like fun."

CHAPTER NINETEEN

Pumping her arms, Jane pushed her heart rate up into the zone as they ran into the rising sun. *Feel the burn, baby.* When she had clocked out of Guardian Storage at 6:14 a.m., it was fully dark. Now, an hour later, the horizon glowed a pure golden mango and it was a tropical 66 degrees. *Sure beats freezing my ass off in New England.*

She felt a whispery kiss of nostalgia. Back on Nantucket, the island's Main Street shops would be decorated with holly wreaths and red velvet bows as they geared up for Christmas. In NOLA, the stores were draped in metallic green, gold, and purple bunting and pushing iced King Cakes for Mardi Gras. *Different cultures, different worlds. How great is it that I get to know both?*

She risked a downward glance. Piddles loped contentedly by her side, his odd blue tongue lolling between his teeth. He was matching her stride for stride and still in the game.

"Hang tough, Biggy P." She wheezed. "We're getting there."

Dodging the crosstown traffic, they left Franklin Avenue and turned right on St. Claude. *Things are looking up. Got the shed squared away for the Ducati and I have a date, a real date, with Ryan Embry tomorrow night.* Butterflies battered her stomach. *How long has it been since I had a real date? Ten, twelve years, maybe? Jesus. Back at the Police Academy with Paulie Burdett? Has it really been that long?* The skin between her shoulder blades needled with panic. *Don't forget to shave.* Jane flushed with irritation. *Stop that! Don't start acting like an idiot over this. It's just a date.*

They looped around The Boat, parked cock-eyed and blocking the driveway. Catching her breath, Jane caught the murmur of voices from the porch. *7:20 a.m. is a little early even for Gee.* She heard Leslie's reassuring tone and then a high-pitched nervous giggle. *Delilah's here, too.* Bending low, she unsnapped Biggy's harness and they jogged over.

Gee saw them coming. She stood and pushed the screened door open. "Morning, Jane. How you doin' today?"

Barking delightedly, Piddles ran up the steps.

"I'm good. Any word on Fancy?"

"Nothing yet." Gee pulled a squealing wicker chair across the painted gray floor. "Come say hello to me, Mr. P." Snapping her fingers, she sat, combing the mop of corkscrew curls between Piddle's ears before cupping his muzzle in her hands. "Where's your mother, Mr. P? Where's Fancy at?" Sitting back, she pulled out her phone, flicking the screen and looking ill. "I'm worried sick. Haven't slept since Saturday. Just lay in bed, staring at the ceiling." She tapped her temple. "Can't turn off my head. Everything just spins."

"I know it's a struggle, Gee." Delilah stared worriedly over her teacup. "But you have to fight that feeling. It will only attract more negative energy. You can't let it bring you low."

"That's easy enough to say." Gee looked haunted. "I can't fight how I feel. Fancy's been gone three days. I have a bad feeling about this."

"We all need to believe that Fancy'll be back with us soon." Reaching over, Leslie patted Gee's arm. "I know you're worried, Gigi, and that's to your credit as a friend, but it does no good to get so worked up when we don't know where Fancy is or if anything has even happened to her. You'll make yourself sick if you go on like this and that won't help anyone."

"Y'all sound so practical." Gee hunched forward, resting her wrists limply on her knees. "I'm not wired that way. I'm not fighting my brain I'm fighting my heart."

I'm with Gee. Jane's sharp-edged interior voice skated across her soul. *Fancy's been missing for 60 hours. Gee's right to be worried. Anything else*

103

sounds naïve.

The skin around Leslie's eyes gently crinkled as she stirred her jasmine tea. "I see that Ken and Ryan finished re-roofing the shed. Didn't they do a nice job? Ken was right for a change. The yard does look better without that coop. It's an improvement."

Gee studied the square of bare earth where the chicken coop used to stand. "I'm glad that thing is gone. Never liked it. Always felt nasty to me." She shuddered. "All those loose pin feathers blowing around and the little piles of white crap on the ground. Gave me the yips."

"That reminds me." Leslie tapped her chin. "Jane? By any chance did you borrow my Wellies? My boots, my rubber boots?" She twisted sideways in her chair. "It's the strangest thing. I always leave them on the mat by the door. Keeps me from tracking garden loam into the house. I can't find them anywhere."

Is that a dig? Jane subtly checked her sneaker treads for mud. *Nope, I'm clean.* "Haven't seen them, Leslie." Standing up, she stretched her cooling muscles. "Is Ken up? I'd like to thank him for fixing the shed before I forget."

"That's another mystery." Leslie replaced her china cup. "I don't know where Ken is. He was up at the crack of dawn, just after five. Got one of those strange calls again. Slipped out of bed and caught the early bus."

"What's Pops up to now?" Gee wondered.

"I have no idea." Leslie shrugged. "Whatever it is, your father is keeping it a secret even from me."

"Wouldn't it be great," Delilah clasped her plump hands, "if Ken was sitting in a coffee shop somewhere writing new songs?" Her kohl-rimmed eyes widened. "If he came out with a new album as a surprise?"

Leslie smiled. "That's a nice pipe dream, dear, but Ken hasn't written a lyric in thirty-five years. He swore he'd never do it again and he is one stubborn man."

"Maman?" Gee toyed with her mug. "Aren't you curious to know what

Pops does when he gets those calls? Don't you want to find out where he goes?" Leaning forward conspiratorially, she lowered her voice. "I could follow him one day and find out."

"No, don't do that, Gigi." Leslie's eyes flared wide. She held up her hand and rainbows from her diamond ring danced over the ceiling. "Your father and I have been married for thirty-three years. I don't need to know what Ken's up to every minute of every day. He'll tell me what he's doing when he's ready."

Wow. Jane blinked. She felt a ripple of cautious unease. *Is that what love is really about? Loyalty and blind trust? Shit. Maybe that's why I never found it. How do you ever learn to trust someone else that much?*

She heard a clatter of footsteps overhead. They began to descend the back staircase into the kitchen and she recognized Aunt Babette's gait.

"Leslie? Leslie! Where y'at?"

The elderly woman scurried around the corner landing, clutching her chest and looking breathless.

"Gigi? Oh! And Delilah, good morning, dear. Leslie? The police are here."

"What?" The wicker chair cracked as Leslie slowly rose.

"The police, *cher*. At the door. I saw them coming. From my window."

"Oh my God." Gee paled. "It's Fancy."

"Don't say that, Gee." Delilah snapped, pointing a sharp red fingernail. "Don't call that bad juju into being. We don't know anything for real yet."

Leslie squared her shoulders. "I'll go let them in."

She led them past the closets and kitchen cupboards, automatically setting her teacup in the deep sink. An eight-note Winchester doorbell chimed as they trooped through the swinging door into the living room. Nervously shaking out her hands, Gee trotted ahead.

"No, Gigi." Grasping her sleeve, Leslie slowly drew her back. "This is my house. If there is trouble coming, I will answer the door."

105

Thumbing the brass spoon latch, she swung the heavy door open. Two men dressed in good suits stood waiting. Raising their right arms in unison, they displayed their NOPD star-and-crescent law enforcement badges.

"Good morning." The bald white man with no neck said. "I'm Detective Felix Bordelon. This is my associate, Detective Antwon Dupree."

Jane recognized Bordelon from NOLA's Missing and Exploited Person's Unit. Dupree, a younger black male with sun-faded natural hair towered over his right shoulder.

Bordelon adjusted his thick glasses. "We need to speak with Gigi Pascoe. We were given this as a secondary address. Is she here?"

CHAPTER TWENTY

"Fuck. I knew it!" Gee groaned. "Something bad's happened to Fancy."

"Why do you say that?" Detective Dupree squinted, his voice a rich baritone.

"Please, step in." Leslie indicated the room. "We're all family here."

"No need to entertain the neighbors any more than usual," Aunt Babette acidly remarked.

Jane felt the balance of possible outcomes tip as Bordelon crossed the threshold. *It's bad. Big bad.* The detective's eyes reflected bitter knowledge and sorrow. *Notifying the families is the toughest part of the job. Look. He's not meeting anyone's eyes.*

Gripping a laptop in one broad hand, Dupree followed. Their leather shoes slapped the floor and their steady tread bounced off the plaster walls like the ticking of a pendulum clock. They took up a standing position, side by side, over the coffee table.

Reaching behind her, Gee felt for the sofa and sat. "You have news? About our friend?"

"Yes." Detective Dupree frowned. "I'm afraid we do."

"Afraid?" Delilah squeaked. Collapsing next to Gee, she reached for her hand, interlacing their fingers and resting their interlocked hands on her lap.

"Please take a seat," Aunt Babette asked. "You two just standing there makes me nervous."

"Thank you, ma'am."

Bordelon choose the ladderback chair. Squeezing into an upholstered armchair, Dupree opened his laptop on a side table. Pulling a notepad and a pen from his breast pocket, Bordelon repeatedly cleared his throat.

"911 logged a call at 6:13 a.m. Metro CSI responded immediately. A K-9 unit recovered the body of Lester Wayne, AKA Fancy Abellard from a storage facility in Mid-City."

Oh, shit. Jane suddenly felt ill. "Which storage facility?"

Bordelon checked his notes. "Guardian Self Storage on Canal Street. Why?"

Gee shifted sideways, looking waxy and green. "Jane? Don't you work there?"

"It is. I mean, I do." Jane's temples throbbed. Pressing them with both hands, her blood pressure spiked so rapidly that she saw silvery stars like a firework display shooting across her peripheral vision.

Dupree studied her suspiciously. He slowly blinked like a tortoise. "And you are?"

Jane licked her parched lips. It didn't help. "Jane Byrne." *CSI found Fancy's body at 6:13 a.m. That means Christophe must've found her corpse and called it in almost the second I left the building.* "I do work at Guardian. Security. Lob shift."

Dupree looked puzzled. "Lob shift?"

"Lobster." Jane shook her head. "Nights. I work nights. Ten to six."

Bordelon checked his wristwatch. "It's eight-eleven now. Where have you been?"

"I went for a run." Tugging her damp T-shirt, she nodded at the poodle. "And came home to find this."

"Home?" Dupree asked. "You work at Guardian Storage, you knew the victim and you live here, too?"

Shit. Shut up! Jane scrambled. *Shut your fucking mouth! Stop volunteering information. It's making things worse!*

108

"Jane rents our tenant apartment," Leslie inserted softly. "It's a separate unit off the courtyard."

Dupree's fingers hovered over his keyboard. "And you had no idea there was anything wrong at Guardian Storage this morning?"

Always cooperate with the police. Jane squirmed. *Always. They're looking for deception, mismatches and lies.* She recalled the missing in-and-out client access details on Guardian's exit log and Cal's unexplainable wad of cash. *That looks suspicious as hell. If I throw Cal under the bus it'll take their focus off of me.*

"There's an issue with one of the exit cams that's been noted in the security log," Jane offered, "but shit like that is always happening." Faking a serenity she didn't feel, she rested her hands on her knees. "Cheap bastard owners won't invest a dime in building maintenance. That whole place needs big work just to get it to code."

Dupree maintained his steady unsettling gaze.

Don't offer them anything more. Silence is a police tactic and they're using it on you.

"What?" She caved. "What more do you want? I don't know anything about this! Where," she stuttered, "where was she found?"

Bordelon thawed first. "Inside a locked storage unit."

"On Level Three?" Jane blurted.

Dupree pounced. "You do know more about this!"

"All I know," she repeated carefully, forcing herself to relax as her thigh muscles trembled, "is what is outlined in the security log. Clients have been complaining for months about the stink on Level Three." *Hold up. It has been months,* Jane realized. *I've processed complaints about the stink from the day I arrived, from my very first day, way before Fancy died. It was the first thing Numa had me investigate on my rounds on Day One.*

"Get a court order." She suggested. "Guardian can release the owner's name on the unit. That's a solid lead. That's where I'd start."

"Warrant's in process," Dupree stated shortly.

Aha. Okay. They're already on it. Jane re-centered. *Waiting for the judge to get to court and sign off on it is more likely and that won't happen until at least noon.* She smiled knowingly. *Judges can be tardy. Nothing new there.*

"I can't believe Fancy's dead." Gee whispered, staring at the floor between her feet. "I can't believe she's gone."

"I know, honey. I know." Leslie's shoulders slumped. "I am so, so sorry."

"How did she die?" Gee looked up suddenly, her voice brittle. "Was it an accident?"

"No." Bordelon checked with Dupree, who nodded grimly. "It was blunt force trauma."

"But what does that *mean*?" Aunt Babette's raised voice cracked.

"The preliminary report indicates a skull fracture with multiple broken ribs. Fingers were broken in both hands." Dupree dry rubbed his palms together. "For what it's worth, Ms. Abellard fought her attacker."

"Someone hit her?" Gee leapt up, her face tightening like a fist. "Some *feet pue tan* beat Fancy to death?"

"Not exactly." Dupree's suspicious gaze returned. "We believe Ms. Abellard was kicked to death."

"Fuck!" Gee shouted. Striding to the window she gripped the frame, her shoulders hunched to her ears. "I hate this!"

"Easy, Gee." Delilah's eyes flared wide. "Stay chill. He's only telling us what happened. He didn't do it." She rose, her face as wan as the moon. "Was it a hate crime? Was Fancy targeted because she was queer?"

Gee spun around. "That is a great question."

Dupree smoothed his tie. "We have no information on that point at this time, but I can promise you we're keeping a close eye on that possibility."

"I hope you are," Delilah insisted. "Because that's the fear we live with

110

every single day." Crossing the room, she linked her arm with Gee's, drawing her back to the sofa. "We've been warned we might see something like this, an increase in violence against LGBTQ because of Trump."

"Fucker." Gee muttered darkly. "Fucking lowlife thug, preying on people's fears. You know he stole that election. You know he did."

"We've been warned things could get worse," Delilah agreed.

"I can't imagine how things could get any worse," Aunt Babette interjected.

"Agreed." Bordelon thoughtfully polished his glasses. "I know that nationally we've seen a slight uptick since the election."

"Uptick!" Gee spat. "Is that what you call it? Fancy is our friend not a fucking statistic!"

"Gigi, please, *sha*." Leslie implored with a frozen smile. "Try to stay calm."

"We're all aware of the hate crime situation," Dupree inserted hurriedly. "My partner misspoke. Human rights are human rights. We don't get to pick and choose. Law enforcement officers are sworn to uphold the Civil Rights Act for everyone," he emphasized, "*including* LGBTQ."

"Correct." Matching his thumbs, Bordelon tented his hands. "If this is a hate crime, we will pursue the charges of that criminal act. Our stated departmental policy is 'even one is too many.' Any acts of intimidation, vandalism, or violence," he ticked the points off his stubby fingers, "gets elevated to the FBI and the U.S. Attorney General's office for investigation."

"That's a crap guarantee." Gee scowled. "We don't know where Sessions stands on LGBTQ rights. The man's a Trump supporter from Alabama."

"*If* Sessions gets confirmed as the new U.S. Attorney General," Delilah added. "The Senate might still reject his nomination."

"Mike Pence is even worse," Gee insisted. "He's a known homophobe." She combed her thick hair with her fingers. "We are fucked with this Administration."

"For what it's worth," Jane offered, "the right people will be handling the investigation. The Fibbies have the talent, the Quantico resources and the national scope to process a hate crime if that is what this is."

"They do." Dupree's forehead wrinkled. "Why do you know that?"

"I've worked with the Bureau before." Jane raised her chin. "In Massachusetts. I witnessed a child abduction and they brought me in."

CHAPTER TWENTY-ONE

"I'm sorry." Leslie gasped. "You what?"

"Yes. Four years ago." Jane's stomach rippled with nerves as she confronted the searing memory. *Stop avoiding this. Look straight at it. Don't be afraid.* "In another life."

"A child abduction, Jane? What happened to the poor *bebe*?"

"She was recovered." *The only way out is through.* "Safely returned to her family."

"Seems strange to me," Dupree squinted, "that you're near the center of things again. Why is that?"

"Random chance." Jane's morning weariness evaporated. *Fear is energy. I can use this.*

"What I want to know is *when* did it happen?" Aunt Babette's face shone with focused intelligence as she twisted her hands in her lap. "That might tell us who did this terrible thing. When did Fancy die?"

Bordelon crossed his arms. "The preliminary report indicates a 46-60 hour window. The Coroner is trying for more detail."

60 hours? Jane backtracked through her sketchy mental calendar. *Saturday night. Fancy was murdered right after Leslie's birthday party.*

Dupree swiped his laptop. "When was the last time each of you saw Ms. Abellard?"

Leslie nervously glanced around the family circle. "She was here for my birthday party. That's the last time I saw her."

"Same with me," Aunt Babette agreed, sadly. "Fancy left wearing the party mask I made for her, special. Walked out looking regal like a queen."

"I was sweeping glass up off the floor," Jane added, "but I saw her leaving like they said."

"I gave her a lift home," Gee stated. "Actually, we both did, Dee and me, since we were already heading that way."

"You did?" Dupree typed a note. "You and Ms. Gardere dropped Fancy Abellard off at her house on Dauphin Street in Marigny on Saturday night?"

"No, Gee. That's not right." Delilah looked puzzled. "Don't you remember? You and Fancy dropped *me* off first because I had to get up early to run the shop inventory on Sunday morning."

"Sorry, that's right." Gee rapped her temple. "My bad. It was a big night. I drove Fancy to the club after we dropped Dee off. Fancy was meeting a Tinder date, I think she said."

"Which club?" Bordelon asked.

"Femme du." Gee blinked. "Where else?"

"Did you go into this club with her?"

"No, I still had my own shift to cover 'til two. At Club Oz. I'm a dancer there." Gee picked at her blue nail polish. "I got home around two-thirty or three, after close. Dee? Isn't that right?"

"I suppose so." Delilah hesitated. "I didn't hear you come in."

"You didn't hear me?" Gee blinked. "I took a shower."

"No." Dee looked apologetic. "I took a couple of Tylenol PMs. I was dead to the world."

"Did anyone else see you working at Club Oz during this time?"

"Only about two hundred people," Gee replied sarcastically. "I'm lit up center stage, climbing a pole."

"Gigi's their headliner," Leslie interjected proudly. "Their star attraction."

"Don't let Fancy catch you saying that," Gee joked. Looking horrified, she covered her mouth with her fingers. "This sucks. I forgot!"

114

"It happens." Dupree scanned his notes. "Did Ms. Abellard have any enemies? Bad blood or grudges? Any hard feelings we should know about?"

"None that I know of." Gee slumped against the cushion. "Dee? Anyone?"

"Fancy could be obnoxious," Dee chewed her lip, "and some girls were jealous of her lifestyle, but I don't think anyone hated her enough to kill her." She glanced at Gigi. "I know she owed some people money. Money was always a problem with her."

Dupree's head snapped up. "Who did Ms. Abellard owe money to? Drug dealers? Pimps?"

"No!" Dee protested. "Bookies, mostly. Fancy loved playing numbers and *bourre*. She was addicted to it. But I think she mostly owed friends."

Leslie suddenly looked haggard. "Gigi? Please tell me you didn't loan Fancy any more money!"

"Maybe a little." Gee shrugged. "She got behind on her mortgage again. You know she loves that house. I helped her out."

"Gigi!" Leslie sputtered. "You promised you wouldn't do that! You *promised* me."

"Maman," Gee implored. "The sheriff posted a notice on her door! The bank was ready to toss her into the street."

"How much did you loan her this time?"

"Not much. A little. A couple of hundred."

"I heard," Aunt Babette inserted, "it was more like six thousand."

"Maman! Aunt Babette, stop! It's my money. I earned it. I can spend it any way I want."

"Did you ask Ms. Abellard to pay you back?" Dupree asked. "And she refused?"

"No! It wasn't like that." Gee squirmed. "I didn't have to ask her for it. I knew she'd pay me back when she could." She squared her shoulders. "Fancy's always up against it at the end of the year. She makes it up in tips

115

during Mardi Gras." She sat up. "She always pays me back with interest. It's no big deal."

"I see." Bordelon flicked a piece of lint off of his sleeve. "When you filed the missing person's report on her, when we talked, you mentioned a fist fight at a party. What was that about?"

"What about it?" Gee shifted sideways. "Fancy got pissy with some cracker working the bar."

"Nothing new there," Delilah eagerly agreed. "He was giving her free attitude." She sniffled into her black lace hankie. "As usual, she gave it right back."

"Who was this person," Dupree asked, "working the bar?"

"Some random friend of Ryan's." Gee looked blank. "Maman? Do you know?"

"You'd have to ask your father that one."

"Tyler Shank," Aunt Babette replied promptly, resting her bony elbows on her knees. "He works with Ryan Embry at Delta Power. Ken asked him to man the bar at the very last minute."

"Tyler Shank." Dupree started typing. "Spelled like it sounds? He live near here?"

"I'm not sure where he lives," Leslie stated uncertainly. "Cheryl would know."

"Cheryl?"

"Cheryl Embry. My dearest friend."

Dupree typed another note. "Let's get back to this party. Who threw the first punch? Fancy Abellard or this Tyler Shank?"

"Neither." Gee casually crossed her legs at the knee. "It was me."

"You did?" Dupree started. "Why did you start the fight?"

"Because that peckerwood insulted my dad." Pulling a thread from a cushion, Gee rolled it into a loose ball before flicking it to the floor. "I don't take that shit offa no one."

"Gigi, watch your temper." Aunt Babette warned, her voice rising.

"Please don't take that out of context." Leslie splayed her hands. "Gigi was provoked. That Tyler Shank fellow was drunk on tequila."

"I see." Snick. Snick. Snick. Bordelon repeatedly clicked his pen. "This is all very helpful. I have one last question." Snick. Snick. He pointed the pen at Jane like a baton. "How long have you two been friends?"

"Us two, who? Me and Gee?" *Why is Bordelon asking me that?* Jane breathed deep as paranoia dug its talons into her guts. *What? He thinks we were in on this together?* "I don't know, a couple of weeks, maybe? Why?"

"No reason."

"I think we have what we need." Closing his laptop, Dupree stood. "Ms. Pascoe? You'll need to follow us to the Coroner's Office."

"Are you arresting her?" Leslie scrambled up. "She's my daughter. I have the right to know."

"No, ma'am. We're not arresting anyone at this time." He buttoned his suit coat. "CSI located Ms. Abellard's purse at the scene. An organ donor card identified Gigi Pascoe as next-of-kin." Tucking the laptop under one arm, the detective rubbed his hands. "You'll need to bring a photo ID to make the identification."

"Wait." Gee hesitated, her face drawn. "I'm not sure," she whispered, "I can do this."

"Why not?"

"I ... I don't want to see Fancy dead." Closing her eyes, Gee pinched the bridge of her nose. "I want to remember her like she was. Fabulous. Alive."

Leslie slipped around the coffee table. "*Cher?* You need to go with these men." She gently stroked Gigi's back. "Fancy needs you, honey. You need to go."

Gee's shoulders slumped. "Dee? Will you go with me?"

"Really, Gee?" Delilah fingered the tiny gold and ruby cross at her neck. "You want *me* to visit the house of the dead?"

"Please, Dee. I can't do this alone. I can't. I just can't. I need your help."

If they don't move on this, Fancy's killer might go free. Jane's fingertips tingled. She dug deep. *Fear is energy, but so is rage. Fancy deserves justice. We all do.* "Give me your keys, Gee. I'll drive."

CHAPTER TWENTY-TWO

Jane gripped The Boat's cherry red steering wheel. It took her a few stop-and-start tries to get used to the gas pedal and to the brakes because of her boots, but the Cadillac's powerful V-8 engine responded quicker and easier than she had feared. Back home, she had slipped out of her running gear into her standard civilian outfit of jeans, T-shirt, and her favorite gray hoodie. Her backpack lay on the floorboards next to Delilah's feet. She felt focused and ready for anything.

"Take the ramp for I-10W." Gee pointed, her hand trembling. "We want US Business 90, then South Claiborne Street." She rested her arm on the passenger side door. "Look at me. I'm still rattled. Thanks for driving."

"Not a problem," Jane said.

"Why are we going this way?" Delilah protested from the back seat. "The morgue's on MLK."

"No, they moved it." The ragtop was down. Gee raised her voice over the steadily whistling wind. "Built a new facility on Earhart. Opened in January."

"They needed one. Jesus! That last morgue they used was a horror show. Remember that, Gee? Rhodes Funeral Home in Central City? They kept Nanna's body in a refrigerated trailer in their parking lot."

"This city morgue thing is a complete cluster fuck." Gee rapped her cellphone against her thigh. "Katrina flooded them out of the courthouse basement, so they had to move to Rhodes. Took them ten years to raise the money for this new building."

Dropping the phone listlessly onto her lap, she studied the

neighborhood passing below. "This feels like some kind of weird dream. Like Fancy's pranking me, playing a joke. I keep looking for her text." Picking the phone back up, she squared it on her fingertips. "It's weird they found Fancy in the same place, Jane, where you work."

"I keep thinking the same thing." Delilah agreed, her voice shrill. "Jane? You never saw anything strange going on there?"

Can't blame them for asking. Jane tightened her grip. *It does look suspicious as hell. If I was them, I'd be asking me the same exact thing. Odd things do happen at Guardian, but I ignore them, don't speak up.* Shame warmed her face. *Maybe I should've paid more attention to things at work, dug a little deeper, cared a little more. If I'd been less focused on myself and my own tale of woe would it have made a difference? Would Fancy still be alive?*

"I don't know if it's suspicious." Jane started slowly, poised instantly to clam up. "But Cal always carries a fat stack on him. I'm not sure where he gets it."

Gee cut her eyes. "Maybe he doesn't trust the bank with his money. Some folks don't."

"Maybe." Jane moistened her lips. "I've been wondering if Cal's working a con, you know, leasing Guardian units under the table for cash? If that's true and Numa finds out, he will go fucking ballistic."

Delilah leaned against the front seat. "Numa's your boss?"

"Yes. The boss, the big boss, the manager." Moving The Boat over, Jane illegally passed a slow moving Toyota blocking the passing lane. "He's friends with the owners."

"You need to figure out what's going on with this Cal guy, if he knows anything about Fancy." Delilah stated flatly, painfully prodding Jane's shoulder with her velvet-gloved hand. "This whole thing sounds dodgy as hell." She sat back. "And we need to know if Fancy was killed because of her lifestyle. You must be stone cold blind if you think this only happens to other people."

Jane checked on Delilah in the rearview mirror. Dee sat huddled in her crimson cutaway coat, black mini-skirt and thigh high patent leather cavalier boots. The breeze kept snatching at the veil on her top hat and snapping it like a pennant. Shrugging, Dee pulled her lapels closer to her throat.

"Uptick!" Gee snorted contemptuously. "Police fucker called it an uptick."

"*And* Washington keeps reversing LGBTQ policy." Dee scoffed. "GLADD called it an all out attack and you know what? I think they're right. It does feel like we're going backwards on things instead of moving forward. Jesus, Gee! What if they roll back same sex marriage? Or Roe *v.* Wade? Think Trump'll go that far?"

"He can't. The Supreme Court judges will stop him."

"You don't know that." Dee argued. "They might not."

"Now you are being paranoid, girlfriend."

"Wanna bet? Oh, no. Those right-wing Republicans don't let go. They're still fighting to kill Planned Parenthood and Obamacare. Such hypocrites! You'll notice they still cover Viagra prescriptions in *their* health care plan. Tell me that's not gender bias."

The Superdome slid past like a silvery hump-backed whale. Rotating the steering wheel, Jane caught the highway split. Checking her mirrors again, she smoothly slid The Boat into the new traffic pattern.

She jumped as Gee flicked her knee.

"Awfully quiet over there, Jane. Still with us? What d'you think about things?"

"Jane's not political." Dee simpered.

"She's right," Jane easily agreed. "I've learned to keep my mouth shut and my head down. It's safer that way."

"Works pretty well for an ostrich." Gee pointedly folded her arms across her chest. "How's that working out for you?"

Jane felt stung by the rebuke.

"Give it time." Dee confidently smoothed her velvet gloves. "You'll change your mind once this shit hits closer to home and you start losing *your* friends and *your* family members."

Jane winced. *You're wrong. Dead wrong. Both of you. I know exactly how it feels to be an outcast, to lose my family and my friends. Four years in now and my heart still grieves for everyone I've lost.*

Delilah straightened her hat. "I feel like a Jew, suddenly trapped in Nazi Germany. I'm a bi-sexual, not a criminal. Why am I being treated like one?"

"It's not just us," Gee stated. "It's Muslims, Jews, blacks, immigrants, anyone off the grid. Trump's normalizing hate. It's Amerika spelled with a KKK."

"I love, love, love how he tweeted his support for LGBTQ during the campaign." Dee's voice rose. "Said Hillary would threaten our freedoms and beliefs. Jesus! Who fell for that one?"

Jane pulled The Boat onto the exit ramp. "Evidently, 26% of the general population did."

"Would you look at that?" Gee gaped. "Jane has actually expressed her opinion."

"Fuck off, smart ass."

"That's because only 51% of us voted," Delilah pursued. "I hope the 49% who didn't bother getting up off their asses are feeling better about the way things are now."

"Maybe," Gee offered sarcastically, "they're hoping to get new jobs building Trump's Mexican wall."

"Good luck with that." Jane straightened the wheel. Earhart Boulevard looked deserted. "And there's another government pork belly money pit we get to pay taxes for. So, where's this morgue?"

"On the right. Keep going."

Jane spotted it. The new Coroner's Office and EMS headquarters had been built on a city block of flattened bulldozed wasteland under a snarl of concrete overpasses. The cross-town traffic buzzed overhead like an angry hornet's nest. With a snap of recognition, she knew where she was. "You should've said it was near Street Made Repair. They fixed the yoke on my Ducati when it rusted out."

"I'll know that for next time." Gee pointed. "Pull in there."

"Next time?" Dee wailed. "Dammit, Gee! Don't say 'next time'! You know words have power! You'll call Death into being!"

"That's hooey." Jane slid The Boat into a parking spot. "Pure idleness and superstition."

"Says you." Delilah snapped, cupping her jaw with her gloved hands. "Can't you feel that energy surge? It's hurting my teeth."

"I'm with you, Dee." Swinging the passenger door open, Gee unlatched the front seat and pushed it forward, politely extending her hand. "Just because Jane's a Yankee doesn't mean she's automatically right."

"Says you," Jane echoed. "Hand me my backpack, will you, Dee?"

Dee handed it up before reaching up and straightening her hat with resolve. Her black-lined lipstick stood in stark contrast to her extraordinarily matte skin. "Alright, girls. I'm not happy about this, but let's get it done."

They marched, side by side across the parking lot for the main entrance. The concrete pavement was still so fresh that the stenciled handicapped space logo looked crisply blue. None of the other parking spaces bore the oily dribs, drabs, blots, or shadowy stains usually deposited by the third hand vehicles from previous visitors. A six-foot tall chain link fence protected the facility from the passing pedestrian traffic on Earhart Boulevard. Out of the range of a pod of security cameras mounted on the roof, some street thug had already scaled the fence and tagged the new building with *Baron Samedi is Waiting for You* in fat purple spray-painted lettering.

Delilah's face paled even more. Staring wordlessly at the graffiti, she reached for the door.

CHAPTER TWENTY-THREE

"This place is sick."

The pneumatic security door softly sighed as Delilah crossed the ultramodern reception area. Unfastening the pearl buttons on her frogged velvet gloves, she tucked them into her burgundy patent leather alligator bag. "What a difference! Sure doesn't look like the nasty ass funeral parlor I had to use."

I've worked with the dead before. Bracing herself, Jane took a hesitant sniff. *Cadaverine, putrescine, skatole, and methanethiol, that stunning combination of shit, mothballs, rotten eggs, garlic and fecal cabbage.* Whether or not she could handle the daily stench had been Jane's only concern over working forensic CSI as a profession. The NOLA Coroner's Office smelled lightly of balsam pine and she relaxed. *Not that working CSI or with the FBI is even an option anymore.* Depression's familiar leaden mental cloud settled on her shoulders like a sodden blanket, and she felt a remorseful pang at the missed lifetime opportunity. *That's the road I should've taken. Too late now.* Bearing down hard she squashed the regret. *Stop thinking like that! I did what I had to do. The past is dust and ashes. That door is permanently closed.*

"There you are." Detective Dupree looked up. He was leaning against the front desk, standing next to Bordelon, who was holding his hat in his hands. "We thought we lost you."

"You almost did, near Tulane." Gee strode over. "You ran that red light."

"It was orange." He blinked.

The detectives were talking to a strikingly tall, mature woman with combed out hair held off her face by a bold multi-colored beaded headband. She was wearing washable slacks, rubber clogs, and a powder blue smock. A Crescent City Coroner's Office badge was clipped to her smock pocket which was stuffed with ballpoint pens.

"*Ms*. Pascoe?" Bordelon emphasized, sliding his glasses up his nose. "This is Dr. Tamerlane Sabatier. She's the PDI, the professional death investigator assigned to the case."

"You're G.G. Pascoe? Next of kin?" The PDI's voice was slowly measured and melodic. She checked her clipboard. "I'll need to see your photo ID."

Gee pulled out her wallet and slid her driver's license from its plastic sleeve.

"I'm confused. This says your name is Paul?"

"It's Gigi, G, I, G, I. I don't use Paul."

"Oh! I see." Returning the license, she corrected the authorization form before handing it over. "You'll need to sign this release. It confirms your identity and allows us to return any personal items to you."

Gee grimly scribbled her signature.

"Very good." Sliding the clipboard under her arm, Dr. Sabatier cocked her head. "Please accept my personal condolence during this difficult time. You can be assured that the Coroner's Office is here to assist the family in any way."

"Thank you." Gee returned the pen. "We appreciate that."

"And these others are family members?"

"Yes." Delilah sniffled into her black lace hankie. "We're all the family Fancy had."

"I'm sorry. Fancy?" The PDI's forehead wrinkled. "That name was registered as," she checked the form, "Lester Wayne Abellard."

"That's an AKA," Jane offered. "Fancy was her nickname."

"That's not true." Gee countered. "She had it legally changed to

Fancy."

"And you're all coming back?" She pressed on, resting the clipboard against her abdomen and studying them carefully. "I need to warn you that this procedure may be disturbing. It isn't necessary that you all attend. We only need one person to make an identification."

Gee suddenly looked frantic. "Dee? Jane? You're coming with me, right?"

"We are, if you need us." Delilah soothed.

"I do. I do."

"Yes," Jane agreed. "We're all coming back."

"Very well. I've reserved a viewing station. Follow me."

Dr. Sabatier pushed through a set of swinging double doors. They trooped down a hallway lit spotlessly white by bands of overhead florescent lights. Other than their footsteps and a scratchy intermittent whisper coming from the air conditioning vents, the annex was eerily quiet.

"I've been tasked." The PDI spoke over her shoulder, her voice echoing off the tiled walls. "With any medico-legal death, sexual assault, and mental health investigations in NOLA and I report directly to the Chief Deputy Coroner. Do you have any initial questions?"

"Are we the only ones in here?" Delilah whispered.

"Oddly enough, yes. We're experiencing a lull." Snatching a folded sheet off of a nearby cart, she tucked it under her arm. "That's not usually the case. Central's the busiest Coroner's Office in Louisiana. We see upwards of 1,000 autopsies a year plus two hundred more from neighboring parishes who request our help." Pausing before a steel door, she twirled her index finger. "Dr. Jeff made some real changes. This is a state-of-the-art viewing facility."

"Top drawer." Dupree snickered.

Cop humor. Jane winced at his pun.

"First class." Dr. Sabatier corrected severely as she opened the viewing room door.

They filed in. Jane caught an unexpected rustle and she jumped, because the room wasn't empty. A sallow morgue attendant stood stock still in one corner as motionless as a zombie. He was wearing a lavender smock with a neon green hairnet. Gray industrial goggles and a paper facemask were loosely slung around his neck.

"Baptiste?" The PDI slid the sheet onto another cart. She scanned her clipboard. "We need Coroner's Case docket D-7493."

"74-93. Yes, ma'am. Be right back with it." Straightening his paper sleeves, he pushed through a swinging side door, shuffling away in his blue shoe booties.

"Everyone? Please take a seat. This may take a few minutes."

Dr. Sabatier pointed to a cluster of plastic chairs. Crossing the viewing room, she grabbed a brown paper bag off a stainless-steel shelf next to a stack of paper towels and an opened pop up box of plastic evidence collection bags.

"Ms. Pascoe? This is Mr.," she caught herself, "*Ms.* Abellard's personal property, recovered at the scene. The DC has released it to the family."

Gee warily hefted the paper bag. It had weight, and she sat down before she opened it.

"What's in here?"

Ripping open the metal staples, she peered in before pulling Fancy's gold wallet out. Flipping it open, she looked up. "It's been picked. Everything but her license is gone." Dipping her hand back in, she snaked out Fancy's pink silk purse. Grief lined Gee's face when she noticed that the silvery chain link strap was snapped in half. She choked as she threaded the slim chain through her fingers. "You said she put up a fight?"

"Yes. We believe she did," Detective Bordelon sympathized sadly.

"Is her phone in there?" Delilah asked.

Gee tipped the bag on its side. "No, I don't see it." Sliding out Fancy's mohair sweater, she gasped, rapidly shaking her fingers like a cat flicking a damp paw. "This has dried blood on it."

"The violence associated with this homicide is what triggered the Coroner's Case registration," Detective Dupree rumbled.

"I've been a PDI for thirteen years," Dr. Sabatier added, "and I'm still shocked by the insane senseless violence that I see in this city."

"Leave Fancy's clothes in the bag, Gee," Delilah suggested quickly. "We'll take care of that later."

The PDI leaned her hip against a stainless-steel table. "We'll hold Ms. Abellard's body until the homicide investigation is complete. That may take several weeks. We have new autopsy protocols in place." She delicately dusted her fingers. "Dr. Jeff has directed us to be thorough."

"That's a good thing." Dupree stopped picking at his nails. "Since we couldn't always believe the evidence or the answers that previously came out of this office."

Dr. Sabatier angrily pushed off the table. "Previous protocols were sloppy." She raised her chin. "We're working very hard to reestablish public confidence, and trust." She picked the clipboard up. "When the investigation is complete, we'll release Ms. Abellard's body to the funeral home you choose. Ms. Pascoe?" She clicked a pen. "We'll send you status updates via email unless you'd prefer a call?"

"No." Gigi rested her forehead on her fingertips. "Email or text work best."

Jane tensed as she caught the sound of rubbery wheels gripping linoleum. There was a pause, a solid metallic clunk, and the side door swung open. Baptiste returned, pushing a loaded gurney into the viewing room over his fully extended arms. Everyone froze. He settled the gurney against the far wall like he was parallel parking a car.

Straightening his shoulders, he unzipped the body bag from head to foot with three ferocious tugs.

ZIP. ZIP. ZIP. Jane grabbed her nose.

CHAPTER TWENTY-FOUR

"Oh-mi-god!" Delilah gagged. "Wait! I'm not ready for this!"

"This one's not so bad." Baptiste rocked steadily from side to side. "December's better for decomp. Not so hot." Shoving his hands deeply into his smock pockets, he wheezed. "He-he-he. This fella look like a human canoe. Look how much they stitched him up. He looks like a baseball."

"Thank you, Baptiste. That's all." Dr. Sabatier inserted quickly. "I'll buzz when we're done."

"Yes, ma'am." He shrugged, shuffling back into the hall.

The PDI reached for the folded sheet. Snapping it open, she settled it neatly over the body bag and the corpse, leaving only Fancy's head and hands exposed. Jane dropped her hand to her side as a powerful wave of chlorine scent scorched her nose hairs. She felt immensely grateful for anything that masked the stench.

"Ms. Pascoe?" Dr. Sabatier faced the room. "Is this Lester Wayne Abellard?"

"Yes." Gee gasped, pressing her fingers to her mouth in obvious horror. "Fuck. It's her. It's Fancy."

Jane automatically surfaced her CSI training, distancing herself from the immediacy of the scene and looking at it objectively. Decomposition was more than started; it had advanced. Fancy's broken fingers were swollen like purple sausages. Her golden fake nails sprang from her fingertips like malformed talons. Jane shifted her eyes up the sheet. Fancy's shaved head was a balloon mask of post-mortem lividity. Skin slippage had already begun. Her cheeks sagged, and the loose skin pillowed against the gurney. The dulled white of her eyeballs gleamed through two blackened slits. Her mouth yawned opened in Death's last grimace, that dark jester's final smile. Her lips were drawn back over her gray gums, exposing her missing teeth.

Gee hesitantly stepped closer. "Where's her hair?"

"I'm sorry, what?" Dupree looked confused.

"Her hair, her wig," Gee insisted. "It's not in the bag. Where is it?"

Snatching up her clipboard, Dr. Sabatier ran her finger down the inventory. "I don't see it listed. She didn't come in with one -"

"Quick!" Snapping her fingers, Gee stared unblinking at Fancy's corpse. "Give me a towel. I'll make her a turban, cover her up." Obviously steeling herself, she took another step closer. "She'd hate to be seen like this, all naked and bald."

"This is horrible!" Delilah wailed, unpinning the rhinestone brooch on her lapel. "Wait, Gee! Use this, too."

"Stop!" Jane leapt up, terrified by the onrushing danger. "Don't step any closer! They forgot to bag her hands."

"She's right." Detective Dupree blocked their way. "Please return to that side of the room. You'll contaminate the evidence."

"I'm sorry, Gee." Delilah gagged again, pressing her hankie to her lips. "I can't take this. I need some air. I'm feeling faint."

"Sure thing, honey." Gee dug out her keys. "Go warm up The Boat. We'll finish up and I'll drive you home. Can you find your way back?"

"Yes. I'm sorry. I'm so, so sorry." Delilah blindly waved good-bye. "I've got to go."

Jane faced the PDI. "Did you scrape her fingernails? Swab for skin residue samples?"

"I believe we did." Dr. Sabatier stammered as she scanned the report. She snatched up a couple of plastic evidence collection bags. "I don't see it listed. I'll bag them now."

"Don't do that. Can't use plastic." Glancing around the room, Jane came up empty. "Humidity degrades DNA even faster. You should be using acid free paper bags. Don't you people know that?"

"How do you know that?" Dupree challenged.

"Who are you to tell me my job?" The PDI chorused.

"I'm ex-CSI. That should've been done at the crime scene. Too late, now. Any evidence you do find will get tossed outta court by any decent defense attorney."

"Is she right?" Gee asked, wide-eyed. "What a cluster fuck! You're supposed to be the professionals!"

"Every department has its own protocol," Dr. Sabatier stated defensively, thumbing a blue button mounted on the wall. "Thank you for your cooperation. We have what we need. This office will be in touch with any news."

"That's it?" Gee demanded.

"That's it. We'll be in touch." Dr. Sabatier repeated, her eyes glinting like steel.

Bordelon caught the door, politely holding it open as they filed into the hall. "And that's it for me, as well." He settled his hat. "I'll close Ms. Abellard's missing person's file and transition the case to Homicide. Ms. Pascoe?" Continuing down the hall, he spoke over his shoulder, buttoning his overcoat from the bottom up. "I'm truly sorry about your friend. I know this wasn't the answer we were hoping for. I hope the family can find closure." He paused. "On a personal note, I'll add you to my prayers and buy a mass for Ms. Abellard. Detective Dupree will be the case lead, going forward, but please don't hesitate to bring me in if you need to. I want to see this case successfully closed, since it's my last one."

"That's right! I forgot." Dupree slid to a stop. "What's today's count?"

"Ten more days." Bordelon smoothed his lapels. "Until I retire. Thirty-four years on the force should be enough for any man. Call the governor. I'm due for parole." He joked gently, tipping his hat, turning on his heel and striding for the door.

Gee's shoulders dropped as she watched him go. "Detective Dupree? You gonna quit on us, too?"

"No, I'm not." Dupree raised his chin. "I want an answer."

"And I'm not going anywhere, Gee," Jane stated. "I'll see this through."

"Good." Gee balled her fists. "Because I'm going to find out who did this to Fancy and make them pay. So, what do we do now?"

Jane considered the evidence. "We know her wallet was rifled. Her bank could tell us if some scumbag tried using her debit or credit cards. If he accessed an ATM, we can subpoena the video."

"Already asked Judge Duquesne for a subpoena this morning." Dupree smirked.

"Subpoena Fancy's phone company records, too. Trace any calls she made or received over the last few weeks. Try to spot a pattern or a singularity."

"Keep going. You're doing my job for me." Dupree sounded sarcastic, but he looked impressed. "Anything more to suggest?"

"Yes. Track down the current location of her phone using GPS. If the killer sold it for scrap, which I'm guessing he did, the recycling center should have security video. If it's a pawnshop, even better. I know they store video. Plenty of them in the Ninth Ward. We might get lucky, get a hit."

Gee looked puzzled. "You're still thinking Fancy was robbed? This wasn't a hate crime?"

That's a good question. Jane paused. *What do I think really happened?* She recalled the grisly details from the viewing room. *Fancy's murder was vicious and deliberate. You don't kick a person to death by accident.* Guilt rippled through her core. *Did I automatically fall into my old comfortable way of thinking because it was easier than engaging my brain and thinking outside the box? I've kept up with the Yahoo headlines. Gee's gender fluid world is under attack from right wing hate groups and extremist evangelicals. LGBTQ civil rights protections are being rescinded by the Trump administration every day. Maybe I need to trim my sails and shift my way of thinking?*

Dupree's cellphone buzzed. Pulling it from his pocket, he frowned. "I need to take this." He sped for the door. "I'll follow up. Be in touch."

Jane watched him go. *What if Dupree doesn't find Fancy's killer? What if he gets busy, and lets it drop?* Her need for justice breached the surface of her rocky emotional plane like a spouting whale. *Hate crimes are on the rise. The wrong element is getting stirred up. Soon enough, this new behavior will become our new norm. What do I want my reality to be?*

She swallowed thickly. "No, you're right, Gee. This has 'hate crime' written all over it. No matter who did this, or why, we need to stop this scumbag before he hurts anyone else."

"We?" Gee asked, wide-eyed. "We need to stop him?"

"Yes." Jane stated flatly. "We."

Ignoring her own rising mindless panic, Jane shut her eyes as she recalled the searingly clear details of her own very, very bad day on Nantucket four years ago, when she scoped down her extended arms and heart-centered a 9MM clip into another monster until he was dead. *And I'm not sorry I did it, not one bit.* She opened her eyes. "We're going to fight this and we need to win. I won't live in a world that has this kind of evil in it."

"I'm in." Gee stared, unblinking. "*Oui.*"

CHAPTER TWENTY-FIVE

"You *reconfrontant* working solo tonight?" Numa Hebert sat hunched behind the security console, scowling. "Had to pull Christophe in early to cover daylight."

"Why?" Jane studied her boss. Numa was sweating profusely, his cheekbones spider-webbed with bright broken capillaries. As usual, he looked like a heart attack waiting to happen. "Where's Cal?"

"Fuck if I know. Probably took off running. The cops are after him." Numa flattened his greasy bangs against his forehead until he looked like Napoleon. Pushing away from the monitors, he freed his suspendered potbelly, which ballooned as he rose. "Caught that fucker working the system. Cops asked me to see who leased #301 and guess what? It's not on the books, but Cal issued an entry fob for it. Turns out Cal's been letting unauthorized people on site." He squinted. "You know anything about that?"

"Absolutely not." Jane lied. *But I had my suspicion.*

"What a cluster fuck." Numa struggled into his windbreaker. "Now the owners want me to figure out which units are leased legit. What am I? An accountant?" He repeatedly pursed his lips. "Level Three's *de'pouille,* a real mess now that the cops got done with it." Snaring a paper printout with his fingertips, he tapped a floor plan schematic. "301, next to the fire door. You stay out of there, sweetheart. Trust me. You don't want to get involved with any part of this."

Oh, but I already am. Fancy was a friend. Jane chanced a random cast for information. *How much do you know, Numa?* "The news said they recovered a body."

134

"Fuck yeah, and not for the first time." Numa zipped his windbreaker to his throat. "Thought we was done with that when we chased the druggies out. That fentanyl is some lethal shit." He massaged his brow. "Cops are thinking this is something different though, something more, I could tell. Owners told me to shut my trap until the cops got a warrant and then be as helpful as heck. Fuck if they didn't show up with one. Spent the whole day crawling up my ass. Who rented #301? How did they pay? Got bank info or a street address? Show us the corridor videos. Had to explain that we didn't *have* corridor videos; took everything in me to convince the cheap ass owners to install security cams in the stairwells last year. Now I look like an ass wipe. I'm cashed." He looked it. "Red will relieve you at six. Text me if there's an emergency," he grimaced sourly, "right after you dial 911." He turned for the door. "I'll be down at The Deuce. I need a drink or two, maybe even three. Fuck. It's been that kinda day."

Got it. Jane watched until Numa turned the corner for the garage. *Anyone else in here with me?* Spinning the chair around, she double-clicked the mouse and opened the SecureVue access log. The last discharge entry read: 9:48 PM, Unit #111. The associated black and white still photo capture was so distorted and grainy it could have come from Mars. Jane relaxed. *Crap software, but at least the exit camera is online again.*

I'm alone. Normally she waited until after she saw Numa's black Honda CR-V on the exit turnstile monitor to patrol, but Jane itched to see the crime scene where Fancy's corpse was recovered. *Because you never know. NOPD CSI might've overlooked something. They were careless about bagging Fancy's hands. What else did they miss?*

Grabbing her security fob, Jane headed for the stairwell, trotting up to Level Three, anticipation pushing her to take the concrete steps two at a time. Swiping the keypad, she shouldered the heavy steel fire door open, her eyes immediately tearing up. *Industrial ammonia-based cleaner. That and bleach are two giveaway crime scene tells.* Pressing her tongue to the roof of her mouth, she blanketed the smell and studied the scene.

Unit #301's rolling accordion gate was down, but the Guardian Storage installed locking bolt had been ruthlessly drilled out. Curly metal shavings littered the floor. The unit was now padlocked secured by a heavy chain, its square steel frame cobwebbed with yellow NOPD CSI roll tape. The court ordered search warrant Numa mentioned was prominently taped to a support pillar. *Standard protocol. Numa was right. Sealed up tight as a clam. No way I'm getting in there.* Jane chewed her lip. *What did CSI find in there besides Fancy's corpse? I might pry that intel out of Dupree, but he'll be keeping the case details close to his vest.* She dropped her hands to her hips. *What's my next step? What more can I do? We need to catch this killer! I need more data.*

Got it. Jane raced back to the office. Sliding behind the security console, she launched the SecureVue application. Scrolling through the menu options, she hovered the mouse over the MasterStore archive. *Probably shouldn't be doing this.* Her conscience prickled uneasily. *Owner records are confidential. Not open to the public.* She settled in. *But I'm not the public. I'm Security, right?*

Shit! Snatching her hand off the mouse, Jane gasped as she recognized the imminent danger. *The second I open this file it'll automatically refresh the time/date stamp. Dupree will know that I've searched it.* Her head swam at the enormity of her near error. Slowly releasing her breath, she pulled the desk drawer open and started searching.

This'll work. Inserting the thumb drive into the PC port, she copied the MasterStore file over. *No going back now.* She double-clicked the mouse.

An orange ERROR message bar filled the screen.

ENTER PASSWORD.

"Shit." Jane fell back against the chair. *Give him some credit. Numa's savvier than I thought.* Pushing away from the console, she walked to Numa's desk and started riffling through his messy stacks of reports and manila folders before spotting an index card tucked face down in one corner of his old school desk calendar blotter. *Wanna bet?* Jane flipped the card over. *Jackpot.* She snorted. *So much for stated client privacy concerns and security.*

Returning to the console, she carefully henpecked GUARDIAN007 into the password field and pressed ENTER.

The MasterStore file blinked twice before it opened. Jane leaned in. Sliding the keyboard closer, she typed Control/F and searched for Unit #301. The spreadsheet immediately rolled to an entry highlighted in yellow:

OWNER *301   OPEN   PAYMENT METHOD: N/A

"No registered owner." Jane released the keyboard. *That confirms what Numa said about Cal taking cash payments under the table. Dead end.* She continued to stare at the blinking single line entry. *Or is it? Hold up.* Her pulse started to hammer as she tabbed through the remaining columns. *Numa said Cal gave out an entry fob for #301. What does the MasterStore vehicle ID column say? If I crosscheck the vehicle ID for #301 against the gate entry camera I'll get a screen shot of the killer!*

The vehicle ID column was blank. "Shit! Cal!" Jane shouted, tightening her hands into fists. *Wait!* She paused. *Think this through. Maybe I've been going at it backwards? The EntryLog file is associated with a unit number. Search* that *archive. EntryLog might give me what I need.*

Quickly returning to the main menu, Jane double-clicked the EntryLog tab and a second spreadsheet opened. Using Control/F she repeated the search for Unit #301.

The search box stalled and pulsed blankly. Hitting ENTER again, harder, Jane repeated the search and got the same negative result. *Zero vehicle entries for Unit #301? That doesn't make sense.* Widening the date range search to cover the previous ninety days, Jane tried again, her shoulders hunched to her ears. *Nothing? How can that be? The killer deposited Fancy's body on Saturday night. He didn't carry her up from the street. We would've captured that on the stairwell cam.*

Gooseflesh crawled up Jane's forearms as another suggestion gelled.

The killer signed in under another, different unit.

Hammering the keyboard, she tightened the date range search to the previous four days. *The killer wouldn't be one and done. He'd keep coming back to check his work.* Selecting SORT, she hit ENTER. The EntryLog spreadsheet automatically refreshed. Holding her breath, Jane studied the repeated visit entries.

There were six in-and-out line items for Unit #515.

#515? Jane sat back, puzzled. *No one's using Level Five. Those are the empty music studios.* Returning to the MasterStore report, she clicked Control/F and initiated a new search:

OWNER *515 ORGANIZATION: ATPP   PAYMENT METHOD: CASH

ATPP? Fuck. Sour dread filled her empty stomach. *This can't be good.* Minimizing the MasterFile report screen, she launched Google. The primary search results confirmed her concern. She double clicked the lead hyperlink and the American True Patriot Party website displayed.

She studied the white supremacist website filled with hate-filled catch phrases and glaringly graphic propaganda. The ATPP's mission statement was clearly stated in bold type: **America was created for white Christian Anglo/Europeans by white Christian Anglo/Europeans. All other ethnicities, races, religions, and demographics are absolutely not compatible with American culture. As such, a mass exodus, isolation, apartheid, or segregation must be restored to maintain our nation.**

"Fuck me. Camps." Her stomach roiled. "They're talking concentration camps again." She slowly lowered her forehead to rest on her folded hands. *Well? I knew they were out there, and I ignored it and now here we are. This shit makes me sick.* She considered the rising human rights abuses and the increase in rage and injustice being reported daily in the news. *The question is: what am I going to do about it? I can't ignore this shit anymore. It's time to speak up, take a stand. This shit is real, and I need to do something about it.*

Reaching for the mouse, she tabbed through the MasterFile log for the license tag associated with Unit #515. This time, she hit pay dirt.

OWNER *515 ORGANIZATION: ATPP   VEHICLE   ID: CV 2M77

She stared at the Confederate flag boldly printed on the special interest Louisiana plate. "'Sons of Confederate Veterans.'" Jane murmured. "State issued plate. Crissakes! How is this shit still allowed?" Realizing the true extent and the plate's full meaning, she felt electrified by outrage. "How the fuck can you still order this plate from a state DMV?"

Rolling the chair closer to the console, she returned to the EntryLog archive, typed 'CV 2M77' into the search field and waited, her shoulders hunched to her ears.

A still photo slowly filled the monitor in banded gray sections, but she got a hit.

"Nailed you, fucker." Jane stared at the battered pickup truck. *Ford F-150. An early one. 1983, '84? Basic trim package.* Half of the Louisiana car tag was in shadow, but it was enough. She released her breath. *I've got something solid here. This could be Fancy's killer.*

She leaned in. *I need to tell Dupree.* She frowned. *But how do I share this intel with him? He'll know I illegally cracked these files. I'll get canned and he can't use this evidence in court.* Tapping her lips, she considered her options. *What if I tell Dupree anonymously? How could that work?* She rose to her feet. *I could lose my job over nothing. I don't even know what's in Unit #501.* Slipping her phone and her security fob into her pocket, she clipped a duty taser to her belt. Crossing the room, she opened Numa's desk drawer and grabbed his set of Guardian's master keys.

Only one way to find out. Let's go see.

CHAPTER TWENTY-SIX

The overhead lighting buzzed on with a snap. *Never liked Level 5. Music studios are spooky as hell like vacant theaters or empty churches and barns. They have a presence.* The corridor was so still that Jane's measured footsteps echoed off the concrete walls as her shoulders instinctively crept up to her ears. *It feels like something big is watching me.*

Unit #501, right? Gripping the master keys, she eyed the three jumbo floor-to-ceiling storage units on the left. The three darkened music studios were on her right, finishing up that row with a built-in two-story reverb chamber whose smooth circular wall rose thirty feet straight up through Level Six like an empty corn silo. The reverb chamber only had one door in and it used the same door out. *That thing gives me the creeps.*

She spotted a line of dried muddy footprints leading to Studio One. *Gotta be Ken's. No one else uses these studios.* She followed them first, cupping her hands to peer through the slotted tinted windows and testing the locks on all three doors to make sure she was truly alone. Studio Three still housed a monster tabbed Legacy mixer deck, but all three studios looked derelict, their isolation booths filled with cast off speakers, mic stands, and amps.

All clear. Spinning on her heel, she trotted to Unit #501.

The locking deadbolt mechanism opened easily under Numa's master key. Bending both knees, Jane rolled the accordion door overhead and out of the way and quickly scanned the contents. The unit was almost empty except for a double-stacked row of taped up cardboard packing boxes and a rolled up blue plastic tarp shoved against the rear wall.

Jane stepped in. The hairs on her forearms rose, individually shifting as if they were charged with static electricity from an unseen summer storm. *Smells like rotten hamburger.* She grabbed her nose. Taking another step forward, she noticed a glistening spray of crimson droplets splattered on the floor. *That's not random.* Ordering her stiffened legs forward, she closed the distance to the tarp, gasping with the sucker punch as her eyes focused and her brain suddenly made sense of what she saw.

Step away! Step away now! Call Dupree! Her CSI training commanded. *Sorry, no can do.* Her knees popped as she knelt. *I can't un-see his shoe.*

"Oh, Cal." Her heart shattered. "What did you do?"

Sliding her jacket sleeve over her hand, she reached for the tarp, the stiff plastic crackling under her fingertips like brittle harbor ice fractured by a rising tide. *Marva will be devastated when she finds out.*

Pushing the tarp aside as one piece, Jane lost her balance, landing hard on her elbow and falling on her ass before scrambling to her feet, her pulse roaring in her ears.

Numa?

Numa lay slumped like a bundle of dirty rags in a puddle of coagulating blood that still seeped from the deep stab wound in his chest. His head lolled against his shoulder, his eyes half-closed, his slack jaw open and his face a chalky gray.

Bending forward, Jane gripped her knees. She couldn't get enough air. *But I saw Numa leave the building!* Her rational mind raised an objection. *No, that's not right. I saw him leave the office. I was in too much of a hurry to watch for his car leaving on the exit cam.* She shivered as needles of dread prickled her spine. *Numa met the killer on the way to his car.* She gasped for breath. *But I checked the entry log! No one else is here.* Her mind swayed drunkenly and then righted as she unclipped the taser from her belt. *That entry log info is dodgy and always has been. The killer might still be in the building with me.* Her hand ached to feel the weight of her service Glock pulling on her wrist the way it used to as she chanced another scan of the unit. *I don't see a knife. Unless it's in one of these boxes the killer took it with him.*

Stumbling into the corridor, her pulse pounding in her ears, she pinned her shoulders against a wide support pillar and speed-dialed Dupree. *Come on. Come on.* She stared at her phone as it refused to connect. *Shit. I need more bars. I'm inside tons of concrete. I need to get to the office or to the roof.* Indecision made her pause. *Do I go up or down? Does that rooftop panel even open?* She fingered the master keys. *It's got a separate chain.* She studied the stairwell, struggling to stay focused but feeling trapped and knowing she needed to make her decision. *Down it is. What are my options? Freight elevator? No, too much noise. Exit ramp? No fucking way I'm outrunning his truck if he's in here. Fine.* Jane swallowed. *Stairwell it is.*

Gripping the taser in her left hand, she swiped the key fob over the security pad, flinching as the shrill acknowledgement beep trilled. *If he's here, he knows I'm on my way down.* Her heartbeat thudded in her ears. *Fuck. I really don't want to do this.*

Pausing on the landing, she rose onto her toes. *I have a taser. He has a knife.* Her previous police tactical training took over like forgotten muscle memory. *I've got six seconds to react when I see him.* She filled her lungs with air. *Six seconds has to be enough.*

Shoving the door open, she started down, alert to the ends of her fingertips.

Eight steps, pause, look, turn became her new mantra as she raced past Levels Five and Four. Glancing down the center railing, the stairwell appeared deserted, her footsteps and her breathing making the only sounds as she rounded the turn for Level Three.

Numa is dead and Cal is still missing bubbled up from her subconscious as she continued her descent. *The killer's erasing anyone who knows he's been using lockers at Guardian Storage.* Slamming the fire door open, Jane raced down the hall, pulling her phone from her pocket. Sliding into the office she locked the door, scanning the monitors as she speed-dialed Dupree.

"Dupree. It's late. What can I do for you?"

"Dupree?" Her pulse pounded so painfully her voice cracked. She had to swallow twice to get the words out. "Guardian Storage, Unit #501. Another homicide, Dupree. Numa Hebert, my boss. Stabbed, less than an hour ago. I need help. The killer may be on site with me."

She heard his quick intake.

"Are you safe? Is your location secure?"

"Yes, I think so." Jane tuned her ears to listen for the slightest whisper of sound. "I'm locked in the office. I have a taser. I want my fucking Glock!"

"Shelter in place. Jane? Don't ... touch ... anything. Stay exactly where you are. Do you copy? Answer me."

"Yes." She heard his scramble. "I copy."

"ETA is twelve minutes, fifteen tops. Stay on the line. I'm leaving now."

"Roger that." Setting her phone on speaker, Jane scrambled up to close the office blinds. They wouldn't stop a bullet, but in some primal way she felt safer behind their slatted screen. *Good luck with that.* Her rational mind scoffed. *Like a child hiding under the covers from the Bogey Man.* "Fuck off." She muttered, pulling a chair away from the center console and sitting with her back to the wall as she repeatedly glanced between the entrance camera monitor and her phone like a ticking pendulum clock.

"Still there? Did you notify anyone? The owners?"

"I don't even know who they are. Numa never shared that intel with me."

"Take care of this first." Dupree's voice sounded distant and grim. "Just so you know, if we can't get ahold of the owners, you're in charge."

"Got it." She heard Dupree's tires squeal.

"Talk to me. How did you find the body? Know where to look?"

"On patrol." She boldfaced lied. "I saw blood splatter on the floor and tracked it to that unit." Her instinct warned her it was time to stop lying to Dupree. *He's an ally you idiot, not a rival.* "Dupree? Wait. That's not right." She confessed. "I researched the ownership records on the unit where Fancy Abellard was found. Connected it to Unit #501. They're both rented by the same group, the American True Patriot Party."

"The what?"

She heard his intake again.

"The ATPP?"

"There's more." Her words tumbled out. "I have a still photo capture of an associated vehicle with Louisiana tag, CV 2M77." For the first time in years, Jane's memory seemed crystal clear and her brain processed the information like a well-oiled machine. "An early Ford F-150 pickup truck. I think it's our killer, Dupree. That's where we should look."

"That's where I should look." The entrance monitor flared as a Crown Vic and an unmarked unit drove up. Dupree's image blinked into the grainy camera next to the security gate's jointed arm. "Let us in. I want to know what's going on."

You and me, both. Jane slammed the entry access button with her fist. *Because this fucker is closing in.* Reaching for the taser, she hurried to join Dupree, gripped by a riptide of relief so great she stumbled as she glimpsed an end to her responsibilities. *Time to hand it over to the professionals. I just want to be left alone again to do my thing.*

No, I don't. Sudden insight illuminated her mind. *This is my thing. I love doing this shit because this is what I do best.* Picking up her pace, Jane remembered: *This is the best version of who I really am. When did I forget that? I'm as fucking professional as it gets.*

CHAPTER TWENTY-SEVEN

Jane dribbled a thin thread of hand lotion around the inside of her new shoes, hoping that it might soften the cheap pleather that kept pinching her baby toes. The open-toed sandals were horribly out of season, but they were almost the right size and they had only been six bucks in the Dollar Store's clearance bin.

She nervously checked the kitchen clock radio. 6:17 PM. *Two minutes since the last time I looked.* Squeezing her protesting feet back under the straps, she studied her hands. *Why am I trembling? It's only a date. I wasn't this fucking nervous running down that stairwell looking for a killer.*

Ryan Embry was due to swing by and pick her up at any moment. Jane kept listening for the sound of his van pulling into the driveway. The Deuce offered live music without a cover charge on their Wednesday Over the Hump Night and he'd scored a table. She looked down at Mr. Piddles, panting happily at her feet.

"What d'you think, Biggie P? Am I ridiculous?"

He thumped his tail against the floor as she finished primping. At least she was happy with her hair. The straightening iron had worked its magic and smooth waves framed her face. She critically studied her dress, still uncertain if she actually liked the loud floral pattern or not. *Am I showing too much cleavage for a first date? What message am I sending? Here I am, love me? I'm thirty-four years old. I'm desperate?* Jane frowned sourly. *Who am I kidding? This isn't the real me. This isn't who I really am.* Closing her eyes, she gripped the bathroom sink. *Stop thinking like that immediately! I need to be open to this, give it a fair chance. If I don't try something new, nothing will change.*

"Piddles?" She reached for her new dangling crystal earrings. "Your mother is a head case."

There was a rap at the door. Her heart leapt into her throat with a flurry of nervous butterflies. Snatching a breath, Jane turned, tripping over the bathroom threshold in her strappy and unfamiliar heels. Piddles leapt out of her way, barking happily and following her into the front room, excitedly pawing the air while dancing on his hind legs.

"Get out of my way, dog." Jane smoothed her hair. Squaring her shoulders, she swept through the living room, lightly tapping a lampshade to level it and shifting the throw pillow from the window seat to the chair. *That's odd. When did I move that pillow there?* Shrugging off the question, she unlocked the door.

"Hey, Jane."

Ryan stood framed in the doorway, his face and shoulders lit golden by the overhead bug light. Jane noticed that in her new heels she could look at him dead on, eye to eye. He sported a new haircut now, too, super mod, his hair left longer on top but trimmed tight to the sides like Chris Martin from Cold Play. His neatly pressed dress shirt collar was open and he was wearing a silver Mercury dime on a black cord around his neck. Studying her, his eyes widened.

"You look great, Jane! That a new dress?"

"It is." She nervously ran a hand over her exposed collarbones to check her bra straps.

"Looks nice." He extended a tissue paper wrapped bouquet of mixed roses and stared at his feet. "My mom insisted I bring you these." He mumbled. "She's old school that way."

"I'll put them in water." *Oh, crap.* Jane swallowed. *Housekeeping failure number 1001.* Stepping into the kitchen, she placed the flowers in the sink. *Do I even own a vase?*

"Your place looks nice. Cozy." Reaching down, he scratched Mr. Piddle's ears. "How you doin', buddy?" Straightening, he awkwardly folded his arms. "I wasn't sure if we should still go out, you know, with Fancy being dead and all, but then I thought Fancy'd be the last one to miss out on a date. Know what I mean?"

"I do," Jane replied, distractedly. "You're right." She started opening and closing the pantry doors, searching for anything that might hold the bouquet. *Woman is a tool-making animal, girlfriend. Find something, quick.*

A random piece of Mr. Piddle's kibble crunched underfoot as Ryan stepped into the cramped kitchen. "Jane? You okay?"

She pressed her fingers to her throbbing temples. "Yes, I am. I'm sorry, Ryan. I don't have a vase for these flowers."

"Use this." Reaching past, he lifted a dusty Mason quart jar off a shelf. Tipping the dried dead spider out of it into the trashcan, he turned the tap on and filled it with fresh water. "I didn't mean to make you more work."

"I'm not much of a housekeeper." Jane flushed. Ryan stood so close that she felt his body heat radiating off of him in waves.

"I'm not looking for one." He flicked the water droplets from his fingers. "You've met my mother. Happiest day of her life was the day she brought home plastic slipcovers and zip locked her furniture inside Baggies."

Setting the Mason jar on the counter, he reached out his hand and gently raised Jane's chin to meet his eyes. She felt the rough scratch from the callous on his fingertips.

"I'm not looking for that kind of girl, Jane. You should know that."

His eyes were a clear and bottomless blue. Jane felt an electric thrill tickle her core in the very same instant she heard the protesting voice in her mind. *I'm not a girl, Ryan. I'm a woman.* She bit back her retort. *Don't be so critical! He's trying to be nice. Give the guy a decent chance.*

Ryan pulled back, cocking his head, and Jane caught the spark of self-deprecating humor in his eyes. Stuffing the roses into the Mason jar, he set them on the counter.

"Dating you is like dating Cinderella." He whispered as she walked by. "We should get going if I need to get you home by nine."

"It's only fair." Slipping into her jacket, Jane patted her pockets to make sure she had her iPhone and her wallet. "I need to give Biggie a chance to pee before my shift starts."

Locking the door, she followed Ryan toward the van, stuffing her hands in her pockets and considering the god-awful brown and orange Guardian Storage uniform waiting for her upstairs. "After ten I turn back into a pumpkin."

"I've admired you in that uniform."

"You have? When did you see me wearing it?"

Ryan laughed uncertainly as he politely held the passenger door open. "We cross paths. I see you on your way to work when I'm coming home. What color is that supposed to be anyway? Shitty brown?" Stepping aside, he waited for Jane to climb in. "Don't mind the van. Delta gives me a solid allowance for gas and mileage. Be a shame to waste it."

"Beats taking the bus." Jane agreed, cocking her thumb at the refurbished shed. "We could always take my bike."

"I'd do that." Ryan scanned the night sky. "Only because it would give me an excuse to grab onto you, but it might rain. I'd hate for you to ruin that pretty dress."

"I'm good with the van." Jane climbed in. Resting both hands limply in her lap, she felt ruffled by irritation as Ryan shut the door. *I know he's being a Southern gentleman, but I hate feeling passive. Who made this stupid rule up?*

Using the side mirror, she watched Ryan circle the rear bumper as she settled in. The van smelled like male funk, burnt hair, and Windex. *Give him credit. He tried cleaning it up.* An unidentified metal bar started prodding her kidneys and she shifted uncomfortably in her seat. *This van would make the perfect covert cover. No one notices a Delta Power van parked on the street.*

Reaching for the seatbelt buckle, her fingers brushed a mound of crumpled paper receipts. Pushing aside a Guardian Storage business card, she studied a red and yellow cardboard box tucked into the center console. *Bengal Tiger Military Classic AK ammo? Steel jacketed hollow point, 124 grains.* Jane sat back. *Cop killers. What's Ryan doing with these?*

Opening his door, he caught her stare. "Sorry about that." The ammo box rattled as he slipped it under his seat. "Carrying those for a buddy of mine."

"With an AK-47? Assault rifles are banned in Massachusetts."

He clambered in. "This is Louisiana. We fight for our rights."

Let it go. Jane briskly rubbed her arms. *He's not doing anything wrong. Stop playing detective and enjoy yourself. This is supposed to be a date!*

Chapter Twenty-Eight

Ryan lightly rested his hand on her headrest as he backed the van onto St. Claude Avenue. "Jane? Do me a solid? Tyler lost his security badge; he thinks on Saturday night. If you see it lying around, will you snag it for him? Delta's gonna tag him sixty-five bucks to replace it if he don't find it by Friday."

"Of course." She agreed. "Hey, sixty-five bucks is sixty-five bucks."

"That's what I say." Crows' feet circled Ryan's eyes as he smiled. "It'd cover more than a couple of cases of good beer."

Jane unzipped her jacket. The heater was blasting and the van was uncomfortably warm. "Saturday night was insane. How's Tyler doing?"

"Gee loosened his front teeth, but he'll survive." Ryan turned right on Lesseps Street. "We might meet up for a beer later." Turning his head, he waggled his eyebrows. "Unless you decide to call off sick and we extend our date."

"Can't afford to do that." Jane quickly defused his suggestion. "No paid sick leave. S'weird to think that Saturday was the night Fancy got killed. Already feels like a lifetime ago. It's only been four days."

Ryan shrugged casually. "Fancy liked living on the edge. Something bad was bound to happen to her, sooner or later."

Jane recalled the shattered human horror displayed on the autopsy table. "No one deserves what happened to her, Ryan. I don't care what kind of fucking lifestyle she was living." Folding her arms, Jane stared out the window into the night. Her ghostly reflection stared back and she felt the steely edge of the guilt and questioning uncertainty she lived with every day. *If no one deserves to die then how do I justify killing Mason Hollister?* Leaning hard on her resolve, the answer came to her like the tolling of a distant channel buoy. *Hollister was a monster, enabled because he had unlimited power and money. He deserved every bit of what he got.* Inhaling a shuddering breath, Jane owned it. *He deserved the death I gave him. I sent him straight to Hell where he belongs.*

Finding an open spot at the curb, Ryan masterfully parallel parked. Leaning over, he shut off the van. The engine started ticking as it cooled. His forehead puckered with concern. "*Chere Mere* said you had more trouble at work?"

"We did. My boss got killed last night. I found him."

"Shit, Jane, are you alright?" Ryan gaped. "I didn't know! We could've done this another time."

"I didn't want to do that." She answered hurriedly. "I gave it a lot of thought. I know it sounds cold, but all I wanted to do was something normal."

"Sounds like you need to find someplace different to work." Ryan rested his forearms on the steering wheel. "Someplace safer than Guardian Storage."

"It's safe enough," she replied grimly. "I've got NOPD on speed dial."

"Two murders in one week? What do the po-po say's going on?"

Jane hesitated. She had repeatedly stated her hate crime theory to Dupree at their interview that morning. "They're investigating. Plus one of my co-workers, Cal is missing."

"They're thinking it's three people now? Got any suspects?"

"It's not like Dupree's going to share any real intel with me." She temporized as the December chill started seeping through the van's steel walls. "I'm not a cop."

"Shit happens though, Jane, right? Life goes on?"

"Yes." She agreed slowly. "Life goes on. And we get left behind to deal with it."

151

"You sound so sad, Jane. Depressed. Sounds like you've been through it." Unbuckling his seatbelt, Ryan shifted sideways. "You don't need to hold back with me. I can take it. I want us to be friends, good friends." His Adam's apple bobbed. "My ex was a bitch." He gestured a denial with both hands. "But I can already tell you're not like her, not one bit. You're something different, something special. I think we could be good for each other."

Jane stopped twining her fingers. *Don't be such a coward. He's just sharing his feelings.* She nerved herself to look up again. Ryan was sharing his adorably winning grin, but his words had sounded insincere to her ears and his smile seemed pasted on. She couldn't find any genuine warmth or connection in it. *Is it me? Or him?* Jane felt gripped by distrust. *Why do I feel like I'm being groomed, like Ryan's memorized a script?*

"Let's see how it goes."

"O-kay." Opening his door, Ryan stepped into the street, drawling the word into two syllables. "Slow and steady wins the race."

Leaving the van, he looked surprised to see her already standing on the sidewalk.

"I would've gotten your door," he stated uncertainly, politely offering Jane his arm.

"I'm still learning this Southern charm thing." Jane grasped it hesitantly, letting Ryan lead her up the slanted sidewalk to the familiar side door.

"Damn, Jane. Any man here would be proud to be seen walking into The Deuce with you."

As he thumbed the entry button, Ryan smiled, looking odd with one half of his face lit red and the other half lit blue from the neon commercial beer sign hanging in the window.

"This neighborhood's called the Bar-Muda Triangle." He joked. "Between Vaughn's, BJ's Lounge and Bacchanal, but The Deuce gets my vote for the best blues music in town hands down, every damn time."

"I agree."

The door buzzed and he pulled it open. "You've been here before?"

An explosion of light, heat, laughter and the rising notes from a heartfelt alto sax spilled into the street. *This is more like it.* Jane immediately felt her spirit rise to match the brassy snappy beat.

"Girlfriend!" Adele swooped over shouldering a tray littered with tipped shot glasses and empty beer bottles. "Where have you been? Haven't seen you in months! Cute dress!" Adele's grin showcased her platinum grill. "Who's this handsome fellow you've got with you?"

"Ryan Embry." He bowed gallantly. "It's our first date. Won't be the last."

Adele slid the tray onto the corner bar. "Who's paying?"

"I am."

"Sugar daddy! He's a keeper." She winked, scanning the room. "I'm going to sit you two at one of my tables. Follow me."

"You already like this place, Jane?" Ryan looked pleased. "Then it was a good pick."

Adele pulled out her notepad. "What can I brang you to drink?"

"Got Covington Amber?"

"Sure do. On tap."

"Bring me a tall one of those. Jane? How 'bout you?"

"Club soda and lime, please, Adele."

"Really?" Ryan raised an eyebrow. "One beer won't hurt you. Call it barley soup."

"No, I can't go to work with beer breath."

"I have mints," Adele offered.

"Club soda and lime, please, Adele. Like I said."

"*Laissez le bon temps,* girlfriend." Adele scribbled a note. "One tall Covington with a 'why bother.'" She cocked her hip. "Chef's special tonight is all-you-can-eat frog's legs. Big fat bullfrogs, too. Saw them getting prepped in the kitchen. Lots of meat."

Hot bile splashed the back of Jane's throat. Her tongue suddenly felt thick and her gorge rose at the thought of chewing on amphibian. "Oh hell, no."

Ryan scooted closer. "You should try them, Jane. They're *good*. Some folks like eating frog better than eating chicken."

"I'm not that kind of folk." *What else have they got?* Jane scanned the menu looking for another choice.

Adele hesitated. "Need a few minutes?"

"I'm ready." Folding his menu, Ryan possessively cocked his thumb. "She's got me on a schedule. I'll take the alligator tail. Jane? What'll you have?"

Tall beer with fried alligator tail? Give me heartburn for a month. "Shrimp and grits, please, Adele. Thanks."

"Coming up." She pointed her pen. "I'll make sure you get extra gravy, *lagniappe.*"

"What?" Ryan caught Jane's eye. "You some kind of vegetarian? You don't eat alligator, neither?"

"Alligator's a reptile, Ryan. Same thing as eating snake."

"Snake's delicious!" Playful humor danced in his eyes. "Tastes just like chicken."

"Seriously, dude? Are you fucking with me?" Jane rested her palms on the table. "If you say that one more time I won't be able to eat chicken again either!"

He howled with laughter.

"Of course, I'm fucking with you, Jane! Eat whatever the fuck you want. It's a free country." He smacked his lips appreciatively as Adele returned with their drinks, raising his beer in a toast. "Chin, chin. Here's to our first date! I'm having fun already."

CHAPTER TWENTY-NINE

Sipping his beer, Ryan studied Jane steadily over his glass. She could see that he was thinking.

"What?" She asked.

His cold glass left a condensation ring on the table. Pointing his finger, Ryan drew a complicated crosshatched design through it.

"I need to be honest with you, Jane. You deserve that." He released a breath that puffed out his cheeks. "I've never met a woman like you before. You're so badass. Work security, ride a boss bike." He cocked his head. "We don't grow women like you down here much."

She twisted the lime wedge into her drink. "That's a good thing, right?"

"Sure is. That's what I meant." His forehead creased into wrinkles. "What's your story?"

"Easy enough." She gave the sparkling club soda a stir. "I'm a Yankee from Massachusetts, from an island off the coast -"

"I knew you were a Yankee from the way you talked." He interrupted, smiling warmly. "Won't hold it against you."

She admired the rising bubbles in her glass. "Used to be a cop. Didn't work out, so I left. I'm in NOLA now, working security."

"A cop, huh? Damn, Jane, that's sexy as hell." He wiped the foam off the corners of his mouth. "Still got your handcuffs? What kind of cop?"

"CSI Specialist." Jane flushed at the fib. She had backed away from stating 'detective' since that title seemed to put people off. "Liked the work. Loved the people. Couldn't manage the stress. PTSD put me out of

155

commission. End of story."

She glanced at the blues band tucked into the corner. The Deuce was overly warm with the accumulated heat from the crowded tables and the many enthusiastic dancers. Her nose tickled, and she caught the scent of Old Spice wafting off Ryan from across the table as she felt the preliminary warning itch. *Oh crap, no. Not now.* Of all of the incense scents, sandalwood was her nemesis. It raised hives on her skin. *Who wears Old Spice anymore?* She fumed. *Did Ryan inherit a bottle from his dad?* She turned aside as Ryan leaned in.

"So, Jane, what're your plans?"

"Plans?" Glancing down, she noted the red welts already beginning to pattern her wrists.

"You gonna stay in NOLA or just passing through?"

"Not sure yet." The temptation was irresistible. Sliding both hands beneath the table, she began to scratch. The immediate sense of relief was exquisite. "Why?"

"Because." Ryan softened his tone. "I'm not playing around. I meant it when I said I think you're something special." He resettled his chair. "I'm looking for a special relationship, the right relationship, and I think you're it."

"Crissakes, Ryan!" Jane scratched even harder. "It's only our first date!"

His eyes turned frosty and he looked affronted. Sliding his chair to the opposite side of the table, he picked up his beer.

"I get it. Red light." He frowned sourly. "Moving too fast again." He sounded sarcastic. "I'll give you credit. You're direct."

"Here you go." Adele arrived with their meal. Sliding the tray onto their table, she used both hands to offload Jane's fragrant bowl of shrimp and grits as the briny seafood scented the air. Next, she hefted an oval platter piled high with a golden mound of fried lumps surrounding a white china bowl of speckled remoulade dipping sauce.

Ryan rubbed his hands together appreciatively. "Let me at it!"

"Another beer?" Adele asked.

"You bet. Fill me up." Snatching a hot nugget, Ryan tossed it from hand to hand. "Jane? How 'bout you?"

"I'm good." She gave her grits a stir. "One club soda's my limit."

"Give me a holler," Adele turned, "if something ain't right."

Jane spooned up a bite. The rich smooth gravy coated her tongue and the fresh Gulf shrimp was so tasty she forgot her rash.

"So?" Ryan speared another nugget, chewing as he exhaled. "What else d'you want to talk about?" He pointed his fork. "Your turn. Last topic was mine."

"I'll play." Jane cooled another spoonful. "What was it like growing up with Gigi as a boy? Gee said you two were best buds. I'll bet that was interesting."

Ryan stopped chewing.

"I mean, must've been kinda crazy when you were kids. Did you two hang out?"

Ryan swallowed thickly. "Of course, we hung out only he was called Paul back then. His dad was a WarBird." He rested his elbow on the back of the chair. "How fucking awesome was that? Like growing up next door to Mick Jagger."

Reaching for his glass, he took a gulp, swishing the beer through his teeth. "None of the other kids had a famous dad. Ken Pascoe was on MTV." He speared another bite of alligator. "Sirius radio still plays his songs."

""Love Power"." Jane agreed. "He only had the one."

"One was plenty." Ryan shrugged. "It was more than most of us had. Our dads worked in the oil field," he smiled ruefully, "or for Delta Power."

I've never thought about Ryan's father. Jane lowered her spoon. "What did your dad do?"

"Fuck if I know." Finishing his beer with one long swallow, Ryan belched. "Took off before I got a chance to meet him."

"I'm sorry, Ryan. Must've been rough. Did your parents get divorced?"

"Seriously?" He snorted. "Chere Mere is devout. She'll stay married until the day we lay her in the dirt. She may already be a widow and not even know it." He rapped the table. "Ken Pascoe is the closest thing to a father I'll ever get. I love that man."

"Did Ken teach you to play music?"

"You know, he never did." Ryan's eyes softened with memory. "Kinda strange, actually. I've never seen Ken hold a guitar." He straightened. "If I hadn't seen him in that MTV video I wouldn't have believe it, but it's Ken Pascoe, alright. Standing in that park with those other guys, slapping that bass around. Looks like he's enjoying himself, having fun."

Jane started to relax. "He told me he gave up on music after the other WarBirds died."

"Yeah, I guess." Ryan polished the grease off his fingers. "That Big House was something to watch, growing up. I was in and out of it nearly every day. They never locked their doors. Miss Leslie's a nice lady, always canning vegetables and baking and keeping chickens, but she's a nut job." He leaned closer. "You do know that Aunt Babette's a witch, right?"

Jane felt a flicker of cold Puritanical fear. "I know she's a voodoo priestess."

"Same difference." He shrugged. "She's a real voodoo queen from New Orleans." Crossing his forearms, he rested his elbows on the table. "Gee and me used to sneak into her room to poke around. She's got candles and shit, an altar, all kinds of stuffed birds and feathers in glass jars, crazy shit hanging in her windows, real hoodoo stuff. Creepy." Dropping his chin, he waggled his fingers. "One time she almost caught us. Gee and me bolted for the back stairs, running hell for leather for the kitchen!"

He laughed. "I didn't sleep for three nights, thinking that every scratch on my bedroom screen was Aunt Babette trying to get me." He pushed the empty platter away. "Chere Mere had to seal my window shut with penny nails blessed by the priest for protection. Thank God I had a box fan that summer or I would've died."

Jane smiled. "You had a strange childhood."

"I surely did." Ryan eased back. "And it only got stranger when things changed with Gee." He met Jane's eyes. "I've seen some strange shit in my life, but nothing like what I saw happen to Gee. One day he's walking around being Paul, a boy." His voice wavered uncertainly. "The next day he's saying he's a girl."

"How old were you?" Jane set her spoon aside. "When her identity changed?"

"Eleven." He replied promptly. "I was eleven. You should've seen the look on folks' faces the first time Gee showed up at the church BBQ wearing that fucking polka dot bikini." Toying with his empty glass, he looked for Adele. "I hid in the shed I was so embarrassed, because they all knew Gee was my friend. Felt like they were blaming me for what happened to him. That somehow, I did it. That it was my fault." He cleared his throat. "Chere Mere straightened them all right out. She said Gee was a changeling and that's why his mother dumped him off."

"I heard another story." Jane leaned on her elbows. "That Ken really is her dad, but her mother was a WarBirds groupie with the band."

"*His* mother." Ryan corrected severely. "Say what you want, but Gee Pascoe is still a man."

"How can you say that Ryan?" Jane sat back. "Gee's a woman in a male-gendered body." She felt this statement with bedrock certainty.

"Nope." He pushed away. "Nope. Never gonna believe that. Gee was born carrying the gear. He's still a man." He repeatedly tapped the table. "In his heart Gee knows that, too. That's why he'll never get that surgery."

"Gee told me she won't get the surgery because she's afraid of dying on the table -"

Ryan mansplained right over the top of her, arguing blindly. "Then *he* needs to get help, do what *he* needs to do to accept the way God made him. Sweetheart, I'm right about this." He absently massaged his tattoo. "And Trump's right to kick them transgenders out of the military. Never should've been allowed in the first place."

Jane felt appalled. "Trump can't do that."

"He shore can." Ryan crowed. "He's Commander-in-Chief. Shouldn't have to spend my tax money, which should be spent defending our borders to pay for their transitions." Snapping his fingers to get Adele's attention, he rudely pointed to his empty glass. "Dumb bitch. Plus they disrupt morale, and every bit of that goes against God's law. Trump's right. It is time to take America back."

"Back to what?" Jane tried to reason. "When has it ever been better than it is right now? We can't change policy on people mid-stream, Ryan, or start treating them like second-class citizens. Trans people went into the military when it was approved. They've built their lives, their careers, and their families on that fact."

"Sure they did under Obama." He emphasized, dismissively waving his hand. "It's probably too complicated for you to understand. Don't worry. Donald Trump will straighten it out."

"How?" Jane's temper flared white-hot. "By stepping on civil liberties? By ignoring our Constitutional rights?" Recalling the permanent loss of her home, her family, and her friends because of her court settlement, Jane leaned in. "Ryan, I have followed the letter of the law my entire life and I have paid dearly for it." She swallowed. "I'm willing to accept that because the letter of the law is all we have keeping us civilized."

"No, Jane. No." Ryan stubbornly shook his head. "God's law is all we have. Gays and transgenders are abomination in the eyes of the Lord and you need to submit yourself to His authority and to His truth."

"Which God?" She raged. Scrambling up, Jane snatched at her jacket. "Which neo fundamentalist group sold you that bucket of absolute crap?"

Ryan stared up, goggle-eyed. "Where are you going?"

"Date night is over." Jane stated. And just like that, she knew it was true.

CHAPTER THIRTY

Too many women put up with this shit. Jane fumed, stuffing her arms into her jacket. *What the fuck was I thinking? What am I even doing with this guy?*

"Where are you going?" Ryan repeated in stunned disbelief.

Jane tugged out her phone. The inbox icon indicated one missed call and a voicemail from Delilah Gardere. *Sorry, Dee. Don't have time for you now.* Jane thumbed the app. "This independent woman is taking Uber. This was a mistake. We are never going to agree."

"No, Jane. Wait." Scrambling up, Ryan opened his wallet and threw two twenties on the table. "You don't know what you're doing."

"Wanna bet?" She strode across the dance floor. Shoving the side door open, she stepped into the night, hearing Ryan's frantic scuffling as he followed. "Don't call me again, Ryan. We are done."

Vaulting lithely over the handrail, he blocked her way.

"Wait. Jane? I can see you're angry. Listen. You're not thinking clearly. I'll give you a ride." He pointed. "Get in the van. It's right there."

"Get out of my fucking way, Ryan." Jane clenched her fists as adrenaline thrummed in her veins. "I'm not kidding. I'll blow through you like the breeze."

"Can you even hear yourself?" His raised voice cracked. "You're hysterical."

Stepping closer, she closed the gap. "I'm not hysterical, Ryan. What I am is truly pissed."

A cruising Crescent City taxi had its dome light on. "Taxi!" Dodging between two parked cars, Jane flagged it down.

Ryan followed her into the street. "Jane, wait! I can't show up without you! Chere Mere will ask what happened to us."

"Tell her you're an asshole." Flinging the rear door open, Jane slid across the brittle leather seat. "And there is no 'us.' You got that?"

"Where to, lady?"

"Bywater. 301 St. Claude Avenue." Jane snapped. Her hands shook as she unzipped the secret inner pocket of her wallet. She plucked out her emergency twenty-dollar bill.

"That's it, cunt?" Ryan shouted. "That's it? Then fuck you! Die, bitch!"

Asshole. Jane collapsed, dropping her wallet onto her lap. *This is fucking surreal.* Gripping her head with both hands, she felt like she was having an out-of-body experience with one half of her brain dispassionately observing their fight and the other half raging to go back and finish it. *Let it go. It's not worth it. Ryan's never going to change. And neither will I.*

She felt the familiar ripple of gut nausea as the whiny voice of her corrosive self-doubt and apologetic reason slipped into her mind like a hot knife. *Maybe I was too hard on him. I should have been more reasonable.* Her temper flared white-hot again. *Why should I be the one to apologize? Why? Because I spoiled our date?*

"Miss?"

The taxi driver nervously eyed her in the rearview mirror. "You gonna get sick? It's two hundred bucks extra if you puke."

"No." Jane collected a shuddering breath. "I'm good."

"Sure 'bout that? Let me know if you need me to pull over quick. I'll get you to the gutter. Done it before."

"Thank you." She still felt dizzy and disassociated. "I will."

"Looks like you was havin' a bad date." The taxi driver commiserated kindly.

"Yeah." Jane scoffed. "A bad date with Satan."

"M'su Diable." He chuckled. "We all been through that one, honey. You just relax now. I'll get you home safe."

"Thank you again." Jane closed her eyes. Her brain was already busily rewinding their argument, trying to recast it to her advantage. *Fuck it! It is what it is. Why should I feel guilty? Ryan's a misogynistic, racist jerk. I didn't do anything wrong!*

The cab sped around a corner, took a hard right, and pulled up short at the curb just as the fare box clicked. Jane looked for her wallet.

"301 St. Claude Avenue." Folding his leathery forearms, the cabbie rested them on the steering wheel, ducking his head to check the address. "Looks like your night ain't over yet. You expectin' another party?"

"What?" Jane stared out the window. The Big House was lit up like the sinking *Titanic* with yellow light flooding from every window. It even shone from the normally darkened rooftop dormers on Aunt Babette's third floor.

Scooting for the door, Jane handed over the sawbuck, struggling to get free of her tangled jacket and her stupid dress. "Keep the change."

"You sure, miss?" He gaped. "That's eleven dollars tip."

"Keep it. You did me a solid." Shoving the door open, Jane scrambled out to find The Boat parked in the driveway. *Gee's here. What's wrong now?* Her ankles twisted as she stumbled across the rough dirt yard. Reaching down, she slipped the cheap sandals off of her feet, chucking them overhand into a curbside trash bin. *Who am I kidding? I'm not this kind of girl. Never was.* "And fuck these stupid ass shoes!"

She immediately felt better as she ran across the cold front porch in her bare feet. Unlatching the front door, she stepped in to find Leslie standing next to Ken, clutching his arm with Gigi and Aunt Babette huddled near the base of the staircase. Aunt Babette was waving a wad of cash.

"What am I supposed to do with this?" She wailed. "I couldn't just leave it laying in the register. She doesn't keep a safe."

"Here, give it go me." Ken reached for the money.

"Oh no, you don't." Leslie blocked his move. "I'll hide it in the dishwasher. No burglar would think to look for it there."

"What's going on?" Jane demanded.

"Jane!" Ken whistled appreciatively. "Look at you! All sexed up." Slapping his hands together he rolled up on his toes. "I like it!"

"Please, Pops. Focus." Gee turned. Her pupils were dilated with excitement or with fear. She had pushed her hoodie sleeves up to her elbows and smeared her mascara into dark circles under both eyes. "Dee never showed up tonight to close up the shop."

"And she never does that! She left me there on my own!" Aunt Babette cried.

"We can't find her anywhere." Nervously sweeping her hair behind her ears, Gee started pacing like a caged tiger. "She's not at the house, she's not at the club. She's not answering her phone."

Jane suddenly remembered. "She left me a voicemail. I forgot."

"See?" Ken rumbled. "I told you. Women! All this worry over nothing."

Thumbing the menu, Jane set her phone to speaker.

"Hey, Jane." Delilah's baby doll voice echoed faintly, like it came from inside an elevator or a tin can. "Do me a favor? Tell Gee it's time for some housekeeping!" She sounded happy and bright. "Her voicemail box is full. Yo, Boo? Wake up. You missed my turn." The speaker crackled with a tussling sound followed by a shrill outraged scream. "Hey! Get off me! Let go!"

Jane looked up, horrified, her mouth as dry as ashes. "I didn't know this was here." She dove headfirst into an abyss of guilt. "You gotta believe me! I knew Dee called, but I didn't know this was here."

The color had drained from Gee's face, leaving her lips transparently blue. "I'm not waiting. This happened to Fancy. Siri? Call Dupree." She clamped the phone to her ear. "Someone is after us."

Aunt Babette moistened her lips. "Or some thing."

CHAPTER THIRTY-ONE

Jane's fingers fumbled as she buttoned her uniform dress shirt. She felt hollow with fatigue. She jealously studied Piddles, contentedly curled up at the foot of her bed. Noting her attention, he thumped his tail twice, blinking sleepily before licking his nostrils clean with his purple tongue.

"That's plain ass nasty, Mr. P." She conquered the final button. "You kiss me with that mouth."

She had grabbed a hurried shower before Dupree's arrival, hoping that it would clear the cobwebs from her mind and put some distance and perspective between Delilah's fearful voicemail message and her disastrous date with Ryan Embry, but the memory of their vicious argument still gripped her attention, leaving her feeling wronged and unsettled. In addition to pitching her sandals, she had balled up her new dress and marched it out to the trash bin. Her actions now felt petty and rash.

Jane pinched the bridge of her nose. *Dr. Warren was right. I'm allowed to make mistakes. What I need to do is stop judging myself over every goddamn little thing.* Her shoulders slumped as she leaned against the vanity. *I'll never make the absolutely right decision every single time. We all have bad days. Days we're tired, days we're sick. Days that are just plain low.* Cricking her neck, she focused her intent. *I need to keep my eyes on the bigger picture like finding Dee.*

Trotting downstairs, Mr. P at her heels, she snatched up the Advil bottle and dry swallowed two caplets before twitching the kitchen curtain aside. The Boat was still parked in the driveway, but Dupree's black Crown Vic Interceptor now blocked it in. Turning on the zinc tap, she cupped her

166

hands for a quick drink before blindly reaching for an acrylic dishtowel neatly folded into quarters on the draining board. The new towel felt oddly rough against her skin. Frowning, Jane studied its gaily printed red poinsettia border. *When did I decide to use this one?* She glanced at the pantry door. *I was saving this for Christmas Day.* Turning the towel over, she checked the Dollar Store tags. They had been neatly snipped off. *Damn, I need to pay better attention.* Jane felt fuddled. *When did I do that?*

"Let's go, Pid."

Locking the apartment, Jane jogged across the courtyard and up the porch steps, rapping her knuckles on the warped kitchen door before turning the tarnished brass knob. "Hello, the house? I'm coming in."

"Front room, Jane." Gee called. "Come on through."

Piddles yelped. Leaping ahead, he pushed the swinging door open and bounded toward Gigi before scrabbling to a stop once he noticed there were two strangers in the group. Slowly circling the ottoman, Pid tentatively avoided Detectives Bordelon and Dupree seated side-by-side on the couch. Skittering clear, he jumped gleefully on Gee before happily settling in by her knees.

"Good to see you, too, buddy." She rubbed his tasseled ears. "She been taking good care of you?" Gee looked up. "Those runs are working. He's trim. Fancy fed him too many treats. Fuck." Her face fell as she raised her fingers to her mouth. "That sucks. First time I've used past tense."

"Any word yet on Dee?" Pulling a chair forward, Jane sat.

Gee glanced at her mother. "I filed a missing persons' report. Just finished giving our statements."

"No luck tracing her location," Dupree inserted, "using GPS on her phone. It's dead. Unresponsive." He quickly amended.

Jane frowned. "I thought you needed a warrant to get historic location information?"

"Not in Louisiana," Bordelon replied easily. "CSLI is unprotected."

Jane realized two witnesses were missing. "Where's Ken and Aunt

167

Babette?"

"Ken gave his statement first. He went to the bathroom." Squinting, Leslie peered down the hall. "Aunt Babette went upstairs to rest."

"We were coming for you next." Dupree tugged his ear. "We're gonna need your phone for evidence."

"What do you mean 'need my phone'?" Jane sputtered. "I'm not giving you my phone."

Dupree leaned in. "Maybe we just take it."

"Don't bully me, Dupree." Jane snapped. "I know that takes a warrant or probable cause. I have the right to refuse consent."

"Jane?" Leslie worriedly wrung her hands. "Maybe you should help these gentlemen? Wouldn't that be best?"

"Why are you being obstructive?" Dupree persisted. "Got something to hide?"

"Let's hear the message and go from there." Bordelon reasonably suggested, polishing his glasses with his tie. "We appreciate your voluntary cooperation as a concerned citizen."

"Fine." Selecting the voicemail icon, Jane thumbed the speaker option and cringed.

"Hey, Jane. Do me a favor? Tell Gee it's time for some housekeeping! Her voicemail box is full. Yo, Boo? Wake up. You missed my turn."

She flinched at Delilah's shrill scream.

"Hey! Get off me! Let go!"

Dupree rested his elbows on his knees. "Who's her 'boo'?"

"Nobody I know, other than me." Gee looked confused. "I can't think of who that'd be, unless it's someone she just met, but Dee would've told me that, I think."

"Ms. Byrne?" Bordelon repeatedly clicked his pen. "It's getting late. Let's get your preliminary statement. When did you last see Ms. Gardere?"

"Physically see her?" Jane crossed her arms, carefully running through the days in her mind since they tended to blur together with her off cycle work schedule. She felt annoyed as Bordelon scribbled a quick note. *What? He thinks I'm a person of interest now because I hesitated? Does he think I'm reviewing my alibi?*

"The last time I saw Delilah Gardere was on Tuesday after Fancy Abellard's identification at the Coroner's Office. The three of us were together. Me, Gigi Pascoe, and Delilah Gardere. After that, Gee dropped me off here at the house." Jane shifted in her seat. "Sorry, Gee. That's a horrible memory to dredge up."

Gigi lowered her head to her hands. "Gotta be done though, right?"

Bordelon pointed the pen. "That corroborates what we already know. Ms. Pascoe was the last person to see Ms. Gardere at their home on Wednesday morning before Ms. Gardere left for work." He slid his glasses up his nose. "Anything more? No detail is trivial."

"I don't think so." Jane reviewed her memory. "I don't recall anything feeling odd or off, other than the fact we were leaving the Coroner's Office which feels wonky no matter how often you do it."

Dupree's head snapped up. "You've made a habit of visiting the Coroner's Office?"

"Not by choice." Jane backtracked smoothly. "I work security. I've witnessed drive-by shootings, attempted break-in accidents, domestic disputes. People do some crazy shit to get their stuff back. On Tuesday, though, I came home, took my nap, got dressed and reported to Guardian for my shift." She flicked her nametag. "Same thing I do every day. Same thing I'm doing right now as a matter of fact."

"Very good." Looking ill, Detective Bordelon rubbed his forehead. Reaching into his breast pocket, he pulled out a stack of business cards. "Everyone? Take one of these. It has my contact information including my personal cellphone number. Call or text me if you think of anything more, if you remember anything more. I don't like the way this is looking. I'm concerned we're seeing a pattern, a trend."

"I'm not sold on that approach," Dupree countered.

Gee snicked the card with her thumbnail. "Define 'trend.' You think someone's targeting my friends? Or targeting our community?"

"I wouldn't say either one, just yet." Dupree held up his hand, looking actively uncomfortable. "Still preliminary."

"Antwon? Two people taken from the same household in two days? Two more based on common location?" Bordelon asked. "What are the odds?"

"Jane? Your boss, Numa?" Gee turned. "Was he queer?"

"Not that I know of, not that he said."

"See?" Dupree looked vindicated. "To my mind that discounts the hate crime angle. It's a false lead."

Jane faced Dupree. "Did you follow up on that car tag I gave you?"

"Car tag?" Gee blinked. "What car tag?"

"I identified a truck at Guardian that might be connected to the murders. Dupree? Did you follow up on that?"

"You don't need to tell me my job." He replied defensively. "We've initiated an APB. It's registered in St. Martin Parish, an address near Henderson. Local is checking into it."

"Where's Henderson?" Jane pursued.

"Swampland," Gee replied.

"What about Cal Johnson? Any word on locating him?"

"His wife filed a missing persons' report yesterday," Bordelon reported.

"I'm not sure I follow," Leslie piped up, looking troubled. "How many people is this?"

"Four," Bordelon noted.

"Four people in four days?" She looked ruffled. "Well, I'd certainly call that a trend."

Gee stood up. "Where do we stand with finding Fancy's killer, since she was the first one?"

"We've successfully traced Ms. Abellard's phone records," Dupree rumbled, "and interviewed her … clients. Right now, her case is pending until we get a fresh lead due to our currently limited resources."

Cop speak mumbo-jumbo. Jane's heart hardened with certainty. *But Dupree's right. It has been over 48 hours. The success rate drops every hour as the murder trail goes cold.*

"That's it?" Gee's voice escalated as two tense cords stood out in her neck. "You're done with her case? Why? Because she's black? Because she's queer? Would a dead white woman be getting more effort outta you?"

"I object to that statement!" Dupree shot up. "That's offensive!"

"I don't give a shit what you object to." Gee spat. "I'll go find Dee and do a better job of it than what I see coming outta you." She repeatedly jabbed her index finger. "I don't see one damn thing you're doing that says finding Dee is going any better than what you did to find Fancy's killer or this other guy, what's his name? Numa?"

"And Cal Johnson," Jane stated. "Cal's missing, too."

"Excuse me."

There was a genteel cough from the staircase landing.

"I overheard what y'all were saying." Gripping the bannister, Aunt Babette descended the steps. "I know I watch too many crime shows on TV, but could this be the work of a serial killer?"

"Ma'am?" Raising both eyebrows, Dupree cleared his throat. "If we thought NOLA had an active serial killer we'd need to elevate the case and notify the FBI."

"Why wait?" Leslie folded her arms sarcastically. "That sounds like a good idea to me."

"I have another suggestion." Aunt Babette coughed delicately into her fist. "Perhaps the cards can assist us?" She thoughtfully tapped her lips. "We could try a Tarot reading or perhaps ask the spirit board for help."

"Ma'am?" Bordelon studied her over his glasses. "Am I hearing you right? You're suggesting that we consult a psychic on this case?"

"I'd be delighted to help." Modestly lowering her eyes, Aunt Babette placed her hand over her heart. "I was born with the gift."

"That's it. I'm done." Dupree snatched up his hat. "I don't have time for a circus sideshow act."

"We'll be in touch with any news." Quickly closing his notebook, Bordelon stood, staring at the floor. Nodding silently, he followed Dupree to the door.

Leslie waited for the latch to fall before she spoke again. "Gigi? Baby? You can't let yourself get angry like that. You lose control."

"I can't help it, Maman." Gee shook the tension from her hands. "Those cops stick in my craw. What the hell do they think they're doing?"

"They're connecting the dots, Gee." Jane warned. "Dupree caught the fact that you were the last person to see Fancy and Dee alive. Bordelon picked up on it, too. And they both know Fancy and Numa were found where I work."

"So what?" Gee looked defensive. "They can't tag me. I didn't do it."

"But they can make your life miserable because they're gonna try." Jane linked her hands together. "I've been on that side of the line. Right now they're pegging you - or me - or both of us as 'persons of interest.' They don't care who the killer is as long as they arrest someone for it. Nothing about this is personal to them. It can't be. They need to stay neutral. They've been trained for it. They just want to close this case and move onto the next one because there's always a next one, like Bordelon said."

"Sweet Jesus." Leslie eyes widened. "Is she right?"

"We need to *do* something." Gee spun around. "Aunt Babette? Will you read the cards for us?"

"Of course I will, *cher*." She pushed up off her chair. "Come up to my room."

172

CHAPTER THIRTY-TWO

Aunt Babette grasped the ebony bannister worn smooth by generations of Broussard family hands over the span of centuries. She spoke over her shoulder as she slowly climbed the stairs.

"Leslie, *cher*? Take the dog with you, please? We need to focus our energies. He'll be a distraction."

"Of course." Leslie made a kissing sound to get Pid's attention. "We'll be in the kitchen."

"Hummm? Tarot deck or Ouija board?" She turned for a narrower set of steps leading to the third floor. "Which should we try first?"

"Ouija board?" Jane hissed, grabbing Gee's forearm. It felt as muscled as a steel hawser. "We're using a Parker Brothers parlor game as an investigative tool?"

"Shut up. She'll hear you." Gee drawled. "We need to use the tools we are given."

"I'll teach you genuine investigative technique someday."

"Sign me up." Gee replied promptly. "I'd make a great detective. I already know everybody and everything."

"Walk, walk, walk." Aunt Babette finally fit her key into the deadbolt lock. "Those stairs are about to do me in, girls. However," she pushed the door open using her elbow, "I refuse to capitulate. Seventy-four years young and I am still making my way through this beautiful, troubled world."

Jane caught her reflection in an age spotted full-length mirror hung next to the door. She smoothed her uniform over her hips. *Hey! Looking kinda trim for a change. Good work!* Warming with pride, she scanned the ornate gilt plaster frame. *Jesus! What a monster. How did Babette carry this thing up the stairs?* Her curiosity gave her a poke. "Strange place to hang a mirror. Aren't you afraid it might get bumped?"

"Took two men to carry that up here when they came to do some other work." Aunt Babette rested her fists on her hips. "It's good protection for M'su Diable. He is so very, very vain. When he sees his own image, he's so attracted to it he's unable to move from the spot."

Goose bumps turned Jane's forearms into chicken skin. "Which spot?"

"Right where you're standing." Lifting her foot unnecessarily high, Aunt Babette stepped into her room. "So far, it's worked just fine."

Gee caught the door flatly with her open hand. "Does Maman know you installed a deadbolt on this door?"

"*Non, petite cheri.* But it was *necessaire* to keep the nosy children out." She hobbled toward a baize covered card table. "*Naturellement,* children are curious, but they need to be protected, kept out of harm's way. Besides, your mother hasn't been to my room in twenty-five years."

Jane caught the flare of sudden knowledge in Gee's eyes. *Babette knows that Gee and Ryan explored her room when they were kids.*

"Don't step in the red brick powder." Gee pointed to a messy line of blood red sand loosely spilled over the threshold.

"The what?" Unsure of what she'd heard, Jane danced in place. "Did you say red bird powder?"

"Red *brick* powder." Gee carefully enunciated. "Used for protection. Keeps evil outside the door."

Jane followed Gee inside. "What's it made of?"

"Ground up red bricks." Gee studied Jane like she had suddenly sprouted two heads. "What'd you think?"

"Ahhhh. *Bien.*" Aunt Babette sank into an upholstered chair with a grateful groan. She reached for an oversized deck of cards. "That's better. Come, girls. Let's get started."

Babette's room ran the length of the Big House from front to back, but it was only half as wide. *Bathroom must be across the hall. I can't imagine she goes up and down those stairs for a quick midnight pee.* The wall facing St. Claude Avenue featured a single dormer, but the rear wall facing the courtyard and Jane's apartment had two expansive double-hung windows that spilled winter light into the room. Babette had installed cheap shelving across these windows and then filled the metal shelves with empty bottles in every color: 7UP green, root beer brown, Milk of Magnesia cobalt blue. Sunlight filtering through the bottles softened the atmosphere, leaving Jane feeling relaxed and unfocused. *I feel like I'm trapped inside an aquarium.* "That's some collection," she noted. "What are the bottles for?"

"To trap the evil spirits." Rubbing her shoulder, Aunt Babette winced. "If they try to crawl in through the window."

"With that many evil spirits floating around," Jane snarked as she sat, "I'm surprised you even dare to go outside."

Aunt Babette cut the deck. "So, Jane. You're an unbeliever?"

"Yes. Of many things."

"Fair enough." She continued to shuffle the cards. "Usually, that's the result of defective intelligence, deficient education, or deliberate misinformation." Squaring the deck between her fingers, she centered it on the table. "What do you already know about voodoo?"

"I know about zombies." Jane mulishly folded her arms. "And some kind of poisonous fish venom, sticking pins in dolls and that old James Bond film my friend John used to watch. That pretty much covers it."

"Hollywood. They so rarely get anything right." Aunt Babette ruminated slowly. Lacing her fingers together, she settled back. "Voodoo is a religion, Jane, equal to any other belief that people practice. Haitian voodoo came here from Africa, brought by enslaved people. NOLA voodoo, which I practice is a blend of Haitian voodoo and French Catholicism."

"Which is why," Gee inserted, "you'll hear her asking Christian saints for their help."

"That's true. I want help from every spirit who works for good."

"Why not?" Jane rolled her eyes. "Can't be too careful. When do the voodoo dolls and the pins come in?"

"That's not true voodoo." Aunt Babette spat three times. "That's hoodoo for the rednecks and the tourists. Hoodoo is *une honte.* It embarrasses me to see it."

"Swamp superstition," Gee agreed. "Pure back door."

"Any other questions before we start?"

Jane pointed her chin at a portrait of a regal black woman with a challenging gaze and a gorgeous copper colored shawl hanging on the wall. "Who's the lady?"

"Who's that?" Gee gaped. "It's Marie Laveau!"

Jane gasped as a line of electric pain blossomed behind her right eye. The needle like agony ran down her ear to the hinge of her jaw before racing down her neck into her shoulder. *What the fuck?* She gasped again, digging her nails into the felt covered table. *Fuck! This is so fierce I can't even think!*

"You've never heard of Marie Laveau?" Aunt Babette cocked her head. "What do they teach you people up north in those fine schools? History is who we are, Jane. How do you know where you're going if you don't know where you've been?"

As quickly as it came, the searing pain evaporated. *Crap. Now on top of everything else I need to find a dentist?* Jane wiped her eyes with her fingertips. "I know plenty of history," she protested, "only we learned about Sam Adams, George Washington and Thomas Jefferson. And Paul Revere."

"Bah! White man's history," Babette scoffed. "Never tells the whole story. Never tells the 'herstory,' the woman's part, like men did it all themselves. Ha! You never see any women or children running around in the movies or in the museums, any barking dogs or smoke from campfires or piles of horseshit. Men like to make it pretty by leaving us out." Chuckling, she smoothed the deck out into one long crescent. "Don't want us around to mess up their uniforms."

I'm a woman. Jane ran her fingers down her buttons. *And I've worn a uniform most of my life.*

"Marie Laveau was my seven times great-grandmother on the Dulayne side." Babette tidied up the cards with her purple fingernails. "The most powerful voodoo priestess NOLA has ever had. I inherited my Creole strength and power from her." She proudly lifted her chin. "She only worked for good, just like me, in spite of what they say. Men are so funny. As soon as something goes wrong, they point as some poor, powerless woman and shout 'witch!'" She shrugged resignedly. "I'm not sure why. Somehow it makes them feel better."

"Say I go along with this hocus-pocus. What's next?"

"*Bien.* I'm going to use this, my favorite Rider Waite deck and the Celtic cross pattern. I've had great good luck with it. Gigi here will select the first card, the significator, since Delilah is our focus and she was Delilah's best friend."

"*Is* Dee's best friend," Gee quickly corrected. "I *am* Dee's best friend."

"But of course." Pulling a single card from the crescent, Aunt Babette flipped it over.

"Very good." She leaned in.

CHAPTER THIRTY-THREE

"Queen of Pentacles. *Bien.* The Tarot is already trying to help us." Aunt Babette slid the wide card to her left. "This is a good card to represent our friend Delilah, I think. This queen is very sensuous. She loves gardens and wine and all the good things Mother Earth has to offer."

Flattening her hands on the table, she mixed the cards up again. "Now, girls, put your thoughts to the other side. Focus your energy on being helpful, good, and kind. Ignore the dark thoughts; send them away. Concentrate your intent on finding Delilah. We're trying to create a unity between us, the universe, and the deck."

Gently gathering the cards together again, she squared them up and flipped the top card over.

"Nine of Swords. The nightmare card." Babette snapped it down on the center of the table. "This card looks bad, but don't give it too much thought right now because the other cards will influence this one. It may mean that Delilah is caught up in something she doesn't understand."

She flipped the next card over. It was blank.

"Yes," she slowly hissed. "That confirms it. This blank card represents the unknown." She placed the empty card on top of the Nine of Swords. "I'm seeing a lot of uncertainty here." Reaching up, she wiped the corners of her mouth. "This next card represents the unconscious."

Flipping the top card over, she carefully placed it below the blank one. "Six of Swords. Now, this card is good. Delilah is moving forward. Yes, she may be uncertain, but she's moving in the right direction. That's fine. Let's look at the past."

"Reversed Justice." Frowning, she slid that card to her left, clipping it thoughtfully with her fingernails. "This card is a trickster. I'm never certain with it." She waggled her head. "It represents karma, bad karma, something that has happened in the past. Something dead, decayed. Something buried." She nervously glanced at the colored bottles blocking her windows. "Something that may be trying to come back to haunt us."

"Let's see what the consciousness card says." She firmed her lips. Turning another card, she slid it over the green felt to the top of the cross. "Judgment. Now this is interesting. Judgment represents a call to action, but that blank card," she tapped it, "is impeding forward movement. All of this is very interesting. Let's see what the outcome card says."

She flipped the seventh card over.

It's Satan. Jane gasped at the depiction of a goat-headed devil seated on a throne.

"This doesn't represent M'su Diable, child." Aunt Babette smiled gently. "It means Delilah is a prisoner, chained by her fears." She circled her right palm over the Celtic cross display. "This is all a very positive reading, filled with energy. I'm seeing a lot of Major Arcana represented. Take heart. The cards are pointing us toward success."

Sounds like complete hoodoo to me but look at their faces. Jane shifted uneasily. *Gee and Babette look entranced. They're buying into every bit of this.*

"Now, I'll set out the wand." Babette laid a single card down on her right. "Six of Wands. *Tres bien.* Something will be resolved or become clearer in six days." Pinching the top card, she flipped it over. "Knight of Cups. Here we go." She smoothed the row with her fingers. "This is the environment card. You're being directed to pursue your quest."

Gee leaned in. "Pursue it how? What should we do?"

"Let's ask the Tarot." Aunt Babette tapped the deck. "This next card is the 'want' card. Concentrate on it, girls. This is the place of hopes and emotion and of powerful devotion." She plucked the card. Studying the card silently for a moment, she slowly reversed it and set it down. "The Fool card, reversed."

"That'd be me." Jane scoffed, time checking her phone. "I'm feeling foolish."

"Don't mess around," Gee stated severely. "This is serious."

"Gigi is right, Jane. This is serious." Aunt Babette studied her with troubled eyes. "Someone is standing on the edge of a cliff. There is a big moment ahead," she inhaled, "not necessarily bad. Trust in the future will be supported." She sucked in another breath. "The problem with this card is that it's reversed. Because of that blank card, we're still seeing uncertainty."

"The only uncertainty I see," Jane stated, "is that we're not getting any hard intel on where Delilah is."

Aunt Babette frowned. "Focus your intent on this card, the last one, the outcome card." She flipped it over. "Page of Pentacles. *Tres bien*. This card is favorable, even lucky. Page cards represent youth and vigor. This particular page serves the Queen of Pentacles." She nodded decisively. "There's your answer. You will see a positive outcome within six days. As for Delilah, the Tarot is telling you to go look for her. Have you checked that club you're always running off to? Have you looked for her there?"

Gee scratched her stubbly jaw. "I'll ask around again tonight. I'm thinking we should go check her shop."

"Why?" Aunt Babette blinked. "She wasn't there when I locked up."

"I'm not sure. I have an odd feeling, a *presentment*."

"Then you must follow it." Bending down, Aunt Babette reached for her purse. "The Tarot doesn't care where you start, *cherie,* as long as you get started." She handed Gee a crystal skull key ring. "These keys will get you in. You might need to work the door a little, it gets sticky after it rains." She slid the cards back into their sleeve. "Now, girls, quickly. I know you're in a hurry. Let's see what the Ouija has to say."

CHAPTER THIRTY-FOUR

Rain began to softly patter against the windows as Aunt Babette stood. *Where's she going?* Turning sideways in her chair, Jane watched the elderly woman drift across the room toward a mid-century teak console. Carefully raising the latched lid with both hands, she ran her fingers over a row of well-worn cardboard sleeves.

"Which one do we play today?" Tapping her lips, she caught Jane's eye. "Music helps with Ouija. Spirits like hearing a strong beat."

Selecting one album from the collection, Babette shook the black disk out of its sleeve, twirling it between her fingers before settling it onto the chrome spindle.

This should be good. What's Babette going to play? I can see the spirits tapping their feet to a snappy zydeco beat. Jane smiled. *If spirits have feet.* She blinked in genuine surprise as a remembered set of tinny chords leapt off the record like a spinning helicopter blade with the very first note.

"The Rolling Stones?" Jane gasped.

""Gimme Shelter"." Babette displayed the birthday cake album cover. "*Let It Bleed*, 1969." She ran her hand across the colorful image. "I bought this album at F.W. Woolworth on Canal Street the day it came out. Heard they had it in stock and grabbed the first streetcar I could. Stood in line for over an hour."

She laughed, and Jane suddenly saw the vibrant girl Aunt Babette had been.

"Cost me $3.49, plus tax. Ha! What you kids pay now for a cup of coffee, but that was real money back then." Picking a boxed board game up, she held it to her chest. "Listen to that Merry Clayton sing! What power! What a voice!"

"Best Stones song, ever." Gee agreed.

Aunt Babette shuffled back to the table. "I'm willing to argue that Merry's actually singing lead vocal over Mick's harmonica if anyone cares to debate me about it."

"Won't get an argument out of me," Jane said.

"Music is the one thing, Gigi, that your father and I agree on." Her eyes twinkled as she set the Ouija board down. "I'd play it loud enough to rattle the roof if Leslie would let me." Shaking the brown lid off the box, she set it aside. "But Leslie likes her peace and quiet and this is her house. She's the queen bee." Catching Jane's eye, she snorted. "What, Jane? You're surprised I like rock 'n roll? That's because you met me when I'm old, like you see me now, and that's sad, because you'll always remember me like this, but I bought this record when I was 25, younger than you are now."

Unfolding the board, she snorted again. "All this talk of racism and hating women, you think that's new? Shit. We had that thrown in our faces when I was growing up with Jim Crow *laws* ruling the land." She smoothed the central crease. "You think you're the first ones to resist? The first sit-in protest happened right at that Woolworth's lunch counter where I got this album in 1960. Oh my, yes. Early days. Seven students, five black and two white sat together in the white-only section." She leaned across the table. "Can you even imagine that? Having white-only seats? Or a white-only drinking fountain?" Shaking her head, she laughed brightly. "What am I saying? You kids buy your fancy water in bottles hauled in from Fiji. No free American water for you."

Jane recalled her training day photographs of white law enforcement officers using German shepherds on black civil rights protesters in Alabama. "Was there trouble in NOLA like in Selma? Were those kids arrested?"

"Oh no, honey. No. This is N'Orleans! We're every damn tint there is." She stroked her bronze arm. "We've been protesting over color a good long time, ever since they pulled us into the Union. Gov'mint never could figure us out, especially Creoles because we were mixed race from the beginning." Her eyes shone with pride. "A free and independent people of color with fine businesses and legal property." She rapped the table. "That's what throws them, all those puckery old white men in Washington. That's what all this is really about. Owning property. Who owns what, or who."

She pointed a purple fingernail. "This mess in Washington ain't nothing new. You two are just too young to remember it, but I remember Selma and Montgomery and Dr. King getting shot." She grew fierce. "And those Washington men should be afraid because it wasn't just marching back in the day, it was riots, mob riots! They set Los Angeles on fire! That's what they're really afraid of, all of those men, because we still got the numbers and they know it." She squinted. "We just need to get ourselves organized somehow. Figure it out and start using that power the right way ourselves instead of being told what to do." She sat back, gasping. "And we can't ever run away, girls, because the day we stop fighting, they win."

She's right. Jane shuddered. *I just plowed my way through the court system. Nothing about it was easy, but I had to believe that at least the court was neutral about my case. Due process was my only hope.* Jane swallowed thickly. *What if I had walked through that courtroom door straight into bias because of the color of my skin? Or because I wore a hajib or my gender? What then?*

Aunt Babette cocked her head as "Gimme Shelter" ramped up. "Get on with your bad self, Merry, girl. You keep screaming until things truly change."

She started sliding the Ouija board back and forth across the felt cover, creating so much static electricity in the air the hairs on Jane's forearms quivered.

"Merry Clayton was sixty years ahead of her time, girls. Listen to that sound. That's the sound of the angry female energy being unleashed on the world today. 'Rape, murder'." Aunt Babette sang. Reaching up, she wiped flecks of foam from the corners of her mouth. "All of those holy rollers who say they walk in fear of God had better pull up their pants, because this, girls, this is the voice of God the Mother, she who sows *and* reaps, she who has been silenced and ignored and shunted aside. She is re-entering our world and she is pissed at what we have done with her legacy."

Shit. Jane grew concerned. *She sounds fucking nuts.* She sucked in a shallow breath. *Mom said spirit boards are demonic and Aunt Babette sure sounds possessed.* Jane glanced nervously across the table. Gee looked unfazed. *Okay, Gee, I'll play. But if this gets any weirder, sorry, I am not comfortable with this. You are own your own and I am outta here.*

Blinking repeatedly, Aunt Babette pulled a notepad and a sharpened pencil from the box. "Now, Jane, think. Never ask Ouija a question if you don't want an answer. The spirits are active and they are listening. This is not a joke or a silly game. This is serious, and our intent is real." She tightly shut her eyes. "We are gathered here today to seek help finding our lost friend, Delilah Gardere."

Jane quickly scanned the tan Ouija board. It had two curving rows of block capital letters in the middle over a straight line of numbers from 1 to 0. The sun was pictured in the upper left-hand corner of the board over the word YES. A crescent moon with a single star was shown in the upper right corner over the word NO. Along the bottom of the board were the words GOOD BYE.

Aunt Babette blinked her eyes open. Reaching into the box, she pulled out a cream-colored plastic heart-shaped planchette. Turning the pointer over, she gently blew away the dust between its tiny tripod rubber wheels before polishing its crystal lens with the hem of her purple blouse.

"Gigi already knows this, Jane, but you'll lightly rest your fingertips on the edge of the planchette, like this. Now, clear your minds, and focus. We'll circle the board three times, once for each of us, and oh! Always remember to say 'Good Bye' when you're done or a spirit may follow you home."

I am really not comfortable with this. Jane hesitated as the tripod pointer skated over the board. YES. NO. YES. NO. The planchette rapidly swung between the sun and the moon images. YES. NO.

"Excellent!" Aunt Babette leaned over the board, obviously thrilled. "Sometimes the spirits prefer Tarot, sometimes they prefer the board." She nodded eagerly, her dark eyes bright. "I don't usually see such a strong response so quickly. Quick! Gigi! Ask your question."

"We are seeking my friend, Delilah Gardere," Gee stated carefully. "She's missing from her home. Her friends and her family who love her miss her. Spirits? Can you help us find Delilah Gardere? Do you know where she is?"

The planchette skated to a dead stop in the center of the board.

Gee looked up, horror reflected in her eyes. "Aunt Babette?" She whispered. "Why does it show us nothing?"

"That's a good sign." Aunt Babette waggled her head. "It means that Delilah is still with us on this side of the divide. She lives, still free from death's clutches."

The planchette slowly inched toward the crescent moon. NO.

Gee choked. "She's dead?"

The tripod circled the block lettering before creeping back up toward the moon, where it chittered to a stop. NO.

"Fuck! Dee's not alive and she's not dead? Where is she then?"

Jane gasped as the planchette began to swing wildly between the letters.

"Write this down!" Aunt Babette stared. "B-I-G-P-I-G."

"What the hell?" Jane sputtered.

"P-I-G," Babette repeated. "M-A-N."

"Big pig man?" She released her pent-up breath. "Are you fucking kidding me?"

"Jane, please. Man? What man?" Gigi demanded from the board. "Which man?"

"T-H-E-M-A-N."

The pointer skittered to at stop at the bottom of the board. GOOD BYE.

Lifting both hands, Aunt Babette released the pointer. Her shoulders slumped and she dropped her hands into her lap. "Do we know who Dee's men friends are?"

"She doesn't really have any." Sweat had gathered in the hollow of Gee's neck. She wiped it away. "Except for my dad. Dee prefers the company of women."

"She has you, Gee," Jane stated. "Technically, you're a man friend."

"Fuck off." Gee looked hurt. "Why? Because I have a cock? Don't be stupid." Turning away stiffly, she faced Aunt Babette. "Try again but ask for Fancy this time. She'll help."

"As you wish." Re-centering the planchette, Aunt Babette waited patiently until Jane had replaced her fingertips on the pointer. "Thank you, kind spirits, for your guidance in our quest. We seek more help finding our friend, Delilah Gardere. This time, we ask our friend Fancy Abellard to guide us, if she can."

The pointer remained still, leaden and unmoving.

"Fancy?" Gigi implored. "Can you help us?"

The planchette started crawling toward the doubled rows of letters.

"She's here." Tears sprang into Gee's eyes. "I can feel it."

"H-E-Y-G-I-R-L."

"Oh, Fancy." Gee wept. "I miss you so much! I'm so sorry about what happened." She sucked in a ragged breath. "Who did it, Fancy? Who hurt you so bad?"

YES NO. The planchette swung rapidly back and forth. YES NO. YES NO.

"Gigi! You're asking too many questions." Aunt Babette scolded. "Focus your intent. You're causing confusion."

"Got it." Gee's Adam's apple bobbed as she swallowed heavily. "Fancy? Are you there?"

"S-H-O-W-M-E-T-H-E-M-O-N-E-Y."

"It's her." Gee giggled, blinking away tears. "Fancy? Where's Dee? Help us find Dee."

"W-I-T-H-M-E-N-O-W-S-A-F-E."

"With you? But you're dead!" Gee released the planchette like it was white hot. The pointer skated to a stop. She quickly returned her fingertips to it. "Fancy? Answer me! Where is Dee?"

The pointer sat unresponsive in the middle of the board.

"You broke the connection." Aunt Babette's breath rattled in her throat. "She's gone."

"Is that it?" Jane asked. "Are we done now? Is it over?" *There's nothing supernatural going on here. Everything about this can be explained by the three of us sitting around this table. Most of these answers don't even make sense.* Her innate sarcasm reasserted itself and she snorted at the preposterous situation. "Anyone else care to speak up while we're sitting here?"

She immediately fell forward over the board as the pointer started picking out new letters.

"She's back!" Gee shrieked. "What's she saying?"

Aunt Babette stuttered as she tracked the letters. "M-U-R-D-E-R-"

"Fancy's giving us the name of her killer!"

No fucking way. Jane's brain spun and she felt lightheaded. *This can't be real.* She stared at the Ouija board in disbelief. *Shit like this doesn't happen.*

"O-U-S-B-I-T-C-H."

BANG. Jane's chair hit the floor as she leapt away from the table.

"Murderous bitch?" Gee's face tightened as she blinked, obviously confused. "Fancy was killed by a woman?"

"No, that's not it." Jane whispered in horror. *Murderous bitch?* Her legs were shaking uncontrollably. *No fucking way.*

"Girls? Are you alright?" Aunt Babette blew on her fingertips, looking wide-eyed and frightened. "Something evil just came through."

"That's it. I'm done. I'm through." Jane gasped. "I'm not doing this anymore. Gee? I'll meet you outside." She raced for the door.

"Jane? What's wrong?" Gee scrambled up. "Where are you going?"

"Say 'Good Bye'!" Aunt Babette shrieked. "Say 'Good Bye!' Don't leave this with me in my room!"

Wrenching the door open, Jane ran into the hall, the big mirror looming on her left. It now seemed to be filled with swirling mist and shadows. She raised her hand to block her peripheral vision. *Get me the fuck outta here. No fucking way I want to see what that is.*

"Jane!" Gee shouted from the doorway. "Wait for me!"

Her bad knee locked. She lost her footing, tumbling down the staircase, grabbing for the bannister and bouncing off the rough plaster walls. *Keep it real, goddammit! Keep it real.* Jane filled her mind with her seventh rule as she fought to outdistance the blinding panic. *Crissakes! Mom was right! I hate this devil shit!*

Scrambling around the landing, she limped for the door. Pulling it open savagely, she stumbled onto the porch and leaned over the railing, filling her lungs with great gulps of fresh, clean winter air. The leaden skies had opened and it was pouring buckets of rain. Jane sucked in another great, shuddering breath. The gutters were overflowing the sidewalks, awash with leaf litter and paper trash. A muddy lake puddled the dirt yard to the street and the leaves of the live oak tree streamed silvery droplets. Because of the downpour, the birds were silent and there was no other sound than her great gasps and the pattering of raindrops in the soft mud. The familiar NOLA scent of acrid clay rose from the earth and smothered her nose, thinned suddenly by the herby perfume of cannabis smoke. Jane heard the rocking chair creak and she flinched.

"Jesus." Ken's voice squeaked as he inhaled. "I'm beat."

CHAPTER THIRTY-FIVE

"Sucks getting old, Jane. Don't ever do it."

Jane shuddered as Ken returned the glowing spliff to his lips. In that posture and with his unruly hair he looked like The Devil incarnate seated on his throne minus the curling rams' horns and the goatish beard.

"Something wrong? You look shook."

"Ken, I need to ask you something." Digging her nails into the rotten railing, she leaned on her investigative training, the one tried and true muscle memory technique that helped her regain her focus in every PTSD crisis situation. "Where do you keep disappearing to? Where do you go? I need to know."

He inhaled again. "Can't tell Leslie."

"I won't." Her heart still hammered, but it had slowed to a steadier beat.

"Got a job." He wheezed a broken laugh. "Stocking shelves at the Dollar Store. I know, funny, right? Joke's on me. Only job I could get. Can't run a computer. Don't have any skills. Needed to pay for her ring somehow."

Really? Could it be that simple? Or am I being played by the whole Pascoe family? "I know you've been using a music studio at Guardian Storage." She confessed. "I spotted you on security cam video."

"No, Jane, not using." Ken sadly shook his head. "I rent one sometimes to sit and think, to remember my ghosts. It's peaceful there, but that's it. Most times I don't even turn on the lights."

"Have you ever seen anyone else on Level Five, when you rented a studio?"

"Can't say that I did. I know there are folks on other floors, but that one's pretty much deserted. Quiet as King Tut's tomb. That's why I like it."

"You never seen anyone using the big storage unit by the fire door?" She pursued.

"Don't you trust me, Jane?" Frowning, Ken studied the burning spliff. "I believe I just said that answer was 'no.'"

The front door wrenched open and Gee tumbled out. Her collar was torn open and her face was flushed.

"Jesus, Jane! You can really move when you want to. You okay? You spooked by what happened upstairs?"

"You're not?"

"Why?" Ken flicked the spliff into the sodden bushes. "What happened upstairs?"

"Aunt Babette used the Ouija board to help us find Dee."

"You got a message?"

"I'll say we did." Jane swallowed past her tongue.

"Goddamn it!" Ken pushed up off the chair to a crouch. "I told Babette she needs to keep that witchy shit to herself. You can't shit where you eat. I'll go talk to her. We need to live in this house."

"No, Dad, relax. It's chill," Gee said. "I asked her to do it. This is driving me *fou*." She did look a little white-eyed. "I woke up this morning sleeping in a chair instead of my bed. Don't remember sleepwalking, but I guess I got up to watch the door. I keep listening for Dee's key in the lock." She extended her phone. "I keep looking for her text."

Ken dropped his beefy hand on her shoulder. "I'm sorry to hear that, Gigi. It's tough losing friends."

Gee wrenched free. "Dee's not lost! Don't say that, Pops! You'll call it into being."

"That's not what I meant." Ken studied Gee warily. "What did the Ouija board say?"

190

Gee stared at the floor. "Fancy came through. Said Dee was with her, but the Tarot told us to search. The message was muddled."

"Jesus!" Ken sputtered. "Babette read the cards, too? No wonder Jane freaked out."

"I think," Gee thoughtfully tapped her lips, "we should go check Dee's store."

"Can't do that right now, Gee." Jane protested. "I need to get to work. If I don't leave this minute I'm going to be late for my shift."

"Call off sick."

"I can't! Not if I want to get paid."

"Shit. Okay. Listen. Hop in The Boat and I'll give you a ride over. We can talk about it on the way."

"You two be careful," Ken warned. Holding his hand under the dripping gutter, he flicked the droplets from his fingers and turned, looking concerned. "Watch your backs, and I mean it. You can stir up some serious shit when you start asking questions. Everyone out there has a secret they don't want to share."

"We'll be careful, Pops." Gee blithely promised.

Dodging mud puddles, they raced for The Boat. Sliding behind the wheel, Gee grabbed a Saints ball cap stuffed between the windshield and the cranberry red dashboard. Combing her bangs off her forehead, she slipped the ball cap on backwards, gangsta style. Checking her mirrors, she backed into the traffic on St. Claude Avenue before snapping her fingers at the glove box.

"Grab my smokes outta there, will you please?"

Jane turned the knob and the glove box fell open into her lap. Digging through the trash, she found a cardboard box sealed in cellophane. "This?"

"That's the one." Using her elbows to keep the wheel straight, Gee unwrapped the cellophane, popped the lid with her thumb and clenched a slim brown cigar between her teeth before pressing the built-in dashboard lighter. "Okay, so here's the deal. I'll ask around at the club tonight and if we haven't heard anything new from Dupree by tomorrow morning we'll go looking. I'll swing by and pick you up at what, like two? Could you be ready by two?"

Jane drummed her fingers on the passenger door. "I'll be ready."

Reaching over, Gee turned on the radio. Jane felt enchanted as an antenna automatically rose out of the right front fender. "This car is awesome. It's like having a robot."

"One reason I bought it." Gee pointed to the dash as the lighter popped. She lit her cigar, speaking through a mouthful of smoke. "Came with a factory 8 track tape player. Those are getting tough to find except at garage sales." Settling the knob on WTIX-FM, 94.3, NOLA's oldies station, she sat back.

Jane continued to drum the door. "Gee? Something's bothering me about this. That message we got back at the house? It's not right. I don't think a woman killed Fancy. It doesn't match the physical evidence we saw at the Coroner's office. The attack on Fancy was too brutal. Women don't typically use their fists or their feet. Sure, they might snatch up a kitchen knife or swing a shovel, but generally women maintain distance during an attack. They don't close in and they don't use their hands, they use a tool." Jane studied the clearing night sky. "I think Fancy's killer is a man."

"Any candidates?"

"No." Jane admitted. "And I understand Dupree's frustration with this case."

"Ouija's not always right. Nothing's guaranteed." Pointing the cigar, Gee smiled. "I like how your inner cop is showing. You're thinking outside the box."

"I've been thinking differently about a lot of things, lately." Jane settled her shoulders against the plush upholstery. "Knowing you has made me rethink a bunch of things."

"Like what?"

Jane picked at her cuticle. "I used to skip over reading the transgender stories in the news. Figured it was none of my business, but now when I see them I dig in. There's some serious political shit going on right now and the science of it, too, like the story the trans wrestler who keeps winning state titles. Knowing you makes that shit personal. I didn't use to care."

"You have been reading." Gee turned The Boat left toward the canal. "How do you feel about that wrestler?"

"It's the feeling part that's tough." Jane tucked her hair behind her ears. "Sure, I think he should be allowed to wrestle, but he's been taking testosterone for his transition, right? Don't take this wrong, but that makes me wonder if that's fair to the girl wrestlers if he has that hormone in his system during competitions? We get all over the Germans and the Russians in the Olympics when they do that."

"True." Gee stuck her cigar in the ashtray and left it to burn. "From what I've read he's being forced to wrestle girls because the state is insisting he's female gendered." She straightened the wheel with both hands. "The problem is people have stopped using their goddamn common sense. We need to look at these things on a case-by-case basis just like everything else and stop making generalizations. That's what keeps hanging us up."

The pickup truck ahead of them turned right. Gee accelerated to close the gap. "I keep wondering where are the adults and the people in charge when this crazy shit happens? Where are the adults? Why don't they speak up?"

"I should've spoken up once." Jane rubbed her damaged knee. "Back in my Police Academy days." Peeling back the lid, she shone a bitter light on the blasted memory. "I had a drill sergeant, a real prick. Didn't like having women on his squad, any woman, not just me. Didn't matter if you were qualified or how hard you wanted it or even how hard you tried. Said women weren't physically capable of doing the job. Said we weren't mentally tough enough. Bastard got my goat, so I decided to prove him wrong."

Gee grinned crookedly. "I'll just bet you did."

"He kept pitting me against the biggest guys in hand-to-hand training."

Jane laughed uneasily. "Shit, I get it. None of us was taking it easy. I spent a hundred extra hours in the gym, lifting weights so I could hold my own." Remembering her dedication, she felt proud of her committed effort. "Him seeing me do the extra work stuck in his craw because I was showing him up, proving him wrong and he knew it."

Gee slowed The Boat for a red light.

"I got warned he said he was going to take me down a peg and I ignored it. At our next one-on-one he flipped me and deliberately crushed my knee. Dropped his whole body weight on it. Crissakes! You should've heard it go like someone snapping celery. The pain was so bad I blacked out. Woke up icing a knee brace in the infirmary."

Gee stared in open-mouthed horror. "Shit, Jane. I hope they fired that bastard."

"Hell, no." She dry-rubbed her palms together. "Didn't even earn him a reprimand, because no one, not even me, spoke up about it." She studied a tourist pod illegally crossing the street. "I didn't want to be seen as weak or a complainer. Fuck. Two surgeries later and it's still not right." She frowned, bitterly. "He's probably still teaching self-defense at the Academy. No, no," she scoffed, "he's probably retired by now and enjoying his pension, the sonofabitch. Probably doesn't even remember my name."

"I get it." Gee shifted uncomfortably. "Why is speaking up so hard to do?"

"It's human nature." Jane bit her lip. "No one wants to get cut out of the herd so we shut up and take it. That's our biggest fear, abandonment. Being alone and getting left behind."

Gee's face pinched shut. "Did you mean to say it that way? About getting left behind?"

"Oh shit, no, Gee, I wasn't talking about you." Jane stammered. *I forgot how easy it is to hurt someone.* "I meant that as a general observation."

"Okay. Well, you might be right. No one wants to get voted off the island."

Jane sucked in her breath. *Did she mean that to stick it to me?* Her instinct was to retract into silence like a clam into its shell. *Dammit! Don't hold this in and turn it into another grudge or a grievance. Speak up!* "Did you mean to say that to me that way?"

"Say what to you, what way?" Gee looked confused.

"Say like getting voted off the island as in my personal case."

"I meant it like the *Survivor* TV show." Gee turned. "I forget we really don't know each other, that's this is still new. You don't know me well enough to know I don't do that backstabbing bullshit to anyone." She raised her chin. "I don't play that game, Jane. If we're gonna be friends, you're gonna hafta trust me and be honest. I'm not smart enough to figure it out any other way."

"Got it." Jane swallowed drily. *It's now or never.* Summoning her resolve, she took a mental giant step forward over the gaping abyss, trusting that her gut instinct and the whole truth would somehow support her. "Then I need to tell you something more." She released her pent-up breath. "I'm the 'murderous bitch.'"

CHAPTER THIRTY-SIX

Gee snatched the cigar as it fell from her mouth. "What?"

"Yes." Jane sucked in another breath. *How the ghosts of the past cling to us no matter how hard we try to hide. I've never told anybody this, not even John.* The dam burst and the words spilled out. "Those were Mason Hollister's last words to me as he died. I'd swear to it on a stack of Bibles. John never heard him say it; he was too busy working on Sarah. But Hollister whispered those exact words to me as he bled out."

Jane shut her eyes tight. She could still recall that crime scene in exact and gory detail. "His blood moved across the floor, came right at me. It saturated the hem of my pants." Opening her eyes, Jane wiped her mouth. "Remember the room you told me about, the one with the bloody handprints on the walls?"

"Yeah." Gee stared in horror. "The hospital room, the one from my dream?"

"This is my version of that nightmare."

"And you think this Hollister fucker came through the Ouija board to speak to you from Hell?"

"I don't know what to think anymore." Jane plucked at her seatbelt. "I only know I shouldn't have sat for that reading. It's the only thing my mother ever forbade me from doing."

"Doing what? The Ouija board or the Tarot?"

"Both. From doing anything paranormal or devilish." Jane laughed uncertainly. "She said I had too much imagination and crissakes!" Raising her hands from her lap, Jane let them tremble. "Look at me. She was right!"

Gee stared thoughtfully ahead. "Jane, what was it like? Killing that man?"

Jane stretched past the PTSD terror to recall the feeling. "It felt like I got caught up in something that was bigger than me." She confessed. "It wrapped me up and carried me with it." She turned sideways as far as her seatbelt would allow. "I'm not making excuses, Gee. I knew what I was doing, and I was doing what I was trained to do. Yes, maybe I was jacked on adrenaline, but I knew what I was doing all the way up those steps. It wasn't some kind of blackout. I ran into that bedroom and I saw Hollister holding that knife to Sarah's throat, eighteen feet away. At that distance, a man with a knife can carve you up faster than you can draw your weapon."

Jane stubbornly shook her head. "You'll never know what it's like until it happens to you. BAM! You lose the first three seconds assessing the situation. BAM! It's right there in front of you and BAM! You react. I don't regret killing Hollister. He was a fucking monster and he was threatening a friend of mine. No, it was more than that. He was threatening my family." She moistened her lips. "He got what he deserved and I'm not going to feel guilty about it. Thank God, the grand jury picked up on that when they dismissed the charges against me."

"I see." Gee rested her folded hands on the steering wheel. "Do you still want to go with me, then, tomorrow to look for Dee? You don't have to help me, Jane. I can do it alone. I don't want you doing anything you're not comfortable with."

"No, I do want to go. I want to help." Jane straightened. As soon as she said the words she knew it was true. *Investigation is my talent. It should be used.* "And Gee? I'm sorry about what I said earlier about you being a man. I know that's not true. Sometimes, though, I slip up and this shit just pops out of me."

"Forget it. I get it a lot." Gee stated wryly. "Oh, wait. Here we go." Switching the cigar to her left hand, she cranked the volume control knob on the dashboard radio.

Jane instantly recognized Mick Kiesling's aggressive drum solo opening as "Love Power" began to play, followed by his famously hesitant snare set that sounded like a round of semi-automatic weapons' fire. Kenny Pascoe's gloriously funkified thrumming bass guitar quickly supported Scottie Brennan's choppy opening lead D electric guitar chord. Lemonhead Meyer wailed in on his high-pitched train whistle harmonica as Scottie began to sing:

> Listen up, people!
> Take some time to expand your mind
> To help you see
> That the way it was
> Is not the way to be.

Marianne Tanner's smoky contralto aggressively elbowed its way forward and to Jane's delight Gee joined in:

> Hold tight, feel the power
> Take control, shape it hour by hour.
> I need you, to get me through it.
> You need me, to help you do it.
> Step by step, let's put up a fight
> Them saying it's so, don't make it right.
> I believe
> You believe
> We believe in
> Love power!

"Crissakes, Gee!" Jane collapsed against the leather seat in amazement. "You have one helluva voice." She pointed at the radio as Marianne Tanner wailed up an octave. "You think maybe you inherited it from her? Your voice? Crissakes! Listen to her. She makes that song work."

"Could be." Gripping the cigar between her teeth, Gee steered The

Boat into the Guardian Storage lot, pulling into a vacant handicapped parking spot. "It's the strangest thing. I've heard her voice all my life everywhere I go, but I've never seen a picture of her. I have no idea what she looked like."

Jane unsnapped her seatbelt. "Ken never kept a photo?"

"No, he said he burned them with his session tapes. Pops says I look a little bit like her, but mostly that I look like him." She plucked a speck of tobacco off her tongue. "I tried pulling a screen shot off the MTV video once. She's mic'd up behind Mick Kiesling's drum kit. It's too grainy to see any real detail."

"What if you backtracked her to Kansas City?" Jane's detective instinct kicked in. "She was in Ken's high school class with the other WarBirds, right? That school should still have a copy of their yearbook in their library or archive."

"I never thought of that." Gee looked hopeful.

"You could also try one of those online DNA testing services. You might reconnect to Marianne that way."

Gee looked doubtful. "I'd need to think about that. I'll walk you in." Stepping from The Boat, she caught Jane's skeptical look. "What? It's complicated. I can't upset Maman. She goes big *fou* when I mention looking for Marianne."

Saluting the security camera, Jane turned for the door. "When did you find out you were adopted?"

"My cousin Ray clued me in when I was eleven. Didn't make much a difference." Gee followed one step behind, grinning crookedly. "I was working through some other issues at the time. Getting abandoned by Marianne Tanner was the least of my worries. I kept waiting for my dick to fall off."

"Sorry!" Jane snorted. "Shouldn't laugh, Gee, but damn girl, you're funny." She dug out her key fob. "Did you ever imagine what she was like as a person?"

"Sure I did." Gee puffed her cigar. "Whenever I had a teenage fight with Maman or Pops. Used to imagine running away to find her only I didn't know which way to go. She didn't leave me a note. Mostly, though, I wanted to ask her why she left me behind."

Dropping the cigar into the watery gutter, Gee studied it as it lay in a puddle, hissing. Resting her hands on her square masculine hips, she looked blank and bereft. Jane's heart went out to her new friend as Gee stepped on the cigar butt with the pointed toe of her loafer and snuffed it out. "Was she trying to give me a better life? Do I have any brothers or sisters? You know, the usual shit adopted kids wonder about." Gee stared unblinking into the night sky. "Maman and Pops are my real parents." She stated. "They put up with all of my shit." She turned, her dark eyes filled with doubt and concern. "I never want to hurt either one of them. Or Aunt Babette. Unless we find Dee, they're all the family I've got left."

CHAPTER THIRTY-SEVEN

Dodging the Decatur Street traffic, Jane followed Gee around the for-hire carriages lining the curb, stepping over a gutter filled with crushed red Solo cups and pyramids of puckish green mule turds.

"Gee?" Jane called, remembering the spare Quaker neatness of her former Nantucket Island home. "Does it ever bother you that this whole town looks like it's falling apart?"

"Decay is a large part of our charm," Gee replied easily, juggling Aunt Babette's glittering skull key ring in her hands. "Can't fight the climate. Reminds you to enjoy the hell out of every day, because the next world is always right there, waiting." Scratching her knuckles, she smiled. "That's a good sign. Means I'm gonna meet an old friend or find some money."

"I'll add that to my growing list of Creole superstitions."

Gee paused before turning for Jackson Square. "What do you believe in, Jane?"

"Me?" She gave it some thought. "I think we're all just really smart monkeys. Everything else, even that hoo-ha going on in that big cathedral over there is a myth. We made up a bunch of stories to comfort ourselves around some campfire and being human, as usual, we took things too far. Excess is what we do best."

"Even after what you saw at Aunt Babette's Tarot reading? And the Ouija board?"

"Especially after what I saw with both of those." Jane stated firmly. "That's the kind of shit that gets people tied to stakes and set on fire."

Gee hooted. "That's your Yankee history, my friend, not mine. We

201

never burnt our witches. We recognize their gifts and we honor them."

"If you're talking Salem," Jane huffed, "we never burned our witches, either. Salem witches got hanged except for one poor bastard who got pressed to death."

"What?" Gee stopped dead in her tracks as her jaw dropped open. "How do you press someone to death?"

"You stick him under a board and you keep piling big rocks on top of him until his ribs crack and he stops breathing."

"Damn, you Yankees are mean." Gee looked cockeyed. "I thought the Spanish Inquisition was tough."

A wrought iron fence surrounded Jackson Square. Local artists used it to display their wares and one artist, an elderly, ruminating white man waved his cane.

"Everything's on sale today," he shouted. "Fifty percent off just for you."

His paintings seemed to be NOLA cityscapes painted in different shades of gray. The wet paint had dripped down his canvases like the city was melting.

"I'll match his offer." A jolly black woman sitting next to him cackled. She was selling 3-D acrylic sculptures made from flattened two-liter soda bottles covered with mirrored beads and chips of colored glass. "If you pay cash."

She sat next to a tattooed blonde psychic who started tapping her Tarot deck against her metal TV tray before she inexplicably started shrieking like a hyena. Her shrill cry bounced off the buildings and echoed around the square. "Me, too! Me, too! Cash only."

"Want a reading, Jane?" Gee asked. "My treat?"

"Fuck off." Jane growled. "You haven't been listening."

"Can't help myself." Gee shrugged unapologetically. "You're so easy to rile. It's irresistible." She spun on her heel. "Dee's shop, Le Maison Grise is on the arcade."

Spanish or French, Jackson Square is a beautiful setting. Jane climbed the concrete steps leading to the covered sidewalk. Her bad knee gave her a twinge and she paused to study the bronze statue of Andrew Jackson on horseback in the middle of the square. He seemed to be tipping his hat at the passing tourist horde heading for the Café du Monde for beignets. Gee had continued on. Jane had to hop and trot to catch up.

"What the fuck?"

Gee stood in front of the black lacquered door. Holding the glittering skull key ring in her hand, she glanced at the doorknob and then looked back at her keys.

Jane strode to catch up. "What is it?"

Gee flicked a spider-webbed key ring already hanging from the lock. Looking hopeful, she thumbed the latch. "You think maybe Dee is in here?"

"Don't touch it!" Jane shouted.

Gee snatched her hand back.

"Now your prints are on it." Swinging her backpack forward, Jane dug for her phone. "I'm calling 911. Reporting a burglary in progress."

"Fuck that. I'm going in."

"No, Gee! Wait!"

Jane choked as golden speckles danced before her eyes. Her fingertips went numb as an icy rising tide of crippling anxiety crept up her calves. *Oh, no. It's going to be bad.* The cold shaking tremor spilled up over her kneecaps and she knew it wouldn't stop rising until its sucking tentacles gripped her stomach and probed her heart. Jane groaned as searing images started flashing through her mind: the golden oak staircase rising to the second floor; the curved ebony bannister; that goddamned opened bedroom door as Sarah's anguished screaming filled her ears. Her molars crunched as she fought to release her clenched jaw. *Fucking PTSD. Not now. Focus, girl. Focus and stay calm. Push through it.*

"Jane? What's going on? You okay?"

"Don't go in." Jane gasped like a fish left stranded by low tide. "Might be click bait."

Gee rocked back. "Click bait?"

"A trap. Might be a trap." Blindly shaking her head, Jane tasted the coppery blood from her bitten tongue. "Call for backup."

"We're not cops." Flexing her elbow, Gee shoved the door open. "It might be Dee."

Le Maison Gris was dim with shadow and she stepped in.

CHAPTER THIRTY-EIGHT

"Dee?" Gee shouted. "You in here? Answer me, girl."

Jane shivered as she stumbled across the threshold. The sound of the tinny bell hanging over the door faded away and the shop returned to a brooding silence.

"Dee!" Gee persisted. "Where y'at?"

A breeze swept through the open door, rustling the paper flowers on their stems and stirring the close, stale air. *Stay focused. I can't let Gee do this alone. She needs me.* Jane's stomach still felt queasy and an unpleasantly greasy sweat slicked her skin, but her mind began to clear. She grabbed her nose as her sinuses filled with a mixed stink of patchouli oil, dried strawberries and rancid bacon fat.

"Goddammit, Dee! Answer me."

Gee flipped a wall switch. The shadows retreated under the glass display counters as the single central milk glass globe lit up and the two gigantic overhead wicker paddle fans began to whirr. Jane took another step forward, her ears cocked for the slightest sound. She turned to check the cash register and her sneakers crunched.

"Watch it, Gee. There's glass on the floor."

She slipped past a line of shattered jars and stick bundles bound by thin strands of multi-colored thread, recognizing the withered stalks of lavender and chamomile. The other dried bundles remained a complete mystery. Evidently, the jars had held some type of natural herbal or voodoo remedies. Squeezing her hips sideways to get past an off-kilter counter, Jane had to turn her back on a cluster of pale manikins wearing gaudy Mardi Gras masks.

"I hate those fucking things." She shuddered. "They look like circus clowns."

"Dee hates them, too, but they pay the rent." Gee moved toward a jewelry display in the middle of the room. Frowning, she fingered the overturned black velvet trays. "Aunt Babette didn't say the place was trashed. Someone's been in the shop since she left."

"Yep." Jane felt like a hunter, intent and focused. *I forgot how much I love the feeling of an active investigation. How can something so terrifying feel so good?* She studied the register. The locked box drawer dangled off its broken hinges, cracked in half. "Someone used a pry bar to hack into the register, Gee. Time to call it in." She thumbed 911 on her phone.

"911 Dispatch. Police or ambulance?"

"Police."

"State your emergency."

"An apparent burglary."

"Your name?"

It took two tries. "Jane Byrne."

"We've recorded this number. What's your location?"

"Le Maison Gris, a shop in Jackson Square. Gee? What's the address?"

"Tell them it's on Chartres Street. They'll know where it is."

"Any sign of forced entry?"

"Not exactly. We found a set of keys in the door, but the owner is missing and the place is trashed. It wasn't left this way."

"Stay on site. A unit is responding."

"10-4." Jane thumbed the red end call button. *How strange it is to be on this side of the thin blue line.* "They're coming."

"Good." Gee suddenly dropped to her knees as Jane spotted something blurry and white moving fast and low to the ground reflected in the store's mirrors.

"Watch it, Gee!"

"Free!" Gee scooped up a gorgeous longhaired Persian cat. Hugging the cat tight, she cradled it against her shoulder. "What's going on, Free, baby? Where's your mother?"

"A cat." Jane sighed. She could hear the animal happily purring from across the room. She was so hyped up it sounded like a two-stroke Evinrude motor. "What's free?"

"She's Free, Dee's store cat." The purring grew even louder. "Can you believe Dee found her living under a dumpster? Brought her in and gave her a home. Isn't she a beauty? Named her Free Pussy."

"Nice."

"Usually gets a laugh." Carrying Free Pussy, Gee strolled toward the rear of the shop. "I still don't get what's going on here." She pointed her chin at a poster of partying Carnivale mummers that lay on the floor, ripped to shreds, and a display of fake matchstick voodoo dolls that had been tipped over, brutally stepped on, and crushed.

"I get that they went through the jewelry. Some of it was sterling; they could sell it for cash. And they hit the register, so we know they were looking for money." Gee stared at the floor. "Buy why trash the poster and crush the dolls? You'll notice they didn't bother the T-shirts or the masks or any of the commercial tourist crap. They only hit Dee's voodoo merchandise." She resettled Free Pussy against her neck. "This looks more like some pissed off teenage vandalism than a burglary to me."

"Maybe so." Jane stepped around the counter. "How did they get Dee's keys?"

"Now that is a good question." Gee turned toward a bamboo curtain partition. Without warning, Free Pussy hissed and spat, growling so demonically low in her throat it sounded like a human moan. Suddenly arching her back like a horseshoe, she fiercely clawed Gee's hand, struggling for release before leaping away.

"Fuck, Free!" Gee shook her fingers. "That hurt!"

"Don't move." The hair on the nape of Jane's neck slowly stirred. "Do you smell that?"

"Jane? You're scaring me." Gee froze. "Why are you looking like that?"

"I smell bleach." Jane sniffed repeatedly. "Chlorine bleach."

"So? Maybe they knocked over a bucket."

"No. Bleach destroys DNA. Criminals use it to cover their tracks. Where's it coming from? Is there a basement?"

"Basement? What basement? The water table's two feet beneath our feet."

"What's back here?" Jane gently pushed a bamboo curtain aside.

"A supply room, where Dee keeps her inventory stuff."

The swinging curtain stirred the overpowering chlorine odor into the breeze. The bitter scent grew so sharp that it singed Jane's nostrils and brought tears to her eyes. Tugging her jacket over her right hand, she flicked the hallway light switch, revealing a stubby corridor crammed with chrome shelving, cardboard boxes and a dinged up half-opened metal storeroom door.

"Stay back, Gee." Jane had a ghastly premonition. "Leave this for the cops."

"Fuck that." She lunged ahead. "I'll go look."

"No." Jane caught her arm. *I can't let her do this alone.* "Follow me."

Turning sideways to minimize her profile, Jane slipped into the hall. They continued toward the storeroom step by cautious step. Pulling her sleeve over her left hand, Jane covered her nose and her mouth, breathing shallowly through the mesh polyester microfiber. Her nostrils burned as the chemical scent grew even stronger and she noted a curling spatter of burgundy droplets on the concrete floor. Using her elbow, she pushed the storeroom door open. Blindly reaching in, Jane slid her sleeved right hand along the strangely stickily resistant wall. Feeling for the light switch, she flicked it on.

Gee screamed.

CHAPTER THIRTY-NINE

Gee's scream pierced Jane's ears, triggering a PTSD memory echo so vivid her knees buckled. The storeroom smelled like a chlorine bomb had exploded. An uncapped gallon bleach bottle lay tipped on its side on the floor. Jane's eyes wept as she captured the searing CSI image like a digital snapshot. She almost heard the shutter click.

A lake of congealed blood pooled from one end of a rolled-up square of mint green rug, oddly turned pile side out. Plum colored splotches had seeped through the weave. Jane spotted the dull ivory tone of open raw bone. Bloody footprints in two different sizes crisscrossed the floor. Hundreds of dried dripping crimson handprints plastered the walls with one long jagged spray where the killer had flicked his blade. Turning, Jane shoved Gee back into the hallway. Gee stumbled and fell to her knees.

"What was that?" She screamed, pushing up off the floor. "Was that Dee?"

Jane's brain spun through the obscene snapshot images like a satanic merry-go-round that she couldn't un-see. "Don't go back in there, Gee. Wait for the cops."

"Let go!" Gee struggled to break Jane's grip. "I want to see."

"No, Gee, no, you don't. We need to call Dupree."

"No, please, no." Gee moaned as her shoulders slumped. "I don't want it to be Dee. Not Dee, too. Not Dee."

"I know, honey. I know." Grasping Gee's shoulders, Jane guided her closer to the wall to avoid further contaminating the scene. "We need to follow protocol." She pushed her through the bamboo screen. "Do this the right way."

209

"Fuck!" Gee shook free. Staggering down the aisle, she threw open the front door and fell against the arcade's cast iron railing.

"Don't move," Jane ordered, digging out her phone. *Pickup, Dupree. I need you.* Her heart hammered so fiercely she heard the two beats in her ears.

"Ms. Byrne? A pleasure. What have you got for me?" Dupree drawled, sounding so self-assured he seemed to be speaking from an alternate universe. "Did you remember something more?"

"Dupree?" Jane squeaked. Shutting her eyes tight, she focused on precise reporting. "Gigi Pascoe and I are at Delilah Gardere's shop, Le Maison Gris in Jackson Square. We found Dee's keys in the door and we entered the shop approximately fifteen minutes ago. I called it in as a burglary." The tension released and she started to tremble. "We found Delilah Gardere, Dupree. You need to get here, stat. It's bad, Dupree, worse than you can imagine. Bring CSI. Hurry."

She heard his chair squeal.

"Jackson Square? ETA ten minutes. Stay put."

Gee puked a Niagara of yellow bile onto the flagstones. A passing tourist couple glanced up with obvious disgust. Groaning, Gee slowly straightened. Wiping her mouth, she aggressively flipped them off.

"He's coming?" She croaked.

Jane rested her hand on Gee's broad back. "Ten minutes."

"Holy crap." Pinching her eyes shut, Gee wiped her mouth with her palm. "You're sure that was Dee?"

"Yes, honey, I'm sure. I saw her face." *I'm not going to mention what else I saw in there.*

"Fuck!" Gee gripped the railing. "You ever see anything like that before?"

"Twice. When I was a cop." Jane admitted. "A DD nailed a Jeep full of kids and the case that tripped me into PTSD."

"But that was meant for *me*." Gee jabbed her trembling finger. "Those handprints on the walls? That's the freak show from *my* dream."

"I agree." *And it gets worse.*

"You do? Good. You agree with me." Gee combed her fingers through her hair. "I'm not hallucinating?"

"No. That set-up was too specific to be random."

"Who did that?" Gee voice rose to a shriek. "Who is after me?" She scrubbed her face with her hands. "Fucker! Come after me then, not my friends!"

A light bulb went off. "Gee? Who did you tell your dream to? Those are the ones we need to be looking at."

"Only everyone!" Pressing her temples with both fists, Gee looked up, startled. "What if he goes after Pops or Maman next? Or Aunt Babette?" Dropping her fists, she paled. "Jesus! My head is splitting. I need a smoke." She patted her pockets. "Left them in The Boat."

"We can't leave. We need to wait for Dupree."

"I'll be right back." She snapped. "I'm only going over there."

Gee purposefully bee-lined across Jackson Square. *How much do I really trust her?* A cool shadow of doubt shaded Jane's soul. *What if she takes off and leaves me holding the bag?*

Her CSI training flashed a red alert as she locked the shop door. "Wait for me!"

CHAPTER FORTY

Jane caught up with Gee by the mule carriage stand.

"I don't need a minder." Gee snapped, ignoring the pedestrian crosswalk and dodging across Decatur Street like a toreador as she snaked around the tent pole stakes of The French Quarter Market shops. "I said I'd be right back."

"I locked it up." Rolling her shoulders, Jane tried to loosen up. Glancing toward Canal Street, she hoped to see the marked NOPD unit or Dupree's Crown Vic. *I need help. Where is he?*

Gee strode around The Boat, heading purposefully for the glove box on the passenger side before gasping and pulling up short.

"What the fuck?" She choked. Her face filled with fury as she pointed at the door. "Who did this?" She screamed. "Who trashed my car?"

Triangle shaped crimson enamel chips lay scattered on the asphalt between the two fat white-walled tires. The words *DIE BITCH* were keyed into the panel's cranberry paint.

Die Bitch? Icy fear prickled Jane's skin like sleet. *Could Ryan Embry be behind this? Because that's what he called me after our date.*

Gee marched toward an Asian vendor selling scarves. "Did you see who did this? Did you see who keyed my car?"

"No, mister." The vendor shrank back, her hands defensively curling into claws. "I didn't see no one touching your car."

Jane grabbed Gee's arm. "He's been watching us, Gee." She knew the stats. *65% of criminals return to the crime scene thinking they've overlooked something critical or because they like watching the event unfold. Taking that risk gives them an extra thrill.* "He was standing here, watching us while we were in Dee's shop. Gee, listen to me." Jane tightened her grip. "Listen! I think Ryan Embry might be the killer, the one we want."

"Ryan?" Gee blinked. "Why do you say that?"

"Because he screamed 'Die Bitch' at me the night of our fight."

"You think Ryan did this?" Gee looked stunned. "Come on! Maybe they saw something." She ran toward the artists clustered in the Square. "Sir? Sir?" She ran up to the artist selling the strangely gray paintings. "Did you see anyone messing with that red Eldorado?"

"I might've seen something, Cap." He toyed with the bristling whiskers on his chin. "If I tells you, will I get a tip?"

Gee's neck flushed mottled red from her shoulders to her ears. She opened her mouth to speak and then snapped it shut. Tugging out her wallet, she flashed her cash. "Fourteen bucks. It's all I've got."

"I don't know that I saw much of anything for only fourteen dollars." The old man cannily studied her need with his rheumy eyes, pointing his knuckly finger at The French Market arcade. "I know they gots an ATM machine."

"Wait." Jane unzipped her backpack. "I'll add another ten."

He grasped the money. "Twenty-four dollars might do it."

"What did you see?" Gee demanded.

"I did see a couple over there admiring your car. She looked pleased, but I don't think she did nothing to it." He tucked the folded bills into his shirt pocket. "They was only standing there for less than a minute."

"What did they look like?" Gee pursued. "Black, white? Short, tall?"

"Distinguishing features?" Jane scanned the crowd. "Ball caps, beards, or tattoos?"

He chuckled at their obvious impatience. "Well, they was both white and she wasn't wearing no beard that I could see. He had a Saints ball cap on, but good luck with that. Half the men walking around the Square are wearing them." Sticking his splayed brush into a coffee can half-filled with turpentine, he gave the oily liquid a stir. "You two cops?"

"No." Jane stated. "But we need to locate them if they're still around."

"There was one other guy, a weedy looking fella wearing a uniform like maybe he was a janitor or something over at The Market."

"A uniform?" Gee looked puzzled. "What color uniform?"

"Don't rightly know, Cap. Might'a been gray, or green, or maybe even blue."

"What do you mean 'maybe even blue'?" Gee shouted.

"Stop yelling." The old man winced. "Nothing wrong with my ears. It's my eyes that're failing."

Jane scanned his odd gray scale paintings. "Gee? He's color blind."

"Only been my cross to bear my entire life. Runs through every boy in my family."

"Would you recognize these people if you saw them again?" Jane asked. "In a line up?"

"Don't rightly know. All them white boys looks about the same to me."

He shifted uneasily as Dupree's Crown Vic Police Interceptor roared up. Dupree had the blue and red strobes flashing below his windshield tint line and from the grill. He was leading a marked NOPD unit and a Coroner's CSI van.

"Definitely not." The old man spat. "If it means talking to the po-lice."

"Don't leave," Jane said as Dupree and team double-parked at the curb. "He's gonna want to talk to you."

"Catch me if you can, sweetheart." Lifting the lid on his plastic toolbox, he started packing up his paint tubes. "That's all I gots to say."

Dupree spotted them. Clambering out of the Crown Vic, he met them halfway across the flagstones, already yelling.

"I told you to stay put." He pointed at The Pontalba Building as he directed his team. "Seal off that sidewalk. The vic is in the shop."

"She's in the storeroom, Dupree." Shutting her eyes, Jane recalled the red horror. "Rolled up in a rug. She's been scalped."

Gee's face turned ashy. "Was that what that was?"

"We think the killer was watching us from Gee's car." Jane pointed her chin. "While we were inside."

Dupree glanced at The Market. "What makes you say that?"

"He left us a message." Gee spat.

"Take me to the freshest point." Dupree noted the black pods hanging from the Jackson Square buildings. "We might catch a break. Maybe we got video."

He followed Gee around The Boat's front bumper. Squatting, he studied the *DIE BITCH* damage and slowly rose. "He's not stupid. This side of the car is sheltered from the cameras and the Square. He could duck down and no one would see him working on it."

"He's getting away with everything." Gee reached a shaking hand into The Boat. "He killed Fancy and Dee, and now this."

"Don't touch it!" Dupree commanded. "Until my forensics team signs off."

Gee snatched her hand back. "What? Like my fingerprints aren't already on it? It's my fucking car, Dupree."

She turned the knob. The glove box popped open like a wampum biscuit can, filled to the brim with crumpled brown paper.

"What the fuck is this?" Gee tugged on the damp SuperCenter grocery sack. "I didn't put this in here."

"No, Gee. Don't." Jane warned as an array of horrifying possibilities filled her brain.

"What *is* this?" Reaching into the stained sack, Gee lifted a shapeless hairy blonde bundle of curls as her face turned battleship gray. "Jesus, God! It's Fancy's wig!"

215

CHAPTER FORTY-ONE

"He's taking trophies," Jane stated.

"He's fucking with me, Jane." Gee finished her café au lait. Setting the empty cup on the tiled floor between her feet, she rested her elbows on her knees. "He's fucking with *us*."

"I agree." Jane chewed her lip. Dupree had summoned them to the Central City station on Martin Luther King Jr. Boulevard for a case update and a follow-up interview. It was standard protocol, but fresh worry bubbled her nerves. She could see Dupree in his glassed-in office, but she couldn't hear him. He was animatedly yelling into his phone while thumping his fist against his desk.

Gee scratched her palm. "Three people dead in less than a week? Dupree'd better give us some fucking details. I want to know what they're doing about this."

"And Cal Johnson's still missing, too," Jane squirmed, shifting uncomfortably on her seat. The rolled edge of the chair kept biting into her thighs. *Did they pick these godawful chairs on purpose? To deliberately keep us on edge while we wait?*

"What if Ryan is behind this?" Gee stood. "Can't they watch him? I know he hates me for being trans. Said I *betrayed* him." She started pacing. "Like it's something I could change. Like I ever had a choice. I could see him doing this, lashing out to punish me." She paused, resting her hands on her hips. "He's plenty smart and wound way too tight. Always has been. Cheryl sees to that. She's on him like a hen with one chick. We need to tell Dupree."

"Tell Dupree what?"

Detective Bordelon turned the corner carrying a Styrofoam cup. Jane smelled the burnt odor of the bitter office brew and her paranoia twitched. *How long was Bordelon standing there? What else did he hear us say?*

Gee pointed her index finger. "We think Ryan Embry might be the killer."

"Interesting." Bordelon stared over the rim of his cup. "What makes you say that?"

"Because he screamed 'Die Bitch' at me the other day," Jane stated.

"And that was keyed into my car where we found Fancy's wig."

"Detective Bordelon," Jane reasoned, "as a POI he connects the dots."

Gee turned, looking curious. "POI?"

"'Person of Interest,'" Jane explained. "A key suspect."

"You may be right." Crumpling the cup, the detective tossed it into the trash. Raising his hand, he flicked a 'come here' gesture at Dupree.

His partner hung up the phone. Opening the door, Dupree stepped into the hall. "What've we got?"

"Tell him what you just told me."

"We think Ryan Embry might be the killer." Gee clasped both hands behind her back.

"He was at Leslie Pascoe's party." Jane started ticking the points off her fingers. "He fought with Fancy Abellard, he has a long-standing grudge against Gee, and Delilah would've trusted him enough to turn her back on him."

"True." Bordelon tugged his ear. "But I don't see a connection to the two murders at Guardian Storage or the ATPP."

"The ATPP is a secret organization," Jane argued. "You're never going to know if he's a member and now he's pissed at me."

"You? Why is he pissed at you?"

"We had a bad date," Jane stated. "Did you see Ryan on the tapes from Jackson Square?"

"No." Dupree pinched the bridge of his nose. "So far they're inconclusive. Spent six hours reviewing them last night. Felix? Let's bring Embry in, have a talk. I want to hear his side of things."

Bordelon checked his wristwatch. "It's still early. I'll run by his house. Might catch him before he leaves for work."

"If Ryan's not home," Jane rolled up on her toes, "he works for Delta Electric. Get a warrant. They can tell you exactly where he is based on the GPS in his service van."

"It's too early to ask the judge for a warrant." Dupree scowled. "We don't have probable cause. And you know a little too much about everything." He pointed to the center of his chest. "It would be a preliminary interview, the same thing we're having with you."

"I'll go bring him in." Bordelon marched sturdily for the lobby.

"Watch yourself, Felix." Dupree stepped back into his office. Grasping his laptop with one hand, he shut the office door with the other. "Follow me. Let's take this to Conference Room A. There's room to breathe." He strode down the hall, pushing a faux maple door open with his elbow. "After you."

Jane followed Gee in. The windowless room was approximately twelve by fourteen feet. It held a Formica-topped table and six ergonomic chairs. Jane sniffed. *I'm impressed. Still smells like fresh paint. Usually interview rooms stink like sweat, shit, and fear.* "Nice digs."

"Still new." Dupree pulled out a chair, but he remained standing. "This building's about the only good thing to come outta Katrina."

Setting his laptop on the table, he hovered one hand over an inset communication panel. "Do either of you object to me taping our conversation? Saves me the trouble of taking notes."

"I don't mind." Gee shrugged. "Do what you need to do. Let's get it done."

Jane leaned forward. "Do we need a lawyer?"

"You can certainly have one present if you like, but this is not an arrest." Dupree sat. "For now, this conversation is purely voluntary."

Jane's paranoia flared up again. "How's this? I'll listen to your questions, but I may decide to not answer them."

"That's entirely your call." Dupree flipped a toggle switch and a dime-sized red indicator light blinked on. "Detective Antwon Dupree, preliminary interview with Gigi Pascoe and Jane Byrne, Friday, December 16, 2016, 9:21 a.m. You start." He settled back. "Do you have any questions for me?"

"Cut to the chase." Gee swallowed thickly. "What did he do to Dee?"

"I need to warn you." Dupree swiped the touch screen. "The Deputy Coroner's report is graphic."

Gee braced her calves against the chair. "This is important to me. I need to know."

Dupree tented his fingers. "First off, we're not sure the killer's a 'he.' That shop is a public space. A lot of DNA got spilled. The CSI said she collected more then 120 samples from that storeroom alone."

"How was Dee killed?" Gee insisted.

Dupree cleared his throat. "Preliminary autopsy results indicate blunt force trauma to the base of the skull. Ms. Gardere also had a defensive fracture in the ulna of her right arm and six broken fingers with cuts and abrasions on both wrists."

"She was restrained." Jane shuddered, horrified. *That's my worst fucking nightmare, getting restrained by zip ties. What could be worse than feeling trapped?*

"Yes. Judging from the bruising, we believe the killer used duct tape and some type of small-bore wire, possibly baling wire or something similar."

Gee straightened. "But Dee fought back?"

"Judging from the defensive pre-mortem injuries she sustained, that answer is 'yes.'"

"I hope she marked him up good." Gee scrabbled her feet against the floor. "By God, if Ryan did this, I'm going to kill him, I swear to God."

Stop saying that, Gee! Dupree is recording your every word and you gave him permission to do it.

Dupree flattened both hands on the table. "The killer used a blade to remove her scalp. Dr. Sabatier found traces of carbon steel on the skull. It was a crude attempt with multiple hesitation cuts. The blade wasn't a hunting knife and it wasn't serrated. She believes the killer used a high-end kitchen knife." He cleared his throat. "CSI didn't find a knife at the crime site."

"But the scalping didn't kill Dee," Jane pursued. "What did?"

"Dr. Sabatier listed asphyxiation as the cause of death."

"Fuck!" Gee slammed her fists against the table. "He tied Dee up and then he strangled her?"

"Yes." Dupree's shoulders dropped. "For what it's worth, we believe the killer took the scalp post-mortem. It's a small thing, but at least Ms. Gardere didn't need to endure that trauma."

"Did he rape her?" Jane asked.

"No. There's no evidence of sexual assault."

"This is a fucking nightmare." Gee pressed her palms to her temples.

"What about Fancy's wig?" Jane asked. "Did CSI pull anything from that?"

"No, unfortunately. The killer soaked it in bleach."

Gee slumped against her chair, scratching a rough plastic patch on the table with the square edge of her thumbnail. "What do we do now? Wait for someone else to die? And who will Ryan go after, next?"

"We don't know that Embry is our POI, yet." Dupree smoothed his tie with his hands. "There's another idea I'd like to run by you." He flicked the intercom switch. "Gentlemen? We're ready for you now. Conference Room A. Come in."

CHAPTER FORTY-TWO

The latch clicked and the golden maple door swung open. Before she even turned, Jane heard the familiar throaty chuckle. She caught the lemony citrus note and the blushing rose tone underlying the rich bergamot of his cologne. *Fuck. Sultan Parfum Musk Aoud. I should have known.*

"Good morning."

His voice sent a shiver through her frame from her earlobes to her toes. Pushing back from the table, Jane took up a protected position, placing her back against an interior wall.

Dupree stood up and extended his hand.

"Special Agent Carter. Good to see you again."

'Carter' was a tall, slender, fit black male, approximately six foot two and 35 years old. He was built long, lean and loose like an NFL running back. His hair was clipped short on both sides and kept longer on top with a clearly shaved diagonal parting his scalp. He was wearing belted khaki slacks with a butter yellow sports shirt and a lightweight navy windbreaker. From this angle, his lapel was folded back so Jane couldn't see if it had the logo or the capital letter acronym written on it. Carter carried a tablet and a couple of flat gray envelopes tucked under his arm and he looked exactly like what he was. FBI.

"Antwon? You good?" Carter grasped Dupree's outstretched hand. "This is Special Agent Cesar Mayas. Cesar's on reassignment from the Boston Bureau. He's a great resource for our team. Knows the ground. I'd like to bring him in."

"Glad to have you." Dupree reached out again.

"Thanks. I'm looking forward to working with you."

221

Cesar was looking sharp. He sported a pencil-thin mustache and looked as dapper as Jane remembered in a tailored broadcloth shirt, platinum cufflinks, lightweight gray slacks and a blazer. *His hair is shorter than the last time I saw him.* Jane hid her smile behind her fingers. *And he's going way gray. How old is Cesar now? 40? 41?*

Gee caught Jane staring. "Man candy." Crossing her legs at the knees, she thoughtfully stroked her Adam's apple. "Tag. I saw him first."

Two chairs squealed in unison as the FBI special agents sat.

"Sounds like a challenging case," Carter offered.

"It has been, so far." Dupree tapped his laptop. "But we'll crack it."

"I have no doubt."

"These are our two principal witnesses. Ms. Gigi Pascoe and Ms. Jane Byrne."

Jane's heart hammered against her ribcage as Mayas turned. The tight conference room grew even warmer.

"I already know Ms. Byrne." Mayas smiled uncertainly. "Hello, CJ. How've you been?"

"You know him?" Gee went goggle-eyed. "You've worked with the FBI before?"

Jane suddenly didn't know where to rest her hands. "Yes, back in Massachusetts. We resolved a child abduction case together."

"The one where you shot that guy?"

"No." She squirmed. "That was another case, a hostage situation. A different thing."

"Don't mind me asking." Gee whispered, slipping out of her jacket and hanging it on the back of her chair. "But did you 'know him' know him, or know him?"

"It was business, Gee."

"Thank you, Jesus." She fanned her blush away. "This was about to get complicated."

"Chief Nunn mentioned you the other day." Mayas smoothed his mustache. "In a good way."

"It's Jane now," Jane stated, lowering her chin. "And I think about her, too. And the team. How's everyone doing?"

"They're good, really good. Anetta's settled in. She's running the show."

"I'll bet she is. And John? And Sarah, and the twins?"

"Also fine. Those kids are growing like weeds. They're four now."

Four. Jane felt sorrow's shadow cross her soul like a dense cloud suddenly blotting out the sun. *That's the choice I didn't take, the opportunity I missed. If I ever do go back, I won't be a godmother to those kids. I'll be a stranger.*

"What's going on?" Dupree looked confused. "Have we tripped into witness protection?"

"No." Jane blinked. "I left." *It crushed my heart to do it, but I needed to leave.* Clenching her fists, she owned the fierce gift of her freedom. *I am Jane Byrne. I left all of that behind me and I'm not going to be afraid of anyone or anything, anymore.*

Mayas carefully folded his manicured hands. "Jane? Will you be able to work with me on this case? Or should I recuse myself?"

"No! Don't do that!" Gee exclaimed.

"I can work with you," Jane replied easily. "Why did you come back to NOLA?"

"Diabetes. My Dad's not doing well." Mayas settled back. "My family needs me. Temporary hometown reassignment offered the perfect solution."

"Welcome home." Dupree cleared his throat. "Special Agent Carter will be opening the zero file for this case. Win? Why don't you lead off?"

"Thank you." Carter propped his tablet against the intercom. Squinting, he adjusted the screen to counteract the glare from the canister lights. "I'm Winston Carter and I'm a hate crime specialist with the NCAVC, the National

Center for the Analysis of Violent Crime division of the FBI." His smile revealed some self-deprecating humor. "It's a mouthful, but it fills up my resume."

"Your resume stands up just fine on its own," Mayas stated firmly.

"Thank you again." Carter flicked the tablet. "Fourteen hours ago, Detective Dupree filed an incident submission on the Fancy Abellard homicide and the subsequent homicide of Delilah Gardere with our NIBRS data collection system."

"Here we go," Gee sassed. "Acronym soup."

He looked up. "NIBRS is an acronym for the National Incident-Based Reporting System, the system we use to collate hate crime statistics. This incident data tripped a flag because of the violent nature of the offenses, the close timing, the known relationship between two of the victims and the potential for bias motivation."

"So, you think this is a hate crime?" Gee asked.

"We believe it's a distinct possibility."

"Then let's get something straight." Gee stared down her pointed finger. "Fancy and Dee weren't victims. They were my friends."

"Pardon me, of course, you're right." Carter had the grace to look unsettled. "I didn't mean to sound insensitive."

"An important thing to remember," Mayas studied Gee carefully, "is that you're not alone in this. Many hate crimes go unreported out of shame or fear." He tapped the table. "Thank you for coming forward and meeting with us today."

"I'm not ashamed." Gee stoutly folded her arms. "Or afraid."

"Glad to hear it." Carter quickly pecked out a sentence on his keyboard. "Intolerance can have a devastating impact on families and communities. It plants the seed of terrorism in our country." He looked up. "Any questions, so far?"

Gee thoughtfully tapped her chin. "You married?"

"Really, Gee?" Jane hissed. "Stop fucking around."

"What? I was asking for you."

"In the interest of full disclosure, I'm not." Carter illuminated the room with a million-dollar smile. Squaring his windbreaker, he side-eyed Mayas and continued. "Before we dig in, we do need to disclose that we've already run preliminary background and security clearance checks on you both."

Jane felt a ripple of unease as Gee straightened.

"Security checks? What for?"

"Standard protocol," Mayas rumbled. "Everything was public information."

"We'll start with yours." Carter expanded a document on his screen. "Gigi Pascoe, age 32, lifelong NOLA resident. Six misdemeanors for public intoxication, two for possession of marijuana less than one ounce and one arrest for assault with intent to do physical harm."

"Bitch was trying to steal my beads." Leveling her gaze at Mayas, she flicked her fingers. "What can I say? It was Mardi Gras and I was young."

Something, something's going on there. Jane's stomach stirred as Carter focused on her.

"Cynthia Jane 'CJ' Allamand, AKA Jane Byrne. Aged 34. No misdemeanors on record, but charged with felony manslaughter during an officer-involved shooting using excessive force."

"Justice was served." Jane stated flatly. "The Grand Jury ruled I had the lawful right to discharge my service weapon during the commission of a crime."

"True," Mayas agreed slowly, "but the court appointed five-year probationary period remains pending."

Fucker. Jane felt stung. *Don't you think I know that?*

"Probation?" Gee's jaw fell open. "Does Maman and Pops know that?"

"No one does." Jane snapped. "And don't let it get out. You'll cost me my job."

"You didn't tell the Guardian Storage people, either?"

"I needed the job, Gee." An aggravating tinnitus started buzzing in her ears. "I still do."

"What I don't get." Mayas' forehead channeled into wrinkles. "Is why take an alias? CJ, you left the state."

"I told you it's Jane, now. Jane Byrne." She battled her temper. *How do I explain this so that it makes sense?* She tucked her hair behind her ear. "I wasn't trying to hide. After the hearing I didn't feel like the same person anymore. When I walked out of that courtroom I felt invisible, anonymous, like a ghost." She plowed her fingertips down the tensed muscles in her thighs. "I needed to draw a line in the sand. I needed to make a before time and an after to get past it, to put that shit behind me, to somehow get to the other side." Jane shook the tension from her hands. "Legally changing my name did that. It helped me finish it and move the fuck on." She straightened. "Is that going to fuck things up and keep me from helping you catch this prick?"

"No, it won't." Carter smiled warmly. "Actually, your prior law enforcement experience as a detective is considered a plus."

"It is?" Jane raised her chin as unanticipated hope lifted her spirit and warmed her soul. *Carter needs my experience. He thinks I'm a value add.* The blush crept outward from her core until it tingled her fingers and toes. *I'll need to brush up on my Logic Tree skills, but maybe my training and my years on the force weren't wasted?*

"Let's pursue this thought." Carter's windbreaker strained as he folded his arms. He glanced at Mayas, who nodded. "We have a suggestion. We need to flush this killer out. Staying inside, locked up tight, won't do it. We need to bring this scumbag into the light. Ms. Pascoe? You seem to be the single commonality, the killer's central focus."

Gee scowled sardonically. "Lucky me."

"What's your ask?" Jane said.

Carter leaned in. "We'd like to hire you and Ms. Byrne as non-law enforcement consultants."

Jane's heart leapt into her throat. "Undercover? You want us to work undercover for the FBI?"

"Yes." Mayas added quickly, tapping the table again. "Hired for this specific case only. Undercover operations have proven to be very effective. You two have access to the LGBTQ community. You can both go where we can't get in."

"Interesting." Gee leaned on one elbow like a poker player holding a winning hand. "What's it pay?"

"The standard Federal hourly contractor rate," Mayas replied smoothly. "Minus state and federal withholding." Removing two envelopes marked CONFIDENTIAL from his blazer, he slid them over the table. "Here's your formal release with a legally binding contract. Review these documents and let us know if you have any questions. I know we dropped this on you." He smiled at Gee. "A federal pay grade scale card is included."

"Let's plan on regrouping tomorrow after you've had time for review," Carter added.

"What about hours?" Jane asked as her brain lit up with fresh possibilities. "Can I quit working security?"

"No! Don't do that." Carter's eyes widened with alarm. He raised his palm. "You need to pursue your normal lives. Undercover duty needs to fit seamlessly into your existing lifestyle and your current schedule. Don't alter anything. If there's a conflict, you'll need to behave as you normally would by scheduling time off for vacation or taking a sick day or leave of absence. Continue to keep everything as transparent as possible. We don't want to spook the killer."

Funny that. Working for the FBI was my dream job. Jane agreed thoughtfully. "What brought this on?"

"Because," Carter settled back, "after reviewing Detective Dupree's case notes - thank you again, detective - we believe the investigation needs to be elevated above the baseline hate crime status."

"About goddamn time," Gee interjected savagely. "Two of my friends are dead."

"And judging from the data." Flicking his tablet, Carter stared. "We believe metro NOLA has activated a serial killer."

CHAPTER FORTY-THREE

"Ryan's a serial killer?" Gee gaped.

Special Agent Carter's head snapped up. "Who's Ryan?"

"Ryan Embry." Gee glanced uncertainly at Dupree. "An ex-friend of mine."

"We couldn't be that lucky," Mayas wondered. "Could we?"

"Since we spoke this morning," Dupree interjected, "we've identified Embry as a potential POI. We're picking him up for a prelim now."

Carter looked surprised. "You have enough evidence to support an arrest?"

"Not yet. It's premise and hearsay, but the logic is compelling. We're still reviewing the crime scene tapes out of Guardian Storage."

"Any indicators?"

"Not so far. There are over 400 hours of tape to review."

"If I work undercover," Gee asked, "will I get a gun?"

"Carrying a weapon is a personal choice you'll need to make," Carter emphasized. "The Bureau will not be issuing you one, no."

"If you do purchase a personal weapon," Dupree inserted. "We strongly recommend that you take a safety training course plus you'll need a carry permit according to Louisiana law."

Gee turned. "Jane? Do you have a gun?"

"No." Jane dropped her focus to the linoleum. "I had to surrender my service weapon as a condition of probation."

"I'll think about it." Gee repeatedly slid the envelope beneath her fingertips. "If we do go with this, what's the next step?"

"You tell us." Mayas smoothly adjusted his cufflinks. "What would you normally do over the weekend?"

"Seriously?" Gee laughed, looking wicked. "How much detail can you handle? Saturday night means Club Femme du Monde. Tomorrow night the club'll be hopping."

"Where is this club?" Carter asked.

"Frenchmen Street," Dupree responded automatically. "It's a known nuisance bar."

"Nuisance, my ass." Gee sent him a sour look.

"That area is solid cover." Mayas nodded grimly. "Plenty of foot traffic. No one will notice a HUMINT surveillance unit."

"Everyone's so high that no one will notice." Dupree scowled.

Gee laughed. "Everyone's so high that nobody cares."

"In any case," Mayas interrupted. "You won't see us, but we'll be there." Reaching into his breast pocket, he distributed a pair of silver sealed foil pouches. "You'll need to wear these."

"Condoms?" Gee tossed the foil pouch between her hands like a hot potato. "How lucky do you think we're gonna get?"

"Those are audio GPS wires," Mayas replied sternly. "Clip them inside your shirt, the hem of your pants or your skirt," he flushed, "whatever you're wearing tomorrow night. Make sure that it's physically attached to your person, meaning, don't drop it in a handbag that might get left behind. We'll use those wires to listen in and track your position via GPS."

"I like a lot of different positions," Gee's teased, flipping the foil packet between her fingers like a cardsharper. "How does this thing turn on?"

"It's always on. Once it's removed from the protective sleeve, we'll record everything you say and track your movements. It's an automated feature."

"Everything, son?" Leaning back, Gee slid the foil pouch into her hip pocket. "I hope you're ready for this. You sure it's legal?"

"It is, as long as you volunteer to wear it."

"No worries from me. Dupree?" Gee straightened. "I'm seriously missing my wheels. When do I get The Boat back?"

"Unfortunately, the Forensics supervisor needs to sign off on it before it can be released from the pound. He took a week's leave. We're looking at sometime next week."

"Well, that sucks for me."

"Let's take my bike tomorrow night, Gee," Jane offered. "It'll be easier to park."

Carter hunched forward. "Shoot for eight o'clock. We want to maximize our window of opportunity."

"P.M.?" Gee snorted. "Sugar, most folks will still be waking up from their naps. The Club Femme Du party doesn't even get lit 'til after midnight."

"Midnight?" Jane remembered her shift responsibility. "Hold up. I'll need to call off sick."

Gee smiled brilliantly. "I'm proud of you, girlfriend. You're finally catching on. Everyone in NOLA who works Saturday night calls off sick. The only ones working are the bar backs and the strippers."

"Let's plan on midnight then for surveillance," Mayas stated, desperately. "Could you both get to the club by midnight?"

"For you, sugar? It's a date -"

"Shit, Silverback." Carter pointed at his tablet. "I got a Yahoo alert. The media just christened the killer."

Mayas leaned across the table. "What name did they pick?"

"The Crescent City Slasher." Carter started punching his keyboard, his racing fingers a blur. "We need to get on this. How's that press release coming?"

"Still with Legal." Mayas pulled out his phone. "I'll send you my draft."

"I wish they wouldn't do that," Dupree stated. "De-humanizes these monsters. Makes them seem bigger than they are. Turns this all into some kind of game."

"Sells newspapers." Carter kept typing.

"Sells advertising." Mayas corrected. "I swear people are sheep."

Dupree stood. "And we're the sheepdogs standing between them and the wolves. You two?" Crossing the room, he unlatched the door and held it open with one hand. "Leave them to it. Don't forget your envelopes."

Gee shrugged into her jacket. "Dupree? Should we say we talked to the FBI or keep it on the down low?"

"Mention it as part of a normal conversation." He ushered them into the lobby. "The killer knows you've been here if he has been watching you."

"Agreed," Jane said. "We need to act normal, Gee. Like those special agents said."

"I'll try," she offered dubiously. Suddenly, she froze.

Jane heard it, too. Two male voices in animated conversation. She caught Detective Bordelon's milder mid-range tone and she flinched as Ryan Embry turned the corner. Ryan was walking with his usual loosed hip grace. Jane was shocked to see that he wasn't cuffed or under any type of restraint. Ryan slowed to a full stop as a wide toothy grin split his face.

"Lookee who we got here." Raising his hands, he waggled all ten fingers at them. "Bye-bye, bitches. Seems like you got nothing on me."

Giving them a cocky, two-fingered salute, he spun on his heels, sauntering toward the exit with an exaggerated casualness.

"Where's he going?" Gee crumpled the envelope in her fist.

"No reason to hold him." Bordelon grimaced, massaging his thumb. "Had an alibi."

Dupree raised both eyebrows. "How solid was it?"

"Rock solid." Bordelon wiped his mouth on his hand. "Waived his right to privacy. Delta's time stamp showed Embry worked a full shift yesterday in the Garden District from 9:17 a.m. until just after six p.m. We have his electronic signature on all seven service calls." He sighed tiredly. "He even showed me a receipt for the shrimp Po'Boy he ate at Lulu's for lunch. Paid cash, but it's time stamped, too."

Hold up. No alibi is ever that solid. Jane's training alert lit up like a Christmas tree. Her mind darted from logical point to point, seeking holes and framing objections. "Who keeps their lunch receipt?"

"Evidently, Embry does." Bordelon rubbed his nose.

Jane recalled her basic rule number two: *follow up and follow through.* "Are you gonna do an old school door-to-door? Walk his photo to those seven stops? Confirm Ryan's the tech who actually serviced those calls, that it wasn't someone else?"

"Seems redundant with the GPS from the service van confirming that Embry was there."

Jane kept drilling. "GPS confirmed that the *van* was there. How about subpoenaing Ryan's phone and confirming the GPS record against that?"

"What do you think I do with my day?" Bordelon snapped, suddenly looked puffy and ill.

"Easy, Pard." Dupree dropped his hand on the older detective's shoulder. "She doesn't know how thorough you are."

"This case is squeezing the juice out of me." He listlessly adjusted his glasses. "We didn't need to subpoena Embry's phone. He voluntarily surrendered it. The 'frequent locations' setting matched Delta's GPS and the seven service calls he said he made." Lifting his head, Bordelon stared out the plate glass window, his face bleak. "Embry's not our killer. We need to keep looking. He's clean."

Chapter Forty-Four

"Six-minute warning." Gee stood perched on the curb. "Uber's on its way." Hooking her finger under the envelope flap, she tore it open.

"You're reviewing that now?"

"Oh hell, yeah. Don't you want to know how much we're gonna get paid?"

Jane felt a flicker of surprise. *For the first time in years, I'm actually more interested in the job than in the money.*

Gee scanned the laminated card. "Federal pay grade G10-B, 'non-service associated independent contractor.' Pays 27 bucks an hour. Sweet!" She squealed, hugging the document to her chest. "I finally found a job I like! Getting paid to party!"

"Getting paid to catch a killer," Jane stated firmly.

"That too," Gee agreed, roughly stuffing the documents back in the envelope. "I like working with the FBI. That Agent Mayas friend of yours is smoking hot."

A-ha. Jane smiled. *I thought I noticed a little something smoldering there.* "He's forty something, Gee. Almost old enough to be your father."

"Hello, Daddy." She grinned wickedly. "I like 'em mature. It's been awhile since I've had a decent date. I'm gonna start working on him."

"Gee?" Jane blurted. "How does that work?"

She looked perplexed. "How does what work?"

"The sex." Jane carefully stepped through her question. "You're biologically male and Cesar's hetero as far as I know."

"You're worried because I don't have a vagina?" Gee dropped her arms to her sides. "It works like anything *ever* works, Jane. When people are interested in each other they figure it out."

"I'm sorry." Jane blushed. "I didn't mean to pry."

"Who taught you there's only one way to love?" Gee tapped her lips. Her voice rose. "And if they did, why are you still listening to them? Did'ya ever think that maybe they're wrong?" She started pacing the curb. "If you were attracted to Carter back there and he asked you out, would you say 'no' to him because he's black?"

"No! Of course not."

"Then what's the fucking difference? Why is my gender identity any different than the color of my skin?"

"I'm not sure why." Jane confessed. "There's just something about it that bothers me. I guess it's the way I was raised."

Gee pointed her finger. "That's an excuse but at least you're being honest. Jane? You're a smart cookie. Use your noodle. Think it through. You're a grown woman. Why are you still giving 'them' that power over you? Why are you letting 'them' make your decisions? Shit. I thought you were smarter than that. You sure come off that way."

I do?

"Back there with Bordelon you really showed your stuff. Mayas was smiling. Even Carter looked impressed." Gee tucked the envelope under her arm. "How solid do you think that GPS shit is?"

"It's technology." Jane frowned. "It could be manipulated."

"Ryan's an electrician. Do you think he's smart enough to do that?"

"You tell me. Is he a gamer? I'd think it'd be more of a programming kind of thing."

"I know Ryan plays games with that cotton-picking buddy of his. He's got that garage tricked out like a man cave."

"Which buddy?"

"That Tyler Shank peanut head." Gee nodded grimly. "Ryan's

changed. He used to be more outdoorsy. Hunting, fishing, I know he had a lease camp in St. Bart Parish. Doesn't go there much. I heard Cheryl complaining about it to Maman the other day. Still paying the lease on it. She said his arsenal was collecting dust."

She cocked her thumb. "Inside the lobby just now? Ryan scared me. I know how he gets. When he starts acting all cocky it's because he thinks he knows something secret, something special." She thumped her chest. Hooking both thumbs under an imaginary pair of suspenders, she lowered her voice an octave. "He knows something that makes him a big, important man."

Sweeping her hair back, Gee laughed before checking her phone. "Two minutes. I hate not having wheels. Uber's getting expensive."

Was that a hint? "I said I'd pay you back half."

"Sure, but you never said when." She shrugged. "Most friends Venmo me right away."

"I don't have Venmo. I'm off the grid." Swinging her backpack off her shoulder, Jane dug for her wallet. "What do I owe you?"

"Right now? Total? You're sitting at about fifty, all in."

"Here's fourteen." Jane proffered her cash. "I'll pay you the rest when we get back to the house."

Gee raised her hands. "I don't want to leave you with nothing."

"Take it, Gee. Seriously. I can get more from my stash before I leave for work."

"If you're sure." She slowly tucked the money away. "Thanks. My wallet was getting thin." Swiping her phone to unlock it, she quickly tapped out a text.

Who's Gee texting? Jane felt uneasy. *It wouldn't be the Uber driver, that's done through the app.* She wrestled with the irrational paranoia that still seemed to rear up at every opportunity. *Stop it. Gee has other friends, besides Fancy and Dee. Not everything is an out-to-get-me conspiracy.*

She heard tires squeal and automatically stepped away from the curb as a white Delta Electric van swung around the landscaped median. Peering through the skeletal crepe myrtles she tensed as she recognized Ryan Embry hunched behind the wheel.

"Head's up, Gee" Jane warned.

Ryan spotted them standing on the sidewalk. Deliberately slowing the van to a crawl, he lowered the passenger window, grinning. "Here bitch, bitch, bitch," he crooned. "Look at that fine pair of cunts we got standing there. Wanna ride, bitches?"

Gee leapt off the curb, arms swinging. "Get outta that van, Ryan. I'm gonna fucking take you apart!"

No, Gee! Don't push his buttons. Jane's hand automatically swept for her side arm and came up empty. *We don't know what we're dealing with.*

"Sorry about what happened to your pussy girlfriends." Ryan hissed. "It's killing you not knowing who done it." Popping his open mouth with his palm, he mocked Gee with a war cry. "Woo-hoo-hoo. Scalping's a bitch." Cocking his thumb and finger at Jane like a gun, he silently mouthed: "You're next. You. Yes, you. Next."

"No, I don't think so." He floored the accelerator as Gee snatched at the door. Howling, he sped away, leaving them choking on a plume of oily smoke.

"See what I mean?" Gee coughed repeatedly. "Tell me he's not involved in this!"

"You're right. I don't care what that GPS said." Jane's sinuses burned at the rubbery stink hanging suspended in the air. "Ryan Embry knows something."

Chapter Forty-Five

Piddles started howling even before Jane slid her key into the lock. *How does he know to do that? It's not like I make a lot of noise walking across the courtyard.* Tugging the door open he bounded outside, hopping on his hind legs and pawing the air in his delight to see her.

"Dog? You are a fool." Jane laughed. "Glad to see you, too, Mr. P."

She gave him a minute to spritz Leslie's garden before stepping inside the apartment. She felt exhausted, bone weary, but it was the good kind of tired, the feeling you got when you overworked your brain with thinking and not the logy version that hung off your shoulders like a soggy blanket from depression. Jane raised her chin. *I forgot how good it feels to be engaged in an active investigation even with the FBI withholding information. It's invigorating.*

She tossed the FBI documents on the upholstered chair before stripping off her backpack and her jacket. Her ever ready inner critic immediately snarked a reminder that she should hang her jacket up or it would wrinkle. Recalling Gee's remark about letting other people make her decisions, Jane wondered: *Whose voice am I hearing now? Mom's? It's my jacket and I'm going to ignore it. When you're busy with real life you don't have time to listen to that perfectionist bullshit.* She tested her decision and it held firm. The interior voice remained silent without a follow up rebuke. Jane realized with surprise that it was because she felt justified in her actions and happy. "Is that what this is, Mr. P?" She whispered, almost afraid to say the words out loud in case she jinxed them. "Happiness?"

He cold nosed her palm impatient at her delay. She headed into the pantry to get him a treat. The kitchen clock read 11:42. *Plenty of time for a run before I grab some sleep.* Her muscles felt stiff and she relished the thought of loosening up. "What do you think, Mr. P? Run to Crescent Park before our nap?"

The pantry door hung open. Folding it back, Jane paused. *That's odd. I always make sure this door is secure to keep Piddles and the other critters out. I'm getting careless in my old age.*

She fed Piddles his biscuit and returned the cardboard box to the shelf, straightening the dish rack as she passed. *How did that get knocked off kilter? I didn't leave it that way. My OCD would've kicked in immediately until I straightened it.*

Not wanting to trail crumbs through the apartment, she waited for Piddles to finish crunching his treat before heading upstairs with the contented dog at her heels. Kicking off her shoes, Jane stripped out of her T-shirt and jeans, tossing them into the overflowing laundry hamper. She stood for a moment in only her bra and panties, enjoying the brush of cooler air against her bare skin. Her running gear hung on a hook on the back of the bathroom door. Pushing the door open, she reached in.

Piddles leapt onto the bed, circling the mattress twice before pawing the comforter into a soft nest as Jane slipped into her Lycra running shorts. *Fool dog.* She smiled. *And he's been sleeping on the bed again while I'm out. Look how he's messed up the pillows. Trust a dog to think I wouldn't notice.* She tracked his previous effort. *Up the stairs and straight to the bed. No surprise there.* She relaxed. *The rag rug is still thumbtacked exactly as I left it.*

She struggled to pop her head through the thrift store nylon top. *That offer from Carter could change my life and I liked seeing Mayas again.* Coming up for air, Jane checked her feelings. *Funny how when I wanted to work for FBI it got denied and now here it is again.* She paused. *I could still learn a lot. And maybe I made too big of a thing out of never going back to Nantucket.* Sitting on the edge of the bed, she laced up her left shoe. *I'm not ready to do that right this red-hot second, but I might go back for a quick visit someday. Don't close any doors, right? I'd like to see my old crew again. Might not be so awful checking in with them.*

Switching her feet, she laced up the other shoe. *It's kinda funny that Gee likes Mayas. Poor bastard.* She chuckled. *Doesn't know the tsunami is coming for him. Good luck stopping Gee when she sees something she wants. He's such a ladies' man and she's some new kind of lady. I can't wait to see how this plays out.*

Cricking her neck, she stood, shaking her shoulders loose. *And Special Agent Carter is one good-looking man. You can tell he really works at staying in shape.* She warmed at the thought. *He seems totally on point for someone his age. It's impressive. You can tell he never fucked up his life.* "Ready to go, Mr. P?" Jane turned, jolting to a full stop. "What are you eating?"

Piddles immediately stopped chewing. He gazed at Jane with the soulful look of certain guilt in his eyes as he slowly licked the black and brown specks off his chops.

What is that? A stick? She reached for the wet twiggy bundle. *What has he got into?* Jane recoiled in horror as her brain made sudden sense of what she was seeing. The hoodoo doll sprang into sharp focus, a rough bundle of peeled bark sticks bound together with a scrap of red bandanna. A three-inch long dressmaker's pin painted lipstick red pierced its neck.

"Shit!" She flung the doll across the room, repeatedly flicking her damp fingers. It thumped off the planked pine floor and skittered to rest against the dresser. Mr. P leapt up and barked, wagging his tail and willing to play this exciting new fetch game.

"No, Piddles! Leave it!" Jane shouted. "Don't."

Grabbing a T-shirt out of the hamper, Jane picked up the crude homemade doll. It had a fierce pointed Sharpie marker face with tiny, pale half-moon fingernail clippings glued to the blunt end of each stick arm and leg. A twisted clump of blonde hair capped its head. A cold creeping horror chilled

240

her bones. *Where the hell did they get my fingernails and my hair?*

Striding into the bathroom, she threw open the particleboard door beneath the sink. *Shit.* The Dollar Store plastic bag was missing from the bucket. *They stole my trash.* Straightening, she dug her fingers through her makeup bag before searching the folded towels on the toilet tank. *Not here, either.* Spinning around, Jane scanned the bathroom. *They stole my hairbrush.*

She plopped down on the lidded toilet, feeling queasy and violated. *Someone's been in my house and I don't know who it was.* A line of cold beaded sweat popped along her hairline. Reaching up, she swiped it away with her hand, slowly grasping the invasion's deeper meaning as she started to shake. *It's more than that. Piddles didn't freak out about letting them in. He knew the intruder was a friend.*

Clutching the hoodoo doll, Jane ran downstairs as her mind flipped through the possibilities. *Who would do this to me? Aunt Babette? Why would she? What have I done to her?* Scrambling down the stairs, she skidded to a stop as her detective training kicked in. *First rule of any crime scene secure the site. Is the apartment secure?* Taking a deep breath, she trotted into the kitchen, pulling the dotted curtain aside. The six panes of wavy glass and the patinated brass bolt were intact. *Check. They didn't gain access through the kitchen.*

Marching back into the living room, she checked the side window. *No sign of forced entry here, either.* Nodding grimly, Jane admitted the unspoken truth. *The intruder used the front door and they used a key. Piddles let them in and they searched through my things.*

Gooseflesh crawled up her arms like an army of tiny biting ants as *they searched through my things* fully registered. Piddles whined uncertainly as Jane dumped the hoodoo doll on top of her crumpled jacket.

She crossed the room on leaden feet. In spite of her public scorning of superstition, she muttered a quick prayer to St. Jude, the patron saint of lost causes, wanting to know and to not know at the same time as she reached for the hollowed out book on the middle shelf. *It's been a week since I checked my cash. Rule Six says I'm not allowed to touch my stash unless it's payday or a genuine emergency.* The book felt roughly the same weight as she remembered. Squeezing her eyes tight, Jane blindly thumbed it open, using her fingertips to search the secret inner cavity. Her questing fingers scrabbled around all four corners and then checked them again as she vainly hoped against hope. A sick thud hit the pit of her stomach. She suddenly felt as hollow as the empty book. She fatalistically opened her eyes. Every cent she had in the world was gone.

CHAPTER FORTY-SIX

Jane burst into the Big House without knocking.

"What on earth!" Leslie almost dropped the free-range brown egg carton in her hands. "Jane! You nearly startled me to death!"

"Who has keys to my place?" Jane demanded as black spots pulsed before her eyes.

"I'm sorry, what?" Ken stood frozen by the sink, his fingers knuckle deep in the yellowy brine of a sweet butter pickle jar.

Gee sat kicked back at the kitchen table, her chair resting against the wall, her right ankle propped on her opposite knee. She sat forward with a thump, narrowly avoiding Piddle's paws. "Why?"

"Someone stole my money and left this on my bed." Jane shook the hoodoo doll. "Is this some kind of sick joke?"

Gee stretched out her hand. "Let me see that."

"No, Gee! Don't touch it!" Leslie shrieked. "Don't put that curse on my house!"

"Fuck, Jane. This is real." Gee slowly turned the twiggy doll over between her ringed fingers. "Someone's practicing red magic against you."

"None of you did this? You didn't leave that doll on my bed?"

"Of course not!" Leslie stared in open-mouthed horror.

"I don't mess with that voodoo shit," Ken added.

Gee handed the doll back. "I was with you all morning."

"What about Babette? Could she have done this?"

"She left for her church meeting before we did," Leslie said. "She won't get back until suppertime."

"Does she have a key to my place?"

"I don't think so." Leslie looked confused. "Why would she?"

"There's no sign of forced entry. The windows and the door are secure. The thief came through the door and they used a key." Jane stated. "Have you seen anyone in the courtyard?"

"Not me," Ken stated slowly, "but we only just got back from Publix."

"Are you sure you locked the door, Jane?" Leslie worriedly wrung her hands. "I hate thinking some stranger was trespassing on the property, but maybe you left the door open and someone from the street walked in?"

"I locked it. I know I did." *You don't know my level of career OCD. I checked that the door was bolted twice before I left to meet Gee.* "Here's another thing: Piddles let them in."

"Sweetheart?" Ken asked. "What about Cheryl? Did you ever give her a spare set of keys?"

"I may have, Ken." Leslie suddenly looked frail and uncertain. She raised her hand to her throat. "If I did, it was so long ago I honestly don't remember."

"That's it." Jane pulled out her phone. "I'm calling the cops."

"The police?" Leslie's pupils dilated until her eyes were almost black. "You're calling the police over a hoodoo doll?"

"I'm calling the police because someone stole my money. That's a felony and I'm filing a report."

Ken placed his monstrously huge hand over Jane's phone. "Wait a second. How much money was it? How much are we talking about?"

"3,600 bucks!"

"Holy fuck." He paled. "$3,600 dollars? You kept that much cash in your place? That's the most dumbass thing I ever heard."

"I had it hidden." Jane snapped. *I don't need to justify my actions.* With a flash she recalled Gee texting in front of the police station that morning. "Gee? Did you text anyone that I had cash at my place?"

"Me?" Gee squeaked as her shock flashed into anger. "Fuck you! You think I'm a thief?"

"Everyone, please." Leslie pleaded. "Calm down. Seeing this much anger scares me."

She's right. Jane scanned the Pascoe family. *I've handled this wrong. I shouldn't have dropped it on them like this.* She sucked in a long breath. "You're right, Leslie. I'm sorry."

Resettling her spinning brain, Jane dropped the hoodoo doll to her side and tried for a steadier gear. "This crazy shit's got me rattled. I spoke before I thought things through." *Wow. These last few years have really fucked me up. My knee jerks into paranoia are turning me into something I'm not.* "I'm sorry, Gee. I didn't mean to say that about the money earlier. I know you didn't take it. I'm sorry I even said that. It just popped out of me."

"At least now I know where I really stand with you," Gee stated bitterly. "Some friend you are. I would never talk to any of my friends the way you just talked to me, with suspicion."

"Gee, please." Jane gripped the doll. "Forget I said that. It's the kind of stupid shit I'm still working through from before. Don't let it ruin our friendship. I'm trying to do better, but it's gonna take time."

"Oh, Leslie." Ken sighed tiredly. "Look what you've done now. I thought we were through with that."

Leslie shrank back against the sink, her face stricken.

"Sweetheart?" His voice softened further. "Did you take Jane's money?"

"Ken! How could you even say such a thing?"

"Leslie, please." He searched her eyes. "Sweetheart? I can tell when you're lying. It'll be fine, but I need to know so we can pay Jane back. Did you already spend it?"

She straightened to her full height. "I don't know what you're talking about."

"Maman?" Gee extended both arms. "You need to give Jane her money. It doesn't belong to you."

"You've turned against me, too?" Leslie cried. "You, traitor! You, ingrate! After all I've done for you?"

"Maman, please." Gee begged. "Don't do this to me right now. I can't take much more."

"Fine." Leslie's eyes flashed fiercely before her defenses collapsed. Striding to the dishwasher, she flung it open. "Here. Take it! Take it all!"

Reaching in she pulled out a Ziploc baggie filled with cash. Marching stiffly across the floor, she thrust the plastic bag at Jane. "I was only keeping it safe. That much money should be in the bank."

Jane folded her fingers around the bag. "Leslie? You went through my things?"

"I have the right to inspect my property as your landlord." She defiantly met Jane's eyes. "I do have that right."

"Why did you leave the doll on my bed?"

"That wasn't me." She stepped back, shaking a finger, still defiant. "I didn't do that."

"So, someone else does have a key," Jane stated slowly as another realization dawned. "That's why Babette bolts her door. It's not to keep the neighborhood kids out, it's because of you." She glanced at the dishwasher. "What else have you got hidden in there?"

"Take it. Take it all!" Leslie snatched Tyler Shank's missing security badge, angrily adding it to the baggie in Jane's hand. "I don't want any of it anymore!"

Jane studied the laminated Delta Electric badge. "Tyler's been looking for this since your birthday party. Why did you keep it?"

"Lost things need to stay safe." Leslie folded and refolded a dishtowel. She began to tremble as her eyes darted around the cabinetry and the cupboards. "Like Ken, like Gigi, like -"

"That's enough!" Ken shouted. "Let her alone!"

"Jane?" Nervously linking her thin fingers, Leslie tested a winsome smile. "Are you still calling the police?"

Jane studied the items clutched in her hands. "No, but I am calling a locksmith. And I'm installing a deadbolt on my door like Aunt Babette did." Firming her lips, she nodded repeatedly. "I'll trust Ken with the new set of keys as my landlord, but Leslie not you." She released her pent-up breath. "The next time you want to check your property, it is your right, you'll need to let me know ahead of time so I can be home." She glanced at Ken. "That's the best I can do, or else I'm leaving."

"We can work with that," he inserted quickly. "Sweetheart? Sound good?"

Ducking her chin to avoid meeting Ken's eyes, Leslie silently nodded her agreement. Holding her fist to her mouth, she started sobbing, a bitter soul deep cry that crushed Jane's heart. Ken took a step toward her, reaching out his hand, but she waved him off, shoving the swinging door open and bolting for the living room.

"Maman!" Gee shoved the kitchen chair out of her way. "Wait!"

Ken caught her arm. "Give her a minute, Gee. She'll be okay, she just needs a minute to herself." He swiped his mouth. "When Leslie gets back, it's best if we don't mention this again." He circled his finger in the air. "We'll all be fine if we just let this move on."

"Poor Maman." Gee plopped onto the chair. Reaching for Piddles, she absently stroked his ears. "It's not her fault. It's something mental. She can't help it when she hides things."

"She's not a bad person." Ken listlessly started tidying up, brushing breadcrumbs off the cutting board onto his palm before tossing them into the trash. "She has the most generous heart of anyone you'll ever meet. She just can't stop doing this crazy hiding shit. She's done it for years," he emphasized, dropping a butter knife into an empty mayonnaise jar with a clank. Setting the jar in the sink, he stared into the courtyard. "God knows what we'd find if we ever searched these cupboards."

"Listen." He turned back. "I'll call Walt, a friend of mine. Ask him to set you a new lock. He'll come right over. I'll eat the cost." He worriedly combed his fingers through his thick hair. "Probably should've done that when you first moved in." Extending his hand, he flicked his fingers. "Give me your phone, Gee. I'll do it now. Okay, Jane? Are we good?"

We're all working through something. Jane set her jaw. *We all get to test the deep end where the monsters swim. The only safe way back to the shore is if we help each other.* "Yes, Ken. I can work with that."

CHAPTER FORTY-SEVEN

Jane headed home through the courtyard with her money, the twiggy hoodoo doll and Tyler's security badge grasped in her hands and Piddles trotting by her side. *Funny how things look different once you start connecting with people.* She scanned Leslie's raised organic vegetable beds and the rebuilt shed that Ryan had fixed up for her bike and the patch of tainted soil where the old chicken coop used to be. *It's only been two weeks since I moved in. Two weeks! And look how much more I know now about the Embrys and the Pascoes and even Aunt Babette. I never really knew Fancy or Dee,* she admitted sadly. *Not really. They were like shadows that passed through my life, but their loss still stings.*

Stooping, she flicked a desiccated pecan to play a quick game of fetch with Mr. P. *Gee must feel lost without her BFFs. I need to be a better friend. She needs me.* Shame heated Jane's face when she remembered irrationally calling Gee a thief. *I need to get a better grip on this case. Catch the killer and remove the threat. That's the best way to help Gee.*

She felt the fluttering edges of fatigue closing in. "Hope that locksmith is as quick as Ken said, Mr. P. I need my nap."

Locking the door behind them and checking it twice, she set the hoodoo doll and Tyler's badge on a stack of security manuals and studied the cash filled baggie. *Where do I stash this now? My bookcase cache got blown.* The perfect solution popped into her mind. She trotted upstairs, humming *Lucy in the Sky with Diamonds* as she headed for the bathroom.

Pawing through her makeup bag, she dug out her metal nail file and returned to the bedroom, dropping to her knees between the mattress and the wall and using the nail file to pry up the thumbtacks keeping the Dollar Store rag rug in place, carefully placing the tacks in a neat pile by her knee. Piddles started whining from his vantage point on the bed.

"First things first, Mr. P. Be right with you."

Sliding the nail file into a crack between two floorboards, she leveraged the shorter board up and popped it loose. Sliding her fingertips into the slim gap, she set the board aside. Reaching in between two floor joists, Jane sighed happily as her hand closed around the familiar microfiber cloth bundle. Crouching on her heels, she cradled the bundle in both hands.

"Hello, Lucy. I've missed you."

Carefully unfolding the cloth, Jane examined the black polymer frame and the blued steel barrel and slide of her Ruger LC9. 'Lucy' was a compact weapon, only 6 inches long and 4.5 inches tall. Smiling, Jane paused for a moment of quiet reflection to remember rule number one: *Protect yourself and defend your family and friends* as she enjoyed the heft of the semi-automatic pistol in her hand. She loved how neatly Lucy fit into her palm. Recoil operated, double action with a locked breech, Lucy had defaulted to a seven-round magazine. Jane had purchased an independent nine-round extended magazine as a backup, just in case. *Sixteen rounds total plus one in the chamber if I need it.* She smiled grimly. *Never needed more than six rounds to fix the problem before.*

Tucking the cash baggie into the floor cavity, she pulled out her appendix carry holster and the box of 9MM steel jacketed rounds. Holding the ammo box against her ear, she gave it a shake until it rattled, sighing with satisfaction. *No worries. Plenty left.* Folding Lucy back into the cloth, she resettled the floorboard, tacked the rug in place and stood, recalling rule number four as she headed downstairs. *Girl power: Ignore the fuckers when they say you can't do something.*

Halfway down the stairs, she stopped to consider the statements she had made about owning a gun. *Sorry, Leslie and Ken. Sorry, Gee. Sorry, not sorry, FBI.* She continued on. *Technically, I didn't lie. I said I surrendered my service weapon as a condition of my probation and I did.* She felt zero guilt. *You never asked me about my backup piece.*

Piddles gazed curiously as she set the bundle on the kitchen counter. Opening the box of 9MM rounds, she loaded both magazines, nimbly snapping cartridges into each clip. An immense muscle memory satisfaction began to spread as her fingers flew and she picked up her pace. *Nothing wrong with me remembering how to do this!* She recalled her shock at finding the hoodoo doll on her pillow. *That was way too personal, too damn close. Bed space is sacred. It's supposed to be safe.*

Ducking her head, she glanced out the kitchen window. *My spidey sense is tingling like mad and I never ignore that feeling. Never.* She felt the tension ease from between her shoulders with each satisfying metallic snick. *Preparation is the key. Whatever it is, bring it. I'll be ready.*

She jumped at a sudden rapping on her door. Piddles raced through the living room, barking sharply.

Jane laughed nervously. "Hold on, Mr. P." *So much for staying present and alert, ding-dong. Forgot about the locksmith coming over.* Snapping open a dishtowel, she modestly covered her project. "Thanks, Ken. That was quick. Let's get this done."

Unlocking the door, she staggered back as Cheryl Embry shoved her way in. Cheryl didn't stop until she stood in the center of the room. Piddles waggled his tail uncertainly before settling onto his dog bed next to the chair.

"Cheryl?" Jane sputtered. "What's up?"

"Saw you come in just now." She stuck her index finger in Jane's face. "I wanted to talk to you!"

"Okay. What's this about?"

"You know what this is about! The police took my boy to jail."

"Hold on." Jane raised her hands. "They only picked him up for questioning. I saw him leave."

"And why would they do that, unless they thought Ryan did something wrong? Now he's got to talk to the FBI." Her beady eyes blazed. "There's nothing wrong with my son. This is going to cost him his job."

"Cheryl, slow down. The FBI interviewed me and Gee, too. You were at Leslie's party. They'll probably call you in next."

"Is that what this is about?" Her voice quavered. "A fight at a birthday party?"

"No, it's about catching the scumbag who's murdered three people."

"We didn't have nothing to do with that!" Her shoulders hunched, and she wrung her hands. "I'm worried sick. Ryan hasn't slept in days. Comes home all hours of the night, stumbling around like a dead man. Won't talk to me or tell me what's going on." She stared at the floor, lowering her voice to a conspiratorial whisper. "I think he's started day drinking the way his father did."

She looked up suddenly. "You are breaking my son's heart!"

Me? How is this suddenly about me? "Cheryl, we weren't going to work out. We're two different kinds of people. We've got nothing in common."

"I knew you was unnatural the minute I laid eyes on you." She hissed. "And I know who you really are. Looked you up on the church computer. You're a murderess! Killed that man in cold blood. Shot him dead."

The Internet lives forever. Jane counted to three. *That's the problem these days. No one reads the whole story. They read the lurid headline, make their judgment and move on.* "If you read about the case you know the charge was dismissed."

"Sure it was! No judge is gonna send a cop to prison." The tiny ruby cross at the base of her throat trembled. "Moral corruption, I'm sure that's all that was."

"A U.S. District Court judge dismissed the federal charge," Jane interrupted angrily. "This didn't happen in someone's backyard."

"I don't care what a federal judge did. Does Leslie know she's harboring a criminal? I'll bet you forgot to tell her that when you moved in." She aggressively jabbed her finger. "That dead boy's father sued you personally in court seeking justice."

Jane struggled to remain calm. "Mason Hollister wasn't a boy and his father sued me in civil court. That charge also got dropped."

"Only because the father had a stroke and died fighting you -"

"Mason Hollister's mother dropped the lawsuit because she sided with me." The mad PTSD hornet started buzzing in Jane's ears. "Why would Marjory Hollister do that if she didn't think I was justified?"

"I don't know why she did that." Clamping her eyes tightly shut, Cheryl blindly flapped her hands at her temples. "It's unnatural, a mother siding with her son's killer." Her eyes blinked open. "What kind of mother would ever do that?"

"Mason Hollister was a monster," Jane stated flatly. "And Marjory Hollister knew it. Nothing she could ever do would fix that and believe me, she tried."

"You need to go." Cheryl stiffened. "You need to leave. You brought some evil kind of juju down on us when you moved in. All of this trouble, all of this death is your fault. All of this evil started with you." She stepped closer. "This used to be a nice neighborhood, friendly." She stared up, unblinking. "Never had a lick of trouble before you moved in."

"Cheryl, I'm sorry you feel that way." Jane crossed her arms. "I'm not leaving."

"You're a devil." Cheryl nervously fingered her cross. "Some kind of demon. You need to be cast out." She swept her arm at the hoodoo doll. "You've been warned."

"This was you?" Jane snatched up the doll. "You did this? You left this on my bed?"

"What if I did?" Cheryl sneered. "Nothing you can do about it."

"I could have you arrested for trespassing on private property."

"Good luck with that." She dug into her pocket. "Ain't trespassing when Leslie gave me the keys."

"Drop them or keep them, it's all the same to me," Jane stated. "The locksmith is on his way. This is the last time you'll get into my place without me knowing and the next time I'll be ready."

"I ain't afraid of you, bitch." She glowered. "You threatening me?"

"Take it any way you like." Jane caught the rattle of an approaching diesel engine. Stepping into the doorway, she saw a Fortress Protection panel van pulling into the driveway. Spotting her, the driver leaned out of his window.

"Ma'am? You called for a locksmith?"

"We did." Jane waved him in. "Perfect timing."

"I ain't done with you." Cheryl rudely dropped the key ring to the floor. "You ain't seen the last of me yet." She muttered, brusquely brushing by.

Whatever. Jane released her breath. *Don't engage. Let her have the last word. Just let it fucking go.*

Grasping the hoodoo doll in both hands, she snapped it in half. It broke in a shower of bark and splinters. The dress pin thrust through its neck etched a bloody welt across her palm that raised a line of tiny perfect crimson droplets. Unlatching the trashcan, Jane thrust the doll in as the welt started to sting like a paper cut. She swiped her palm against her pants. *What's the voodoo protocol for this? Should I have burned the doll or buried it like a dishonored flag?*

"Superstition." She scoffed. *I'll need to ask Aunt Babette. And I am through apologizing for my life!*

CHAPTER FORTY-EIGHT

Gee tightened her grip around Jane's ribcage. "Gimme! I want one of these! Don't tell The Boat. She'll get jealous."

The Ducati Monster clicked and growled as Jane changed gears, weaving the sporty motorcycle around an illegally parked car near the Old Ursuline Convent on Chartres Street. Tapping her shoulder, Gee pointed to the classical French building that covered half a city block.

"That convent used to be a vampire prison. Did you know that?"

"A what?"

"A prison. For vampires. Nuns locked 'em up on the third floor. Those shutters are nailed shut with silver nails blessed by the Pope."

More voodoo hoodoo. I can't get away from it. "You're shitting me, right?"

"Oh hell, no! Shutters blew open during Katrina. Folks avoided Chartres Street like the plague until the Pope sent a new keg of blessed silver nails and they got hammered shut again."

I'll play. "Did the vampires get out?"

"They surely did. Heard they flew to Houston. They like it better there. S'less humid. Doesn't mess with their hair."

"And the nails?"

"What?"

"The nails? The Pope's new nails. Were they silver-plated or sterling?"

"Girl? You crazy? Pure silver, of course! Plated nails wouldn't stop a vampire for more than a minute."

Jane swerved to avoid a drunken amorous couple stumbling along the curb. "Sounds like a solid con for getting money outta the church to me. How many of those pure silver nails actually made it to the shutters?"

"Shame on you, Jane, for thinking that way! Not everyone's running a game. Where's your faith in humanity?" Gee rested her bony chin on Jane's shoulder. "Cut right after Kerlerec. Grab the first spot you find. We'll need to walk in."

Jane slowed as a mournful brassy horn began to wail its lonesome notes into the night. *NOLA is the only town where you can hear trumpets playing at midnight and nobody minds. What is it about that sound that makes me feel like I've forgotten something important?* She braked to a stop in front of a space between two SUVs. "Hop off. I'm backing in."

Gee dismounted and strolled to the sidewalk, pulling a cigarette case from her breast pocket and looking very James Dean-ish in her denim jacket, white T-shirt, ankle boots and skinny jeans. Flicking her lighter, she lit a toothpick thin spliff.

"Puff, puff, pass. You want some of this?"

"No, thanks." Jane carefully muscled Monster into the narrow gap. "You do recall the FBI is listening to your every word, right?"

"I do." Gee popped a perfect smoke ring that hung in the air until she stuck her finger through it. "Carter said 'act normal.'" She inhaled sharply through her teeth. "This is normal 'Nawlins, Saturday night." Exhaling, she pointed at the bike. "You forgot your key."

"Keyless ignition. Monster doesn't have one. Pings off the fob in my purse within fifteen feet. One reason I bought a Ducati." Jane surreptitiously checked the concealed carry holster clipped to the waistband of her leather skirt. *Now that I've ditched my belly fat, I'm loving this appendix carry again. Tucks Lucy away where no one would expect to find her.* She reached up to straighten the spaghetti straps on her shimmering silver halter-top.

"Speaking of technology," Gee eyed Jane's outfit, "where d'you pin your mic? Not for nothing, Jane Byrne, but you're walking around in public half naked. Looking all sexed up there, girlfriend. When we get to Femme du, they're going to eat you alive."

"I pinned it to the underwire in my bra. Where's yours?"

Gee slipped the denim jacket off her shoulders like a striptease, waggling her eyebrows as she flipped the lapel. "Testing, one, two, three." She lowered her voice an octave and growled. "Mayas? Carter? You boys there?"

"Don't do that, Gee. Don't fool around." Jane quickly scanned the deeper shadows of the alleys. "You don't know who's watching."

"You're right." Gee strolled for the blazing lights of Frenchmen Street. "Where do you think they're at?"

"Wouldn't be surveillance if we could see them." Jane trotted in her unfamiliar heels to catch up.

"Smart ass." Gee stepped aside as a courtyard door on her right unexpectedly opened and two women stepped onto the street.

"Can't wait to show you this club, Liselle." The woman with the hot pink hair drawled. "It's totally lit. My favorite place in all of NOLA."

Wiping her nose, her heavily tattooed friend sniffed. "How did you come to find it?"

"As soon as I got to town, I asked: Where them gay bitches at? Took me about a minute and a half to find the lavender line where all the LGBTQ clubs are."

Gee grasped Jane's arm. "Follow them. We're still safer walking in groups. There's been some new stupid trouble since the election."

They merged into the sidewalk traffic flowing toward Frenchmen Street. The jazzy NOLA energy was electrically palpable. Jane's head swam as she felt her elevated heartbeat thumping in her throat and in her ears. *Look at all these people. I feel like a salmon swimming upstream.* She got shoulder-checked by another laughing partier and spun around. The night sky was a blurry smear of red, white and green neon light spilling from the bar signs. The thumping beat ebbed and flowed with each step she took as they passed the panhandling musical buskers camped out on every corner. A lone, maniacal drummer using peeled sticks pounded a drum set of overturned plastic pickle buckets, his setup in perfect alignment with the crumbling curb. Spotting Jane, he pointed one drumstick, threw his head back and laughed, his teeth gleaming like a beacon against the shadowy streaming crowd.

Gee paused. "Jane? You okay?"

"I think I'm tripping."

"Don't you love it? Isn't it great?" Gee looked aroused, her eyes wide with excited delight. "Look at all these humans being human. We're all part of the same zoo, right? Part of the same team?"

The crowd parted for a couple waltzing down Frenchmen Street. The woman was dancing topless. Her freely swinging breasts were painted with a garland of silver and gold stars and her cheeky red shorts left nothing to the imagination. Her male partner was more formally attired in a tuxedo jacket and a glittering gold top hat. A note pinned to his back read: *Will Pose for Tips.*

"This is what people really want. Life!" Gee triumphantly raised her fists. "Real life and being free to do whatever they fuck they want to do." She squinted. "Why do we make it so fucking hard on each other? Why do we keep doing that?" She rapped her temple. "That's what's really wrong with us. You do know that, right?" She knit her fingers together. "We turn everything into a competition and then we judge *everything*. It's such a fucking waste of time and energy." She pulled Jane toward a chrome door set into a black stucco wall. "We should enjoy the time we have. Enjoy being with our friends and our family. That's the fucking point." Her mascaraed eyes filled with sorrow. "That's what Fancy knew. And Dee."

Jane gasped as their souls touched, as lightly as a feathered puff of tomb dust.

"Welcome, ladies." A bald, beefy bouncer held the door open for the two women ahead of them. "You two, hold up. Not so fast." He raised a hand the size of a Virginia ham. "Can't let you in right now."

258

"Come on, Muscles. Don't be like that." Pulling out her wallet, Gee palmed a ten-dollar bill. "She's with me."

"No can do, Gee. Keeping a count. It's capacity." His tight black T-shirt stretched transparent as he folded his arms. "Can't let you two in 'til somebody else leaves. Don't want no trouble with the Fire Marshal tonight." Lumbering to his feet, he folded Gee in a bear hug, squeezing her until she coughed. "It's good to see you, girl. How you been?" Stepping back, he kept a grip on Gee's biceps as he lowered his bowling ball head to search her eyes. "Heard the hard news about Fancy and Dee-Dee. Heard we might got a serial killer. That true?"

"That's only a theory," Jane inserted quickly.

He looked at Gee quizzically. "Anything I can do to help?"

"Thanks for asking. I'll let you know. Meet my friend, Jane."

"Hey, Jane. Looking fleek, sweetheart. That's a good look on you. I like it."

"Muscles?" Gee rested her hands on her hips. "What are you still doing here? I thought you got deployed to Afghanistan."

His shoulders hunched to his ears. "Change of plans. Trump banned my transition. Said I didn't have a 'medical need.' Fucker dropped me smack dab between my surgeries." He pointed to his crotch. "Obviously, I can't go back like this, half-cocked."

"That sucks!" Gee looked outraged. "What are you going to do?"

"This." Muscles laughed bitterly. "Let the courts and the Justice Department duke it out." Raising both fists, he pretended to spar. "Some judge in Baltimore issued an injunction, saying Trump's order violated the equal-protection guarantee in the Constitution, but we've already seen how well that Presidential motherfucker responds to that. Does anyone know if he can even read?" Shaking out his hands, Muscles dry-rubbed his palms together. "Nobody tells me not to serve my country. Nobody. I don't care who the fuck you are. I can tell you my C.O. was pissed. Doesn't give a shit what gender I am as long as I keep up my sniper skills."

"Muscles holds the long-distance kill record for his brigade," Gee stated.

"Fuck that. I hold the long-distance kill record period at 1,700 meters."

One point oh six miles. Jane was impressed. *That's crazy good.*

"Fuck them little Taliban motherfuckers. Never see me coming." Muscles smiled proudly. "My C.O. had to reach out to another unit to find my replacement. Upset my combat team." He ran his hand over his head. "FUBAR way to run a military program, IMHO. Bustin' up a team increases the risk, but what the hell, not my call. Up to our clueless Commander-in-Chief. Him with the bone spurs, motherfucker."

The door to Club Femme du Monde swung open. Muscles quickly retreated to his stool as an intoxicated couple stumbled out to the techno beat of Rihanna singing *This Is What You Came For*.

"Slide on in." Muscles gripped the door with one huge hand. "No cover charge for you tonight." He winked. "Just catch the scumbag who hurt Fancy and Dee-Dee." He waved them in. "Don't forget we're the good guys. Don't let that motherfucker win."

"Which one?" Gee sidled by. "Trump or the serial killer?"

"Both!" Muscles barked, bumping his fists together, one on top of the other before cocking his fists like a prizefighter. "Be the change you want to see."

CHAPTER FORTY-NINE

The street door slammed shut, cutting off the outside ambient light. Jane tried to adjust to a disorienting pitch-black darkness so profound it felt like she had stumbled into an occupied coalmine. "Gee?" A chilling PTSD frisson spiraled up her spine. "Where y'at? I can't see."

"Blink a few times. It'll help." Gee's voice trembled with excitement. Reaching back, she grasped Jane's outstretched fingers. "I forgot! You've never been here before. Follow me."

Jane tapped Gee's heels as they turned a right-angled corner down a sloping tunnel lit by bands of blinking neon rainbow light strips set in arches high above their heads.

"Almost there!" Gee danced on her toes, laughing with delight. "Honey? I'm home!"

Jane's retinas swam as she followed Gee's silhouette down an eerie black-lighted path created by the imprint of thousands of glowing florescent green footprints stamped on the club's uneven concrete floor. Jane registered a niggling memory, but in a flash it was gone. Her eyes watered and her nose rebelled at the sudden surging scented tsunami of male cologne, female perfume, funky human perspiration and sex. The walls seemed to be vibrating to match the club's raging techno beat as Jane fought to stay focused.

"Gee? Have you known Muscles long?"

"What?" Gee's trilling laughter carried over the music. "Oh, yes! Long enough to remember when he was still being called Michelle!"

They slipped past an anonymous cluster of partiers and turned left. Jane gasped as they left the pitch-dark tunnel and she looked up.

Club Femme du Monde was one voluminously huge floor to ceiling space approximately four hundred feet square. An old warehouse had been gutted to the bricks, leaving only the outside shell standing. The dance floor was on the ground level with a separate and private club floor balcony cantilevered overhead. A drum-shaped glass elevator serviced the VIP balcony with its entry secured by two of Muscle's bouncer friends.

Jane felt deafened by the solid wall of thumping bass provided by the disc jockey entertainer, a laughing woman with swinging waist-length golden braids. Raising her champagne flute, she toasted the dancing crowd from her soundboard on an inset stage behind a mirrored bar that ran the length of the rear wall.

"Whazzup, party people?" She shrieked into her Bluetooth headset. "Are you ready to par-tee?"

She was met with a roar of approval from the heated dancers on the floor which appeared to be a chessboard of Plexiglas squares that randomly lit up in time to the thumping beat she put down. The VIP guests above scanned the dancers below, drinks in hand, laughing and pointing out anything exceptionally outrageous. The entire partying crowd gasped in unison as a rising techno alarm sounded and multiple ceiling installed smoke machines fired off, blanketing the club in a dense cloud of pink fog, which was then split up and lit by a flashing multi-colored laser light show like lightening seen from above as from a plane.

"Head for the bar." Gee pointed.

Jane shouldered through the sardine can packed crowd. The brick wall on her right towered straight up undisturbed for thirty feet. It housed two hundred evenly spaced alcoves in ten rows with a single, flickering yellowy candle perched inside each one. In the very center of the wall an opaque backlit screen showing the living and moving silhouettes of three people, two women and one man, kneeling on a head-boarded bed and strenuously fucking.

Jane flashed red-hot as her mind processed what she was actually seeing and she turned away appalled. The music's techno beat was so poundingly loud she couldn't hear herself think. Twisting her head aside, she tried to spare her eardrums, but the heavy beat pounded her skull no matter which way she turned. The thrumming bass beat rattled the fillings in her teeth. It tickled her vagina.

"Still watching carbs?"

"What?" Jane screamed.

Gee placed her mouth next to Jane's ear. "Drink? What d'you want to drink?"

"Beer. Lite beer. Anything light."

Gee flicked two fingers. A bartender caught her gesture and trotted over. She was wearing a skimpy black lace bra with silk tasseled nipples and a red bow tie. Leaning over the counter, she displayed her ample foot-long cleavage and matching dragonfly tattoos.

"Gee? What'll you have tonight?"

"Keesha, one Mick Ultra, one house pinot gris. I'm running a tab."

"Coming up." Keesha grabbed a jug of wine and filled a stemmed glass. Reaching into a cooler, she twisted the cap off a bottle. "Y'all want a glass for the beer?"

"No! I'll take it like that." Jane answered uneasily, berating herself for wondering where Keesha's fingers had been. "Bottle's fine."

Gee turned her back to the bar, enjoying a healthy sip of her wine as a secretive smile plied her lips. "So, Jane? What d'you think?"

"This is insane." Jane swallowed a mouthful of icy beer. The brew left her breathless and it made her choke. Gee pounded her back as she coughed her air pipe clear. "Damn, that's good! Been weeks since I've tasted a beer."

"Hey, girl." A lovely young man sauntered over, studying Gee from under his exceptionally full eyelashes. "How you been?"

"Hey, Jeffrey." Gee saluted him with her wine glass before she frowned. "Been a rough couple of weeks."

"So I heard." Fingering his lower lip, his eyes softened with sympathy. "Sorry to hear 'bout them bad things happening to your friends."

"Thanks. This is Jane."

"Hey, Jane." He drawled. Jeffrey's skin was as flawless as a bar of creamy milk chocolate. "Gigi? I heard we got a serial killer in NOLA. That right?"

"That's because of what happened to Fancy and Dee. The FBI asked us a bunch of questions."

"It's true?" Jeffrey's jaw fell open. "I thought it was fake news. What did them FBI fellas say?"

"Said we need to be careful. Keep our eyes open." Gee stared into the crowd. "Or maybe he's just after me."

"You?" Jeffrey's eyes widened even more. "What do you mean maybe he's after you?"

"I found some things left in my car." Gee shuddered. "The FBI thinks I might be his focus."

"Well then excuse me, sugar. I'm not standing here. I will see you later."

"Jeffrey, wait. Have you heard anything about Fancy or Dee on the street?"

He danced nervously in place. "A little, maybe, but it's strange." He extended his phone. "The topic is totally buzz, girlfriend, but everyone only wants to text it." He glanced over his shoulder. "No one wants to mention the killings out loud like it might jinx them into being the next victim or something."

Herd mentality. More superstition. Jane shivered. *Let the lightning strike the next guy and spare me.*

"It's bizarre." Jeffrey toyed with his lower lip. "Because you know how this crowd usually loves drama and Instagram. It's all we live for, really. Everyone's playing it safe."

The blue screen on his phone suddenly lit his face. Jeffrey glanced at the number. "I need to get this." Raising the phone, he tucked it against his ear, strolling toward the bathrooms. "Yes, Mom. It's me. Who else would it be? You called my number. What are you still doing up?"

"Jane?" Gee suddenly sputtered. She clutched Jane's elbow. "Am I seeing things? What's *he* doing here?"

Chapter Fifty

Gee tipped her wine glass toward a section of roped-off tables directly under the wall of shame. Jane turned. Seeing them, FBI Special Agent Winston Carter crossed his legs at the knees as he raised his lowball glass in a toast.

"Carter? What are you doing?" Jane strode toward the cordoned off section of banquettes. *He's blowing his cover.*

"Hiding in plain sight. Call me Win." He coolly signaled club security. "It's okay. Let them in. They're with me."

Gee slipped around the red velvet rope as lithely as a sea otter in a kelp bed. "Where's Mayas?"

"Bathroom." Carter gestured toward a darkened hallway to the left of the bar. "Be right back. Care to join us?"

"You bet! Move over. This is sick." Sitting primly, Gee pinched the wine stem between her fingers and her thumb, obviously admiring the fabulous new vantage point in her favorite club. "I've never been allowed in the VIP section before. Fancy will be so jealous - " She choked. "Would've been. She would've been." She stared blindly at the floor. "This *sucks*. I *hate* that I get to do this now when Fancy's not here to enjoy it with me." Her shoulders hunched to her ears. "Or Dee."

"I know, Gee." Jane commiserated, struggling to keep from following her empathy down the rabbit hole. Her immediate instinct was to reach out and comfort her friend, but she knew that would distract her from their mission and the task at hand. Her police training offered her the emotional buffer she needed to retain critical arms-length distance and dispassionate perspective, but Jane suddenly feared that made her appear heartlessly cold. She felt the conflict

266

keenly. It was a losing proposition either way. Out of habit, she opted for the mission. "Carter? If you're in here where's the response team?"

"You mean besides Mayas and me?" His eyes crinkled attractively as he tapped his ear. "SSG is listening. They're saying it's tough filtering our voices over the music." He laughed. "They want to know why you keep challenging my decisions."

Cutting her eyes, Jane scanned the club. Nothing looked obvious or out of place.

"Relax." Carter refreshed his drink from the private vodka bottle. "They're outside. In a Delta Electric emergency service van."

"That's actually pretty good cover," Jane admitted.

"Thank you." He proudly flicked his chest. "It was my idea."

She flinched as she felt a presence hovering at her shoulder and looked up.

"How are you two ladies this evening?" Mayas folded his hands.

Cesar was dressed more casually than Carter in a buttoned-down collared shirt with belted trousers. He had trimmed his mustache and his sideburns were razor-clipped to a smooth black shadow that ran along his jawline. He wore square cut high caret diamond studs in both ears and it worked. Critically studying Jane's skimpy outfit, he judgmentally raised one eyebrow.

"We're fine." Gee straightened. "Surprised to see you here but delighted."

There was a heartbeat's pause in the overwhelming sound as the DJ cut in on her mic. "Time to get sexy, people. Let's change it up." Spinning a vinyl record between her fingertips, she switched to an up-tempo salsa beat song with plenty of brassy trumpet. "Okay, animals. Show me your moves." Lowering her voice, she growled. "How 'bout some Miami heat?"

Mayas looked surprised. Glancing at the dance floor, he quickly looked back at their table. "Care to dance?"

Jane blinked. *Mayas likes salsa?* She felt sideswiped by this fresh insight into the normally reticent special agent she had known for five years. "You dance salsa?"

"And merengue." He extended his hand. "Sorry. I was asking Ms. Pascoe."

Gee's mouth fell open. "I'd love to." Plunking her wine stem down so quickly that the cheap glass rang off the tabletop, she repeatedly poked her finger into Jane's hip. "Move over, Jane. Move. Get out of the way. I need to get up."

Scrambling to her feet, she slipped out of her denim jacket and tossed it aside. Grasping Mayas' hand, she followed him toward the dance crowd silently mouthing 'OMG' over her shoulder. Reaching back blindly, Jane felt for her seat.

"He's got some depth, that one," Carter stated. "The more time I spend with Mayas the better I like him." He rattled his ice cubes. "I hope he accepts permanent NOLA reassignment."

"So does Gee," Jane blurted as she sat.

"Really?" Carter looked startled. "That's fresh news."

"Don't tell Mayas I said that." She quickly shifted the topic to cover her intel slip. "What happened to the anonymous cover idea we discussed yesterday?"

"We gave it more thought after you left the station." Carter pointed his finger at the densely packed room. "No one in this club knows who we are. If we see anyone we've already interviewed that drops the suspicion on them. Anyone new watching us would think it's just another easy Saturday night pickup."

Jane glowed at the burn. *Is that what Carter really thinks of me?*

He shifted uneasily. Leaning forward, he poured another healthy two fingers of vodka into his glass. "Wasn't that our plan? Just another normal night at Club Femme du with everyone looking for love?" Noting Jane's beer bottle, he tapped his glass against the stainless-steel ice bucket. "Want some vodka? We've got a full setup. I mix a nice martini."

"No, thanks. Beer's fine."

"Vodka's low carb." He smiled winningly. "It'll help you relax. You look tense."

"I said I'm good."

"Okay. I asked." He shrugged, easing back and stretching his arms out along the banquette. "See anyone you recognize?"

"Only you and Mayas." Jane rescanned the tumultuous crowd. "But this club's full of Gee's friends. They all know each other. They're part of the same community. It's tight."

"Makes sense. This club is ground zero for NOLA's LGBTQ."

The dynamic salsa beat ratcheted up even louder. Cocking his ear against it, Carter leaned closer. His shirt popped open at the neck and Jane felt his body heat radiating off his chest. She smelled his bold citrusy cologne and she felt an unexpected and delightful tingling between her thighs. Snatching up her beer, she killed it quickly, pointing the empty bottle at the crowd. "Haven't registered anything odd or strange except for, you know, the obvious."

"True." Carter laughed easily. "There's certainly a lot of 'free to be me' in the house tonight."

Get a grip, girlfriend. Jane's pulse kept fluttering erratically as she pulled back from the abyss. *Remember rule number seven: Keep Your Distance, Keep It Real.* Playing for recovery time, she turned to watch Gee and Mayas dancing. The dance floor crowd had opened up a tiny bit to give them room. Mayas looked as focused and intent as a professional gymnast as he gripped Gee's hand and her hip, spinning her on her toes while holding his elbows high. *Gee looks ecstatic. I've never seen her looking so happy. Is that what love looks like?* Jane fell back, amazed. *And I barely recognize Mayas. Who knew? Just goes to show you really don't know people until you see them in action.*

"Be careful tonight." Carter studied the riotous scene. "It's a dense crowd. Limited visual always makes me nervous."

"Roger that," Jane admitted. Studying his strong profile, she nervously fingered her spaghetti straps to make sure they were straight and that the FBI wire was secure. *Is this all we have between us, Carter and me? Strictly business?* Releasing her breath through pursed lips, she checked her desires. *Okay. Let's be honest. What do I want? Do I want this thing with Carter to be a real thing or not? What if he's not attracted to me?*

She nervously smoothed her skirt as the salsa song ended, looking up from her lap as the snappy rhythm transitioned to the finger-popping disco beat of Alex Newell's *Kill The Lights*. Out on the dance floor, Mayas paused. Holding Gee at arm's length, he obviously asked her a question. Raising both hands palm side up, Gee laughed and playfully shook her head. Jane gasped as her heart twisted like a wet sponge and she felt an ugly prickle of envy as Mayas cradled Gee's boyish waist with his arm as he escorted her back to the table. *That's not fair. Cesar was my friend first!*

Gee danced loose hipped through the crowd, her rosy face slick with sweat. Reaching down, she tugged Jane's hand. "Jane, come with me. I need to pee."

She scowled. "You need me to go to the men's room with you?"

"Don't do that." Gee laughed happily, pulling Jane to her feet. "Femme du is non-binary, you idiot. It's just a *pissoir*."

"OMG." She continued to chatter as they wove a path through the massed block of drinkers stacked three-deep at the bar. "I think Mayas likes me, really likes me. Can you believe my luck?" She joined the lengthy bathroom queue lined up against the wall. "He said next time we go dancing I should wear a red dress." She pressed the back of her hands to her overheated face. "I'm not making this up! I swear to God he said, 'next time.' Pinch me. I feel like I'm dreaming. What am I going to do?"

Jane's tongue curled with aspirin bitterness. *It's not fair. I want to feel that happy. When is it my turn?* She bit back her snarky retort. *What's wrong with me? I should be feeling happy for Gee, not jealous.* She studied her blasted shipwrecked soul and swallowed away the thick taste. *Something decent in me got broken. Whatever that was, I need to fix it again, pronto.* She reached for the right answer. "We'll need to go shopping and find that dress. I've never known Mayas to say something he didn't mean."

"Seriously?" Gee bit her lip. She looked so innocent, so goddamn hopeful and expectant that Jane flushed. "Jane?" She squinted. "You okay?"

"No." Bracing herself, Jane dug for honesty. "I'm not, Gee. I think I'm jealous."

"Of me?" Gee's face blossomed like a rose. Laughing, she flipped her right hand palm side up. "You have everything I want including a pussy and great hair and you're jealous of me?" The bathroom line swayed. Gee stepped forward, looking perplexed. "Did you want Mayas, Jane? Is that it? Why didn't you say so?"

"I don't want him like that," Jane replied quickly, "but I do want to keep him as a friend."

"Why would that change because of me?" Gee settled her stance. "Wait a minute. I know what this is. This isn't jealousy; this is commitment. You're stuck between having a relationship with Mayas and making the commitment to do it." She painfully prodded Jane's arm. "Why are you so afraid of that idea?"

"I'm not afraid of anything." Jane blustered.

"The hell you are! You're terrified about making commitments. I've noticed that about you, before. So did Dee. That's why we tested you by giving you Piddles. Figured he might help you crawl out of your shell, force you to get outside, meet new people, make new friends. If nothing else, he got you out of your chair twice a day." She cocked her head. "Stop dicking around. If you're not interested in Mayas, okay, then how about Carter?"

"What about Carter?" Jane sputtered.

271

"Girl? You blind? He's a sexy beast. Go after him."

"I'll think about it."

"Why the fuck not? Because he's black?"

"I already said that doesn't matter!"

"Then why?"

"Because." Jane hissed. "Because it fucking *hurts*. Getting close to people fucking hurts. You get too close and then they leave you or they fucking die. If I'm going to live my life alone, okay then, fuck it." Jane turned away. "I'm fine with that. Leave me alone."

Ducking her head, Gee studied Jane's face. "You can't live that way, girlfriend. Can't live all shut up like that. That's zombie land." Releasing her painful grip, she stepped back. "As much as life hurts, you gotta fight back. I don't know much, but I do know that -"

The bathroom queue opened up again. Jane quickly counted the number of people standing in the line and came up with thirteen. Lucy was uncomfortably pressing on her bladder. "I'll think about it."

"Even if Carter's not the right one for you," Gee persisted, "he might lead you to the one who is. I'm going to keep on you about this as a friend." Gee shared some serious side eye. "Did Carter say anything about me and Mayas while we were dancing?"

"No." Jane lied, growing even more uncomfortable as she remembered her careless slip of the lip. "But he's been all business."

"That's what I'm saying." Gee shoved her playfully. "You need to act friendlier with him. Carter's a stand-up guy, but he's still a guy. Men are fucking clueless. It's unbelievable. You need to encourage him, show him you're interested. Trust me. Carter's a player. Give him a lead. He'll take it from there."

Maybe Gee's right? Did I create my own problem? Is that why I feel so goddamn dissatisfied with my life? Because I built the cage I'm trapped in and then I locked the door from the inside and tossed the key?

272

"Dude! Quit shoving." A man's voice in line up ahead complained.

The emergency exit door flashed open into the alley. The bathroom crowd howled in outrage as the blindingly bright halogen lights kicked on, illuminating the hallway. Jane's pupils shrank to pin dots and she clapped both hands over her eyes as a hammering alarm pierced her eardrums.

"Fire!" A woman shrilly screamed. Her voice rose to shrieking horror. "Fire!"

The static bathroom line collapsed into a shoving shouting melee as people scrambled for the exit. Jane flattened against the wall as the ghastly images of the recent Ghost Ship dance club flashed through her mind. *That Oakland fire killed 36 people.* She fought to stay calm. *Panic is fatal. Why don't I smell smoke?*

"Jane?" Gee screamed. "It was him." She started shoving her way through the crowd spilling into the alley. "Ryan's friend! Tyler. He saw me, Jane. Come on!"

The bathroom door swung open in her face and a confused and stupefied couple stumbled out. Pulling them clear, Jane slammed the door shut. *How did the Fire Marshal miss this hazard?* "Police!" She screamed, using the points of her elbows to force her way through the mob. "FBI. Make a hole."

The crowd carried her down the hallway, almost on tiptoe. Jane felt compressed to the point of breathlessness as PTSD triggered a blistering memory. She saw the rising golden staircase and the black bannisters that looked like dead iron bars.

"Gee! Wait for me!" She screamed. "We need backup! Don't go it alone." *Jesus, Mary and Joseph, M'su Diable, anyone who is listening, help me!* Jane implored. *Don't take Gee. I need her.* Her legs turned to water as the struggling mass of people swept her off her feet and she completely lost sight of the door.

CHAPTER FIFTY-ONE

"Carter! Mayas!"

Jane shrieked into her wire. Gripping the emergency exit doorframe with both hands, she squeezed herself gasping through the mass of people struggling to escape Club Femme du Monde. "It's Tyler Shank. He's with Gee."

She bounced off a man's broad back and skidded through a muddy puddle that slathered her boots with slime. The panicking horde thinned as it spilled out of the alley into Frenchmen Street. *Where's Gee?* Her view was blocked by a pulsing mass of screaming, sobbing people and a dumpster piled high with bagged trash. She ran on.

The heels on her cheap new boots collapsed. She fell against the brick wall, shredding the skin off both palms like confetti. Jane hobbled forward, shaking the scorching pain from her hands. *I need to find Gee. She's chasing a killer.*

Mayas suddenly blocked her way. He grabbed her arms.

"Which way did they go? Jane, look at me. Point it out. Which way?"

"I don't know!" She howled in frustration as she twisted free. "I didn't see them hit the street. I lost her, Mayas. I lost her!"

"Was it Tyler Shank?" Cesar stared unblinking. "You saw him? You know that, CJ? You saw him?"

"I don't know that." Wincing, Jane pressed her bloodied hands to her skirt. "That's what Gee said. That's what I heard her say."

Carter ran up, skirting the dumpster like a feral cat. Cupping his ear, he lowered his voice, bellowing over the street noise. "SSG thinks he's heading for the Bourbon Street. Makes sense he'd try to lose himself upriver in the crowd."

"Use the technology," Mayas barked, looking as intent as a hunting bird of prey. "What does her wire say?"

"Negative. GPS indicates she's still in the club."

Jane flashed on Gee's discarded denim jacket. "You're pinging her coat. She left it behind. I'll text her." She swung her bag forward. "Shit! She left her phone, too!"

"SSG go active." Carter spoke into his cuff. "Code Orange. We've lost contact with Gigi Pascoe. Initiate immediate foot search. Distribute the suspect profile on Tyler Shank." His eyes scanned the milling crowd. "Apprehend with extreme caution. I'll meet you on the street."

"Let's go." Jane ran two steps forward. She pulled up short as Carter and Mayas exchanged a knowing look. "What? What?"

Firming his mouth, Mayas looked at Carter and shrugged. "You're the lead. I'll meet SSG." He melted into the crowd.

"What is it, Carter? Tell me." Jane insisted. "What?"

"You need to stay put. Civilians would only get in the way."

Jane widened her stance. "I am not a civilian."

"You are and you're already slowing me down."

"Fuck you. I don't have time for this." Jane stubbornly shook her head. "I know what I'm doing."

"Do you?" Carter grabbed her hand. "You need to do what I say. I can't run the team, track Shank and protect you at the same time. Jane? Stay put. Stay safe. That's a command." Releasing her hand he slid off into the night. "I'll update you ASAP."

Protect me? Why does the FBI need to protect me? I'm not an LGBTQ target. Jane gasped as the complete truth dawned. *This isn't FBI protocol. Carter's worried I'll get hurt. He's worried about me. Huh.* She paused. *Do I follow his command?*

She took two hesitant steps toward the flaring rainbow of neon light that lit the sky before her instinct flagged the play. *Tyler was smart enough to avoid the surveillance cameras around The Boat at Lafayette Square.* She slowed her steps even more. *Would he head for Bourbon Street? He'd do the opposite of what we think he'd do.* She spun around. *He'd go deeper into the Lavender Zone and try to slip out down Decatur.*

And he's with Gee.

"Sorry, Carter. I don't take orders from you."

She started trotting toward the river, crossing the street to avoid a gang of smokers blocking the sidewalk outside a stripper bar. Stepping up to the curb, her ankle turned and her left boot heel snapped clean off. Jane limped on. *Fuck! Fuck! I'll never catch them wearing these stupid boots. Do I try running barefoot?* She scanned the filthy street and the stained sidewalk glittering with broken glass. *How long before I nail something with my foot?* Inspiration sent up a flare and turning back, she cut down an alley. *Grab the Ducati.*

Monster's dashboard lit up like a Christmas tree as she drew near. Swinging her cross-body bag forward, Jane hiked up her skirt, straddled the seat and thumbed the ignition button. Monster coughed to life before settling into a contented purr. Heeling the kickstand, she cocked the throttle, leaned over the deck and sped back into the Lavender Zone.

At the intersection, she dropped Monster into neutral and pulled up short. Scanning left, Jane noted the intermittent red and blue strobe lights of the first responders at Club Femme du Monde's front door as Gee's voice echoed inside her head. *He saw me, Jane! Come on.*

A singing bachelor party scattered with a combined shout as she straightened her line down the center of Frenchmen Street. Multiple Google map images started clicking like an insane slideshow in her mind as she desperately tried to re-orient herself. *What's next? Esplanade Avenue?* She ground her teeth, berating herself. *Shit. I got lazy. Should've memorized the streets by now. I knew every towpath on Nantucket in my sleep.*

She roared into the traffic at the next wide intersection, scanning the groups clustered in the doorways and the sheer mass of people parading from bar to open bar. Monster's digital dashboard clock read 1:17 AM as the trumpety brass sound of NOLA jazz serenaded the night. Laughing groups strolled along the sidewalk. Nothing looked violently disturbed or out of place.

Was I wrong? Fear drilled her bones hollow as she imagined Gee lying in an alley, throat-slashed, covered in blood, already scalped and dying or dead.

"Gee!" Jane screamed, double-clicking the clutch and pushing on, slowing only to peer into each dank courtyard. "Answer me! Gee?" *Was I wrong?*

Her focus began to wobble as rubbery panic sickened her stomach. *If anything bad happens, take me instead of her.* She implored the voodoo gods. *I'll do anything you want. Just don't hurt Gee because of me.*

"Yo, bitch! One-way street! Wrong way!"

A protesting bouncer lunged at her from a tavern on the corner. Jane swerved and Monster growled as she notched it up a gear to avoid his grasp. Her ears caught the tinny ringing of overturned metal garbage bins and a beaky looking silhouette skittered out of an alley onto the sidewalk to her right.

It was Tyler Shank.

Jane smoked Monster's tires as she roared forward, the rapture of a successful hunt blossoming in her chest and tightening her focus like a laser beam. *Got you now, you bastard!* Leaning over the handlebars, she shrieked into her wire. "Carter! Mayas! Embry's on Esplanade heading for North Peters!"

Gee stumbled out of the alley on Tyler's heels.

"Jane!" She screamed, pointing. "Get him. Get him!"

Seeing Gee still on her feet, Jane felt a rush of relief so strong it felt orgasmic. *Thank you, voodoo gods. I owe you big.*

Pushing off a lamppost, Tyler shoved a path through a huddled midnight NOLA ghost tour. Gee followed, crouched low and as intent as a panther. She made a quick grab, but Tyler dodged sideways and she missed. Off balance, Gee fell to one knee, executing a controlled shoulder roll, springing back up and lunging again.

The tour group scattered like a flock of frightened pigeons as Tyler reached behind his back. Jane's core froze solid as an emerald green bar sign flashed like neon lightning off the steel blade he suddenly held in his hand.

"Gee!" Jane raced forward. *Shit! I'm not going to make it. It's over thirty feet.*

Waving the knife uncertainly in Gee's face, Tyler unexpectedly kicked out his leg and sank his shoe into Gee's gut. She took it hard, retching and reaching out one hand to block her fall as she collapsed onto the sidewalk.

"No!" Jane roared. *I've got to stop this.* "Gee!" She screamed. "Gee!"

Tyler heard the Ducati coming. Turning, he bent his knees and settled his stance, staring down the wicked steel blade and pointing the kitchen knife like a lance. Smiling ghoulishly, he flicked his left hand, beckoning her on.

"Come on, bitch." He spat thickly. "You want some of this?"

Jane skidded the Ducati to a sideways stop. Wrenching her skirt up over her hip, she slid her fingers over her belly feeling for her appendix carry. Pulling Lucy free, she cupped the 9MM in both hands, sighting down the stubby barrel, her focus suddenly so hyper tight she experienced tunnel vision as she aimed for Tyler's skull. She knew a center shot offered better take down odds, but she had never felt more certain of her action.

CRACK.

Tyler flinched as the bullet chipped the cement block wall behind his head. Raising his hand to his cheek, he blinked stupidly. Jane saw the dawning of stunned realization reach his eyes as his fingers limply dropped the kitchen knife. The steel blade rang like a buoy bell when it hit the pavement. Stooping, he snatched the knife back up before sprinting across the street for The French Market.

"You had a gun?" Gee retched. Clutching her ribcage, she struggled to rise, pushing up off the street with her elbow and her toes. "Where the fuck did you hide that?"

I missed. Jane felt stunned. *Why did I pull my shot?* "Are you okay?" She shouted.

"Fuck that." Gee retched drily again. "Shoot him, Jane. *Shoot him.*"

Jane slipped Lucy back into the appendix holster. Straightening the yoke, she gripped the Ducati, twisting the throttle and roaring the wrong way down N. Peters, weaving in and out of the traffic hazards with a focus so intent it felt surreal. She felt unbeatable like an avenging fury, like a great pantheon of pagan gods were suddenly on her side and they were cheering her on.

Tyler tumbled over a wire guy rope supporting a tented booth. Falling to his knees, he raised the knife to fend Jane off, his eyes widening with sudden knowledge and open fear. Leaning over the dashboard, Jane felt the glorious tidal might of true oncoming justice, shrieking like a Valkyrie as she closed in.

She heard the blaring air horn in her left ear. Looking up, she saw the looming chrome bulldog logo centered on the massive grill, registering the screeching locked air brakes and the freight driver's panicking pale face behind his high windshield.

Shit! Shit! She swerved Monster so viciously she lost control. The front tire and yoke dropped into a jagged pothole jolting Jane so hard she bit her tongue as the Ducati jackknifed.

Still gripping the bike, she skidded along the street, her ears filled by the sound of squealing brakes and even more blaring horns. Monster's steel foot peg started carving a groove into the asphalt road surface and seeing sparks, Jane raised her left foot as she continued to slide, screaming as the red hot flame of gravel road rash shredded her bare skin from knee to thigh. *Oh, shit, no! Not my knee again. Not my knee!*

Releasing the Ducati, she surrendered to centrifugal force, limply rolling off of her shoulders and her butt and raising her arms to protect her unhelmeted head, staring out from between her elbows at an oncoming row of antique cast iron horse head ring posts above four fat concrete steps. Throwing her arms out to slow her roll, she felt a thump that jolted her skull. There was a single tiny bright white pinpoint of light and it winked out.

CHAPTER FIFTY-TWO

"God help me." Jane groaned, gently pressing her eyelids with her fingertips. Her skull felt ready to split. She desperately wanted to dive into oblivious slumber, but the ringing pain held her suspended in a dozing limbo land halfway between awake and asleep, a bizarre neutral dimension where even the passage of time lost its meaning.

She recalled opening her eyes to find Gee kneeling by her side. Crimson blood splashed Gee's hands to her wrists.

"Don't move." Gee cried. "911 is coming."

"He'll get away."

"Carter and Mayas are on it."

Jane had almost blacked out again when she tried rolling over to get up. That move had been instinctive. *Get back on your feet and you'll be okay. No matter what it costs you, stay up, stay on your feet, stay with the herd.* Her head had lolled drunkenly. Gee had caught her when she collapsed.

"No hospital. No insurance. Take me home."

Gee had ignored her, glued to Jane's side while the paramedics fitted her with a neck brace and then watching as they strapped Jane to a backboard before lifting and loading her into an EMS van. The trip to New Orleans East Hospital's emergency room was a blurred memory now, strangely out of rational sequence. At Admittance, she remembered Gee saying that Jane had no health insurance as she handed over her VISA card. When the RN asked Gee if Jane was family, Gee had firmly answered 'yes,' claiming Jane as a sister.

Cautiously leaning forward, Jane resettled the gallon Ziploc baggie full of melting ice cubes on her swollen knee, resentfully staring at her new tripod cane before reaching for and scanning, yet again, the hospital's statement receipt. *Fuck. What am I supposed to do with this? Frame it as a souvenir?* Over Gee's protest, she had pridefully paid Gee back every cent of the VISA charge in cash as soon as she got settled back home. Gee had tried refusing it, but Jane had screamed 'Take it! Take it all!' and thrown the money at her. Gee had backed down, promising to come back and check on Jane at least twice a day and to bring her treats.

"What am I? A dog?" Jane had snapped.

She had the total hospital debt memorized. The out-of-network emergency ambulance, transportation plus ground mileage charge came to $1,062.53. Critical care ill/injured patient 75 minutes (bill code 94761) was an additional $1,574.96. The CT scan, of all things, was the cheapest charge at $967.74. The extremely sympathetic examining doctor had given Jane free samples of antibiotic ointment for her gravel rash saving her $32.05. Jane carefully rested her sore head against the chair. The total from her wreck came to $3,605.23. Her entire cash cushion was gone. She was negative $5.23 in the hole with payday still three days away and the rent due again by the end of the month.

She studied the orange prescription pill container on the kitchen counter, a dozen steps away. After picking the gravel and ashes out of her hide with local anesthetic and a needle probe, the doctor had scolded her for not wearing a helmet. *No shit, Sherlock.* He had warned her against taking any painkiller, even over-the-counter Ibuprofen or Tylenol while following a concussion protocol. He had also ordered 48 hours of rest, with no running or other strenuous activity, although light exercise was permitted. Looking at her soccer ball sized knee and the handlebar shaped plum colored bruise on her thigh, Jane snorted. *Like that's going to happen anytime soon.* Raising her hand, she counted the stitches in her newly shaved scalp. *Lucky thirteen. I'm bald on one side like Delilah was only she claimed fashion.*

Jane shifted uneasily in the chair. *Maybe I should try getting cleaned up.* She stared at the steps leading up to her loft and the shower. The thought of navigating the staircase clutching her cane drained her desire and left her feeling limp and depressed. *I could use the kitchen sink and a dishtowel. Do a quick spit wash.* She slumped deeper into the chair. The thought of that much effort overwhelmed her. She felt like she was peering up from the bottom of a well. *Fuck it. Everything I touch turns to shit. Why even try?* She returned her gaze to the prescription OxyContin bottle on the counter. *Twenty-one pills left over from my knee surgeries. What if I swallowed all of them right now? Would that finally fix everything in my sorry ass life and turn my fucking head off?*

She felt the narcotic's magnetic allure. *Closing my eyes would be so easy, so sweet.* Reaching for her cane, she scrabbled up. Hobbling to the counter, she snatched up the pill bottle with its dire warning label: LIFE-THREATENING RESPIRATORY DEPRESSION. For opioid-naïve patients, initiate with one 30 mg tablet orally every twelve hours. DO NOT EXCEED MAXIMUM RECOMMENDED DOSAGE. Her hand trembled as she tightened her grip. *How did it get this bad? Even during my court hearing I never thought of giving up.*

She limped to the sink. Reaching for glass in the dish rack, she turned on the tap, studying the silvery water streaming clockwise down the drain. It felt hypnotic. *It could be that easy. Twenty more minutes, lights out, nighty-night. No more pain.*

Blocking her protesting mind to any rational objection, she thumb-popped the white plastic cap and shook the round tablets marked either OP or 30 onto her palm. *Twenty-one would do it.* She paused as another option crossed her mind. *Street value for these babies should be around $630. That would help me out.* Inhaling deeply, she made her decision, tipping her hand and spilling the tablets down the drain, counting out loud as the dark hole swallowed each one.

Whatever it takes, I'm not going that way. Not now, not ever. And that

I swear to God. Pushing the curtain aside, she studied the courtyard and Plessy Street. The mid-December sunlight was dappling the treetops and the sky was china plate blue. The Bywater neighborhood looked and sounded Sabbath day quiet. She could see the Embry's shotgun cottage at the intersection. Their driveway was empty. *I wonder if Carter and Mayas are done with Ryan yet? He'll be ready for a little peace and quiet once they get done grilling him over his boy, Tyler.*

Anxiety gave her a jab and her heart skipped a beat thinking of Tyler Shank's escape. Dropping the curtain, she shrugged it off. *Fuck it. I did what I could. Leave it to the pros. They have the national manpower. Carter thinks Tyler's heading out of state. They'll catch him eventually.*

Stifling another groan, she limped back to the chair, feeling green and nauseous from the effort of simply crossing the room. Another suggestion flickered along the edge of her mind and just as suddenly it was gone. Jane tried reaching for it, tried recalling what the idea was even about, but her mind drew a complete blank. She fumbled for the chair. The harder she tried to focus on what the idea might have been, the less she remembered. *I hate this foggy feeling. Is this normal from the concussion or should I be more worried? The ER doctor said I might experience concentration or memory complaints and irritability. Well, this is me, complaining. Why do I keep feeling like I've forgotten something critical?*

She lifted her chin off her chest at a rap on her door.

"It's open." She stated flatly, doing her best not to reawaken the throbbing pain currently coiled up and breathing heavily behind her right eye.

"Jane?" Leslie Pascoe gently pushed the door open. Standing on the threshold uncertainly, she held a cake pan covered with tin foil in her hands. "Gigi told us about your accident. How are you feeling? May I come in?"

"Of course, Leslie. Come in."

She hesitantly entered the room. "You sure I'm welcome?"

Jane turned sideways, as much as she could. "Why would you say that?"

"Well, you know, dear, we had that trouble over the money."

"Find a chair, Leslie." Reaching up, Jane pressed her throbbing temples. "We all make mistakes."

"Thank you. I did some baking this morning before church." Leslie slid the aluminum cake pan over the counter before lightly tapping the tin foil with her fingertips. "Made you a hummingbird cake with buttercream frosting."

"I can't eat that," Jane replied roughly. "It's pure carb." She caught the wince of rejection on Leslie's face. "Don't mind me, Leslie. I feel like crap. I'm being a jerk."

"Apology accepted." She murmured. "Oh! Look what they did to your pretty hair."

"Yeah, I know." Jane fingered her stitches. "Looks pretty grim, doesn't it?"

"I won't lie, my dear. It does." Dragging a rush-bottomed chair across the floor, Leslie sat, resettling the silk scarf around her shoulders and looking motherly and concerned. "So, tell me. How are you doing?"

"I'm fine."

"You don't look fine. You look like you lost the war. A nice slice of homemade cake might make you feel better."

Jane smiled at her persistence. She thought of the empty hole her own mother's passing had left in her life. *Gee's lucky to still have her mom around. I know family is a complete pain in the ass, but there's nothing better.* "Maybe later. My stomach's feeling wonky right now."

"Of course. I'm sorry to hear that." Leslie flattened her skirt over her knees. "Listen. Gigi told us about your outrageous hospital bill." She peered at Jane like a curious sparrow. "Why on earth didn't you carry health insurance?"

Jane squirmed. "It was optional with Guardian. Sixty-five bucks a pay. Decided to skip it and take the risk."

"We can see how well that decision turned out." Leslie sat back. "That's a decision only a thirty-year-old would make, when you're young enough to still think you're bulletproof." She pursed her lips. "Now, I've already talked with Ken and we don't want you worrying about your rent. We've both agreed to give you all the time you need to get back on your feet. We can float your rent for a month or two, take partial payments, whatever you can afford until you build your savings back up. We want to do what we can to help."

Jane almost wept. *Shit. These are such decent people.* "Thanks, Leslie, I really appreciate it. And please thank Ken for me. That's very kind of you both."

"Good, then, that's settled. You need to focus on healing and getting better." Leaning forward, she rested her elbows on her knees. "What did Guardian Storage say when you told them? How much time off are they giving you?"

Jane's lower lip started trembling uncontrollably. "None. They fired me."

"They what?" Leslie looked shocked. "Fired you? Why?"

"Because they saw my wreck on the news." Jane confessed. "Chapelle said he can't trust me anymore because I called in sick and lied about it and he has the proof." Her head started to throb. "I get what he's saying, I do. The self-storage business is based on trust, since we're storing people's personal stuff." She sniffled. "He can't have people questioning the integrity of his security guards. Said it would crush his business. Friday's paycheck is the last one I'll get."

"Any severance?"

"Not a dime."

Leslie nervously smoothed her hair. "What about unemployment? Can you get that?"

"No, because I got fired for cause. I already checked." Jane reached for the tissue box. "I'm hosed, Leslie. I'm so fucking hosed. I'm at the end of my rope."

"Oh, honey. Don't cry. I had no idea it was this bad." Leslie plucked a handful of tissues. Handing them over, she patted Jane's hand. "You need to learn to ask for help. You're not alone in this, you know." She smiled warmly. "We're not going to toss you into the street, well, not while I have any say in the matter. Don't worry, dear. We'll figure something out. We always do."

"Like what?"

"Like," she scanned the stale apartment, "getting you up and moving, getting you some fresh air. No wonder you're all depressed, cooped up in here with nothing to do except think on your worries. I know what we'll do." She lifted the dripping ice bag off of Jane's knee and marched for the sink. "We'll walk this cake over to Cheryl. She loves pineapple and hummingbird cake is her favorite. Can you hobble that far?"

"No, I don't think so, Leslie." Jane sank deeper into the chair. "I'd rather just stay here."

"Hooey." Leslie scolded, picking up the cake pan. "On your feet, soldier. I know you've had words with Cheryl over Ryan, she told me. You have to understand, Jane, she's worried about Ryan as any mother naturally would be, because she loves him so much." Standing over Jane, she shrugged. "Being human is tough work. We need to get along. Sure, there'll be disagreements, that's natural, but we need to listen to each other and learn to forgive." She prodded Jane's shoe with her foot. "No more excuses. What did your doctor say?"

"He recommended light exercise." Jane admitted.

"There's your answer." Setting the cake pan down again, she untied her scarf. "Now, dry your eyes and grab your cane, grandma. I'm going to wrap this pretty scarf around your head like a turban, just like this, and we'll go." She suited her actions to her words. "Hold still. I'm trying to be careful. Don't let me hurt you."

She studied her work. "*Bien.* You look as regal as Marie Laveau." Picking the cake pan back up, she propped the door open, standing next to it and tapping her foot. "You know, sometimes just doing something unexpectedly nice for someone else is all that it takes to make you feel better."

Grabbing her cane, Jane tucked her phone in her running shorts pocket and limped for the door. Being vertical again made her feel giddy. "You sound like Aunt Babette."

"Which is not a bad thing." Balancing the cake pan like a pizza box on her open left hand, Leslie gently cupped Jane's elbow with her right, helping her navigate the uneven garden path. "That's the spirit, Jane. Step by step. Take it slow. You're doing great."

Her tough love advice had been solid. Jane immediately felt better and more in touch with the overall world as a crisp breeze refreshed her skin. Gripping the cane, she limped past the barren ground that had been the chicken coop as they headed for Plessy Street. Unexpectedly, the winter rain had skipped a day. Jane noticed that they were leaving fresh footprints in the soft garden soil.

"You know," Leslie paused on the sidewalk, looking both ways before leading her across the street, "they're calling that friend of Ryan's The Crescent City Slasher, saying he murdered Fancy and Delilah and that man from your work. Can you imagine? A serial killer in my house and at my birthday party?"

"Carter mentioned it." Jane tentatively stepped off the curb. "When he called this morning to check on me."

"He called? That was nice of him. What else did he say?"

"They've got Tyler on a security camera stealing a car near Jackson Square." Jane limped on, but her knee was loosening up and honestly feeling better. "They've issued a national APB. Best guess is he's heading out of state."

"I'm not wishing trouble on anyone else. I'm just glad he's away from Gigi and you. That's my selfish concern. Mother Mary, let's hope this trouble is over."

They turned up the Embry's driveway. Jane shivered. The Delta Electric van was gone, but it had left a permanent oil stain shaped like a grinning skull on the concrete pad.

"Careful, dear." Leslie started up the steps. "Use the railing, that's what it's there for." She rang the doorbell precisely. "Cheryl may need this cake more than I thought. I'm sure she hates all the police attention. She's very private that way."

Jane heard shuffling from behind the door before it slowly cracked open. She braced herself for her reception, not knowing what to expect as Leslie raised the pan.

"Morning, Cheryl. I did some baking. Thought you might enjoy a hummingbird cake."

Cheryl blocked the narrow gap with her body. Trembling, she peered out, making no attempt to open the screen door.

"Thank you, Leslie. That was very kind of you to think of me."

Why is she talking like that? It sounds so stilted, artificial.

Even Leslie looked confused. "May we come in?"

"No! Not today." Cheryl gripped the door. Her smile looked as stiff as a death's head rictus. "The house is *beaucoup crasseux.*" She smoothed her patterned housecoat. "I'm not prepared to receive guests."

Really? Jane recalled the single other time she had been inside the Embry's house with its neatly slipcovered furniture, the pillows aligned perfectly on the couch, the metal crucifixes distinctly centered on each wall. *Cheryl keeps her house as neat as a pin.*

"Cheryl? What going on?" Leslie demanded sharply. "Are you alright?"

Cheryl suddenly unlatched the screen door. "Give me the cake." Reaching for the pan, she whispered: "Tyler's here. Call 911." She raised her voice to its normal level. "Thank you, again, Leslie. I'll return the pan when we're done." Whispering again more urgently, she stared, her watery blue eyes pleading and intent. "Tell Ryan to keep away. Please. He's got a gun."

289

Chapter Fifty-Three

Cheryl Embry stepped back, her face a clown mask of terror as she shut the door.

"What do we do?" Leslie hissed, raising her curled fingers to her lips. "That crazy man is inside her house! We can't leave her with him. We need to do something!"

"Keep moving." Fumbling with the cane, Jane started down the steps. "Act normal. He might be watching." *Tyler could take us out before we hit the street.* She could almost feel the madman's beaded sightline wavering on her spine between her shoulder blades. Her initial instinct was to minimize the potential targets by moving Leslie under cover, to keep her safe. Sweat rolled off Jane's face from pure effort as they re-crossed Plessy Street. "Get in the house, quick. We need to call Carter, the FBI. He'll notify the NOPD force. Send a SWAT team."

Jane almost toppled as Leslie clutched her arm.

"Wait! You have a gun. Where is it?"

"Bad idea. I'm in no shape for action." Jane herded Leslie through the dormant winter garden, hobbling as fast as she could. She pointed the cane up the back porch steps. The Big House's clapboard walls were thin, but they might be sturdy enough to stop a .22 caliber round. "Bordelon confiscated Lucy at the hospital. I don't have a carry permit."

What weapon does Tyler have? What are we dealing with? Jane paused. *And where did Tyler get a gun? The Slasher's been using a knife.*

"Who's that down there?" Aunt Babette shouted as the porch door slammed shut. "Leslie? That you? Where y'at?"

"Babette? Stay in your room." Jane called. "Keep back from the windows." Unlocking her phone, she speed-dialed Carter's number.

"Says who?" The elderly woman clambered down the kitchen staircase.

"Oh, Babette!" Leslie wailed, snatching up a dishtowel and anxiously twisting it between her fingers. "That crazy man, that killer is inside Cheryl's house!"

"You saw this?" Aunt Babette braced herself in the doorway.

"No, but that's what Cheryl said."

Pressing her phone against her ear, Jane turned aside as Carter picked up.

"Special Agent Winston Carter. You're on a recorded line -"

"Win?" Jane concentrated on presenting a concise report. "Cheryl Embry just stated that Tyler Shank is in her house. We've got a hostage situation." The adrenaline was singing in Jane's veins, her favorite feeling. She snapped her fingers. "Leslie? What's the address?"

"219 St. Claude Avenue." She responded automatically.

"Get that, Win? Cheryl said Tyler's armed. I don't know what weapon he's got."

"Are you safe?"

"Yes. We're in the Pascoe's kitchen, back of the house. Secure."

"Stay put." Carter commanded. "I'll find Mayas. Don't do anything foolish or rash."

She heard his chair squeal.

"Keep your people safe, Jane. Keep away from the scene. That's your job now. Do it."

"It would be easier if I still had my Ruger." She protested.

"Not negotiable. I'll notify Metro. ETA is … twenty minutes, maybe less. Jane?"

"Yes?"

"Stay safe." He repeated, hanging up.

She turned to catch Leslie dialing the old school rotary wall phone.

"Who are you calling?"

"Ryan." Leslie ran her finger down a list of penciled numbers scotch taped to the wall. "He needs to hear this before he sees it on TV."

A car horn honked from the driveway like the Queen Mary. Aunt Babette ducked before peering out the laundry room window. "Gigi's home. Oh! And she's got Ken and that dog with her."

Leslie hung up without completing the call. Tossing the dishtowel at the sink, she tugged the kitchen door open and ran onto the back porch, frantically waving both arms and shouting through the rusted screen. "Ken! Gigi! Get inside, quick!"

"*Bonjour,* Maman." Gee raised a white waxed paper bag, whistling Piddles to the ground. "I brought beignets. Wassup?"

Leslie was off the porch like a shot, quick stepping across the side yard toward The Boat. Jane caught the screen door as Aunt Babette slipped under her arm.

"Gigi! Ken! Get inside, quick! That Tyler fellow is holding Cheryl Embry hostage in her house!"

Ken slowly closed the passenger door. "What's that you're saying?"

"Ken! I'm telling you! That maniac killer is holding Cheryl hostage! We need to get inside where it's safe. Now."

Ken spun around to face St. Claude Avenue as two marked NOPD units barreled through the intersection, their overhead blue and white strobe lights flashing as they squealed to a stop, forming a nose-to-nose V and blocking Plessy Street.

"Holy shit." His jaw fell open. "You weren't kidding."

Piddles began to whine as four uniformed officers spilled from the cruisers. Drawing their weapons, they took up defensive positions behind their opened doors, the words NEW ORLEANS POLICE emblazoned in bright yellow lettering across their Kevlar vests.

"Dispatch: 10-97. Arrived on scene. Copy back."

The woman officer spoke into her hand-held radio, her handcuffs gleaming like silver half moons next to the folding baton on her duty belt. A bald, heavy-set sergeant popped the trunk on the lead unit and reached in. Jane's hands felt oddly empty as he hefted an M-16 rifle, slinging the gun strap over his right shoulder. The two remaining officers never shifted their focus off of the Embry's house.

"That was my old world, Gee." Jane turned as her nose caught a whiff of cherry tobacco, marijuana and Polo cologne. "How stoned are you?"

"Medium rare." Gee moistened her lips. "Pops and I enjoyed a wake and bake on the ride home. Sure wasn't expecting to come home to this. Hope they shoot that motherfucker dead."

Distant church bells started clanging as a black Crown Vic raced up, Detective Bordelon behind the wheel. Seeing them clustered in the driveway, Dupree opened the passenger door and got out, striding across the side yard and extending his arms like he was herding sheep.

"Move away from the street, folks." He ordered. "Let us do our job."

His Kevlar vest had a large gold crescent seal like a bull's eye target printed directly over his heart. Jane instantly decided that this was not a good look.

"Christ! It's a fucking circus." Ken muttered as a Delta Electric van pulled in behind the Crown Vic. "I need a cigarette."

Leaning over the wheel, Ryan Embry gaped at the unfolding scene. Opening the driver's side door, he slid out of sight before jogging around the van's rear double door, his face pale with shock. "What's going on here?" He demanded, pointing at the blockade. "Why are cops blocking the street?"

"Sir?" Bordelon moved to intercept him. "You need to join these other folks. Stay out of the way."

"But that's my house!" Ryan sputtered. "What's going on?"

"Sir? My partner was right," Dupree stated firmly. "You need to move away from the street for your own personal safety. We have a hostage situation."

"Hostage situation? Christ! I just went to the store for smokes. Who's in the house with my mom?"

"A person of interest in a double homicide." Grasping Ryan's arm, Dupree led him aside. "An HRT negotiator is on the way."

"When did Tyler get here?" Standing on tiptoe, Ryan shouted over Dupree's shoulder. "Tyler? Dude? What are you thinking?" He pulled out his phone. "I'm going to call him."

"We've tried." Dupree noted. "Shank disabled his phone. And the landline in the house."

An insistent two beat 'Woo-EEE' siren grew shrill as a steel-plated Lenco Bearcat armored vehicle rolled down the middle of St. Claude Avenue like a 9,000 pound bank vault on wheels, its red, white and blue overhead and grill panel lights flashing, followed closely by two unmarked Ford SUVs. Front doors and shutters cracked open as curious Bywater neighbors stepped onto their porches and stoops to watch the tactical SWAT vehicles establish a support position behind the two NOPD units facing Plessy Street.

Jane caught her breath as Win Carter stepped out of the lead SUV. His navy Kevlar vest read FBI and he held an electronic public address bullhorn in one hand. Mayas followed on his heels. Teaming up, they ran over to meet Dupree and Bordelon.

"Status report?" Carter barked. "What have we got?"

Detective Dupree glanced uncertainly at the Embry's house. "44-H. Hostage situation in progress."

"Have you attempted direct contact with Shank?" Mayas asked.

"Not yet. Waiting on the HRT negotiator. Thought that would be best."

"What's that timing?"

"Unknown. He's on his way." Dupree frowned. "One potential

hostage. Mrs. Cheryl Embry is inside."

"Alright." Carter scanned the landscape as the FBI SWAT personnel swarmed out of the Bearcat carrying tactical weapons and shields. Every single team member was in full gear including MP5 submachine guns or Colt M4 carbine assault rifles. The last man out carried a steel battering ram if needed to break down the Embry's door.

"We're not waiting," Carter stated flatly. "This is our show. FBI mandate takes jurisdictional precedence for this event. Agreed?"

"But we appreciate your support," Mayas inserted quickly.

Detective Dupree glanced at Bordelon, who nodded. "Agreed."

Jane froze as she watched the FBI sniper setting up the stabilizing tripod for his Remington 700 SPS Tactical rifle. The weapon looked as lethal as it was. She grabbed Gee's arm. "Gee? This shit just got real. That's .308 caliber."

Aunt Babette looked horrified. Reaching down, she grasped Piddle's collar. "I don't want to see this. We're going up to my room."

"Stay back from the window." Jane said as her PTSD kicked in. Her peripheral vision started alternating between red and green colored dots and wavy lines like mascaraed eyelashes as the sniper adjusted his scope. Tearing her eyes away, she noted the arrival of an ambulance. The white van had a huge golden fleur-de-lis painted on it and the EMS techs wore T-shirts printed with the words New Orleans Paramedics across their chests.

Leaning forward, they studied the scene through their windshield as a woman officer unrolled yellow police tape between two lampposts on St. Claude Avenue to block off the growing crowd of rubber necking bystanders drifting into the bike lane.

"This is different," one said, raising his red Solo cup.

"Wasn't really expecting to see this on a Sunday morning, but okay." His neighbor agreed.

Hefting the bullhorn, Carter pointed it at the Embry's house.

"Tyler Shank? I'm FBI Special Agent Winston Carter. Can we talk?"

The house remained shuttered and silent.

"Tyler? We know you're inside. We need to talk. Come on out, now."

The FBI sniper inhaled as the Embry's front door cracked open. Cheryl stood framed in the gap, her hands clutching her faded housecoat at her throat.

"He wants a car," she shouted, glancing fearfully over her shoulder. "He says he wants a car now."

The bullhorn squealed feedback. "Tyler? Take it easy, man. You're making this too hard. Just let her go and we'll talk about it."

"Y'all need to back off," Cheryl yelled.

"Tyler?" Carter repeated. "Come on out, 'bro. Let me see your hands. I can make it easy for you. Tyler? Let's do this easy. Let it go. Ain't worth it, man. I'm telling you. Let Mrs. Embry go and we'll talk."

"I didn't do nothing!" Tyler shouted hoarsely.

"Drop your weapon," Carter insisted. "Let me see your hands. Nobody has to get hurt. Tyler? Listen to me, 'bro. This ain't the way to go. I'm telling you. Don't do it this way."

Cheryl suddenly got snatched back inside the house and the door slammed shut. Jane ducked as the long window to the left of the front door shattered.

CRACK. CRACK.

"Shots fired! Everybody down!" Mayas yelled.

The bystanders in the bike lane scattered like chickens.

"Dispatch?" The woman officer shouted into her hand-held radio. "12:17. Shots fired. Code 4. Repeat. Code 4."

"Hey!" Carter visually checked the SWAT team. "Everybody okay?"

"Man down!" Dupree yelled, his voice ragged. "Medic! I need help."

Aware of their cover, the EMS techs raced forward, bent low over their rolling stretcher and forming an almost perfect horizontal line. Peering through the gap between the SWAT vehicles, Jane could only see Dupree. He had bright red arterial blood splashed up the front of his Kevlar vest to his chin.

"Bordelon!" Dupree dropped to his knees. "Stay with me, man. Stay with me!"

The Embry's front door re-opened. Cheryl tottered onto the porch, openly sobbing. Using her as a human shield, Tyler gripped her neck with his left hand, pushing a cocked sawed-off shotgun into her right ear.

"You made me do this!" He cried. "I didn't want to! You made me do it."

Jane caught a sudden blur of movement. Zigzagging left and right between the tactical SUVs, Ryan bolted past the SWAT team focused on the scene. Agent Mayas saw his action and made a grab for him, but Ryan dodged right and evaded his reach, running out into the middle of Plessy Street.

"Tyler? Bro?" Slowing his step, Ryan raised both arms wide. "No need to do this. We'll do whatever you want."

"Fuck!" Carter cursed. "Sight him. Sight him!"

The SWAT sniper adjusted his scope and settled back. "Done."

"Dude?" Tyler's lips quivered. "You told them I was here, man? You gave me up?"

"No, bro! No! I didn't. It wasn't me, I swear. Mom? You okay?"

"Ryan? Son?" Cheryl tried to turn her head under Tyler's fierce grip. "I love you, son. No matter what happens, don't forget that I love you!"

"Goddammit, Tyler." Ryan stepped closer. "Look at the shit show you got going on here." He took another step forward. "Let her go, 'bro. Let my mom go and take me, instead."

Jane caught Carter flicking his flattened hand at the sniper as he made up his mind. *Oh, shit.* Her heart caught in her throat. *He's going to do it.*

Carter raced flat out like an NFL running back through the two lead NOPD units. Ryan heard Carter's pounding footsteps and he turned. Grabbing Ryan by the shoulders, Carter wrapped both arms around him and using brute force strength and his Kevlar vest as a limited shield, he dragged Ryan kicking and struggling back behind the police barricade. Ryan fought back, using his fists and his feet.

"Let go! Let me go!"

"Hold this fool." Carter chucked Ryan at a uniformed officer. "Cuff him to a bumper, I don't care what you do, but keep him secured." Panting heavily, he turned.

"Ryan?" Tyler called, wiping the snot running from his nose on Cheryl's hair. "Dude? I thought we were partners!"

Cheryl's knees gave out and she started to slip. Still pressing the shotgun into her ear, Tyler wrapped his fingers in her hair. He tightened his grip as she cried out.

"Don't fucking move, bitch! I'll blow your fucking head all over this neighborhood. I'm not stupid. I know what you did."

"He did it!" Cheryl screamed shrilly as she collapsed into a heap. "He said he killed those people!"

"Shut the fuck up!" Tyler fumbled his grip. "You set me up -"
CRACK.

Jane jumped at the concussive snap of the Remington .308. Suddenly freed, Cheryl Embry fell forward, hunching into a boneless ball. Covering her face with her hands, she started shrilly keening as Tyler flopped onto the porch like a limp rag doll.

The high caliber Remington echo bounced off the houses in The Bywater neighborhood. Street corner spectators froze in wide-eyed shock, slowly raising their hands to cover their gaping mouths. Even the ravens fell silent in the bare black trees.

"N.A.T." Jane whispered.

Gee inhaled brokenly. "What does that mean?"

"Necessary action taken. It's done, Gee. It's over."

CHAPTER FIFTY-FOUR

Turning her head, Jane listened to the rain softly pattering against the apartment's wavy glass windows. *How long has this place been standing? A hundred and fifty years?* She thought of Tyler Shank shot to death on the Embry's front porch across the street. *NOLA is crammed with history although we sure never learned much of it in school. What else has this place seen?*

A somber hush had clung to The Bywater neighborhood yesterday long after the tactical SWAT unit had dispersed and the FBI had rumbled away. Initially, the EMS team had taken charge of the cleanup, carrying Cheryl Embry to New Orleans East Hospital and transporting Tyler Shank's body-bagged corpse to the Crescent City morgue. After the FBI signed off on the crime scene, a NOFD 3rd District fire engine had pulled up next to the Embry's driveway. Firefighters had very considerately hosed Tyler Shank's pooled blood off the front porch before it had a chance to set and permanently stain the paint.

Piddles snorted in his sleep. Opening his eyes, he rose from his bed, licked his nose, yawning and stretching more like a cat than a dog before trotting for the door, whining.

"Need to go out, Mr. P?" Jane stretched, too. "You're gonna get wet."

Reaching for her cane, she scrambled up. Her stiff knee still looked puffy, but it was half the size it had been the day of the accident. Her gravel rash had scabbed over into a golden serum crust without any sign of green infection and her big bruise was fading from plum to black and banana yellow. The only real remaining aggravation were the stitches in her scalp because they itched like crazy as her stubbly hair grew back in.

Piddles raced outside through the dormant garden, yipping through the puddles as Jane leaned against the door. Despite the spitting rain, the December breeze refreshed her overheated face. Reaching up, she tested her cheeks using the back of her hand. *Is this a fever?* Her skin felt cool, but not clammy. *What do you know? Damn, girl. I'm on the mend.*

She gazed at the Embry's shuttered house. *Tyler Shank is dead and The Crescent City Slasher threat is over. Fancy and Dee and Numa have been avenged. Dupree finally traced that pickup truck tag from the locker back to Tyler's mom's address. Case closed. Gee and the LGBTQ community are safe again, well, as safe as they ever were.* Jane thoughtfully rapped the cane against the chipped limestone threshold. *Justice has been served. Pretty swift justice for Tyler Shank and that's a fact. When Dad died, I learned that life's not fair, but Lady Justice? She is one intent bitch. She may be blind, but she never waivers and she's not afraid of using that sword in her hand.*

Lifting her chin off her chest, Jane studied the dripping silvery rain. *Isn't it funny how Justice is always shown as a woman? The Punisher is a she. Somehow, somewhere, we lost sight of that.* She shook her head. *And if this really is over, why do I feel so unsatisfied?*

She noted The Boat parked in the driveway, canvas top up and a pink polka dot umbrella drying outside the kitchen door. *Gee must've stopped by for lunch.* Jane's stomach grumbled at the thought of hot food. *How about a smoked turkey and cheese roll-up?* She turned, leaving the front door open for Mr. P's return and to catch more of the welcome breeze.

Her peckish appetite got hosed as she limped into the kitchen. The drain had backed up again because of the rain. A neon orange ring of congealed grease floated like a life preserver on top of six inches of brown water filling the sink.

"Crap. Just what I needed! One more thing."

Piddles yipped uncertainly as he skidded back into the apartment. Pausing in the exact center of the living room, he shook the raindrops off of his wiry coat, spraying the furniture and the walls with droplets before searching for Jane, finding her in the kitchen and tracking a fresh row of muddy paw prints across the floor, obviously hoping for a biscuit or a cheesy rollup treat.

What the fuck. Jane laughed. *Welcome to my crazy ass life. Guess what? It's messy. It's inconvenient. It's a fucking pain in the ass, but I'm living it and it's all mine.* Reaching for the roll of paper towels, she frugally tore off two sheets and dropped them to the floor, leveraging her cane and using her good right foot to mop the paw prints up. "You made a mess, Mr. P -"

She paused as a niggling idea breached the surface of her foggy brain. *Paw prints? Muddy paw prints? Is that it?* She squinted, snatching at the vague, whispery suggestion while struggling to link her thoughts into something cohesive. Her gut instinct started sending up warning flares as she homed in on yesterday's hostage situation, a sensation she never ignored. *Shit. I missed something yesterday. Something big. What was it?*

Leaning against the counter, she recalled Tyler pressing the shotgun to Cheryl's head. Tyler had looked hesitant, uncertain, obviously in fear for his life and clearly out of his depth. Jane stepped the memory back to his assault on Gee on Frenchmen Street, this time using a knife. Tyler had looked equally uncertain then, fumbling and dropping the blade before fleeing the scene.

If Tyler Shank was The Crescent City Slasher wouldn't he be more on point?

A light bulb went off in her mind like fireworks over Nantucket harbor on Independence Day as she made the connection.

Not muddy paw prints, bloody footprints. Her heart began to hammer as she recalled Delilah Gardere's horrific crime scene with its hundreds of dripping crimson handprints stamped on the walls and the *two* sets of bloody footprints circling Dee's corpse on the floor.

Two sets of footprints means two killers. Not one, two.

'Dude! I thought we were partners!' Tyler had screamed before dying.

Jane froze. *Tyler Shank had an accomplice in the hate crime murders.*

301

The Crescent City Slasher is a serial killer team.

She grabbed her phone, still plugged into its charger, speed-dialing Carter's number.

"Hey, Jane. Pleasant surprise. Everything okay? You're on a recorded line."

"Win?" She snatched a quick breath. "Just before he died, Tyler Shank called Ryan Embry his partner. Did you catch that? Think back to Delilah Gardere's crime scene, Win. Pull it up in your mind. Too much shit has happened for this to be the work of a solo killer." She sucked in another breath. "We have an active killer team here, Win. Tyler Shank and Ryan Embry worked together to commit the murders like Leonard Lake and Charles Ng did. They're a team, a serial killer team."

"Jane, I'm sorry. What?"

She pressed the phone to her ear. "I think Tyler Shank and Ryan Embry committed the hate crime murders as a serial killer team," she repeated. "Look at Delilah Gardere's crime scene photos. Do you have them? Pull them up."

"Give me a second. Hold on. They're on my laptop -"

"Check the footprints next to her body. I'm telling you, Win, forensics was my thing. That crime scene had two different footprints. I only just now remembered it."

"One minute. Okay, Jane, I'm in. I'm looking at 'em now."

She heard his soft breathing in her ear.

"You're wrong. It's not two sets of prints. Some of these are partials from when the killer walked on tip-toe."

"That can't be." Jane clutched her forehead, her spinning brain pulsing with pain. She pushed through it. "Check the treads. You need to pull Ryan Embry in again. Press him on it. I know I'm right."

Carter sighed heavily. "Jane? It was an interesting idea, it was, and you really had me going there for a minute, but you need to let this go. We caught the killer, Tyler Shank. Forensics fingerprinted the Glock Cheryl Embry surrendered up. It had Shank's fingerprints on it. Everyone's in agreement, signed off on it, up and down the line. It's done. We need to focus now on other things."

"Oh, really?" Jane snapped. "Like what?"

"Like Detective Bordelon's funeral." Win softened his tone. "Remember that?"

Oh, shit. Her gaffe was so blatant that Jane choked. "I forgot. How's Dupree doing?"

"Taking it hard. To be expected. They were partners for twenty-six years. Most marriages aren't that solid."

"Remind me again." She swallowed thickly. "When's the funeral?"

"Saturday at one. St. Patrick's Church on Camp Street. D'you need a ride? I can swing by and pick you up."

Jane hesitated. *Bordelon's funeral will be a full court press including Mayor Landrieu and the police union reps. No one will miss me if I'm MIA.* "I'll think about it."

"There'll be a second line parade after Bordelon's funeral with his family and friends if you wanted to join that. You know, celebrate his life?" Win paused. "Call me with what you decide, either way. I want to keep in touch, know how you're doing."

"Will do."

Jane tapped out. *Carter's right. Fancy and Dee and Cal and Numa aren't the only victims here.* Her shoulders slumped. *With violence, there's always collateral damage, intended or not. Hatred has a ripple effect. Wrong place, wrong time, catch a bullet and now Detective Bordelon, that nice guy on the edge of retirement dies from Tyler's hatred, too. Now his family and friends and the people who loved him like Dupree are suffering. And Cal's still missing, too.*

She studied the floating orange grease ring in the filthy sink. *But I do need to let it go. Life rolls on, things bounce back and return to normal and I've got my own set of problems to fix like this fucking sink.* She straightened. *That's the practical thing to do. Keep it real and go tell Leslie she needs to call the plumber again.*

Shaking the cardboard box to check on the biscuit inventory, Jane fed Piddles a treat. "Be right back, buddy." Picking up her cane, she hobbled for the Big House, carefully navigating the six back porch steps. The inner kitchen door was open and she heard Ken's rumbling voice.

"Sweetheart, I need to go out for a couple hours. Should be back in time for supper."

"Ken?" Leslie teased. "Where do you go on these mysterious excursions?"

"She's right, Pops. Where do you go?" Gee probed. "You have to admit it looks highly suspicious."

"If you must know, I got a job." Ken blustered.

"A job!" Gee laughed brightly. "Sure you did. Doing what?"

"Restocking shelves at the Dollar Store. Pays nine bucks an hour."

"But why, Ken?" Leslie sounded perplexed. "Why on earth would you do such a thing?"

"Because, sweetheart," his voice softened. "I needed to pay for your diamond ring."

"Oh, Ken. You're adorable. I didn't need that ring to make me happy and you know that!"

"It's worth every penny, Leslie, just to see your smile."

Shit! Jane blushed. *I feel like an idiot standing out here.* She glanced back at the steep set of steps. *But I don't have the energy in me to sneak away and make two trips.* "Hello, the house." She rapped the cane against the warped porch floor. "Can I come in?"

CHAPTER FIFTY-FIVE

"Sorry to interrupt." Jane pushed the kitchen door open. "Leslie? The drain's backed up again. It's filling my sink."

"Quickly, Gee. Go tell Aunt Babette." Snapping her fingers, Leslie pointed. "Nobody flushes a thing until we get the plumber to take a look at it." She snatched up the wall phone. "I want to stay ahead of this."

"Hey, Jane. Zup?" Gee rose. "How you feeling? Better?"

"Much better," Jane admitted. "On the mend."

"That reminds me." Leslie pushed a woolly pink bundle across the counter with her free hand. "Aunt Babette knitted you this cap to cover your stitches." She returned her focus to the phone. "Yes, I'm here. Yes, it's an emergency. Yes, I'll hold."

Jane held the soft pink pussy cap in her hands. *Why not?* She tenderly settled it over her shaved head. The expensive cashmere yarn instantly warmed her sore, stubbly scalp like a buttery baby blanket. *Aunt Babette is the bomb. Instant comfort like a solid hug from a good friend just when you need it.* Jane smiled. "Gee? If you're going up, please thank Aunt Babette for me until I get a chance to do it in person myself."

"Check." Gee snorted, tapping her pointy chin. "I'm not sure why that works on you, but it does, in a strange girl resistance fighter kinda way."

"That's because I'm a rebel," Jane stated.

"Gigi! Focus!" Leslie snapped her fingers again, pointing at the swinging door. "Go tell Aunt Babette that we have a problem."

"Sorry! Wait for me, Jane. I'll walk you out."

"That goddamn sewer line has been a pain in the ass for thirty years."

305

Ken grumbled, tapping the counter with his fingers. "If it's not the water table, it's goddamn tree roots or some other fucking shit. It's always something with this house."

Leslie clamped her hand over the phone. "Ken, please. I'm taking care of it."

Gee trotted back through the swinging door. "Aunt Babette's on board. She won't use any water until she gets an all clear." She checked her phone. "Jane? You ready?" Courteously holding both the inner and outer kitchen doors open, she picked up her damp umbrella. Easily bounding down the steps, she held up her palm to check on the rain. "Might be clearing up."

Jane limped down the steps. "I see you got The Boat back."

"About fucking time." Gee tossed the umbrella onto the floorboards. "Don't get me wrong. Uber and Lyft are great, but I missed having my own wheels. Missed the independence, know what I mean?" She paused. "Need a quick trip to the corner store for groceries before I go? You good for supplies?"

"I'm good, but thanks for asking."

"You let me know if you need a ride." Gee stared at the Embry's house, jiggling her key ring in her hand. "S'weird to think of what went on over there yesterday." Rolling her index finger in the air, she tapped her temple. "Feels like a bad dream."

"I was just thinking the same thing."

"I still can't wrap my head around the fact that Tyler Shank, that little peckerwood shit murdered Fancy and Dee."

"And Numa," Jane added.

"Exactly! Or that he shot Detective Bordelon. I know he said he did it, but it still seems off to me."

"He didn't say he did it," Jane countered. "Cheryl Embry said that he said he did it. It's hearsay actually, not the same thing."

"Oh, sure." Gee scoffed. "Blame the dead guy. How easy is that?"

Tyler Shank never said that he did it. Jane's instinct underlined her earlier protest over The Slasher's identity. "Gee? I know this is gonna sound crazy but let me talk it through. Fancy weighed what? Two-twenty, right? Dee was wrapped in that heavy carpet. Tyler Shank weighs what, one thirty, tops?"

"If that." She scoffed. "Soaking wet."

"So how did he shift that weight by himself?"

"What d'you mean?" Gee looked perplexed.

Hanging her cane off her forearm, Jane linked her fingers. "I keep thinking that Tyler didn't act solo, that The Slasher was a unit, part of a kill team. That somehow Ryan Embry was involved."

"Ryan was involved?" Gee repeated slowly as knowledge dawned in her eyes. "That actually makes sense. I could see Ryan doing that, especially if he was using Tyler to hit back at me. He always was a little chickenshit bastid. Smart enough to not get caught, but happy enough pulling the strings on someone else to do the work. Shit, Jane. You might be right. You need to call Mayas and tell him this."

"I've talked to Carter. He dismissed my idea."

"Fucker. Why? What did he say?"

"That everyone has signed off on it and it's time to move on."

"He's wrong." Gee planted her hands on her hips. "I'm with you. We'll need to do this ourselves."

"Do what ourselves?" Jane asked warily.

"Investigate Ryan. Check his van for starters." Spinning around, she marched through the garden. "He's home for lunch. The van's right there. Come on."

Jane limped quickly to keep up. "Gee? They catch us on their property without permission, it's called criminal trespassing -"

"Then we need to make sure they don't catch us." Ducking low, Gee trotted across Plessy Street. "Learned this when I was a kid, back when Ryan and me had sleepovers. If we come to the Embry's house from this side, they can't see us. None of their windows face this way."

"Anything we do find is inadmissible in court." Jane followed, her internal warning system hiked to red alert. "We don't have a search warrant or probable cause."

"We haven't found anything yet. Would you get over here?" Gee swept her arm forward like an oar. "We'd be done by now if you'd hurry."

"Fuck off. I'm limping as fast as I can."

Gee slid up the blind side of the Delta Electric van like a ninja. "We'll check this first, then check his garage. Ryan's always messing around in there. Calls it his man cave. Makes sense, he's such a fucking troglodyte." Pressing her broad hand against the rear cargo door, she turned the handle and quietly popped it open, scanning the interior. "Jumper cables, bungee cords, big metal toolbox. Ryan's got a case of duct tape. Is that suspicious?"

Jane's eyes watered and her nose burned. "And bleach. I smelled it before on our date. Ryan's an electrician. What would he need bleach for?"

"No reason I can think of. Strike one. Let's check the cab."

Shutting the cargo door with a click, Gee slid along the van. Opening the passenger door, she leaned in and felt under the front seat before unlocking the glove box and poking her fingers through the paper trash. "Gas receipts and a church key. What do you think? Should we risk it and check his garage?"

Jane turned. PTSD snapped her rubber band tight nerves as she studied the standalone structure, a 12x12 foot framed unit approximately twenty-five feet from the back of the Embry's house. The faded asphalt shingled roof swayed in the middle. Tufts of dried grass formed a solid barrier in front of the rickety off kilter overhead door. Cobwebs studded with dead bugs hung from the lintel like a banner of Spanish moss. *No one's parked a car in this garage in years.* The six single windowpanes were painted an opaque black from the inside.

"This here's the tricky part." Gee whispered. "I need to get the key. Ryan keeps it locked. If they step outside the house, they'll see me."

"Where's the key?"

"I'll take that as a 'yes.'" Gee grinned. "Twenty years ago they hid it under that planter. Be right back."

Sweet Jesus. What are we doing? Jane held her breath. Pushing the pussy cap off her forehead, she winced as the yarn tugged at her stitches. Peering around the corner, she watched Gee bolt for the Embry's patio, tip a concrete pot and race back, skidding through shallow puddles and clutching the key in her fist.

"Hope it still works." She huffed, wiping the rain off her face. "I'll go first. You follow me as fast as you can."

"In and out though, Gee, right? In and out and we're done. Outta here?"

"They'll never even know we was here."

Pinching the key between her fingers and her thumb, Gee rolled around the splintery corner, unlocking the side door with a quick and certain twist and noiselessly slipping inside.

What the hell am I doing? Jane paused. *This isn't even my fight. Don't I have enough shit on my plate already?* Her knee throbbed steadily like a two-stroke Evinrude motor as bright silvery orbs haloed her vision. She swallowed the bitter taste coating her tongue. *Suck it up, sister. Enough of the pity party! When did I start whining instead of doing?* She inhaled a ragged breath. *Just get the fuck on with it. Gee needs my backup.*

Tightly grasping the cane, she stepped inside the garage.

CHAPTER FIFTY-SIX

"Quick! Shut the door!" Gee's voice sounded hollow. "Before you hit the switch. It's on the wall to your left."

Jane walked her fingers down a cool plastic cable until they slid over a cold steel plate. "Got it." She flicked the switch and two overhead florescent bar panels flared, illuminating the garage with brilliantly artificial white light.

"Jackpot." Gee whistled softly. "Would you take a fucking look at this?"

Ryan's man cave was immaculate in contrast to the derelict outside public shell. A stout homemade worktable ran the length of the left wall. It held an organized cleaning station and two 9MM Glock Gen 4 pistols.

On the right, directly under the blacked-out windows was a tactical weapons armory housed in custom mounting racks. Of the two-dozen rifles on display, Jane recognized three Remington M700s with sniper scopes, a Browning X-Bolt Medallion with its detachable box magazine and a Daniel Defense Ambush .308 Semiautomatic Kryptek Highlander. A second gun rack held a nice Mossberg Model 500 pump-action shotgun and two Remington Model 870s. Cardboard ammo boxes were stacked in handy overhead cubicles directly over each weapon.

"Ryan's a gamer, huh? I don't think so." Gee scoffed. "What game would this be? Mass destruction?"

Jane studied the massive inventory. "He's got enough weaponry in here to win a war."

"Fuck. That's probably what he's planning on doing." Gee's voice sounded gravelly. "America First, right? This white supremacy shit makes me

310

sick."

Jane turned. Gee's face had turned ashen as she gazed in horror at a Nazi banner hanging on the rear wall. Jane shivered as the image of the crimson flag with its flat black swastika on its big white dot seared her retinas. *How the fuck did we end up back here again?* She shut her eyes to block the hate-filled image. *Isn't that why we fought both World Wars? All that fucking horror, all those helpless dead people. Did all of that mean nothing? What are we, stupid?*

"Is owning this many guns even legal?" Gee spat.

"Could be." Jane blinked her eyes open. "If Ryan bought them through an FFL dealer. These are considered hunting rifles. You can buy most of them at WalMart."

"Fucking NRA." Gee's voice rose. "Jane? You don't think this sick shit is right, do you?"

"No, I don't." She leaned on her cane. "But Ryan has the Constitutional right to express himself on his own property."

"Even when he believes sick-ass shit like this?" Gee replied sarcastically, shaking a glossy flyer. "'Our single goal and focus must be the salvation of our Homeland. The continuity of our white Christian nation is perfectly natural. Any political or personal decisions counter to this belief must be opposed at all costs without mercy.' Seriously? What the fuck?"

"Put that back, Gee. We need to get outta here. This is sick shit, but it's not illegal. He's within his rights."

"One minute." Gee tossed the flyer onto the worktable with disgust. Stepping toward a walnut trophy rack in the corner, she tugged on its camouflaged dust cover. The heavy canvas resisted and giving it a more insistent tug, it ripped free from its Velcro tabs, clearing the rack's upper edge and sliding to the floor with a hiss.

What are those things? Jane inched closer. *Dream catchers?* Her brain spun like a pinwheel as she processed the fresh horror that met her eyes. *Holy fuck. They're scalps.* Acidic bile burned her sinuses. *Human scalps.* One display held gray shoulder-length dreadlocks. *That's Cal!*

Gee retched, pointing a finger at a scalp with long black tresses. "Fuck! That's Dee!"

Jane stared at the scalps hanging from a lower row, her mouth suddenly tasting like copper. She scanned the two mounted scalps on the left and the four more in the row above. *The Slasher was credited with five kills: Fancy, Dee, Cal, Numa and Bordelon. Who else has Ryan murdered?* Jane gulped the bitter taste away. *Fuck. There are six more kills we don't even know about?*

Her scalp prickled and her right hand itched. *That's it. I need a weapon.* Propping the cane against the worktable, she reached for one of the 9MM pistols. The oh-so-familiar Glock grip settled comfortably against her palm. *Sweet.* Releasing the magazine, Jane pulled the slide back to the catch, noting with satisfaction that the standard 17 rounds were represented. *That should do it. Now I feel better.* Re-seating the magazine with a slap, her right index finger extended along the frame, she released the slide lock with her thumb and chambered a round with a snap.

"Keep behind me, Gee. We're getting outta here -"

Reaching for the cane, Jane pulled up short.

"Zup?"

She studied the weapon in her hand. "Win Carter said Cheryl surrendered a Glock after the event. It had Tyler Shank's fingerprints on it. Win said Forensics proved the Glock was used to murder Detective Bordelon."

"So?"

Jane narrowed her focus. "Why did Tyler switch from using a Glock to a shotgun when he held Cheryl hostage?"

"I don't know. Maybe ... because it's bigger?"

"Shotgun's less effective defensively long range, not more." Jane hefted the 9MM pistol. "A handgun would've been a better choice especially when he was managing a hostage." She recalled Tyler Shank's multiple fumbles as Cheryl collapsed on the porch as an alternate idea gelled. "Gee? We're getting played. Who said the Glock that killed Bordelon belonged to Tyler Shank? No one." Jane heard a sibilant whisper behind her left shoulder, and she turned. "Maybe it was *hers*."

"Ryan?" Cheryl Embry called back toward the house. "Come on out here, son. Look who I just caught trespassing on our property."

Shit. The Slasher isn't Tyler and Ryan. It's Tyler and Ryan and Cheryl.

Cheryl raised the Mossberg 12-gauge shotgun, planting her feet firmly in the doorway. She looked perfectly at ease.

She's got three rounds of steel shot, maybe four with one in the tube. The safety's off. Where's Gee? What are my odds?

"Don't raise that Glock on me, girlie. Set it aside on that table and push it away. Yes, just like that."

Ryan suddenly loomed behind his mother. Looking over her shoulder, he unsheathed a gleaming Bowie knife. "Gonna have to call in sick to work for me, Ma. Got my headache again." He cracked a toothy smile. "This looks like more fun."

Cheryl stared at Jane's cap with a withering hatred. "Aren't you a sight? I knew you was trouble the minute I laid eyes on you. Ryan? Should've listened to me, son." She leveled the Mossberg at Jane's abdomen. "I could shoot you both right now for home invasion. Justified."

Gee pointed at the scalp rack. "You are two sick fucks."

"You're the sick fuck, freak." Ryan snarled, shouldering his way into the garage. Tossing the buckskin sheath on the worktable, he raised the ten-inch blued steel knife.

"You people forgot your place." Cheryl tightened her grip on the shotgun. The double barrel looked like a train tunnel. "We let you live in the shadows, but no, you had to have 'rights.'" Her face twisted into a venomous mask of spitting hatred as her voice grew shrill. "You and your kind, you don't

313

get rights. You're deviants. Perverts. Your lifestyle is an insult to God and our nation!"

"I hope you enjoy Hell, bitch." Gee spat. "Because that's where you're going."

"Shut your mouth!" Ryan shouted. "You don't get to talk."

"Grab some zip ties, son." Cheryl ordered. "Same plan as before." Her tone was chillingly reasonable. "Drive them out to Honey Bayou and feed 'em to the gators, like you did them others. Easy-peasy."

"I'm not so sure 'bout that." Ryan tapped the knife's blunt edge against his lips. "These two disappear and you'll bring the cops down on us twice in two days. I know they're stupid, Ma, but they won't overlook that."

Cheryl dropped her chin. "You got a better suggestion?"

"How 'bout we … march them back to their house and burn it down? Place is a firetrap already. A little arson will cover everything."

"Leslie Pascoe's my best friend!" Cheryl protested, looking perplexed. "I'd hate to take her house from her. She didn't do nothing wrong -"

"Sure she did." Ryan pointed the knife at Gee. "She planted that evil seed right there when she took him in to raise. You need to listen to me this time, Ma. It's the best answer we got."

Fuck that. Jane heard a pebble rolling under Gee's shoe. *She's ready to make a move. We need to do something.* Her ears popped and she heard an oddly thrumming *wah-wah-wah* sound like a hovering helicopter. *Shit. Fucking PTSD. Not now.* The shotgun wavered from her chest to her navel as Cheryl's shoulders dropped.

"I trust your opinion, son," she stated uncertainly, "but things are getting outta control. It's getting messy."

"I'll say it is," said Aunt Babette.

Stepping into the garage, she neatly folded her dripping red umbrella. "Saw what you two girls was up to from my window. Called 911. The police are on their way."

"You fucking nosy old bitch!" Ryan raised the knife.

"Watch him!" Gee rose up on her toes, ready to leap. "Watch him, Aunt Babette!"

"What are you going to do, Ryan? Kill us all?" Aunt Babette alertly cocked her head. "I should've stopped you years ago when I caught you stomping on Leslie's chickens. Cheryl?" She squinted. "Shouldn't have let it get this far. Shouldn't have let him do it." She lightly tapped her heart. "I should've said something, but I didn't know you two were killing people." Dropping her arms to her sides, she straightened to her full height. "I won't let you harm my family. This all stops right now."

Jane ducked as the row of blacked out glass panes simultaneously shattered.

"Everybody down!" Win Carter shouted. "On the floor! FBI."

CHAPTER FIFTY-SEVEN

Hearing the backhoe's start-up high-pitched whine, Jane glanced at the kitchen clock. 8:09 a.m. *A little early to be making this much racket, but if it means I can stop peeing in a bucket I'm not complaining.*

She flicked the dotted curtain aside to check on the plumber's progress. Leslie's tidy kitchen garden looked like a trenched-out war zone. The mustard yellow digger growled a deeper note as it started scooping up and setting aside shovelfuls of sloppy muck. Ken and Gee were supervising the project, their arms solemnly folded across their chests. Their family resemblance was even strikingly obvious since they wore matching scowls.

Mr. Piddles perked up expectantly as Jane picked up the cane.

"Walkie, Mr. P? Want to go outside?"

She limped across the courtyard, taking it extra slow and carefully picking solid ground for every step. The backhoe's caterpillar tread had churned the garden's mushy ground into treacherously unstable muddy ruts and she had an entirely new set of sore muscles to explore after yesterday's strenuous exercise. Gee spotted them coming.

"Hey, Jane. How you feeling today?" She grinned devilishly. Bending low, she scratched the itchy spot between Piddle's shoulders. "Yesterday sure raised the bar. Never been part of an FBI raid before. Got me so wound up I couldn't sleep. Hanging out with you sure is exciting. Anything more I should be getting ready for next?"

"Fuck off." Jane planted the cane, wincing as her nostrils filled with the mushroomy odor from the disturbed clay. "How's it coming?"

"What's it look like?" Ken noted sourly. "Fucking sewer line."

316

"Come on, Pops. You must've known this was gonna happen sooner or later. That pipe's a bazillion years' old. Look at it. S'made out of cast iron."

"Sure, but I was hoping for later." Ken scratched his neck. "Do you have any idea how much this is going to cost us? Fifteen thousand dollars just to rent the equipment and it goes up from there." He snorted. "Fifteen grand to dig a ditch. I'm in the wrong fucking business."

"What business is that?" Gee teased.

"The stacking shampoo cases in aisle four business, smart ass." He flicked Gee's bicep. "Jokes on you. This takes too much longer to fix and we'll all need to move in with you for the duration. You get to sleep with Aunt Babette. You ready for that?"

"I'll sleep with Maman." Gee countered quickly.

"Oh hell no, you won't." Ken tapped his broad chest. "I sleep with your mother. That's not going to change."

Jane hid her smile behind her fingers. *Ken's feeling a little prickly today and I'm not surprised.* She glanced at the Embry's property, still cordoned off with yellow crime scene tape. *The FBI didn't wrap it up until after 3:00 a.m. Gee's not the only one who didn't get much sleep.*

Gee followed Jane's sight line across Plessy Street.

"I'm just glad it's over." She grew pensive as the backhoe clanked forward like a German panzer tank. "Now maybe Fancy and Dee and those other people can rest in peace." She shook her head. "I still can't believe how bad it got with Cheryl claiming she was The Slasher and that Ryan didn't know anything about the killings, that he wasn't involved."

"She's just trying to protect her son." Ken studied Gee thoughtfully. "Parents do weirdo shit like that."

Jane resettled her stance to spare her knee. "It would've been more convincing if Ryan hadn't loaded snuff videos on the dark web off his phone. Makes it hard to claim he had no prior knowledge when his account had password protect."

"Who ever said criminals were smart?" Ken scoffed.

"They're not." Jane agreed. "They're just desperate people pushed beyond their limits or people feeling threatened or trying to protect someone or something they love. That criminal mastermind bullshit is Hollywood. At least the FBI can start working on the other IDs for those families to get some closure."

The burly backhoe operator leaned out of his Plexiglas bubble, craning his neck at something beneath the toothy scoop and shouting something unintelligible. Leaning back into the cab, he shut the diesel engine down. It died in a descending series of rattling chuffing coughs.

"Oh, shit." Ken grumbled. "Now what?"

Unbuckling his safety belt, the operator grasped an overhead chrome handle and swung to the muddy ground. "Yo, Ken? Something funky going on here."

"Xavier?" Ken strode closer to the trench. "What is it?"

"Some kinda tarp." He rolled the dirt off his palms. "Got bones sticking out of it."

Stumbling over the dirt clods, Jane followed Gee to the trench. Crossing her arms, she shivered. *Yep, that's a human leg all right.* The backhoe had apparently disturbed the skeletonized remains of an adult human being. *Judging from the width of that hip basket, I'd say it's female.* The unhinged skull grinned crookedly through the plastic sheet and strands of curly black hair still clung to the ivory skull.

Xavier hawked and spat wetly. "No real surprise." He circled his finger to indicate the general area. "Bodies popping outta this ground every day, leftover from Katrina. Plus, they kept pushing the graveyards back to build these neighborhoods. Could be a yellow fever victim from a hundred years' ago."

"It's more recent." Jane cocked her head. "The tarp's got a graphic on it."

318

"What the fuck?" Gee gasped. "Jon Bon Jovi? It's a shower curtain."

Ken slowly covered his mouth with his fist. "Holy hell."

"Sorry, Ken. That makes it modern era. I'll need to call it in." Arms akimbo, Xavier started stepping over the ruts, shouting over his shoulder as he returned to his truck. "Can't be helped. County regulations. Not my decision to make."

Leslie and Aunt Babette, their arms filled with grocery sacks, rounded the corner of the house as Xavier opened his door and climbed in.

"Ken? We've brought breakfast." Leslie announced, stopping stock-still. "Look at this mess! Why y'all tearing up my garden?"

"Sweetheart?" Ken's voice sounded oddly hollow. "He had to follow the sewer pipe. It led this way from the street."

Gee pointed at the trench. "We found a body."

"A body? What kind of body?" Quickly setting her sack down on the porch steps, Leslie reached for Aunt Babette's burden and set it down neatly, side by side before trotting over. "In my garden?"

Clutching her beaded necklace, Aunt Babette slowly followed.

"Ken?" Peering into the trench, Leslie grasped his arm. "I don't understand what's going on." She inhaled sharply. "That *is* a body. What's it doing here?"

She fell back a step as the color drained from her face, leaving it pinched and as gray as clay. "That's a shower curtain." She slowly turned to face Aunt Babette. "You bought one just like it at Weldon's Five and Dime, Babette, remember? Jon Bon Jovi. You had such a crush on him."

The skeletonized foot hanging outside the protective plastic sheet was still wearing a stacked platform shoe with a band of colorful plastic flowers sewn on its toecap. Leslie's eyes glazed over. She started to shake. "Wait a second. I recognize those shoes."

"Quickly, Ken," Aunt Babette ordered. "Cover her back up."

"Too late." Ken stared unfocused into the pit. "I know who this is."

"Sweetheart?" Leslie's eyes filled with sorrow as she faced Gee. "I'm sorry you had to learn about it this way." She twisted her fingers together. "I can't even begin to tell you how sorry I am."

"Maman?" Gee's face fell slack. "How do you know who this is?"

"I didn't know about this!" Leslie pointed her finger. "I didn't even know Marianne was dead until just this very minute."

"How could you not know?" Gee shouted. "She's buried in your garden!"

"I don't know how she got here." Leslie wailed, looking panic-stricken as she glanced between Aunt Babette and Ken. "Yes, I hit her, but when I came back outside she was gone. I thought she woke up and left! You've got to believe me! I've been waiting for her to come walking back into my house for thirty years!"

"Someone buried her," Gee stated. "Pops? Was it you?"

"Me?" Ken looked startled. "I don't think so, Gee." He coughed nervously. "I might have. I don't even remember our fight."

Jane checked on the backhoe operator. Xavier was still on his phone, talking animatedly. *He's reporting a homicide and he thinks one of the Pascoes did it.* "He's talking to the police. Leslie? From what I've heard so far, they're gonna tag you for murder and arrest Ken as accessory."

"They can't do that! He's innocent!" Leslie clenched her fists. "Ken had nothing to do with this. It was all my doing!"

"Not all of it," Aunt Babette inserted softly, clutching her beads. "I buried her. I heard the fight and saw what happened from my room. I saw you hit her with the shovel, Leslie. I did see that. I ran down and found Marianne laying in the driveway, right where you left her." She kneaded the beads with her thumbs. "I had to do something. Couldn't let them take you, *cher.* Had to protect the family. You're all that I've got."

She nodded repeatedly. "We'd just tilled the garden. The ground was nice and soft. I dragged her there on my shower curtain and I laid her to rest."

She smiled uncertainly. "*Cher?* I felt much happier when you built your chicken coop over her grave. That way, no one would till her up in the spring."

Jane felt a rising ripple of horror. She hated even asking the question, but her forensic experience with head wounds and concussion protocols raised a terrifying possibility. There was something more that she needed to know. "Aunt Babette? Before you buried Marianne did you make sure she was dead?"

"*Mon Dieu*! What do you mean make sure she was dead?" The elderly woman looked confused. "I never checked her pulse. You mean I might have buried her alive?"

"The coroner may be able to determine that," Jane emphasized. "In any case, it may throw doubt on who actually committed the homicide."

"And that's a good thing, right?" Gee stated quickly, glancing between the two other Pascoe women. "If they can't prove who did it, isn't that reasonable doubt?"

"This is your birth mother we're talking about here, Gee." Jane stated.

"I know that! But I'm torn." Gee clapped both hands to her face. "I have two mothers. And I never really knew this one."

"Hold on a second." Ken squinted with fierce concentration. "If Marianne Tanner never left this house, then who stole my axe case with all of The WarBirds songs in it?"

Leslie gasped. "Oh! I've still got that, sweetheart. I kept it for you all this time, safe."

Ken looked thunderstruck. "Leslie? You've still got my axe?"

"Yes. I kept it in the broom closet with my cleaning supplies. I knew you'd never look for it there."

"My axe." Ken repeated doubtfully. "You've got my axe."

"Yes, dear. Do you want to see it?"

"Of course, I want to see it!" Ken thundered as he trailed her across the courtyard. "Leslie? It's been thirty years. Why didn't you tell me this before?"

"How could I, Ken?" Picking up the grocery sacks, she started up the steps. "It got too complicated." Opening the porch door with her elbow, she slid inside. "How could I explain that I kept your guitar safe and not tell you about that night, what happened to Marianne? It was so much easier to just put it away. Out of sight, out of mind. Gigi? I am sorry you had to find out about this, this way, like I said," she smiled winsomely, "but darling? That is how we got you."

"Fuck." Gee massaged her forehead. "This is a shitload to process."

"I'll bet it is," Jane agreed.

Stooping, Leslie opened a low cupboard door. Reaching in with both hands, she pulled out a vintage sweeper, unsnarling a gray cord before rummaging through the bottles and buckets stored further inside.

"We need to be practical." Aunt Babette leaned against the sink. "Get our stories straight for when the police arrive. We're going to say that I killed Marianne Tanner, right? Can we all agree on that?"

"I hate that idea, Babette." Ken protested. "When I'm the one who brought this goddamn problem down on us."

"Doesn't matter what you like or hate, Ken." She tapped her chest. "I need to protect this family and I'm seventy-four years old. What more can they do to me?"

Jane heard an approaching siren. "Time check, people. We've only got a few minutes to figure this out."

"Got it!" Leslie slid a black guitar case across the linoleum. "Look at this thing! It's filthy! Let me wash it off. I'll get a sponge -"

"Never mind that." Grasping the cracked leather handle, Ken hefted the case to the counter, nervously fingering the heavily pitted chrome locks. "Don't tease me, Leslie. My heart can't take it. Is my axe really in here?"

"It was the last time I checked it, dear. Open it up."

Using his oddly splayed thumbs, Ken unsnapped the case. Cracking the lid, he peered inside before flipping it back and reaching for the gleaming candy apple red jazz bass with its creamy tuxedo front and its Fender chrome plate.

Ken almost looks afraid to touch it, like it isn't real, like it might turn to dust or vanish if he blinks.

"Hello, Ramona." Ken grasped the guitar, his voice a caress as he lifted it off the plush black shag liner. "I've missed you, baby. How've you been?"

"Ramona?" Leslie blinked repeatedly. "Who's Ramona?"

"The only redhead I've ever loved." Inhaling shakily, Ken held the jazz bass between his hands. "That's a private thing between her and me." He rumbled. "The way B.B. King loved Lucille, the way Stevie Ray loved Number One."

The musty leather case also housed a dozen curling yellow legal pads and a scattered handful of #2 pencils. "Pops?" Gee reached in. "Are these your other WarBirds songs? The ones you wrote besides "Love Power"?"

Ken sighed. Clutching Ramona to his chest, he shut his eyes and swallowed heavily. "Yes, Gee, those are the other WarBirds songs."

Jane looked up as an unmarked NOPD unit, red and blue grill lights flashing pulled into the driveway behind The Boat. Sliding from his truck, Xavier pointed toward the kitchen door. The police unit's driver's side door swung open and Detective Dupree stepped out. Jane noted with surprise that Dupree's normally dark hair had turned completely white overnight.

Decidedly tucking his chin, Dupree marched for the back porch, raising his NOPD detective's badge in his left hand.

"Police!" He declared, starting up the porch steps. "Alright, people! I'm coming in. What have you got going on, now?"

CHAPTER FIFTY-EIGHT

The warped floorboards and the decrepit rush rocker creaked in tandem as Jane pushed off her toes. The December day was unseasonably mild. She smelled the warming earth on the breeze. The Pascoe's plumbing problem had been resolved. The NOPD forensic team had finished their CSI and moved on. Leslie's garden still looked battle scarred, but the yard had been releveled and the morbid sewer trench filled in.

Gee sat curled up on the wicker couch, a fuzzy afghan draped around her shoulders and her feet tucked beneath her knees. She unconsciously chewed the eraser on a #2 pencil as she hum-tested the different melodies from the unrecorded WarBirds songs.

She looked up. "You know what, Pops? These are good. Really good. You're a fucking genius."

Ken stopped tuning Ramona, lowering the red jazz bass guitar onto his knees. "No, Gee. They're fucking great."

"Strange thing, though." Gee frowned, repeatedly tapping a legal pad. "This ain't your handwriting."

"No, it's not." Ken sighed, closing his eyes. "That's because Marianne Tanner wrote every goddamn one of 'em. I never wrote a single lyric or note. It was a lie. Marianne wrote every goddamn song."

"Excuse me?" The afghan slid to the floor as Gee sat up.

"S'right." Ken dropped his chin to his chest. "Those songs are hers, every bit of 'em. I used the plane crash as an excuse to quit writing because I knew fans would notice if I tried writing a WarBird's song. Fans notice shit like that. Critics, too." He pointed at the legal pads. "Marianne got stifled by what we did, but all of those songs and that music belongs to her."

"Oh, Pops. That is fucking pathetic."

"I know it is, Gee. That's just the way it was back then. Part of the times."

"So, who do those songs belong to now?" Jane asked.

Ken looked startled. "Never thought of that." He idly scratched his chin. "I guess they belong to Gee. You were Marianne's only child. She didn't have any other family. I think that makes you her heir."

"Really?" Gee eagerly stacked the songs, straightening them neatly. "Then I have an idea. I think you should record a comeback album, Pops. I'll produce it - if you play bass."

"I don't know, Gee." Ken looked troubled. "I haven't recorded a note in thirty-five years."

"It'll come back to you." She stood. "I know it will. You just need to practice. I'll help."

"We could rent a music studio from Guardian Storage," Jane suggested.

Gee turned in surprise. "Would you really go back there after the shitty way they treated you?"

"Why not? I'm through closing doors. Fuck it. If they've got what we need, I say let's use it."

Laughing loudly, Ken shook his head, his eyes bright with excitement. "What a crazy fucking idea! But we can't call it *Blood Sport*. That's done. That's over. We'd need to come up with a new title, something different, something fresh."

"*Street Angel*." Jane blurted. "Name it after Marianne because it's her voice that got lost."

"Hot damn." Ken snapped his thick fingers. "I love this idea! What a hook! With that backstory it'll sell like hotcakes! People'll remember Scottie and Mick and Lemonhead again. The advance'll cover the bail bond for your mother and Aunt Babette." Leaning forward, he tapped Gee's knee. "What the hell. Why stop there? We might even get enough money to open that dance club you wanted, Gee. I could invest in it, be your silent partner."

"I'm already seriously doubting the 'silent' part of that." Gee smirked. "Just saying."

"Holy shit!" Clapping his hands, Ken popped off a crack that startled the ravens from the trees. "We might have a real shot at this!"

ABOUT THE AUTHOR

Martha Reed is the Independent Publisher ("IPPY")
Book Award-winning crime fiction author of the John
and Sarah Jarad Nantucket Mystery series. She is an
active member of Sisters in Crime, Inc., Mystery
Writers of America (MWA) and in a moment of great
folly at Bouchercon 2016, she joined the New Orleans
Bourbon Society (N.O.B.S.) Visit her website
reedmenow.com for more information. You are invited
to follow her on Facebook and Twitter @ReedMartha.

www.ingramcontent.com/pod-product-compliance
Lightning Source LLC
Chambersburg PA
CBHW050551260626
47157CB00002B/518